I WAS A TWEENAGE WEREWOLF!

CHAPTER
ONE

Welcome to

FULL MOON HOLLOW

PARANORMAL CAPITAL OF THE WORLD

Something stranger than usual haunts this small town.
Adults either can't see it, can't remember it, or go crazy from it.

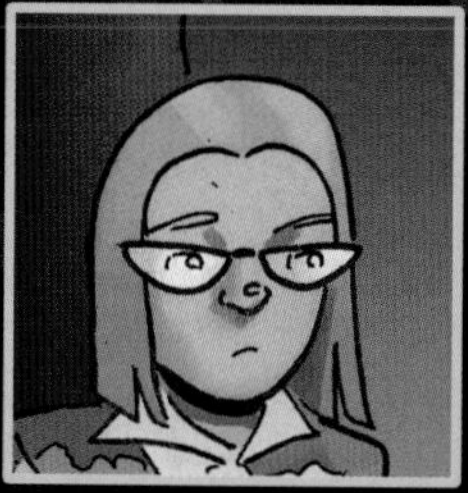

Becky

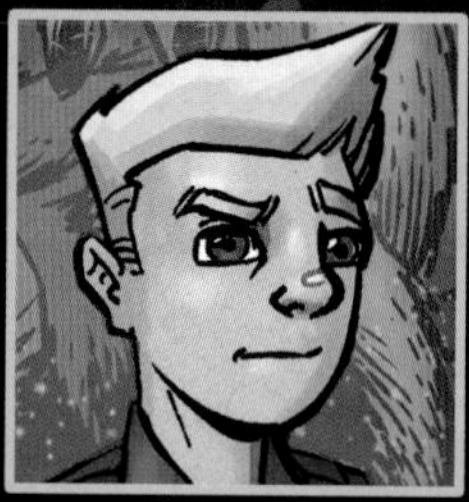

Chase

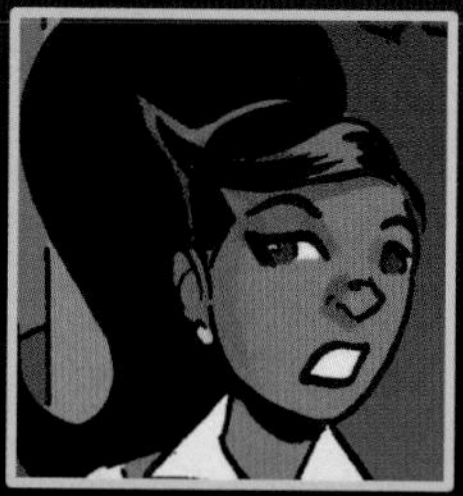

Claudia

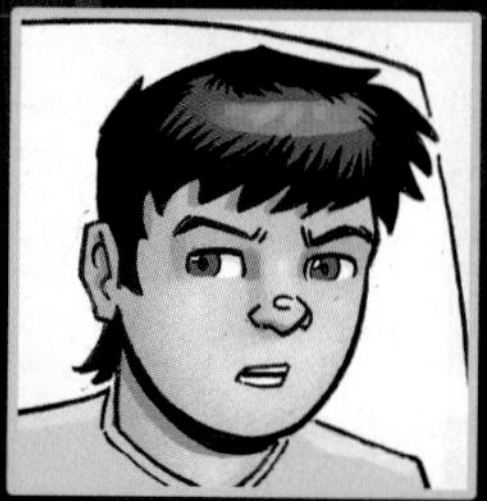

Peyton

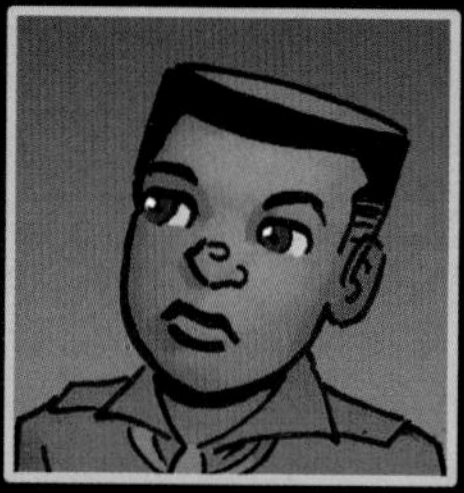

Trey

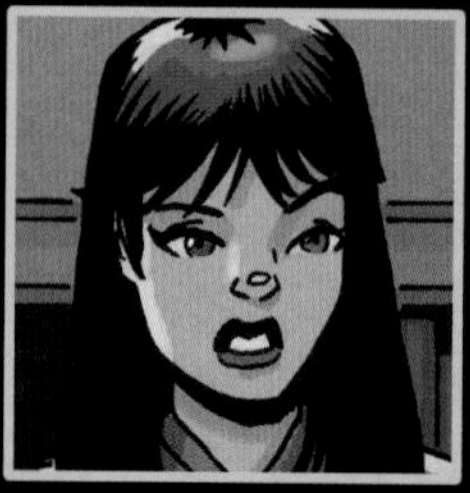

Ms. Chung

Three months ago, a sudden zombie outbreak threatened Full Moon Hollow, but five quick-thinking scouts banded together to save the town. Along the way, they learned that there's more than meets the eye in this sleepy town.

The scouts were assisted by the town librarian, Ms. Chung, whose missing childhood memories may hold the key to solving this mystery…

Story and Letters
STEVE BRYANT
@SteveBryantArt

Art
MARK STEGBAUER
@MarkStegbauer

Colors
JASON MILLET
@Jason_Millet

Edited by
CHRIS MURRIN
@ChrisMurrin

Color Assist
DREW BROWNE
@TheDrewBrowne

Cover
MARK STEGBAUER
& JASON MILLET

Bryan Seaton: Publisher | **Dave Dwonch**: President of Marketing & Development | **Shawn Gabborin:** Editor In Chief
Jason Martin: Publisher-Danger Zone | **Nicole D'Andria:** Marketing Director/Editor
Jim Dietz: Social Media Director | **Scott Bradley:** CFO | **Chad Cicconi:** Werewolf Wrangler

GHOUL SCOUTS: I WAS A TWEENAGE WEREWOLF #1.

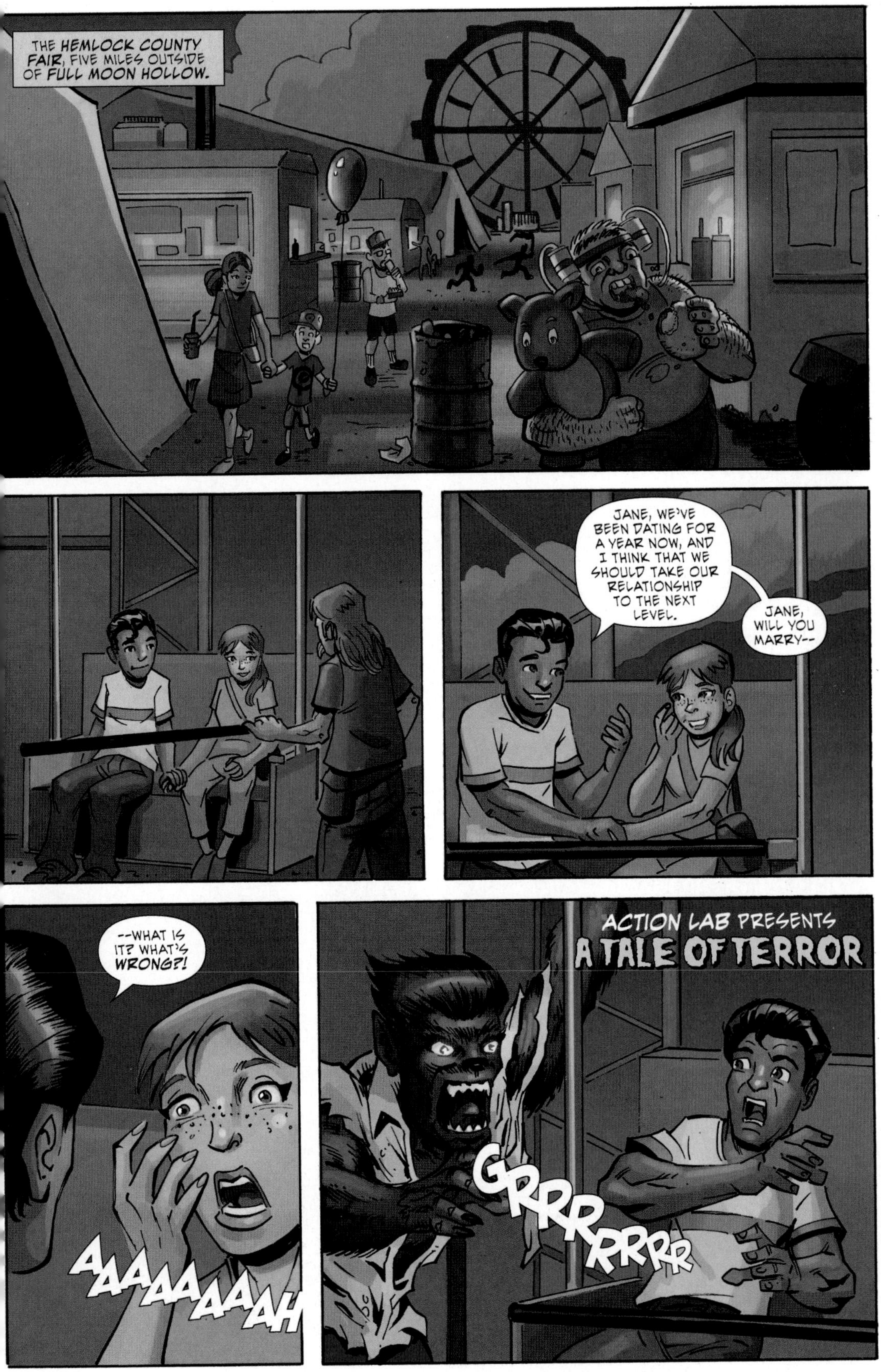
THE HEMLOCK COUNTY FAIR, FIVE MILES OUTSIDE OF FULL MOON HOLLOW.
JANE, WE'VE BEEN DATING FOR A YEAR NOW, AND I THINK THAT WE SHOULD TAKE OUR RELATIONSHIP TO THE NEXT LEVEL.
JANE, WILL YOU MARRY--
--WHAT IS IT? WHAT'S WRONG?!
AAAAAAAAH
ACTION LAB PRESENTS
A TALE OF TERROR
GRRRRRRR

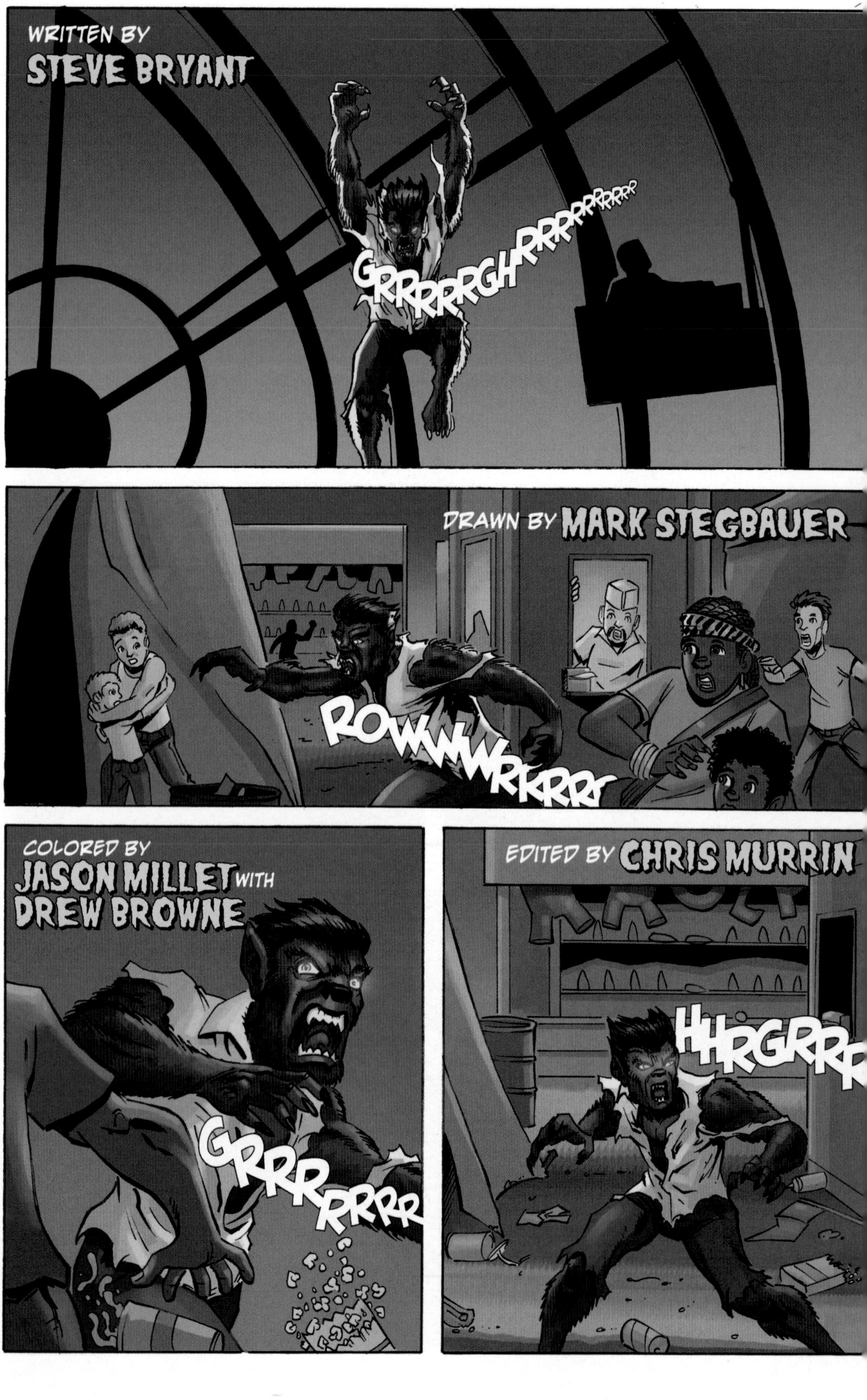
WRITTEN BY
STEVE BRYANT
GRRRRRGHRRRRRRRRRR
DRAWN BY MARK STEGBAUER
ROWWWRRRR
COLORED BY
JASON MILLET WITH
DREW BROWNE
GRRRRRRR
EDITED BY CHRIS MURRIN
HHRGRRR

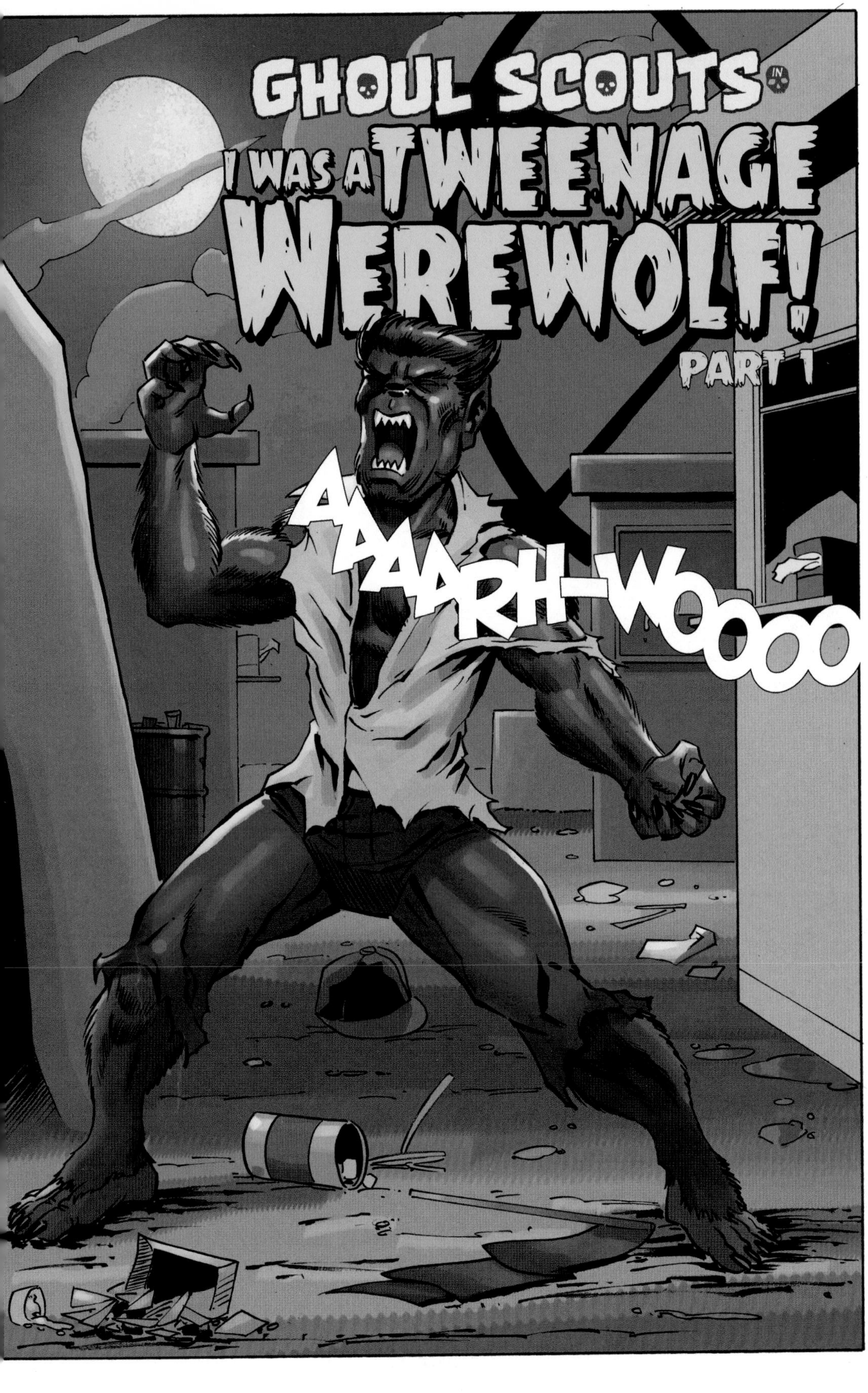
GHOUL SCOUTS IN
I WAS A TWEENAGE WEREWOLF!
PART 1
AAAARH-WOOOOO

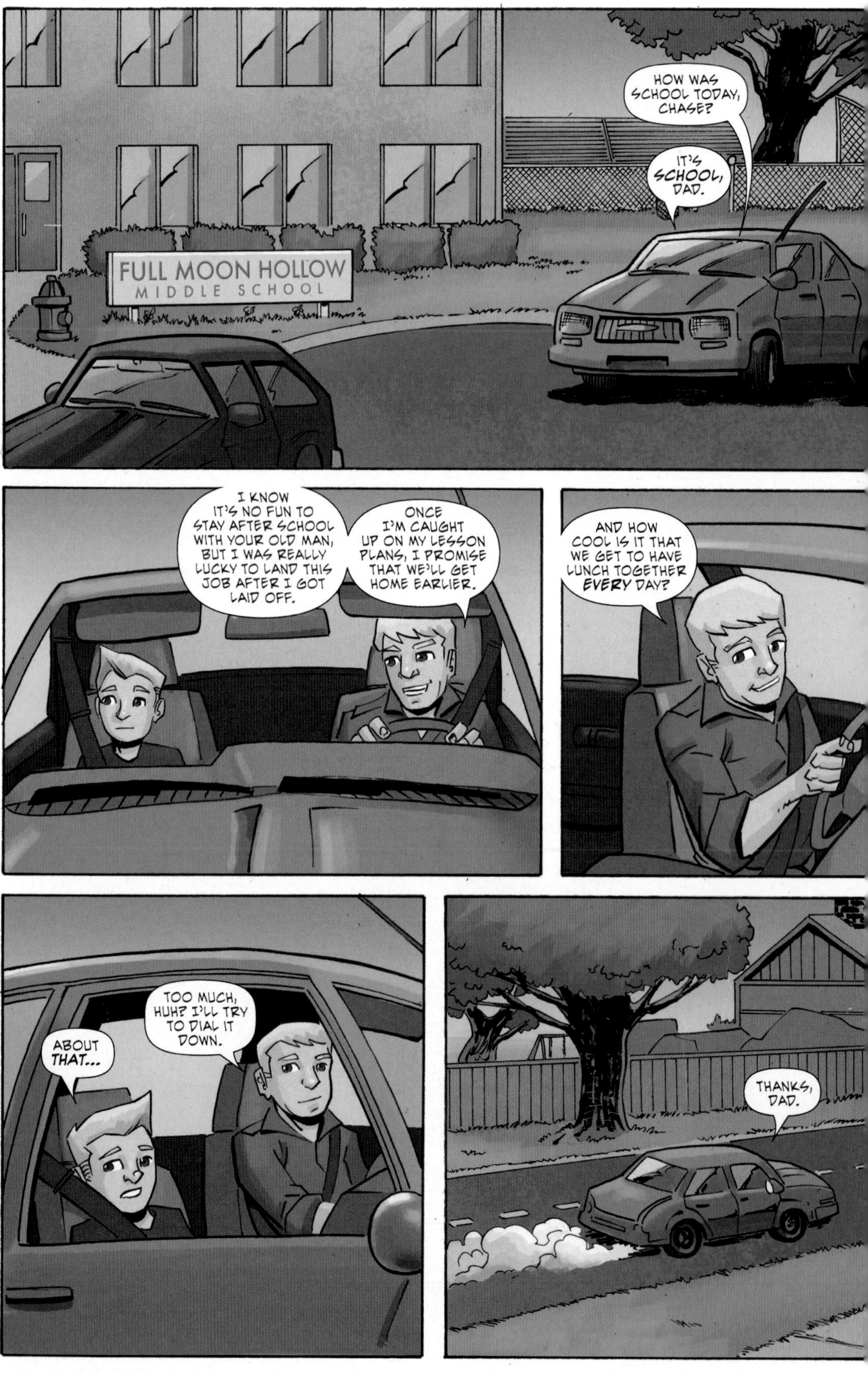
FULL MOON HOLLOW
MIDDLE SCHOOL
HOW WAS SCHOOL TODAY, CHASE?
IT'S SCHOOL, DAD.
I KNOW IT'S NO FUN TO STAY AFTER SCHOOL WITH YOUR OLD MAN, BUT I WAS REALLY LUCKY TO LAND THIS JOB AFTER I GOT LAID OFF.
ONCE I'M CAUGHT UP ON MY LESSON PLANS, I PROMISE THAT WE'LL GET HOME EARLIER.
AND HOW COOL IS IT THAT WE GET TO HAVE LUNCH TOGETHER **EVERY** DAY?
ABOUT **THAT...**
TOO MUCH, HUH? I'LL TRY TO DIAL IT DOWN.
THANKS, DAD.

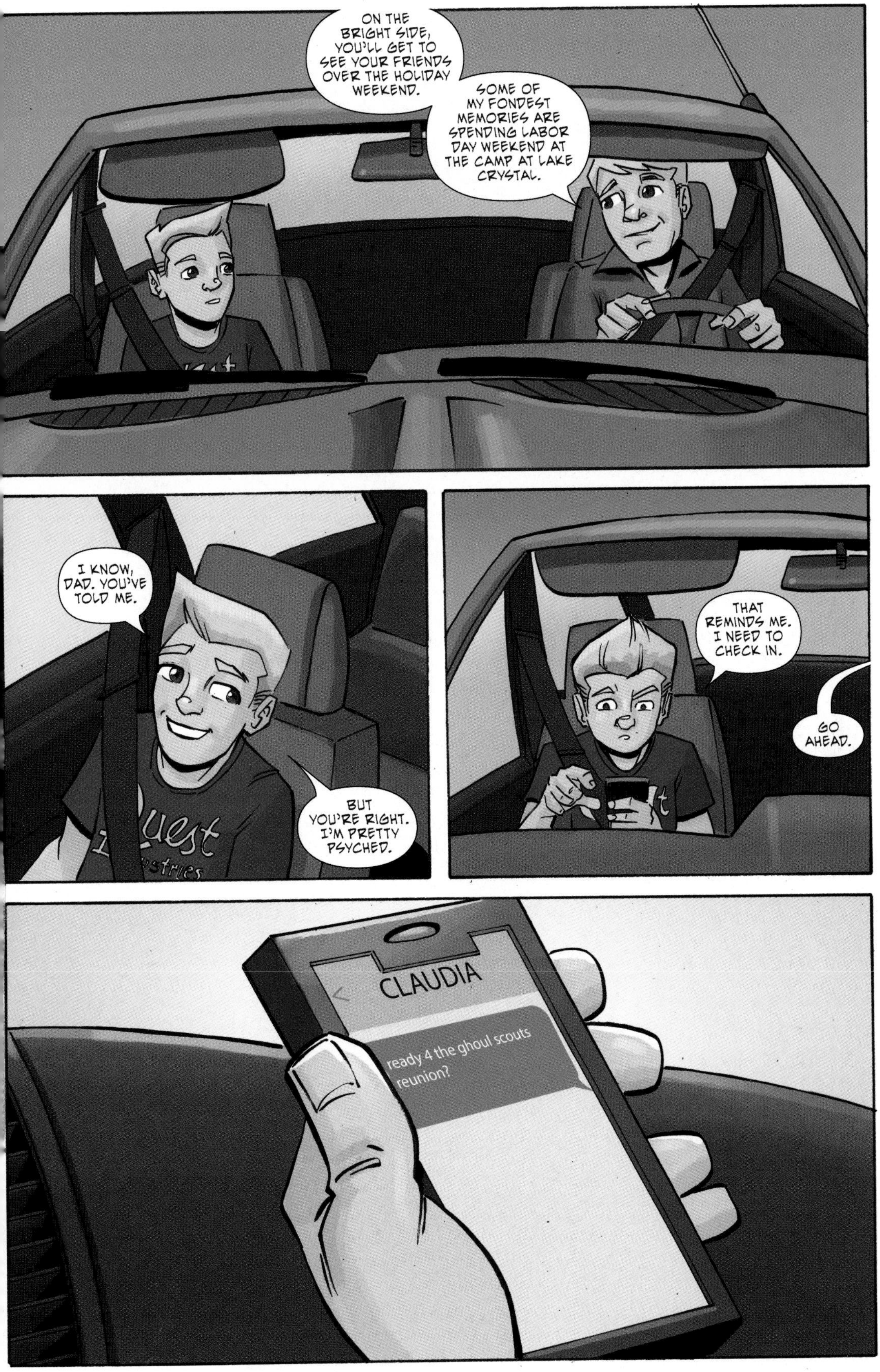

ON THE BRIGHT SIDE, YOU'LL GET TO SEE YOUR FRIENDS OVER THE HOLIDAY WEEKEND.
SOME OF MY FONDEST MEMORIES ARE SPENDING LABOR DAY WEEKEND AT THE CAMP AT LAKE CRYSTAL.
I KNOW, DAD. YOU'VE TOLD ME.
BUT YOU'RE RIGHT. I'M PRETTY PSYCHED.
THAT REMINDS ME. I NEED TO CHECK IN.
GO AHEAD.
CLAUDIA
ready 4 the ghoul scouts reunion?

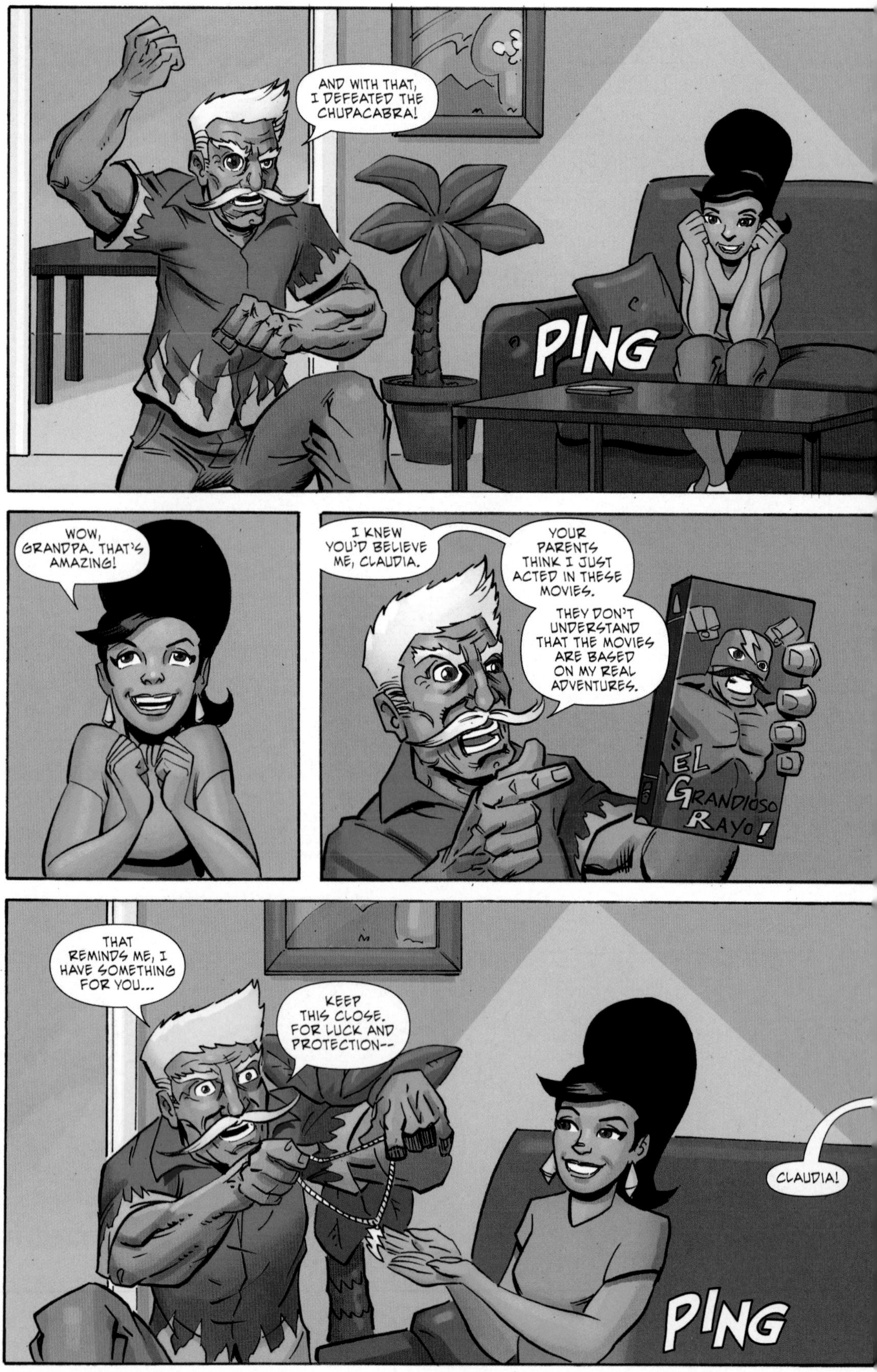
AND WITH THAT, I DEFEATED THE CHUPACABRA!
PING
WOW, GRANDPA. THAT'S AMAZING!
I KNEW YOU'D BELIEVE ME, CLAUDIA.
YOUR PARENTS THINK I JUST ACTED IN THESE MOVIES.
THEY DON'T UNDERSTAND THAT THE MOVIES ARE BASED ON MY REAL ADVENTURES.
EL GRANDIOSO RAYO!
THAT REMINDS ME, I HAVE SOMETHING FOR YOU...
KEEP THIS CLOSE. FOR LUCK AND PROTECTION--
CLAUDIA!
PING

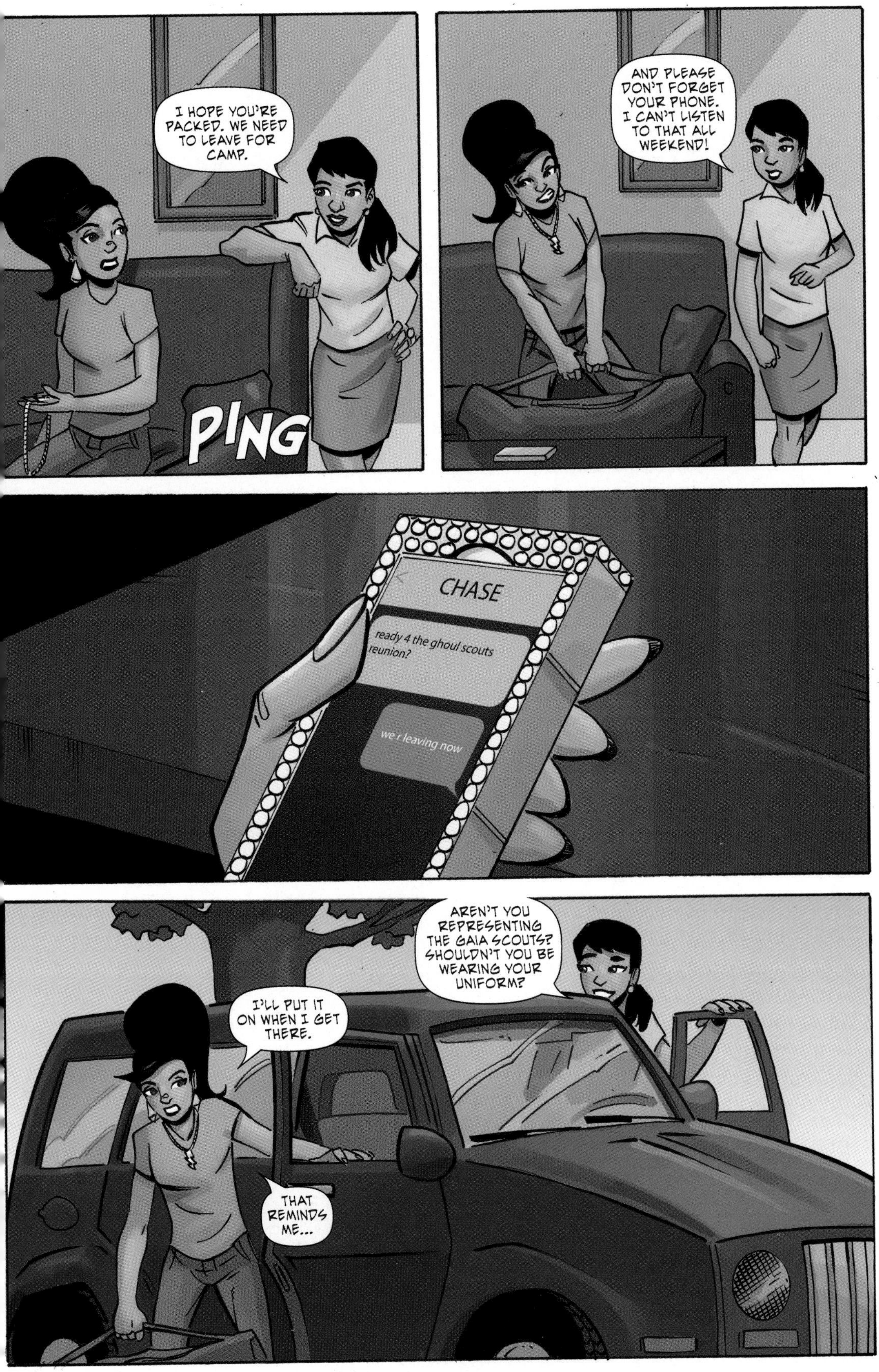
I HOPE YOU'RE PACKED. WE NEED TO LEAVE FOR CAMP.
PING
AND PLEASE DON'T FORGET YOUR PHONE. I CAN'T LISTEN TO THAT ALL WEEKEND!
CHASE
ready 4 the ghoul scouts reunion?
we r leaving now
AREN'T YOU REPRESENTING THE GAIA SCOUTS? SHOULDN'T YOU BE WEARING YOUR UNIFORM?
I'LL PUT IT ON WHEN I GET THERE.
THAT REMINDS ME...

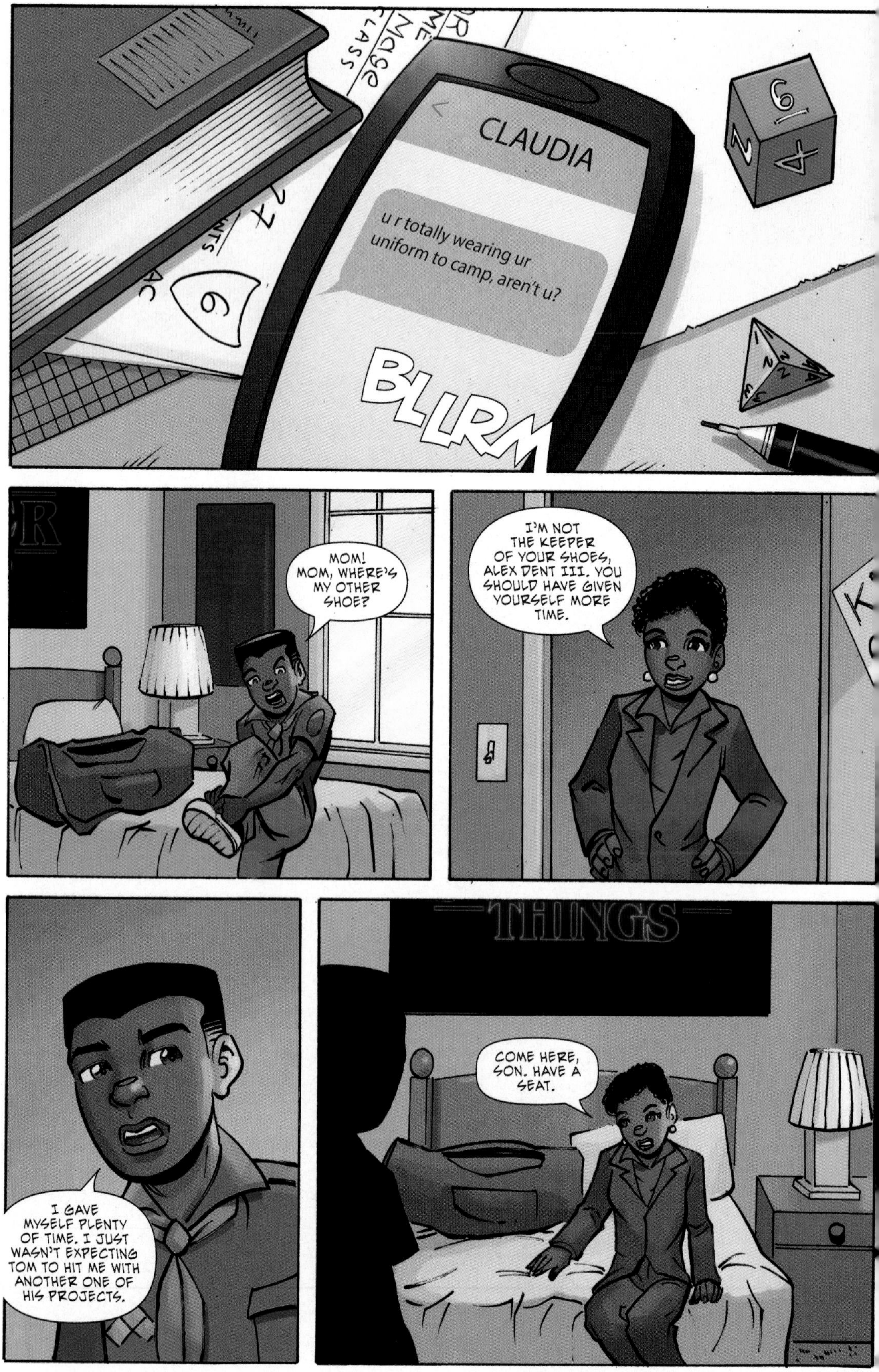
CLAUDIA
u r totally wearing ur uniform to camp, aren't u?
BLLRM
MOM! MOM, WHERE'S MY OTHER SHOE?
I'M NOT THE KEEPER OF YOUR SHOES, ALEX DENT III. YOU SHOULD HAVE GIVEN YOURSELF MORE TIME.
I GAVE MYSELF PLENTY OF TIME. I JUST WASN'T EXPECTING TOM TO HIT ME WITH ANOTHER ONE OF HIS PROJECTS.
THINGS
COME HERE, SON. HAVE A SEAT.

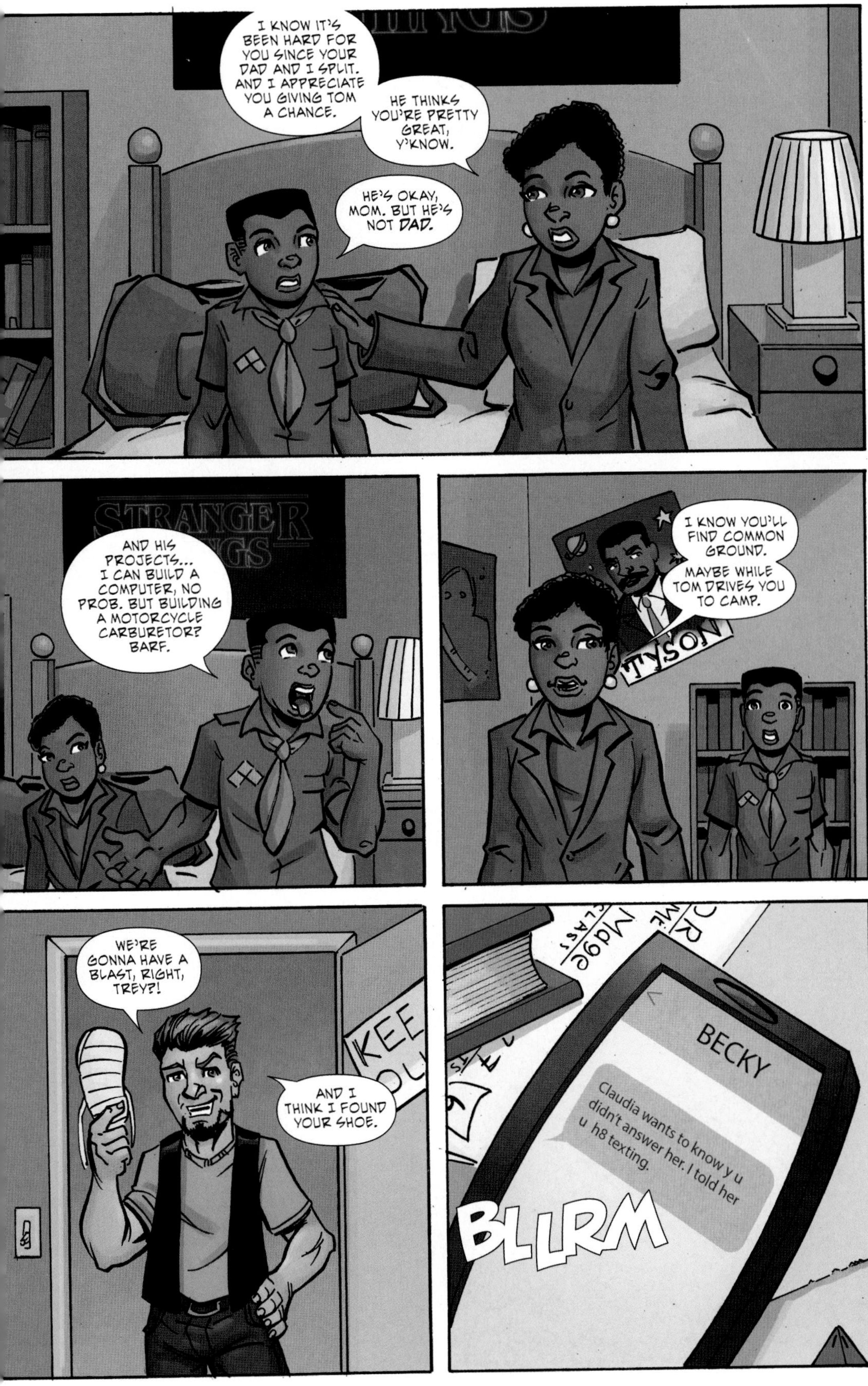
I KNOW IT'S BEEN HARD FOR YOU SINCE YOUR DAD AND I SPLIT. AND I APPRECIATE YOU GIVING TOM A CHANCE.
HE THINKS YOU'RE PRETTY GREAT, Y'KNOW.
HE'S OKAY, MOM. BUT HE'S NOT *DAD*.
STRANGER
AND HIS PROJECTS... I CAN BUILD A COMPUTER, NO PROB. BUT BUILDING A MOTORCYCLE CARBURETOR? BARF.
I KNOW YOU'LL FIND COMMON GROUND.
MAYBE WHILE TOM DRIVES YOU TO CAMP.
TYSON
WE'RE GONNA HAVE A BLAST, RIGHT, TREY?!
AND I THINK I FOUND YOUR SHOE.
BECKY
Claudia wants to know y u didn't answer her. I told her u h8 texting.
BLLRM

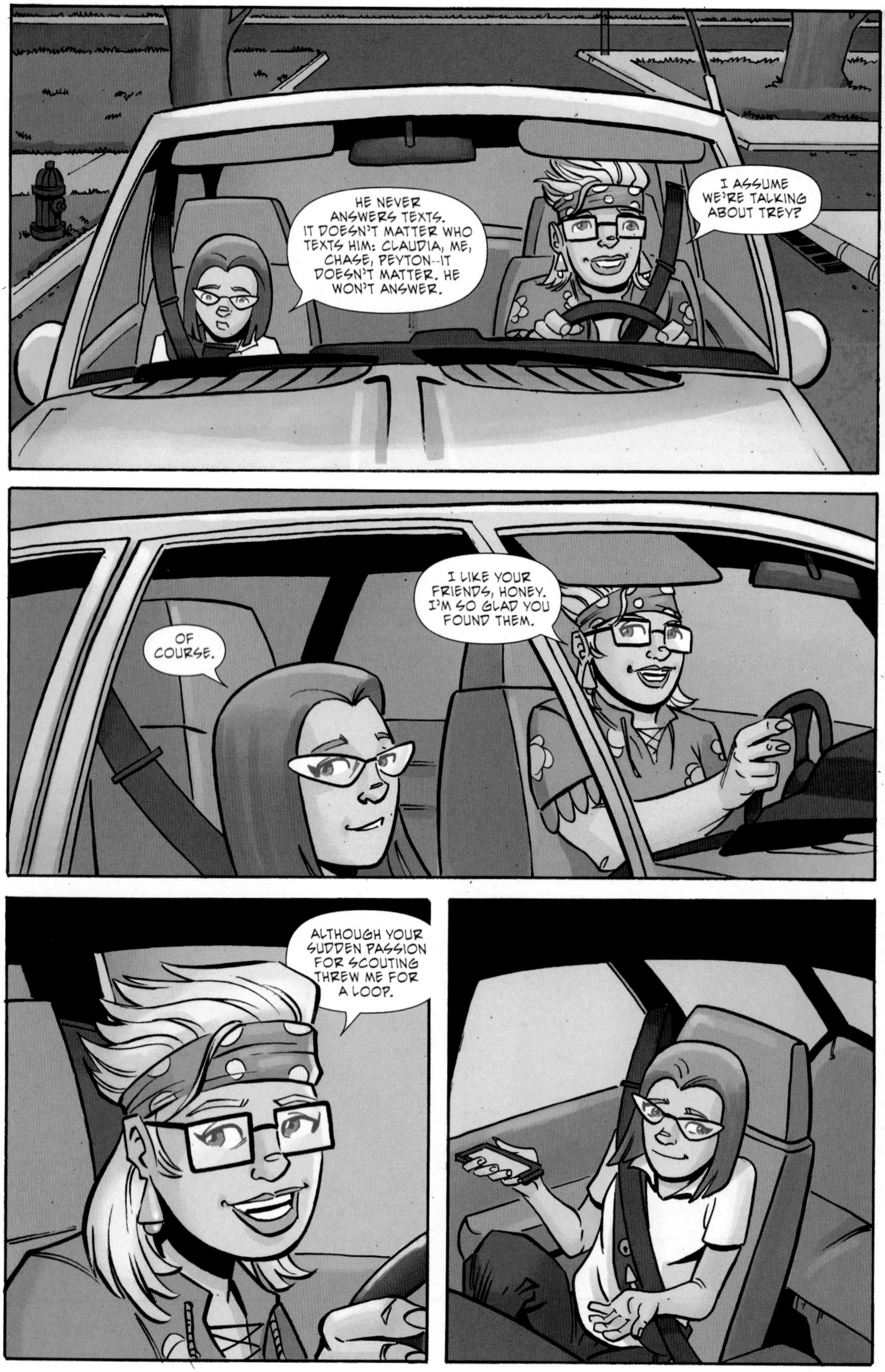
HE NEVER ANSWERS TEXTS. IT DOESN'T MATTER WHO TEXTS HIM: CLAUDIA, ME, CHASE, PEYTON--IT DOESN'T MATTER. HE WON'T ANSWER.
I ASSUME WE'RE TALKING ABOUT TREY?
I LIKE YOUR FRIENDS, HONEY. I'M SO GLAD YOU FOUND THEM.
OF COURSE.
ALTHOUGH YOUR SUDDEN PASSION FOR SCOUTING THREW ME FOR A LOOP.

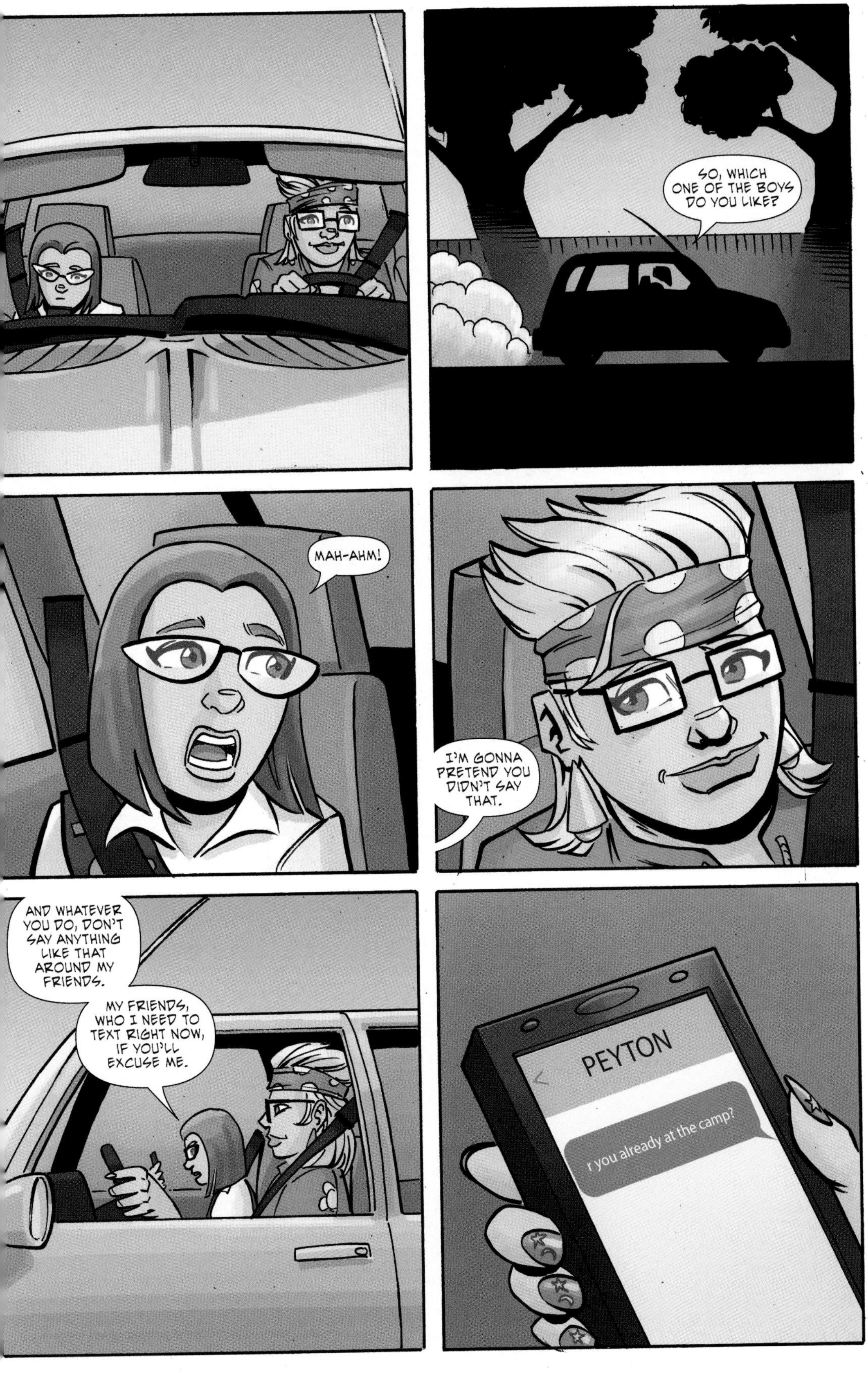
SO, WHICH ONE OF THE BOYS DO YOU LIKE?
MAH-AHM!
I'M GONNA PRETEND YOU DIDN'T SAY THAT.
AND WHATEVER YOU DO, DON'T SAY ANYTHING LIKE THAT AROUND MY FRIENDS.
MY FRIENDS, WHO I NEED TO TEXT RIGHT NOW, IF YOU'LL EXCUSE ME.
PEYTON
r you already at the camp?

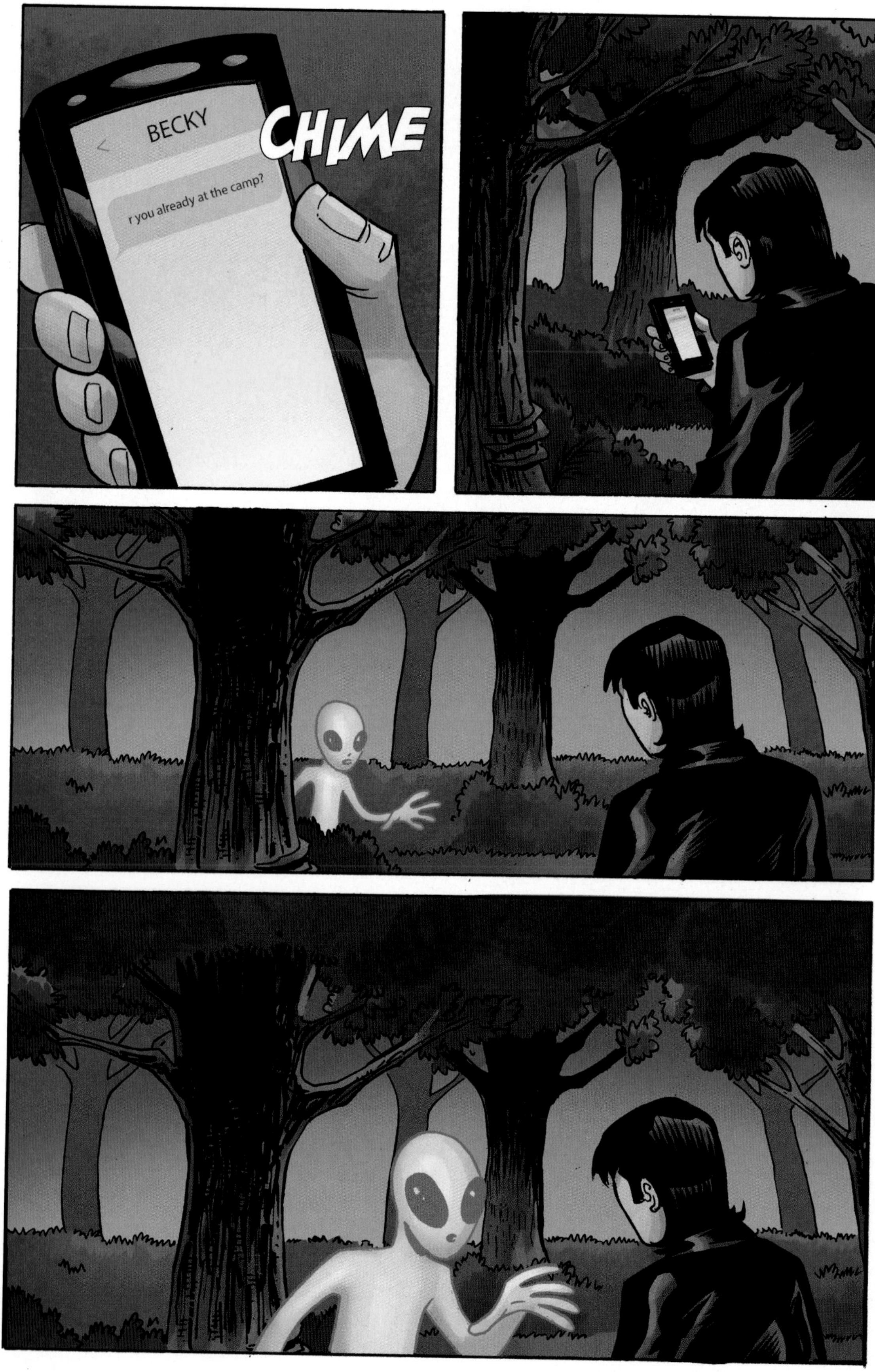
BECKY
r you already at the camp?
CHIME

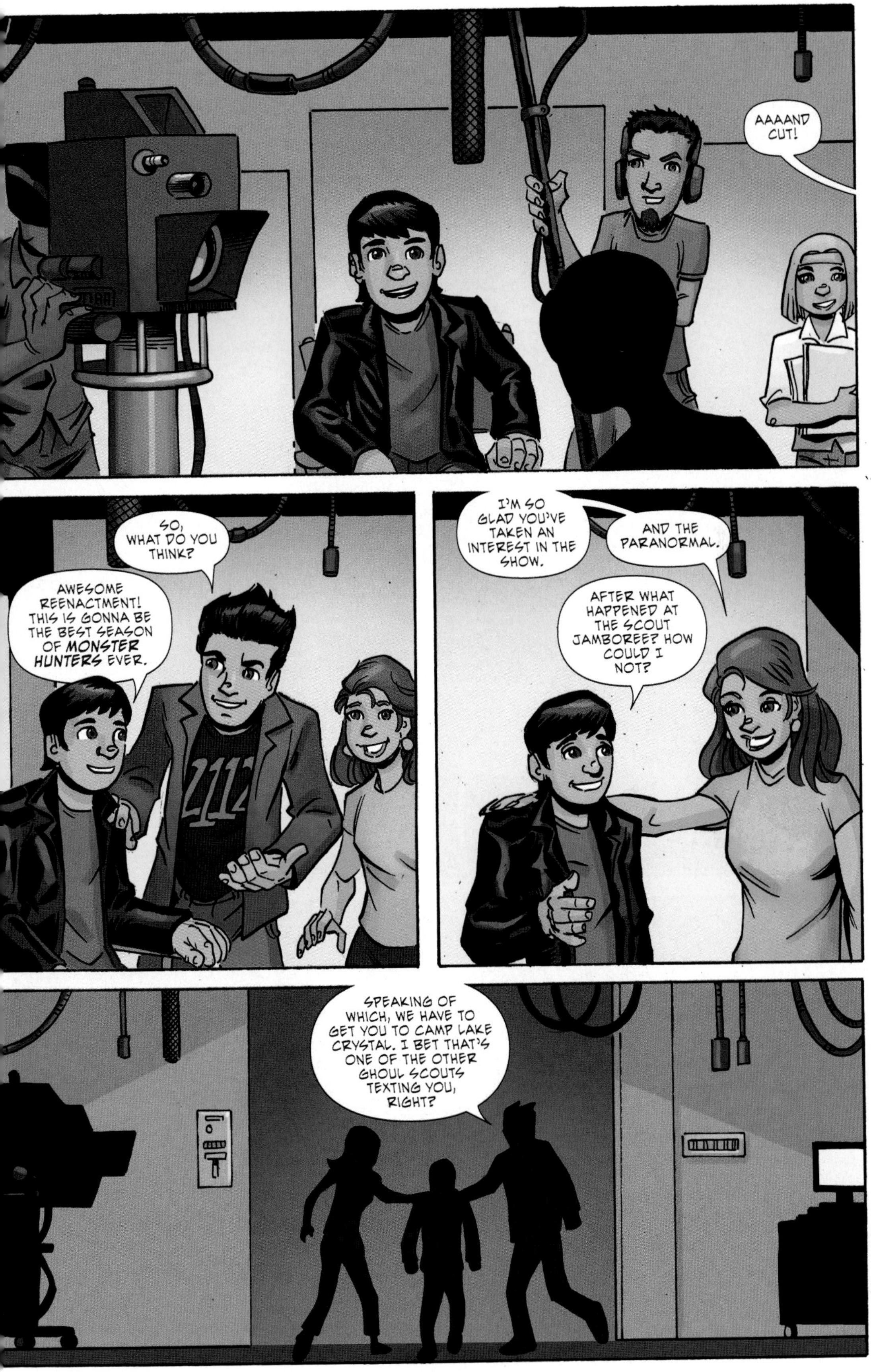
AAAAND CUT!
SO, WHAT DO YOU THINK?
AWESOME REENACTMENT! THIS IS GONNA BE THE BEST SEASON OF **MONSTER HUNTERS** EVER.
I'M SO GLAD YOU'VE TAKEN AN INTEREST IN THE SHOW.
AND THE PARANORMAL.
AFTER WHAT HAPPENED AT THE SCOUT JAMBOREE? HOW COULD I NOT?
SPEAKING OF WHICH, WE HAVE TO GET YOU TO CAMP LAKE CRYSTAL. I BET THAT'S ONE OF THE OTHER GHOUL SCOUTS TEXTING YOU, RIGHT?

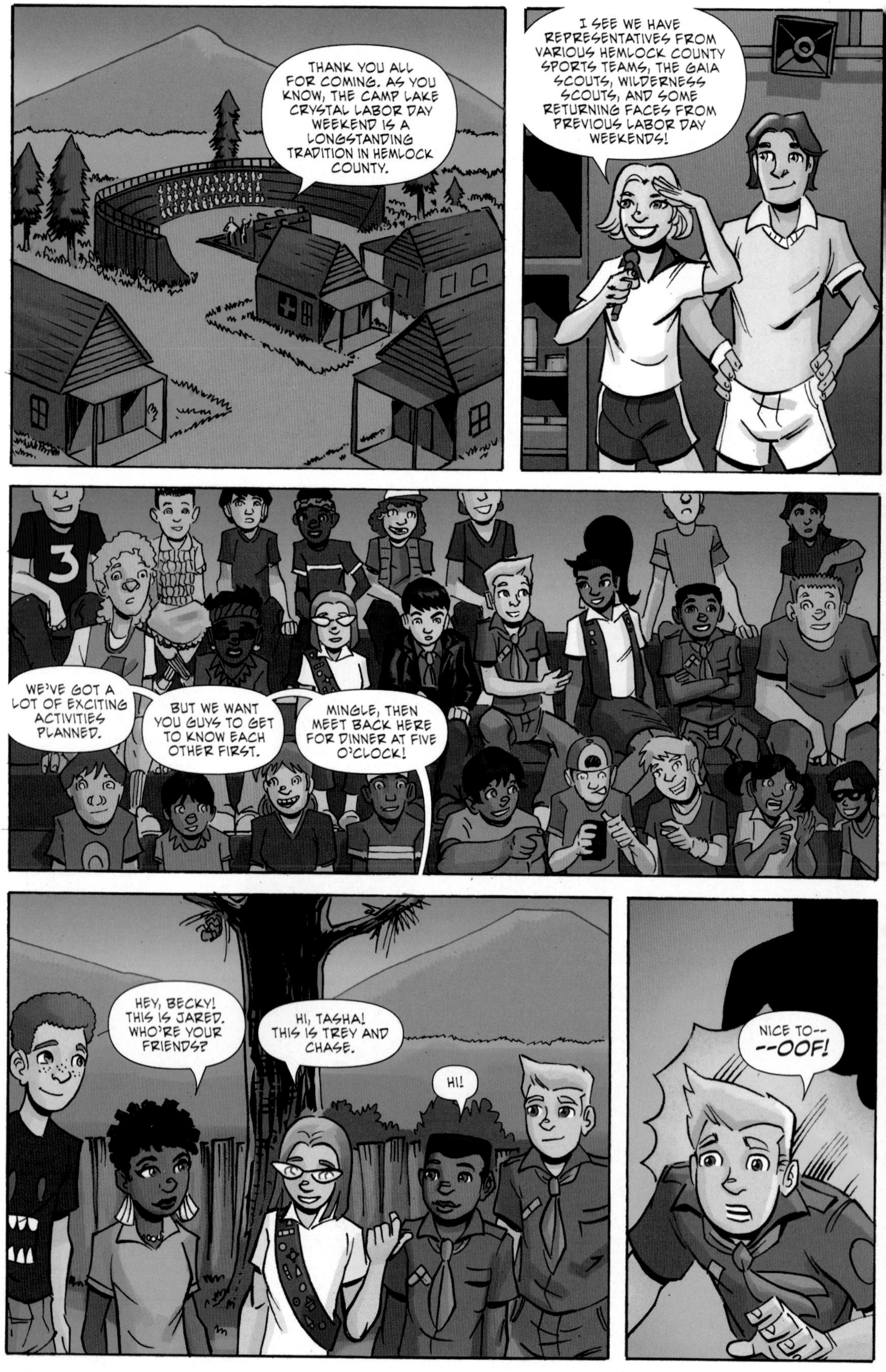
THANK YOU ALL FOR COMING. AS YOU KNOW, THE CAMP LAKE CRYSTAL LABOR DAY WEEKEND IS A LONGSTANDING TRADITION IN HEMLOCK COUNTY.
I SEE WE HAVE REPRESENTATIVES FROM VARIOUS HEMLOCK COUNTY SPORTS TEAMS, THE GAIA SCOUTS, WILDERNESS SCOUTS, AND SOME RETURNING FACES FROM PREVIOUS LABOR DAY WEEKENDS!
WE'VE GOT A LOT OF EXCITING ACTIVITIES PLANNED.
BUT WE WANT YOU GUYS TO GET TO KNOW EACH OTHER FIRST.
MINGLE, THEN MEET BACK HERE FOR DINNER AT FIVE O'CLOCK!
HEY, BECKY! THIS IS JARED. WHO'RE YOUR FRIENDS?
HI, TASHA! THIS IS TREY AND CHASE.
HI!
NICE TO--
--OOF!

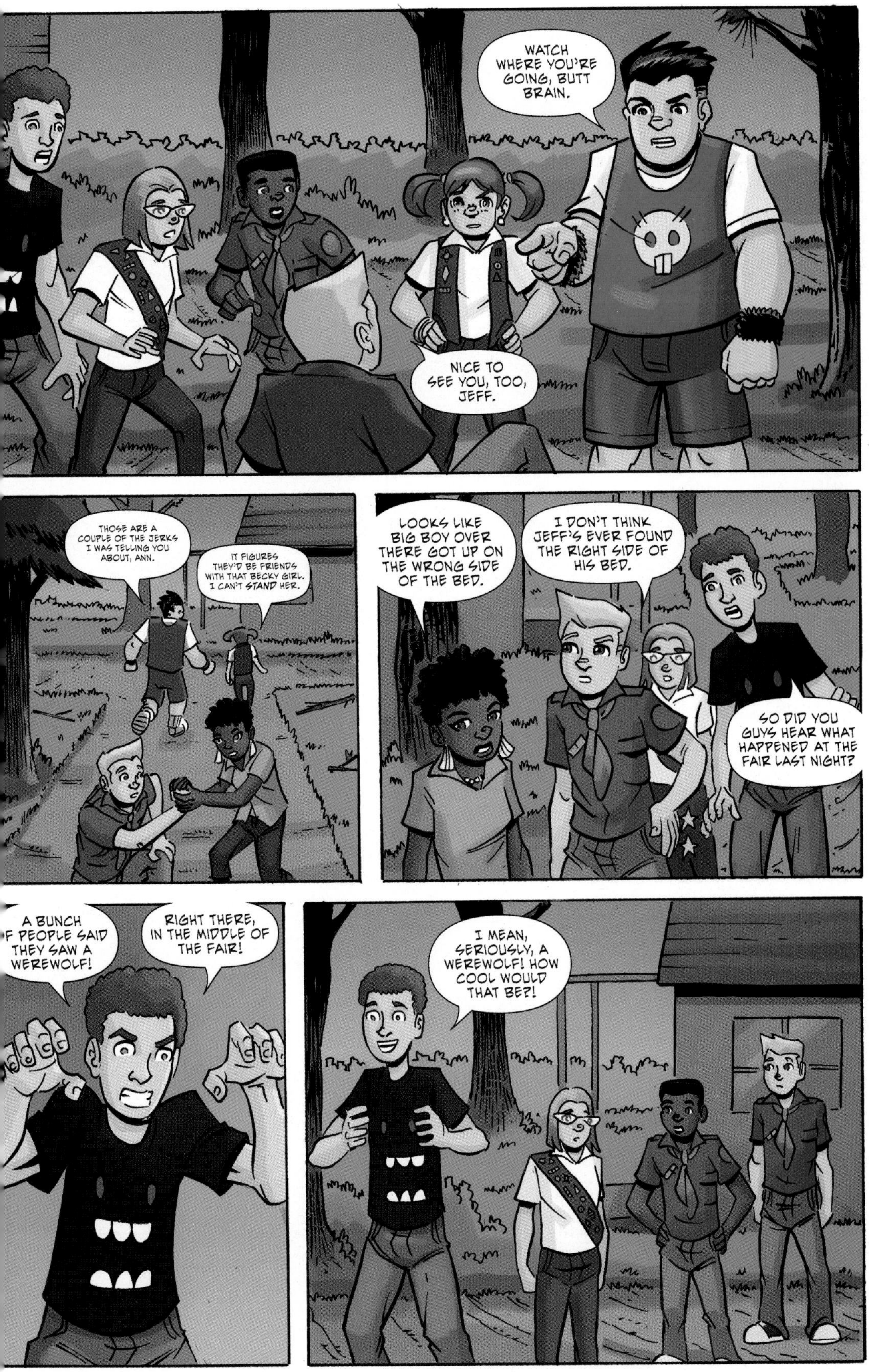
WATCH WHERE YOU'RE GOING, BUTT BRAIN.
NICE TO SEE YOU, TOO, JEFF.
THOSE ARE A COUPLE OF THE JERKS I WAS TELLING YOU ABOUT, ANN.
IT FIGURES THEY'D BE FRIENDS WITH THAT BECKY GIRL. I CAN'T STAND HER.
LOOKS LIKE BIG BOY OVER THERE GOT UP ON THE WRONG SIDE OF THE BED.
I DON'T THINK JEFF'S EVER FOUND THE RIGHT SIDE OF HIS BED.
SO DID YOU GUYS HEAR WHAT HAPPENED AT THE FAIR LAST NIGHT?
A BUNCH F PEOPLE SAID THEY SAW A WEREWOLF!
RIGHT THERE, IN THE MIDDLE OF THE FAIR!
I MEAN, SERIOUSLY, A WEREWOLF! HOW COOL WOULD THAT BE?!

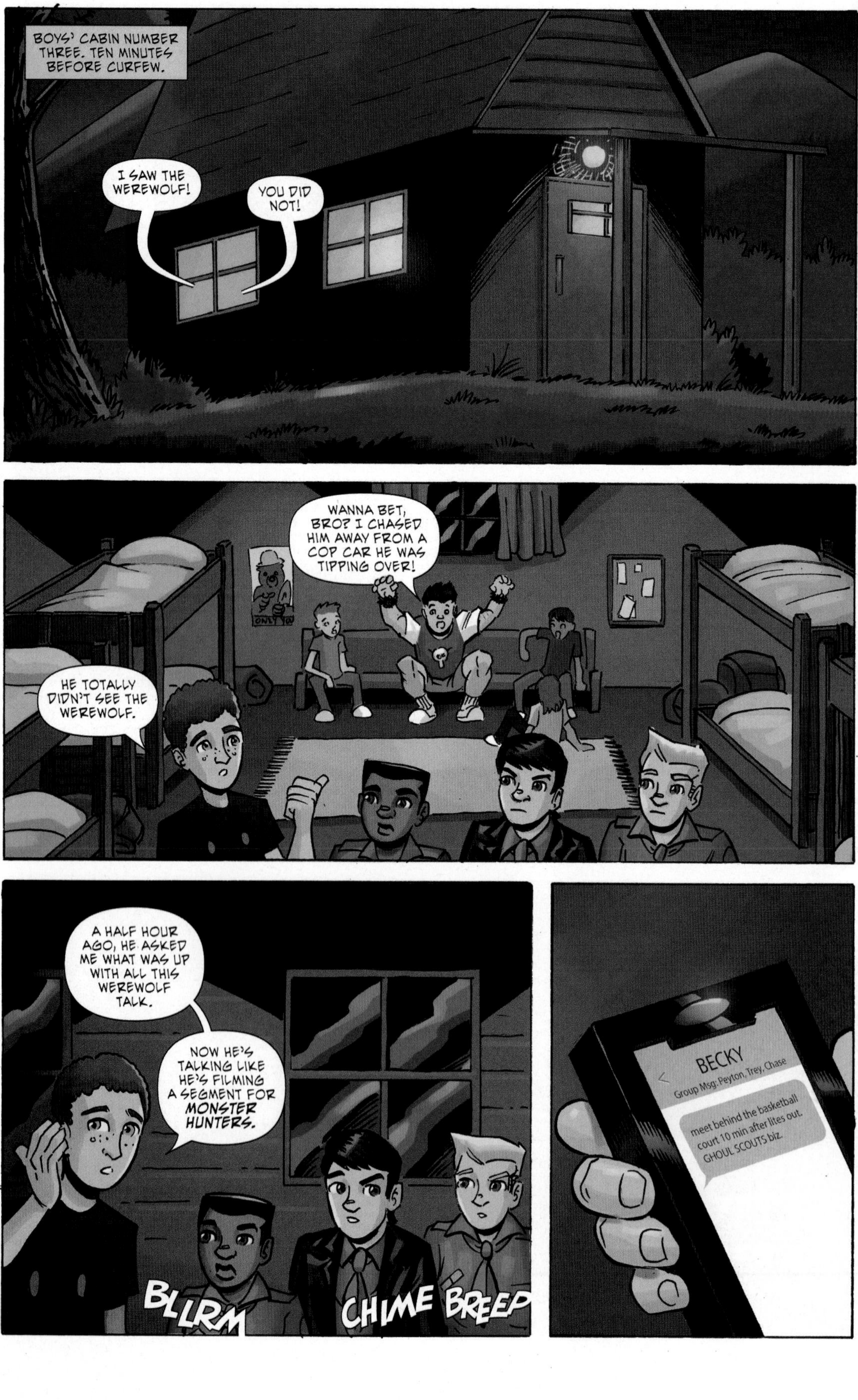
BOYS' CABIN NUMBER THREE. TEN MINUTES BEFORE CURFEW.
I SAW THE WEREWOLF!
YOU DID NOT!
WANNA BET, BRO? I CHASED HIM AWAY FROM A COP CAR HE WAS TIPPING OVER!
HE TOTALLY DIDN'T SEE THE WEREWOLF.
A HALF HOUR AGO, HE ASKED ME WHAT WAS UP WITH ALL THIS WEREWOLF TALK.
NOW HE'S TALKING LIKE HE'S FILMING A SEGMENT FOR MONSTER HUNTERS.
BLLRM
CHIME
BREEP
BECKY
Group Msg: Peyton, Trey, Chase
meet behind the basketball court 10 min after lites out. GHOUL SCOUTS biz.

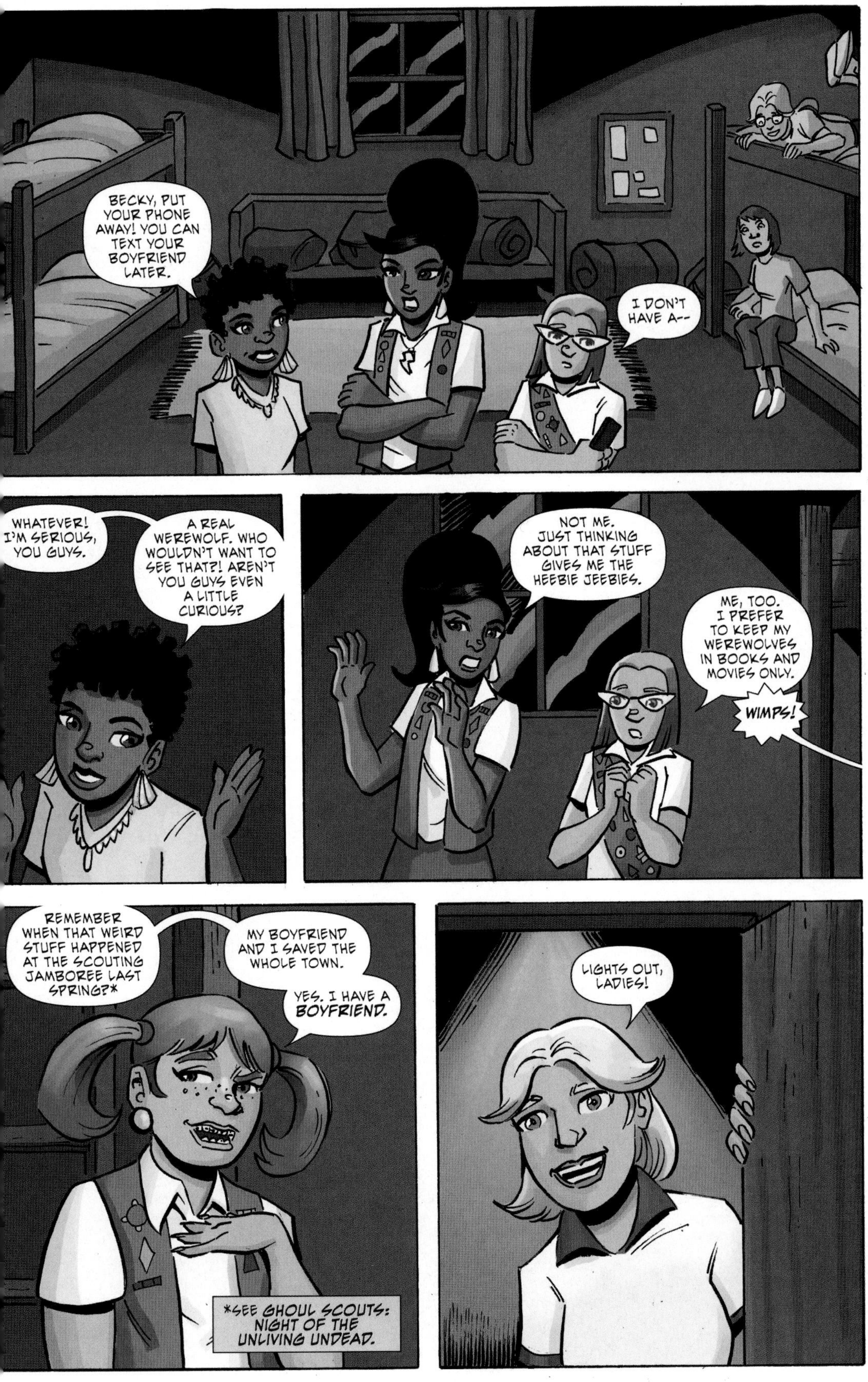
BECKY, PUT YOUR PHONE AWAY! YOU CAN TEXT YOUR BOYFRIEND LATER.
I DON'T HAVE A--
WHATEVER! I'M SERIOUS, YOU GUYS.
A REAL WEREWOLF. WHO WOULDN'T WANT TO SEE THAT?! AREN'T YOU GUYS EVEN A LITTLE CURIOUS?
NOT ME. JUST THINKING ABOUT THAT STUFF GIVES ME THE HEEBIE JEEBIES.
ME, TOO. I PREFER TO KEEP MY WEREWOLVES IN BOOKS AND MOVIES ONLY.
WIMPS!
REMEMBER WHEN THAT WEIRD STUFF HAPPENED AT THE SCOUTING JAMBOREE LAST SPRING?*
MY BOYFRIEND AND I SAVED THE WHOLE TOWN.
YES. I HAVE A BOYFRIEND.
*SEE GHOUL SCOUTS: NIGHT OF THE UNLIVING UNDEAD.
LIGHTS OUT, LADIES!

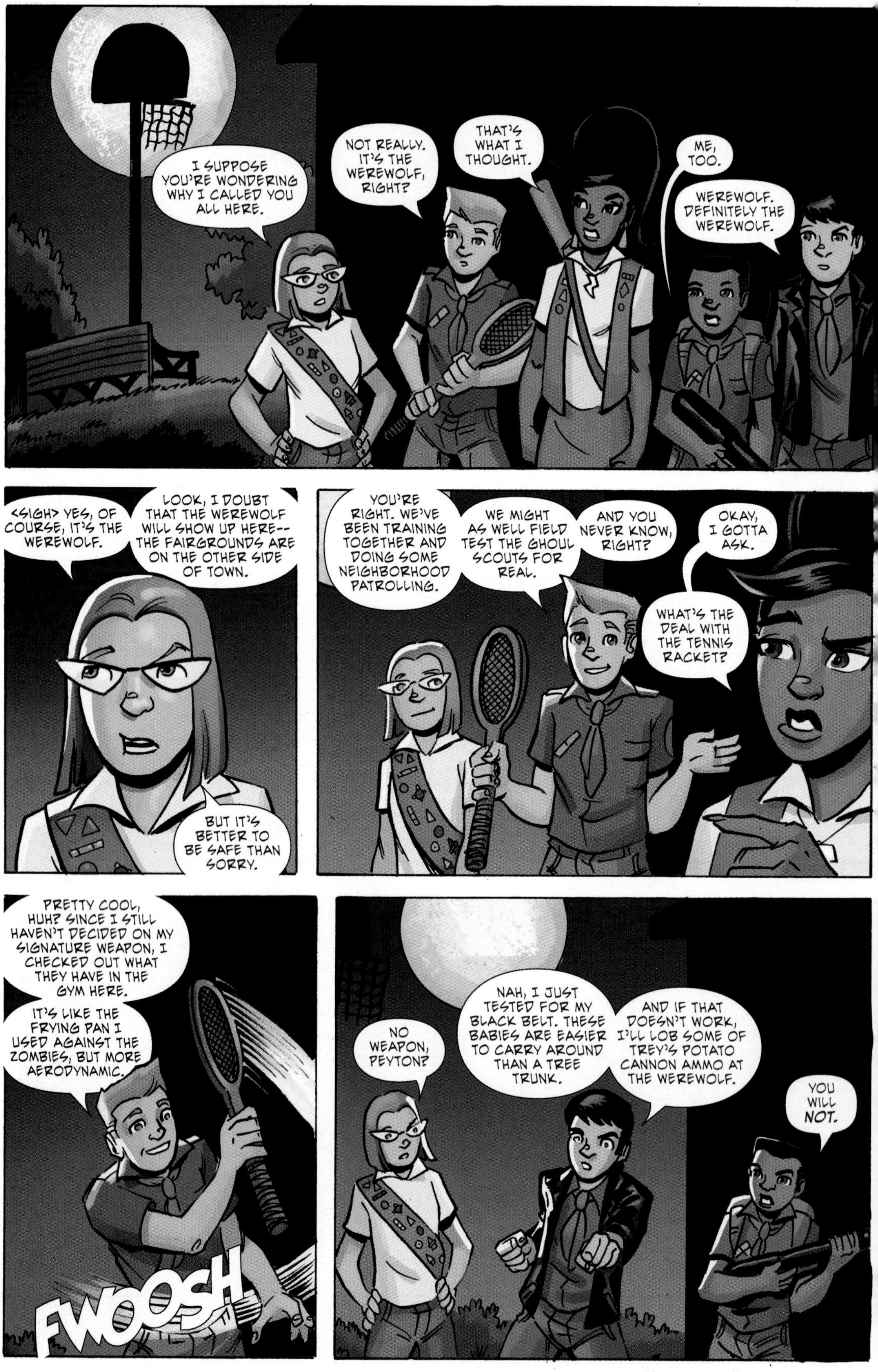
I SUPPOSE YOU'RE WONDERING WHY I CALLED YOU ALL HERE.
NOT REALLY. IT'S THE WEREWOLF, RIGHT?
THAT'S WHAT I THOUGHT.
ME, TOO.
WEREWOLF. DEFINITELY THE WEREWOLF.
<SIGH> YES, OF COURSE, IT'S THE WEREWOLF.
LOOK, I DOUBT THAT THE WEREWOLF WILL SHOW UP HERE-- THE FAIRGROUNDS ARE ON THE OTHER SIDE OF TOWN.
BUT IT'S BETTER TO BE SAFE THAN SORRY.
YOU'RE RIGHT. WE'VE BEEN TRAINING TOGETHER AND DOING SOME NEIGHBORHOOD PATROLLING.
WE MIGHT AS WELL FIELD TEST THE GHOUL SCOUTS FOR REAL.
AND YOU NEVER KNOW, RIGHT?
OKAY, I GOTTA ASK.
WHAT'S THE DEAL WITH THE TENNIS RACKET?
PRETTY COOL, HUH? SINCE I STILL HAVEN'T DECIDED ON MY SIGNATURE WEAPON, I CHECKED OUT WHAT THEY HAVE IN THE GYM HERE.
IT'S LIKE THE FRYING PAN I USED AGAINST THE ZOMBIES, BUT MORE AERODYNAMIC.
FWOOSH.
NO WEAPON, PEYTON?
NAH, I JUST TESTED FOR MY BLACK BELT. THESE BABIES ARE EASIER TO CARRY AROUND THAN A TREE TRUNK.
AND IF THAT DOESN'T WORK, I'LL LOB SOME OF TREY'S POTATO CANNON AMMO AT THE WEREWOLF.
YOU WILL *NOT.*

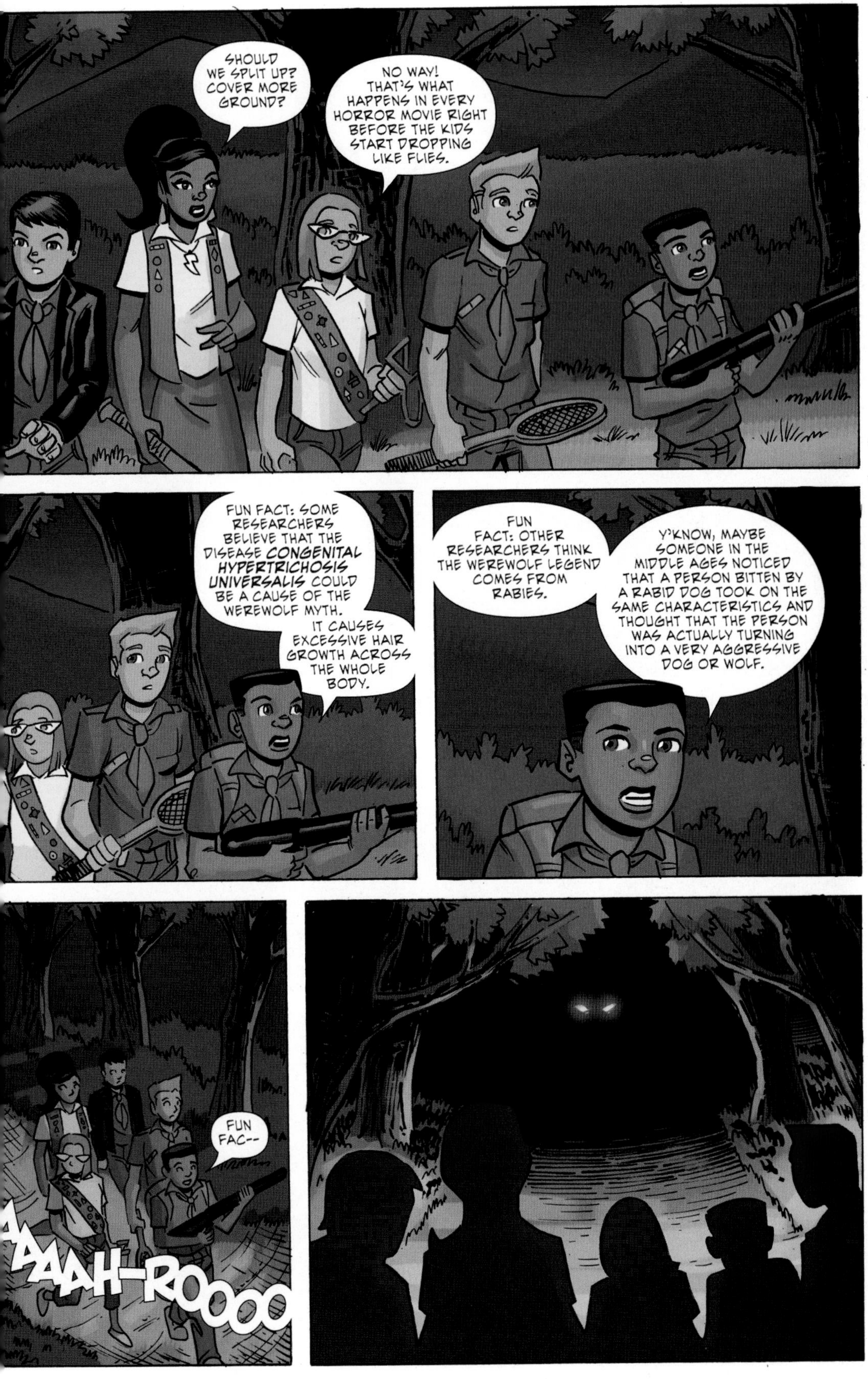
SHOULD WE SPLIT UP? COVER MORE GROUND?
NO WAY! THAT'S WHAT HAPPENS IN EVERY HORROR MOVIE RIGHT BEFORE THE KIDS START DROPPING LIKE FLIES.
FUN FACT: SOME RESEARCHERS BELIEVE THAT THE DISEASE **CONGENITAL HYPERTRICHOSIS UNIVERSALIS** COULD BE A CAUSE OF THE WEREWOLF MYTH.
IT CAUSES EXCESSIVE HAIR GROWTH ACROSS THE WHOLE BODY.
FUN FACT: OTHER RESEARCHERS THINK THE WEREWOLF LEGEND COMES FROM RABIES.
Y'KNOW, MAYBE SOMEONE IN THE MIDDLE AGES NOTICED THAT A PERSON BITTEN BY A RABID DOG TOOK ON THE SAME CHARACTERISTICS AND THOUGHT THAT THE PERSON WAS ACTUALLY TURNING INTO A VERY AGGRESSIVE DOG OR WOLF.
FUN FAC--
AAAAH-ROOOOO

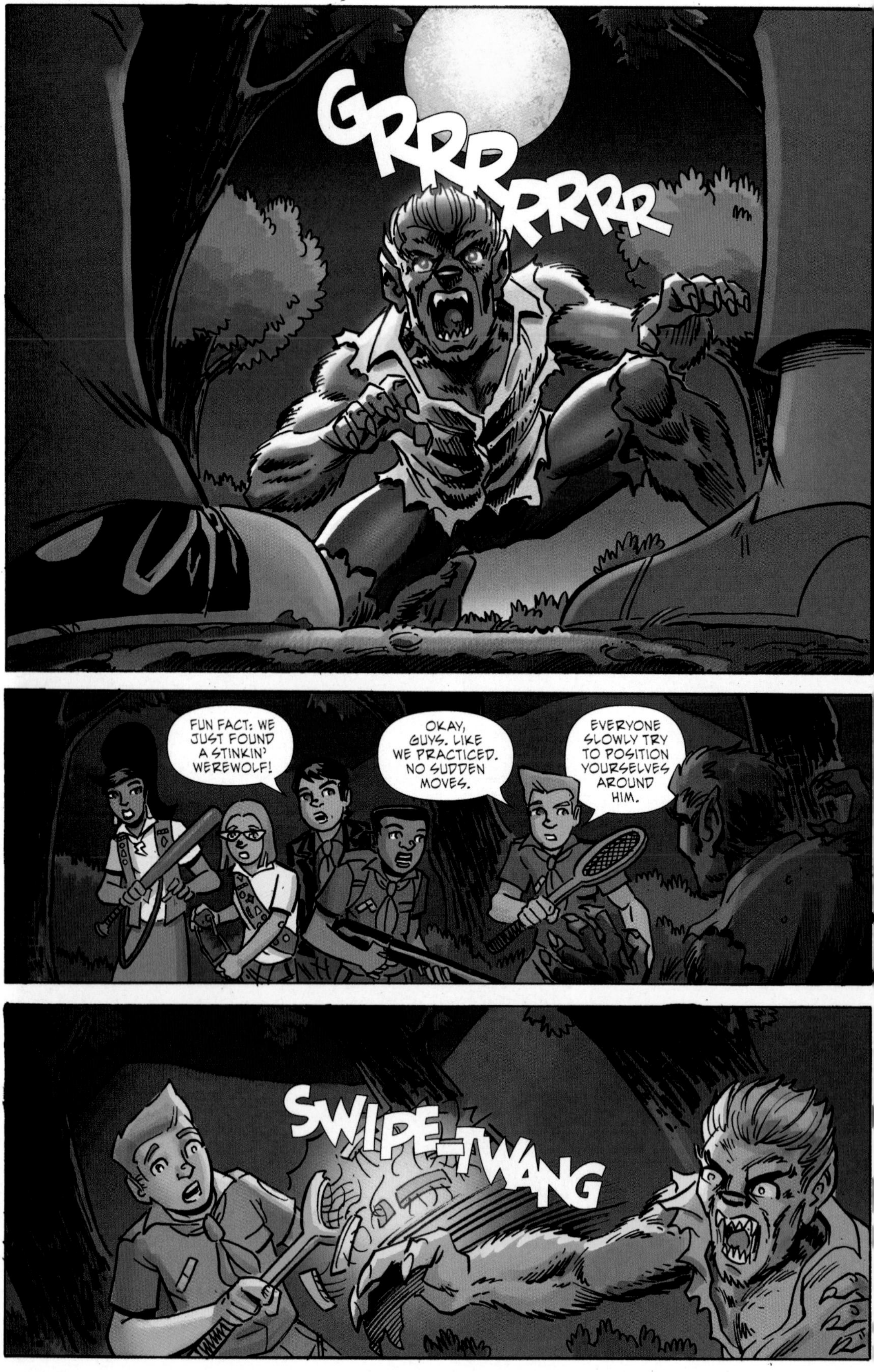
GRRRRRRR
FUN FACT: WE JUST FOUND A STINKIN' WEREWOLF!
OKAY, GUYS. LIKE WE PRACTICED. NO SUDDEN MOVES.
EVERYONE SLOWLY TRY TO POSITION YOURSELVES AROUND HIM.
SWIPE-TWANG

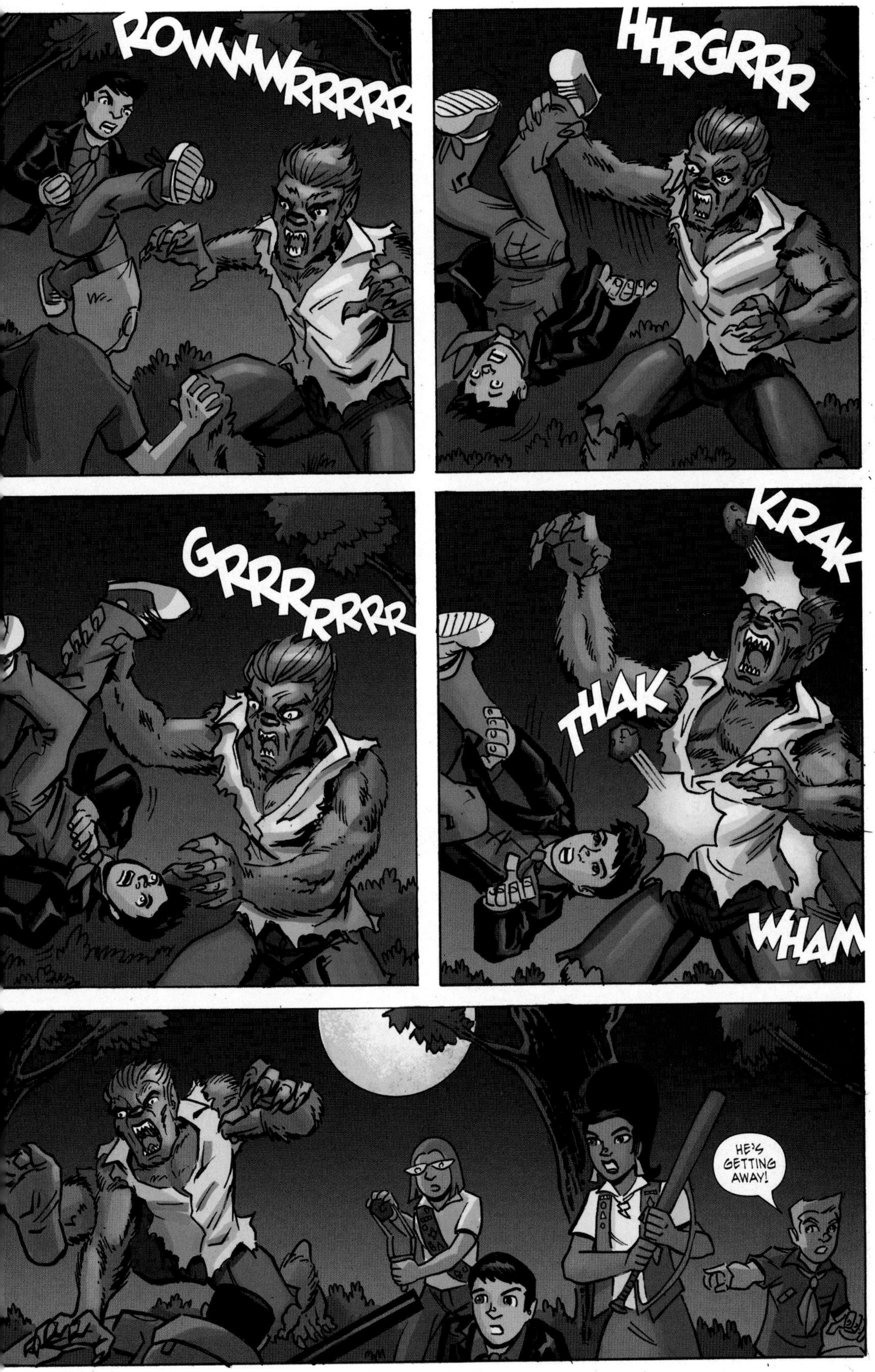
ROWWWRRRRRR
HHRGRRR
GRRRRRRR
KRAK
THAK
WHAM
HE'S GETTING AWAY!

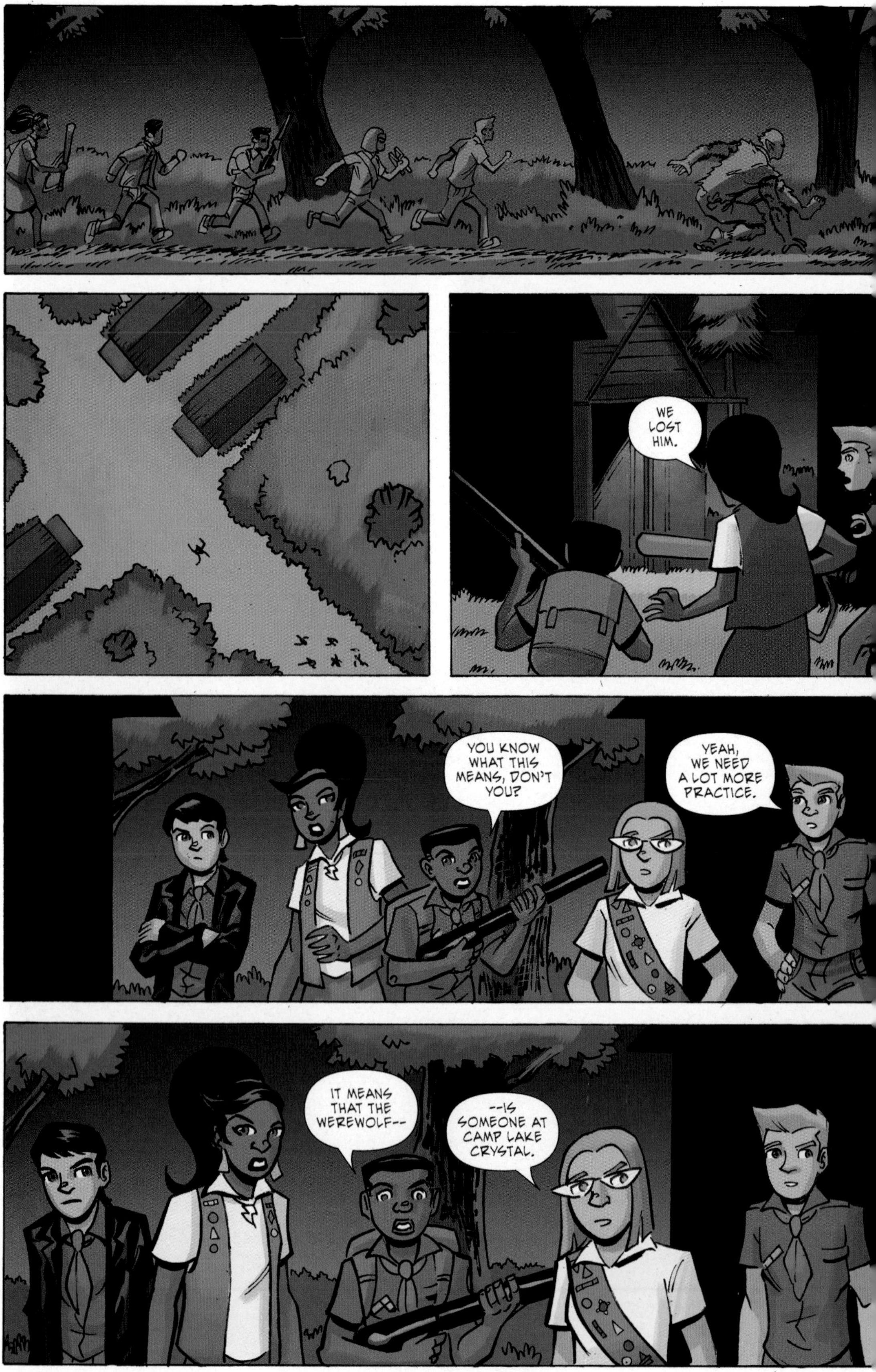
WE LOST HIM.
YOU KNOW WHAT THIS MEANS, DON'T YOU?
YEAH, WE NEED A LOT MORE PRACTICE.
IT MEANS THAT THE WEREWOLF--
--IS SOMEONE AT CAMP LAKE CRYSTAL.

GHOUL SCOUTS™

WHERE'D JEFF GO?

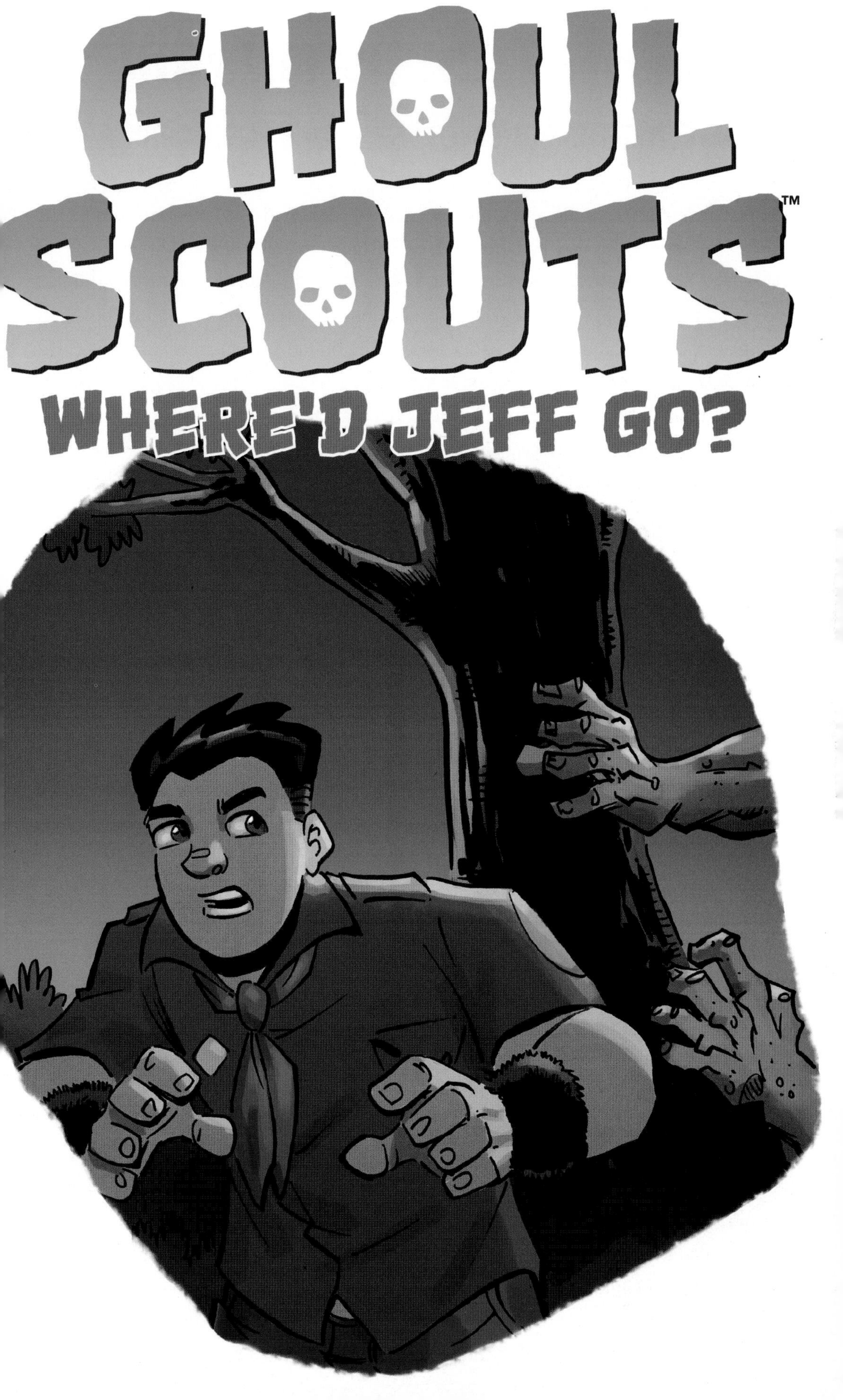

WRITTEN BY **CHRIS MURRIN**
ILLUSTRATED BY **MARK STEGBAUER**

Monsters spilled from the forest into the clearing. Terrified, the boys ran from their campsite. Jeff stopped short when one of the gruesome creatures blocked his escape path. Right behind him, Peyton snagged his right foot on a spiny root, tripping right into Jeff's broad back on his way to the ground. Jeff turned and ran away from the oncoming creep. Looking back over his shoulder, he saw Peyton lying on the ground and said, "Later, Bro! Every man for himself!" He ran into the forest.

Jeff barreled through the moonlit woods. Low branches and tall shrubs scratched his arms and grabbed at his Wilderness Scout uniform. Even over the sound of his own running, Jeff thought he could hear movement all through the forest. He ran for what felt like ten minutes, though it had only been two. Ahead, a low-hanging branch of a willow tree blocked his visibility. He stiff-armed it out of the way and almost ran into another of the monsters!

Still a dozen feet ahead, the creature ambled straight toward Jeff. Its skin had a greenish pallor made all the more sickly looking in the shadows. It grunted through yellow teeth, "WWRREEEEHHH."

"Aaagh!" Jeff screamed. He pivoted off his right foot and turned to his left. The creature slowly pursued Jeff as he fled. After running about twenty yards, Jeff saw a gap between the trees ahead, and through that gap, a path! That's gotta go somewhere safe, he thought. He headed straight for it, but just before he got there, the gap closed.

"BLAAAAAAR," uttered yet another creature as it shambled between the trees. Jeff stopped. He couldn't help himself. He laughed. So that's how it feels when I close the hole on a running back, the star linebacker thought to himself.

"AARRRAAHHHH." Jeff had forgotten about the monster behind him! He thought, all this noise'll bring—

"NNMMMSSS," now another one approached to his left!

"GRNNAAAA," a fourth creep boxed Jeff in, and he could see two more of them following behind it. Jeff spun in a circle, looking for a safe direction to run, but he didn't see one. The monsters had him surrounded. They closed in.

Gotta get to the path, Jeff thought, but how, with that thing in the way? His mind returned to football. He was still playing running back, and what would a running back do in his situation? Jeff thought about his football hero. What would Walter Payton do?

Jeff backed as far away as he could from the creep blocking the gap without getting caught by the one behind him. He bent his knees and bent at the waist, like a runner in the starting blocks. He grinned. "Bring it," he said under his breath. He ran toward the creature. Though he only had a couple dozen feet of open space, Jeff reached top speed quickly.

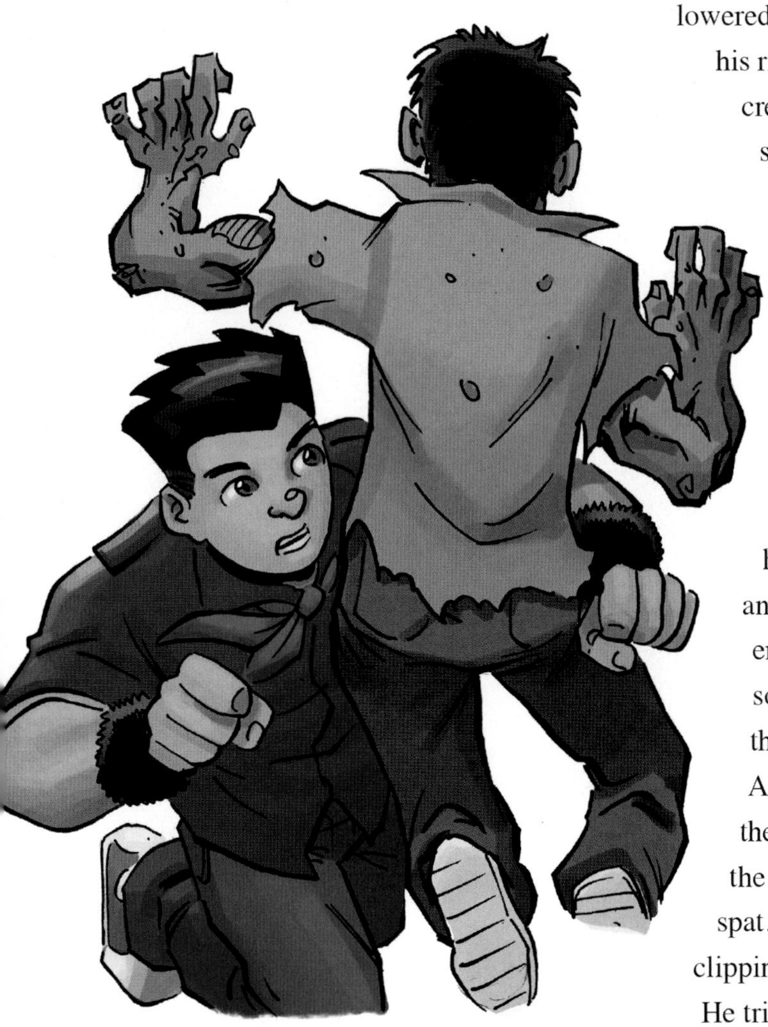

Right before he got to the monster, Jeff lowered his head and jutted out his right shoulder. He hit the creature at full-speed, his shoulder catching it right in its abdomen.

SPLUT!

Everything went dark. The impact pushed Jeff back upright, and he could feel the uneven woods give way to the smoother path beneath his feet, but he couldn't see anything. Something covered his head and shoulders, something drippy, something that smelled like old moss. A trickle of goo ran down the side of his face and into the corner of his mouth. He spat, "Blagh!" Tastes like grass clippings, he thought.

He tried to wipe his face with one of his wristbands, but his arms got tangled in what felt like thin vines covering his head. He could hear the groaning of the creatures coming up behind him, but without his vision, Jeff could only stumble along the edge of the path, feeling his way with his feet. More of the goo seeped into his mouth. He blew it back out with a "PHEEHH!"

Suddenly, Jeff felt something grab his shirt near his shoulders. He felt pressure on his stomach. The world turned upside-down. Jeff felt himself flying through the air, flipping head over heels. He landed flat on his back, hard. Ooof! The wind rushed out of him. Stars briefly interrupted the blackness. Jeff gasped, trying to catch his breath. He could only manage to whisper, "Ow. What the--?"

A girl's voice came from where Jeff had been standing a moment ago. "Ah, crud!" the voice said. "I thought you were one of those … things."

Jeff just lay on the path. He exhaled, "No."

"Well can you blame me?" the voice asked. "Look at you. You look just like 'em. You're stumbling around, all covered in this gunk, making weird sounds." Jeff could feel pulling at the vines around his head. He felt them come free and saw a speck of moonlight.

He
rubbed
his eyes
with his wrist-
bands, clearing the
goo out of them. When his
vision cleared, he saw the smiling face of a girl around his age hovering over him.
"You all right, big guy?" she asked, and then answered her own question. "Yeah, you're all
right. Come on." She stood up and grabbed Jeff's left forearm, putting her own in his hand.
She backed up and pulled, using leverage to hoist Jeff back to his feet. Only when he was
fully standing did Jeff realize just how short she was. The top of her head barely made it
to his chest, but she had a wide, sturdy frame much like his own. He saw that she wore the
uniform of a Gaia Scout.

"I'm Ann," she said.

"Jeff," he replied, still grimacing as he pulled the last tendrils of whatever it was from
his shoulders. "What did you do to me?"

"That? That was a circle throw," she said, "Judo."

"Oh. Cool," was all Jeff could come up with. He wanted to say more, but drew a blank.
Fortunately, horror saved him from an awkward silence.

"GGNNNAAARRRRR," one of the creatures moaned from behind him. Jeff had
forgotten about them in all the blindness, flying, and pain. He turned and saw all six creeps
still chasing after him, but one of them looked different. Where its right hip should have
been, there was a Jeff-shaped hole with vine-like veins hanging down, oozing a dark, green
syrup.

"Let's go," Jeff said, starting to run down the trail away from the monsters.

Ann chased after him and grabbed his shirttail. "Wait," she said, "that just leads deeper

into the forest." She pointed a thumb back the way they came. "Everyone else went the other way."

"Everyone else?"

"Yeah. Your scoutmaster called ours. Everyone's heading to Peart Elementary to hole up."

"So what do we do?"

"Over, under, around, or through," Ann said.

Jeff looked puzzled. "Huh?"

"You're a bright boy, aren't you? Only four possibilities, and since we can't dodge them, we're going to have to fight through these guys."

"Oh, okay. But hey, wait a second." Jeff pointed at the deformed creature. "I hit that one a minute ago and look at it. I don't think these are guys at all. They just look like it."

"You know what that means, don't you?" Ann asked. A blank stare from Jeff was the only answer she got. Her eye sparkled in the moonlight. "No holds barred."

Jeff understood that. He punched a fist into his left hand. "Let's do this."

They walked back down the path, closing the distance between them and the trudging, growling creatures. They stopped about ten feet back. "Ladies first," Ann said, bowing to Jeff.

"Hilarious," Jeff said. He took a few jogging steps toward the deformed monster, then leapt in the air and brought his right knee up. The knee landed in the center of the creature's chest, and with it already off-balance due to its missing midsection, it toppled backward. The creature flopped around on its back like a turtle, unable to get up, growling and scratching toward the stars.

Ann walked past them with a determined look. "Not bad, but check this out," she said. She let the nearest monster get close. In a blur, she grabbed its right wrist and spun toward its right side. She stopped with its arm barred across her chest and its right shoulder in her left hand. The pushed the creature forward and down. When its momentum started pulling it to the ground, she let go of its arm and brought a knee up, hitting it directly between the eyes with a dull thud! The creature fell in a heap, flat on its face, and didn't move or make a sound.

"Looks like they don't like head shots," she said, standing over it.

"Good to know." Jeff moved his wristbands up to his hands and wrapped his knuckles in them. Taking a boxer's stance, Jeff sized up the next monster, looking for an opening.

"RRRNNNGG—" the monster started to growl, but Jeff stepped forward and hit it square in the nose with a left jab. It looked surprised by the punch. Jeff stepped back, bouncing on the balls of his feet. The creature advanced, and Jeff again stepped up, delivering a one-two punch: a straight left, followed by a right cross. The creature's head spun to its right, and it was out cold before it even began to fall.

Jeff turned back to face Ann, his hands raised like he had just won the heavyweight championship. "Wooo!" He didn't notice how close behind him the next monster was.

"Watch it!" Ann shouted. Just before the beast could get its hands on Jeff, Ann shoved him out of the way. She grabbed the creep by the left wrist, hooked her left arm underneath its left arm, and turned so it was draped over her back. She bent forward, expecting the monster to flip over her. Instead, she heard a sound like a tree branch snapping as its hand came off in hers. The creature grabbed onto Ann with its remaining hand and opened its mouth for a nice, tasty bite of Gaia Scout.

"No!" Jeff said. He threw a flying tackle at the monster, driving it away from Ann. All three of them toppled to the ground. The creep hit its head against a rock, knocking it unconscious. Jeff felt a hand grasp his ankle. He had fallen too close to the deformed creature he had kneed, and it now had a hold on him! It pulled itself toward his leg, and opened its jaw to take a bite. Out of nowhere, a fist flew in and hit the creature in the temple, stopping it instantly.

"Nice throw," Jeff said.

Lying propped up on her elbows, Ann said, "Thanks!"

"KKRRRAAAAAGGGH." Two more creatures approached, one ahead of the other. Jeff picked himself up. "You got another one of those circle throws in you?"

Ann did the same. "Sure. You want me to take the front or the back?"

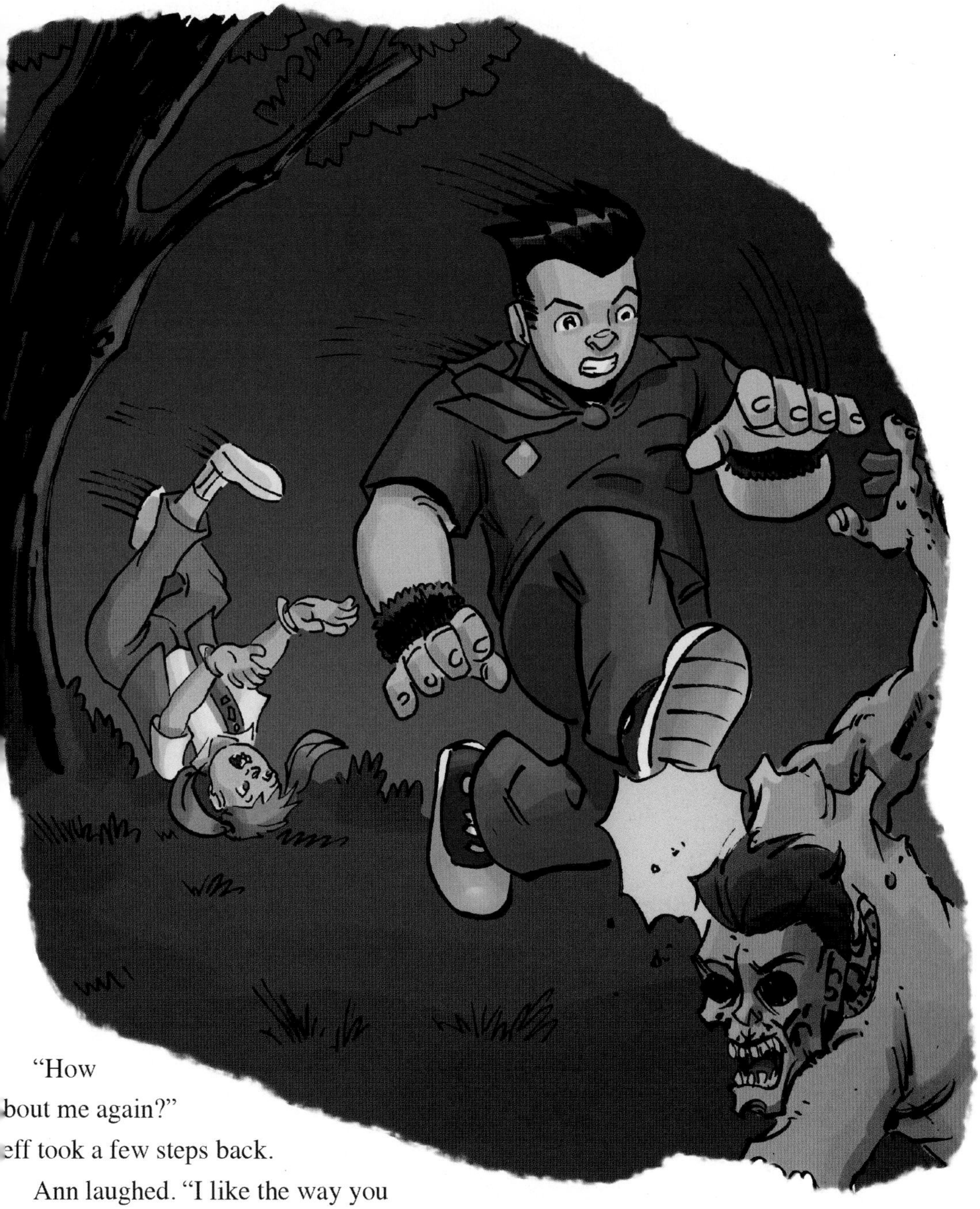

"How
bout me again?"
eff took a few steps back.

Ann laughed. "I like the way you
ink." She turned her back to the creatures as Jeff lined up the shot.

"Ready?" he asked her.

"Come at me, Bro."

Jeff rushed toward Ann, and just as she had before, she grabbed his shirt near his shoul-
ers, planted a foot in his abdomen and rolled on her back, sending him flipping over her
ead. This time, though, Jeff was ready for it. As he flipped over, he aimed for the closer
monster, hitting it with a vicious drop kick. With Ann's throw adding to his own momen-
um, Jeff's kick hit the creature hard enough to knock it a few inches off the ground and
end it flying backward, headfirst.

CROONK!

With a hollow, cracking sound, the two monsters' heads collided. They fell in a heap, knocked out. Jeff stood over them, laughing. "That was fun," he said.

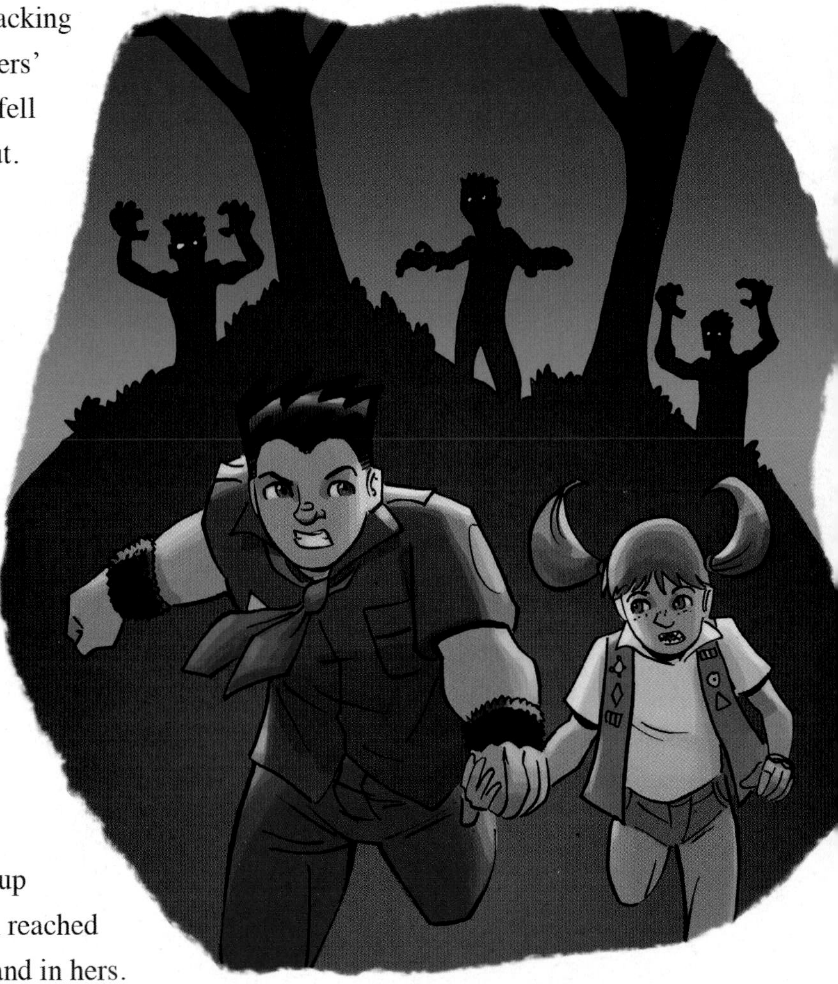

Ann joined him. "Yeah," she said, "we make a pretty good team." She looked up at Jeff and smiled. A loud, rustling sound came from just beyond the tree line, reminding them that they still weren't alone.

"We better catch up with the others." Ann reached out and took Jeff's hand in hers. All of a sudden Jeff's face felt hot and he felt a little unsteady, as if he was standing on a boat instead of solid ground. "Come on!" she said as she pulled his hand, dragging him into motion. Jeff's head cleared a bit as they began to hurry down the path. He could still feel the warmth in his cheeks, though. He struggled for something to say.

"How'd you end up all alone, anyway?" he asked.

Ann slowed her pace and looked down. "Oh … uh … the other girls, they uh … they forgot …" she hesitated, then corrected herself, "they asked me to uh … to walk behind everyone else." She regained her stride as she started to believe her own tale. "They needed me to bring up the rear. You know, cover our six. One of those things popped out of the woods. I stopped to take care of it, but everyone else ran ahead."

Jeff couldn't believe it. "They just left you behind?"

Ann nodded.

Jeff frowned. "What a bunch of jerks!" he said, as the two continued down the path to safety.

The events in this story take place immediately after page 5 of **Ghoul Scouts:** ***Night of the Unliving Undead.***

I WAS A TWEENAGE WEREWOLF!

CHAPTER
TWO

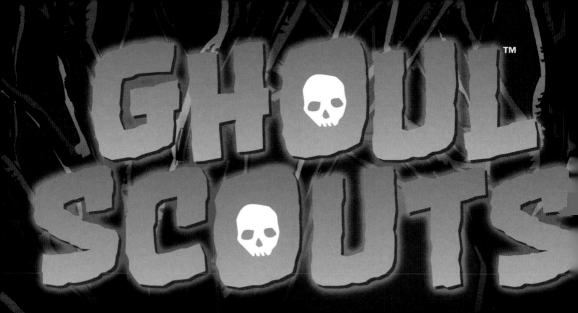

GHOUL SCOUTS

TM

Story and Letters
STEVE BRYANT
@SteveBryantArt

Art
MARK STEGBAUER
@MarkStegbauer

Colors
JASON MILLET
@Jason_Millet

Edited by
CHRIS MURRIN
@ChrisMurrin

Color Assist
DREW BROWNE
@TheDrewBrowne

Cover
MARK STEGBAUER
& JASON MILLET

Bryan Seaton: Publisher/CEO **| Shawn Gabborin:** Editor In Chief **| Jason Martin:** Publisher-Danger Zone
Nicole D'Andria: Marketing Director/Editor **| Jim Dietz:** Social Media Manager **| Danielle Davison:** Executive Administ
Chad Cicconi: Camp Counselor **| Shawn Pryor:** President of Creator Relations

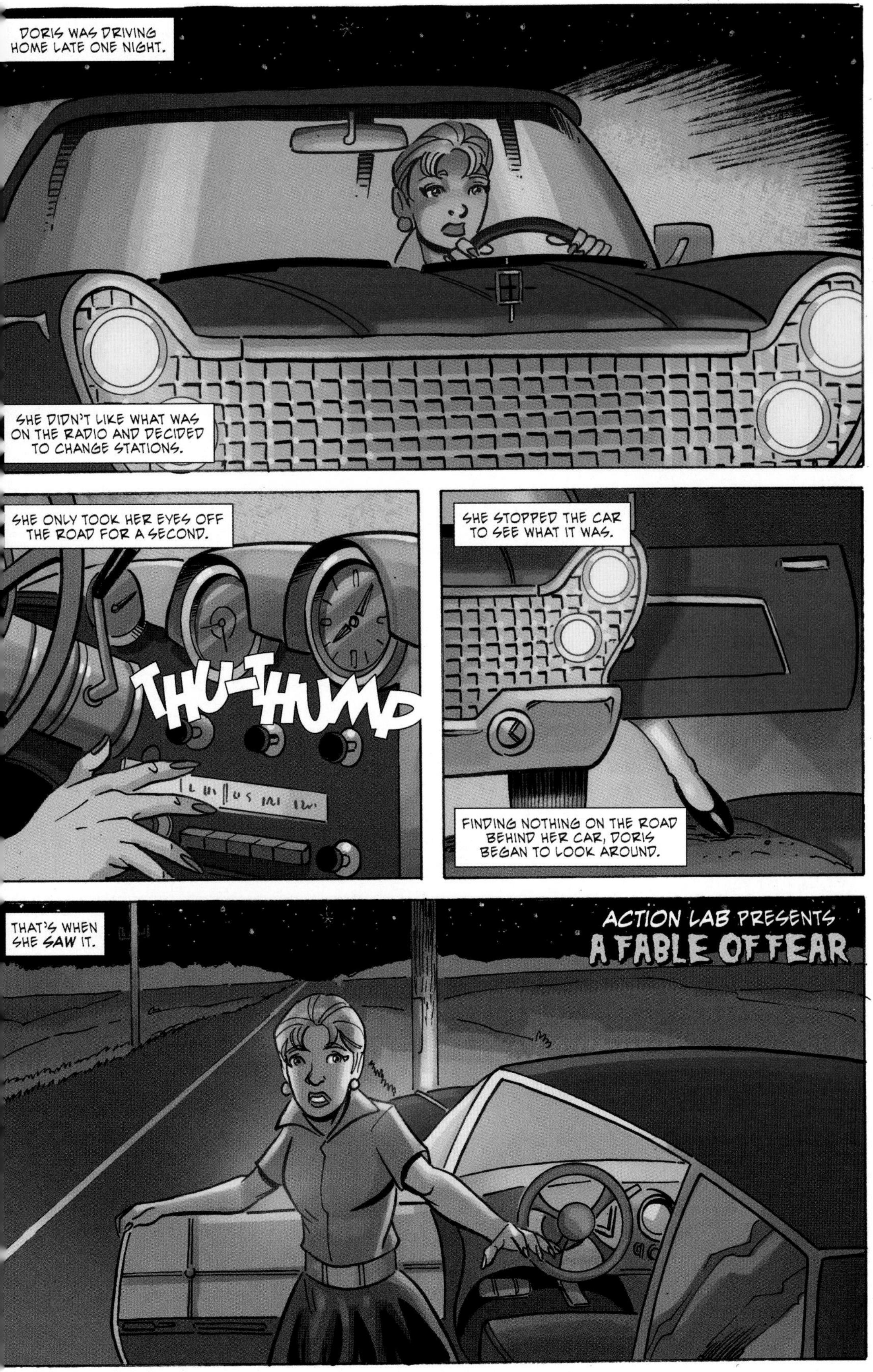
DORIS WAS DRIVING HOME LATE ONE NIGHT.
SHE DIDN'T LIKE WHAT WAS ON THE RADIO AND DECIDED TO CHANGE STATIONS.
SHE ONLY TOOK HER EYES OFF THE ROAD FOR A SECOND.
THU-THUMP
SHE STOPPED THE CAR TO SEE WHAT IT WAS.
FINDING NOTHING ON THE ROAD BEHIND HER CAR, DORIS BEGAN TO LOOK AROUND.
THAT'S WHEN SHE SAW IT.
ACTION LAB PRESENTS
A FABLE OF FEAR

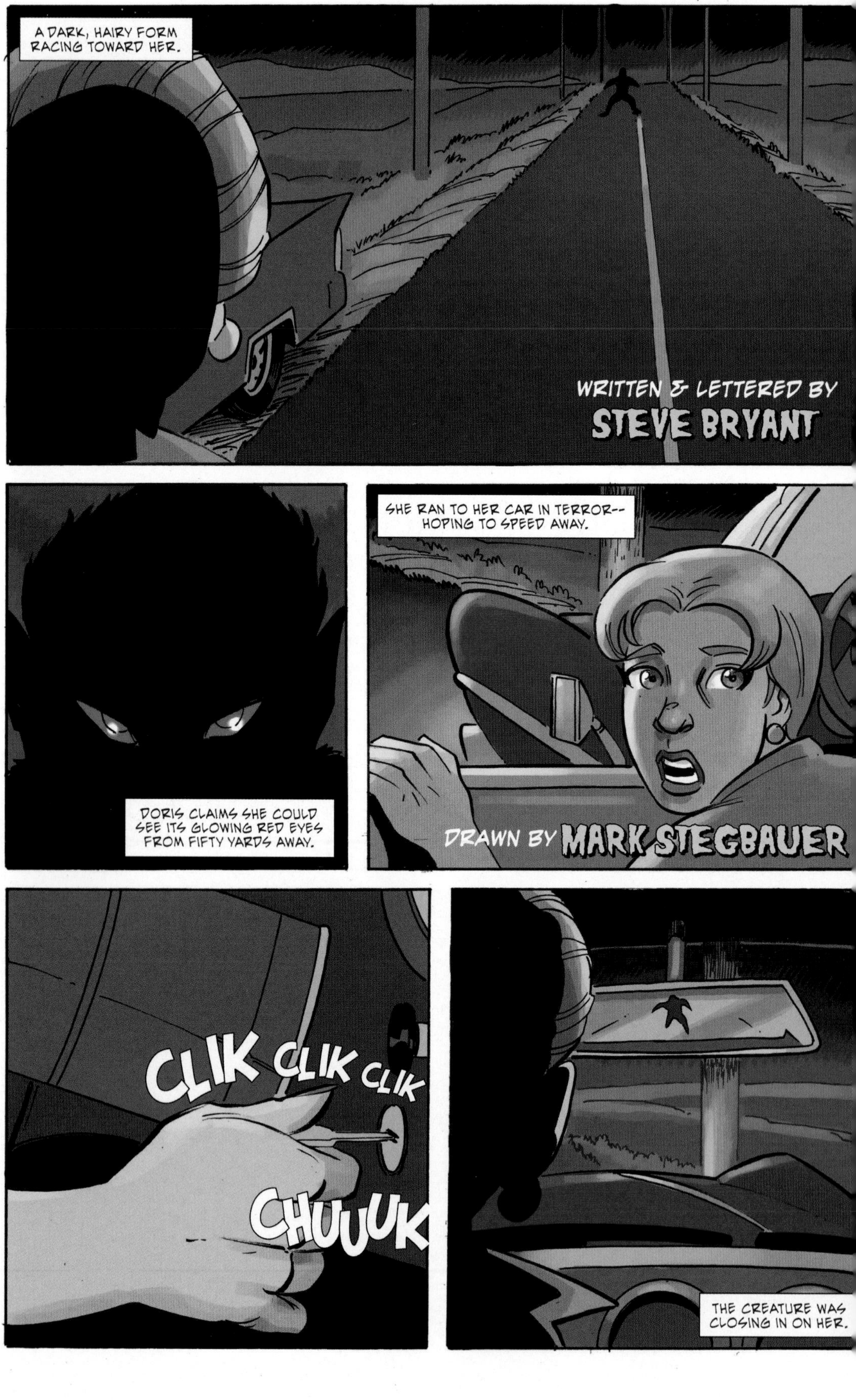
A DARK, HAIRY FORM RACING TOWARD HER.
WRITTEN & LETTERED BY
STEVE BRYANT
DORIS CLAIMS SHE COULD SEE ITS GLOWING RED EYES FROM FIFTY YARDS AWAY.
SHE RAN TO HER CAR IN TERROR-- HOPING TO SPEED AWAY.
DRAWN BY MARK STEGBAUER
CLIK CLIK CLIK
CHUUUK
THE CREATURE WAS CLOSING IN ON HER.

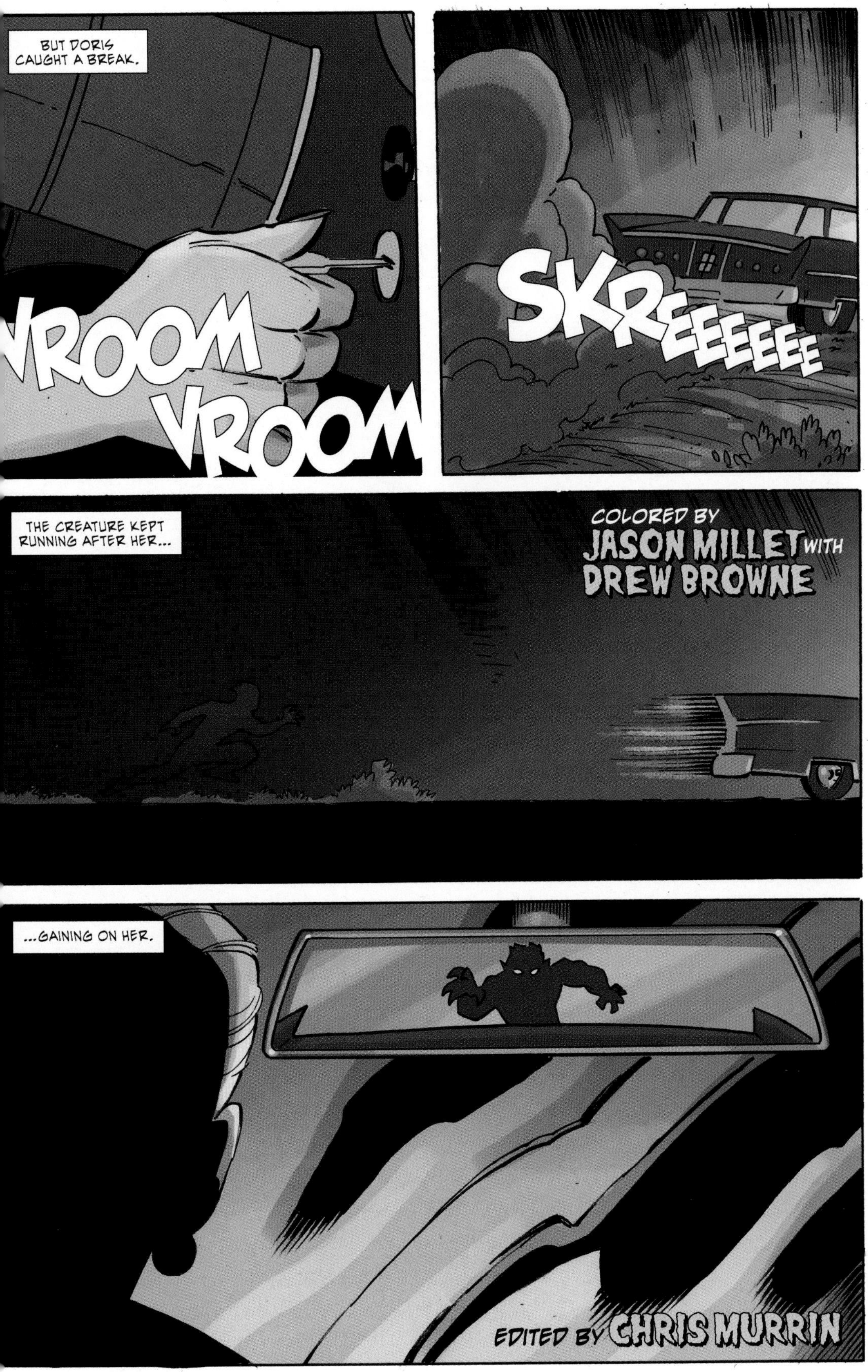
BUT DORIS CAUGHT A BREAK.
VROOM
VROOM
SKREEEEEEE
THE CREATURE KEPT RUNNING AFTER HER...
COLORED BY JASON MILLET WITH DREW BROWNE
...GAINING ON HER.
EDITED BY CHRIS MURRIN

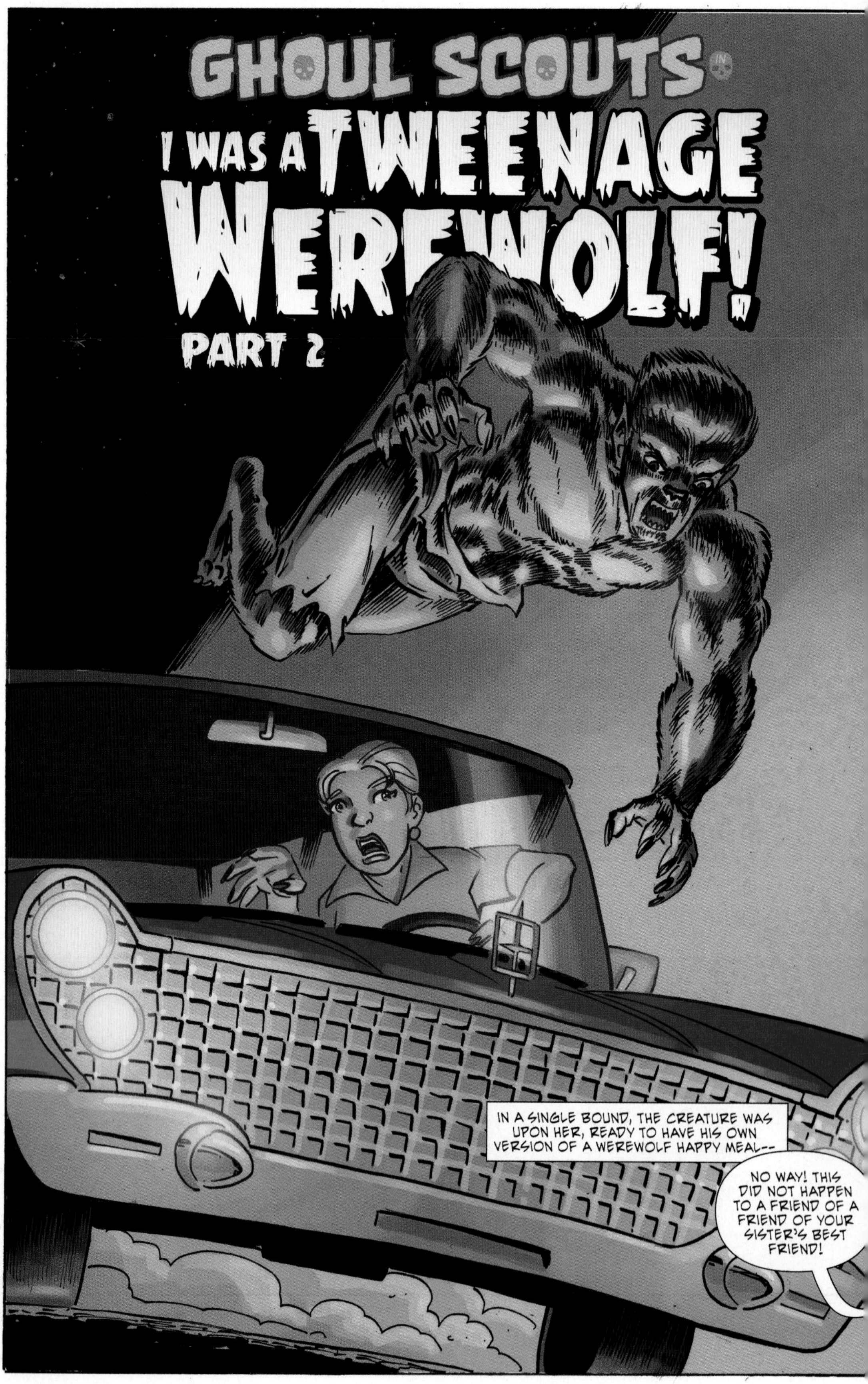
GHOUL SCOUTS IN
I WAS A TWEENAGE WEREWOLF!
PART 2
IN A SINGLE BOUND, THE CREATURE WAS UPON HER, READY TO HAVE HIS OWN VERSION OF A WEREWOLF HAPPY MEAL--
NO WAY! THIS DID NOT HAPPEN TO A FRIEND OF A FRIEND OF YOUR SISTER'S BEST FRIEND!

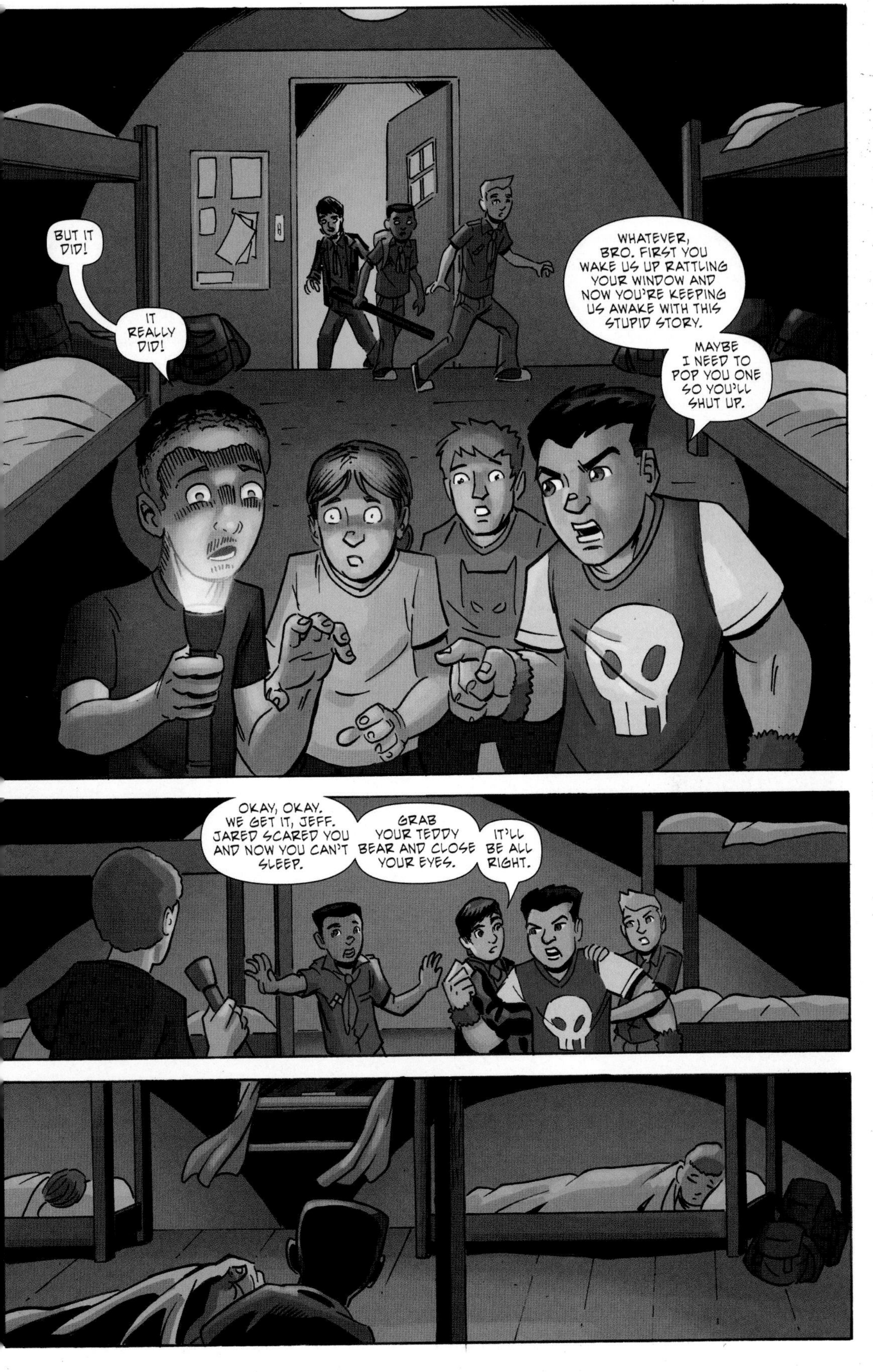
BUT IT DID!
IT REALLY DID!
WHATEVER, BRO. FIRST YOU WAKE US UP RATTLING YOUR WINDOW AND NOW YOU'RE KEEPING US AWAKE WITH THIS STUPID STORY.
MAYBE I NEED TO POP YOU ONE SO YOU'LL SHUT UP.
OKAY, OKAY. WE GET IT, JEFF. JARED SCARED YOU AND NOW YOU CAN'T SLEEP.
GRAB YOUR TEDDY BEAR AND CLOSE YOUR EYES.
IT'LL BE ALL RIGHT.

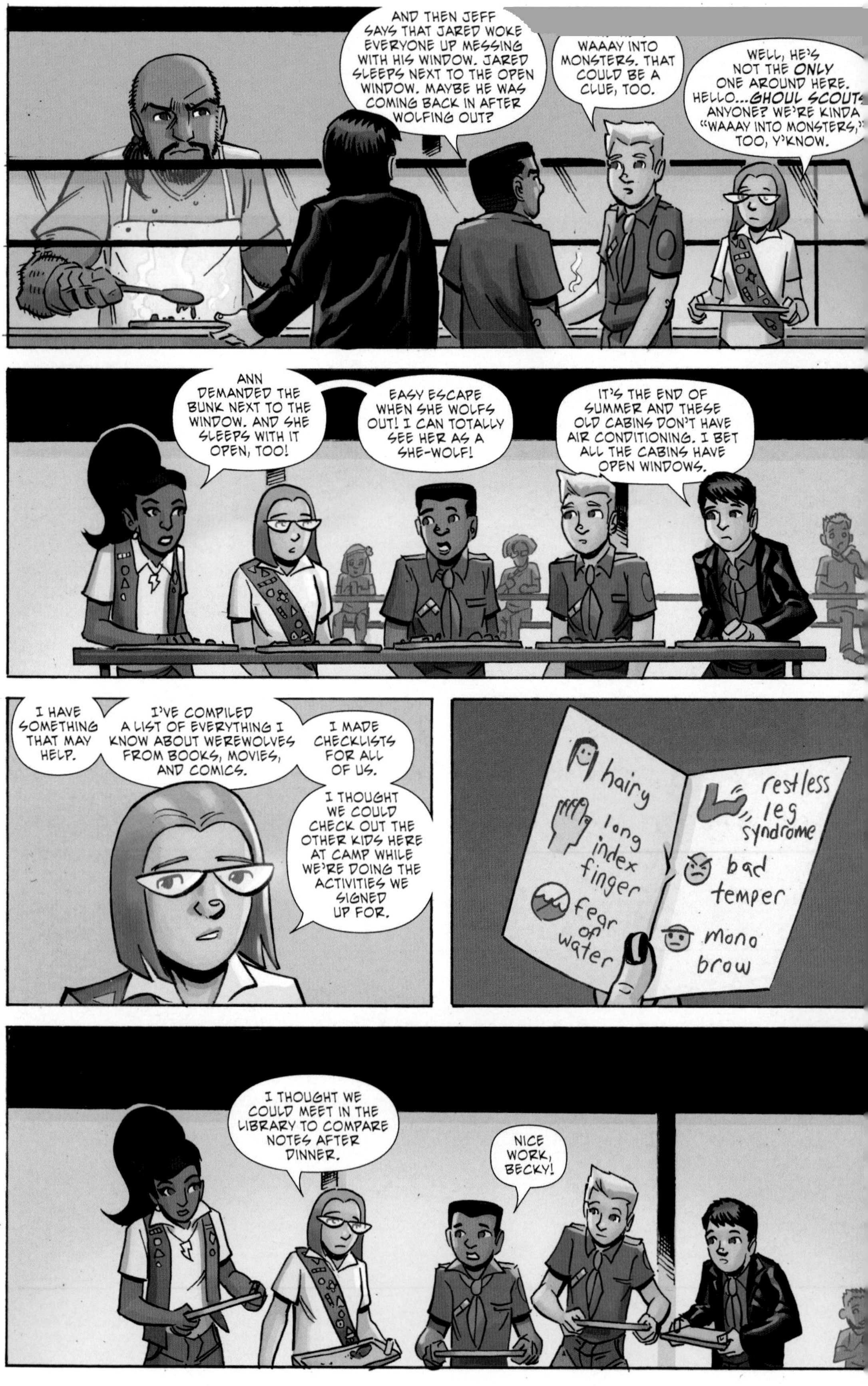
AND THEN JEFF SAYS THAT JARED WOKE EVERYONE UP MESSING WITH HIS WINDOW. JARED SLEEPS NEXT TO THE OPEN WINDOW. MAYBE HE WAS COMING BACK IN AFTER WOLFING OUT?
WAAAY INTO MONSTERS. THAT COULD BE A CLUE, TOO.
WELL, HE'S NOT THE ONLY ONE AROUND HERE. HELLO...GHOUL SCOUTS ANYONE? WE'RE KINDA "WAAAY INTO MONSTERS," TOO, Y'KNOW.
ANN DEMANDED THE BUNK NEXT TO THE WINDOW. AND SHE SLEEPS WITH IT OPEN, TOO!
EASY ESCAPE WHEN SHE WOLFS OUT! I CAN TOTALLY SEE HER AS A SHE-WOLF!
IT'S THE END OF SUMMER AND THESE OLD CABINS DON'T HAVE AIR CONDITIONING. I BET ALL THE CABINS HAVE OPEN WINDOWS.
I HAVE SOMETHING THAT MAY HELP.
I'VE COMPILED A LIST OF EVERYTHING I KNOW ABOUT WEREWOLVES FROM BOOKS, MOVIES, AND COMICS.
I MADE CHECKLISTS FOR ALL OF US.
I THOUGHT WE COULD CHECK OUT THE OTHER KIDS HERE AT CAMP WHILE WE'RE DOING THE ACTIVITIES WE SIGNED UP FOR.
hairy
long index finger
fear of water
restless leg syndrome
bad temper
mono brow
I THOUGHT WE COULD MEET IN THE LIBRARY TO COMPARE NOTES AFTER DINNER.
NICE WORK, BECKY!

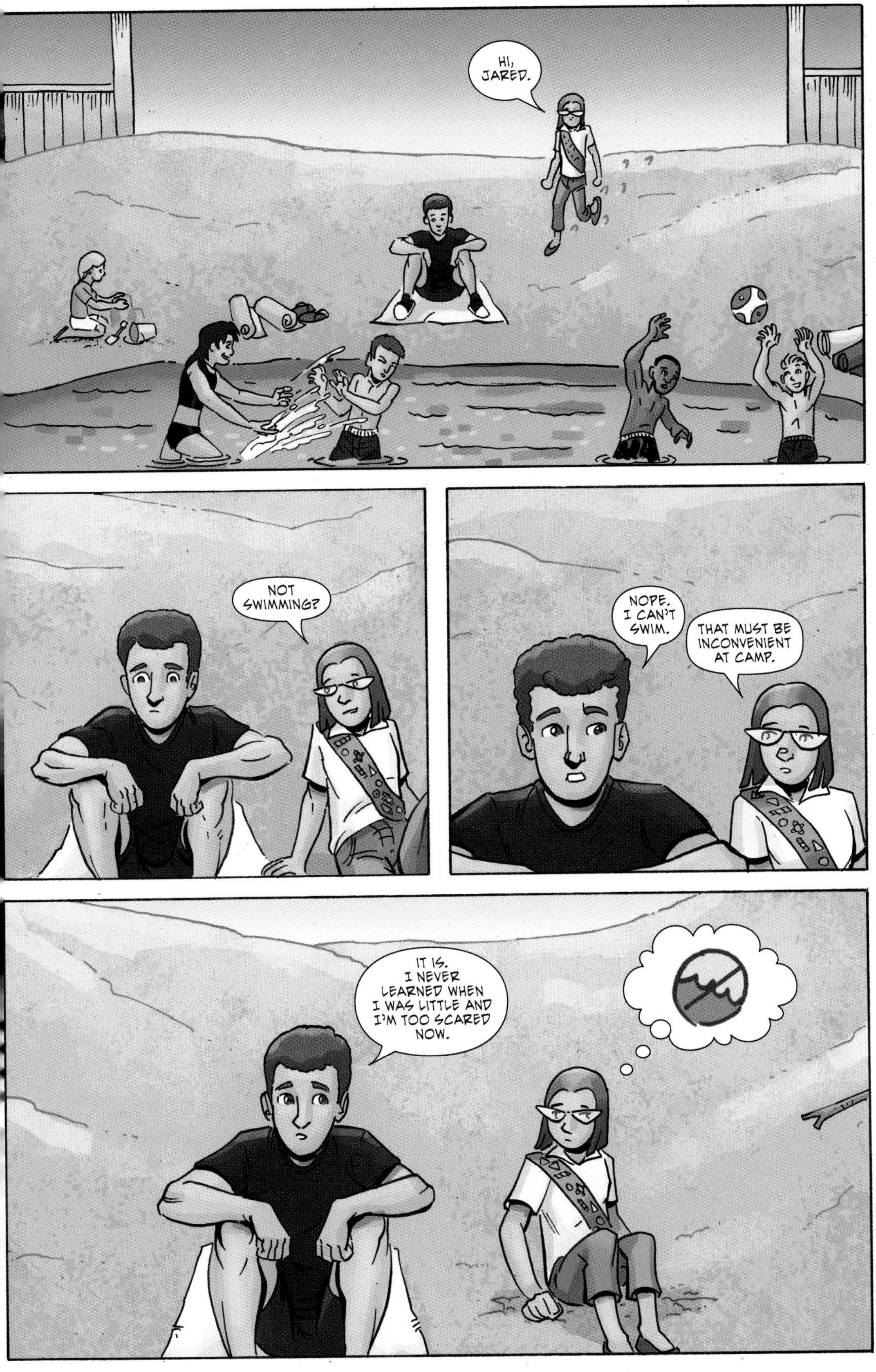
HI, JARED.
NOT SWIMMING?
NOPE. I CAN'T SWIM.
THAT MUST BE INCONVENIENT AT CAMP.
IT IS. I NEVER LEARNED WHEN I WAS LITTLE AND I'M TOO SCARED NOW.

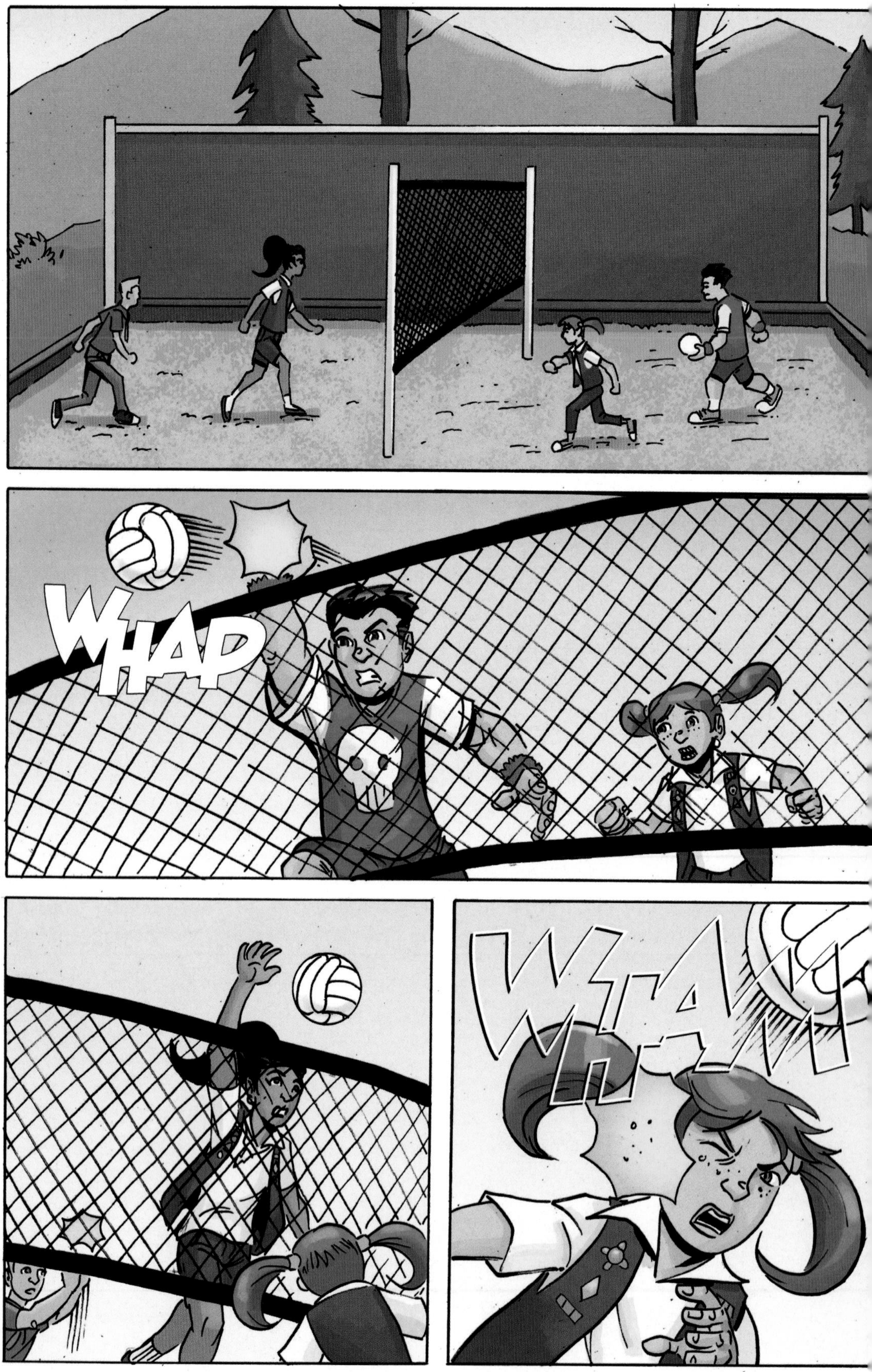
WHAP
WHAM

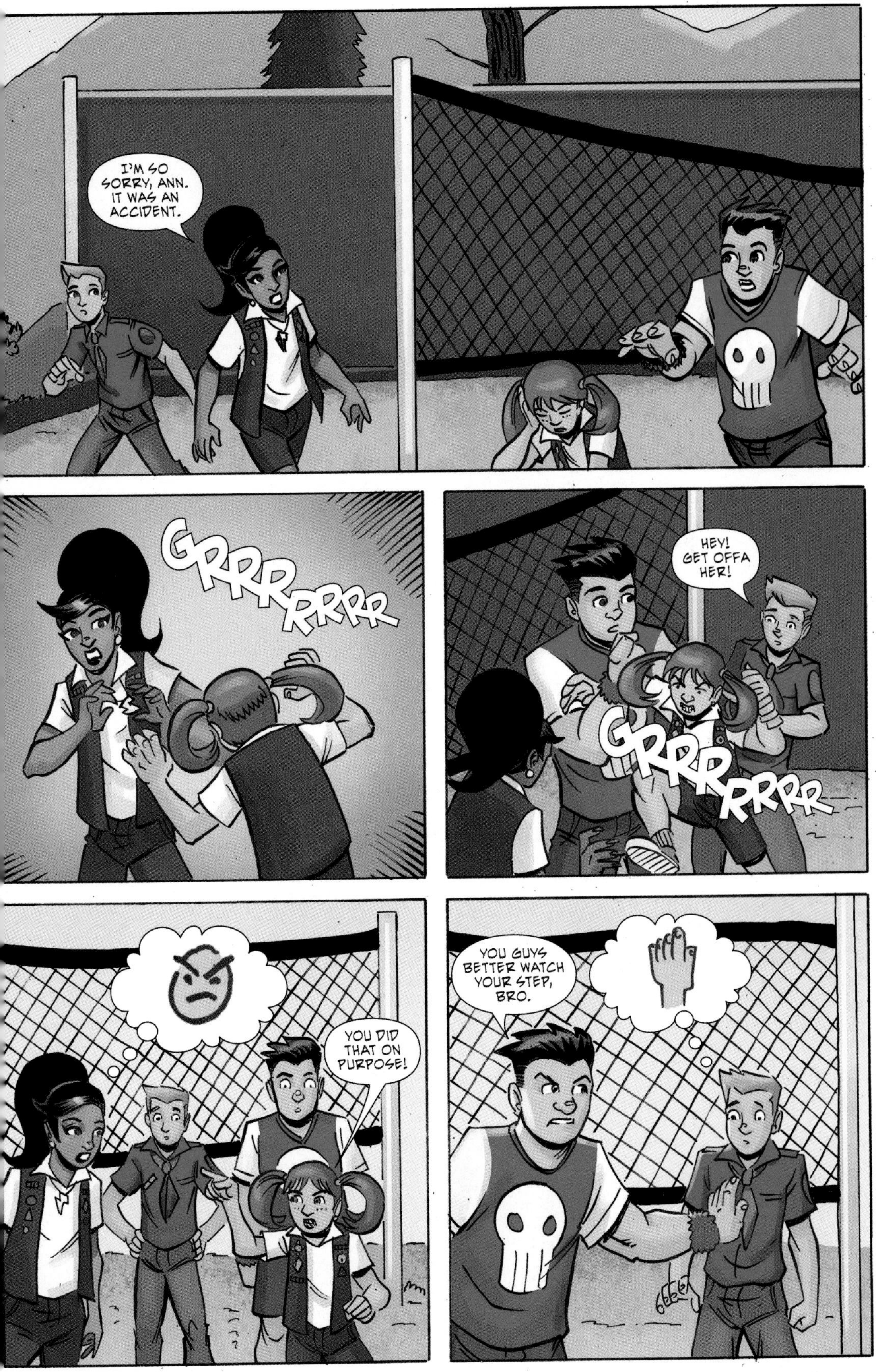
I'M SO SORRY, ANN. IT WAS AN ACCIDENT.
GRRRRRRR
HEY! GET OFFA HER!
GRRRRRRR
YOU DID THAT ON PURPOSE!
YOU GUYS BETTER WATCH YOUR STEP, BRO.

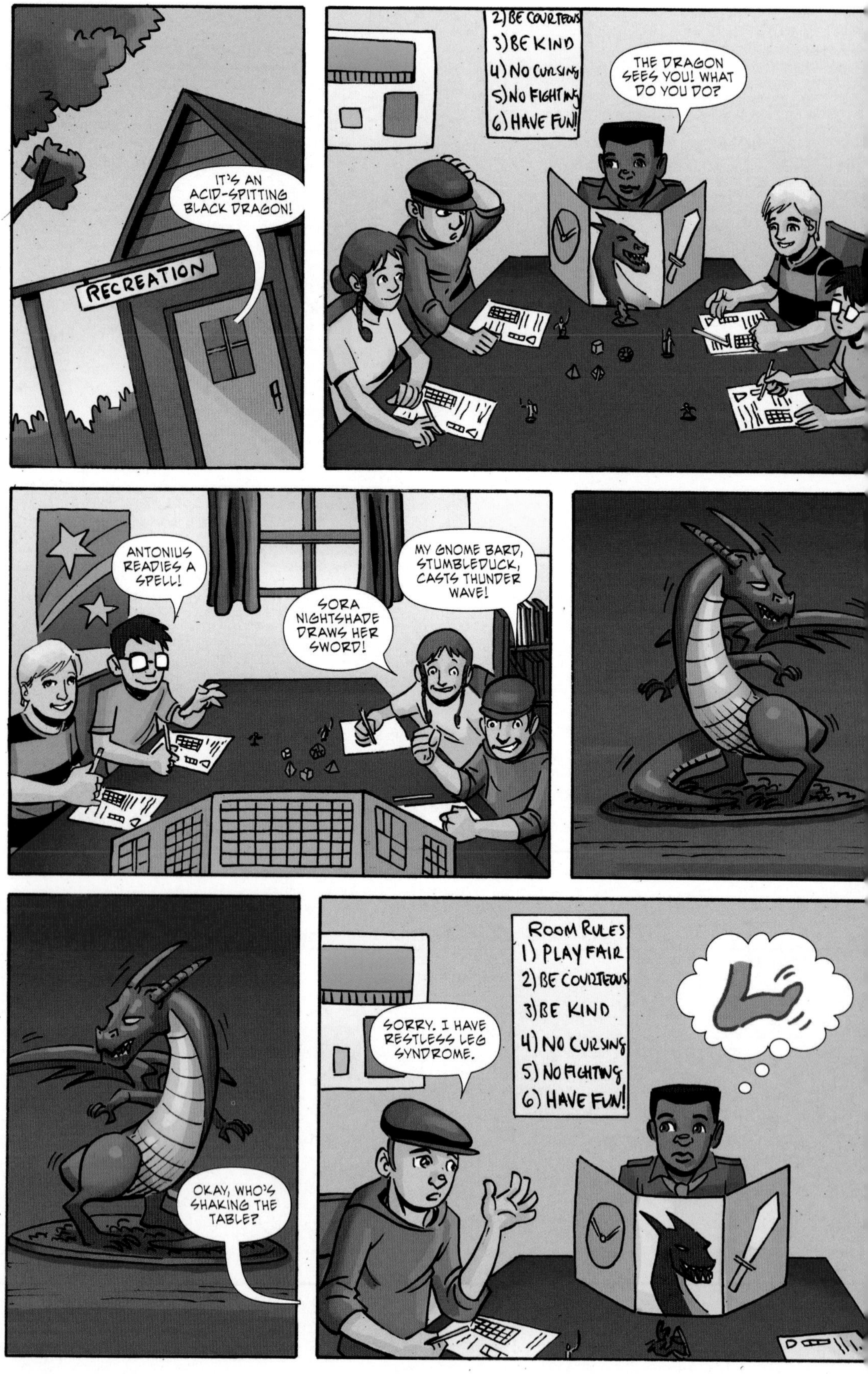
IT'S AN ACID-SPITTING BLACK DRAGON!
RECREATION
2) BE COURTEOUS
3) BE KIND
4) NO CURSING
5) NO FIGHTING
6) HAVE FUN!
THE DRAGON SEES YOU! WHAT DO YOU DO?
ANTONIUS READIES A SPELL!
SORA NIGHTSHADE DRAWS HER SWORD!
MY GNOME BARD, STUMBLEDUCK, CASTS THUNDER WAVE!
OKAY, WHO'S SHAKING THE TABLE?
ROOM RULES
1) PLAY FAIR
2) BE COURTEOUS
3) BE KIND
4) NO CURSING
5) NO FIGHTING
6) HAVE FUN!
SORRY. I HAVE RESTLESS LEG SYNDROME.

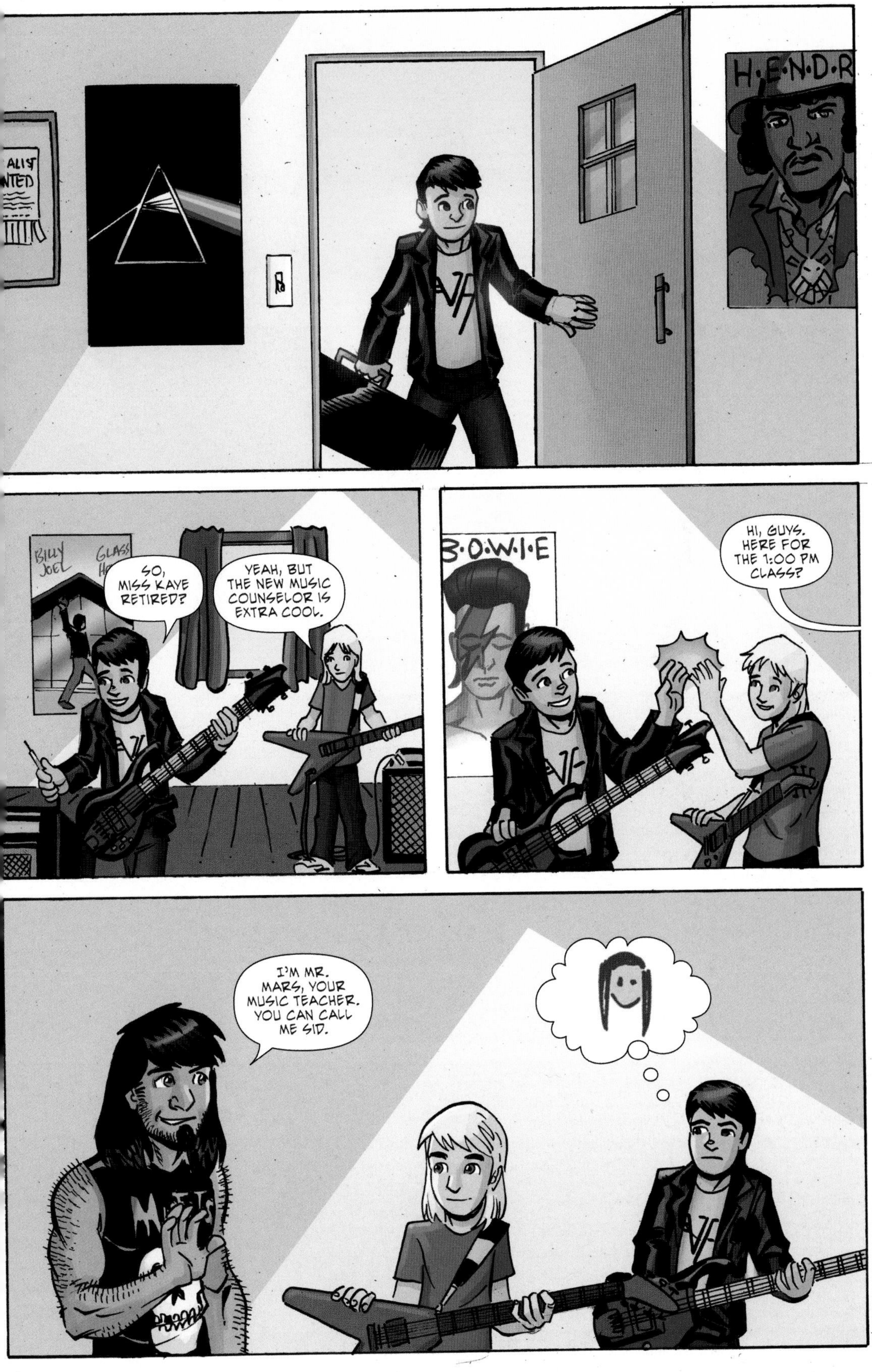
H·E·N·D·R
BILLY JOEL
GLASS
SO, MISS KAYE RETIRED?
YEAH, BUT THE NEW MUSIC COUNSELOR IS EXTRA COOL.
B·O·W·I·E
HI, GUYS. HERE FOR THE 1:00 PM CLASS?
I'M MR. MARS, YOUR MUSIC TEACHER. YOU CAN CALL ME SID.

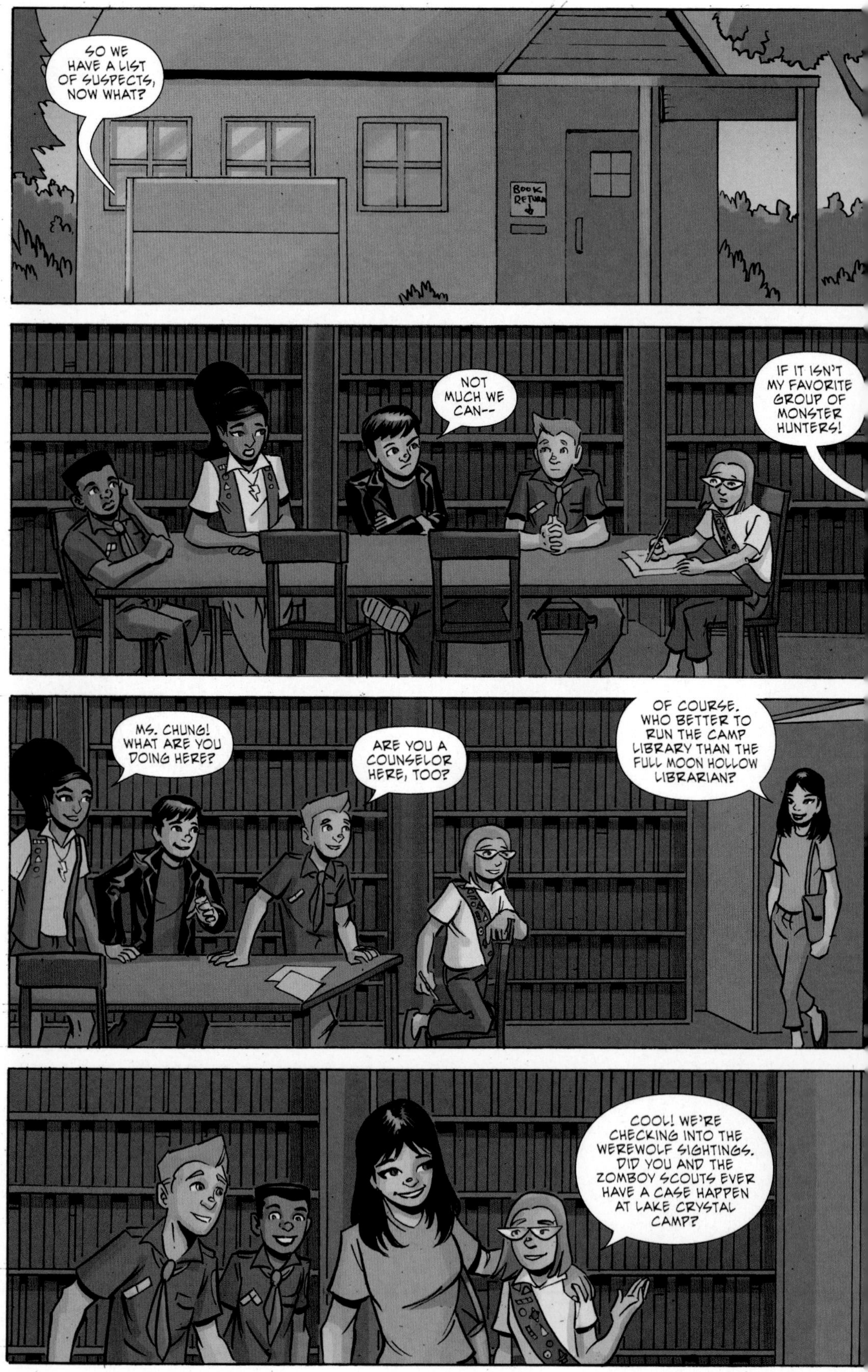
SO WE HAVE A LIST OF SUSPECTS, NOW WHAT?
BOOK RETURN
NOT MUCH WE CAN--
IF IT ISN'T MY FAVORITE GROUP OF MONSTER HUNTERS!
MS. CHUNG! WHAT ARE YOU DOING HERE?
ARE YOU A COUNSELOR HERE, TOO?
OF COURSE. WHO BETTER TO RUN THE CAMP LIBRARY THAN THE FULL MOON HOLLOW LIBRARIAN?
COOL! WE'RE CHECKING INTO THE WEREWOLF SIGHTINGS. DID YOU AND THE ZOMBOY SCOUTS EVER HAVE A CASE HAPPEN AT LAKE CRYSTAL CAMP?

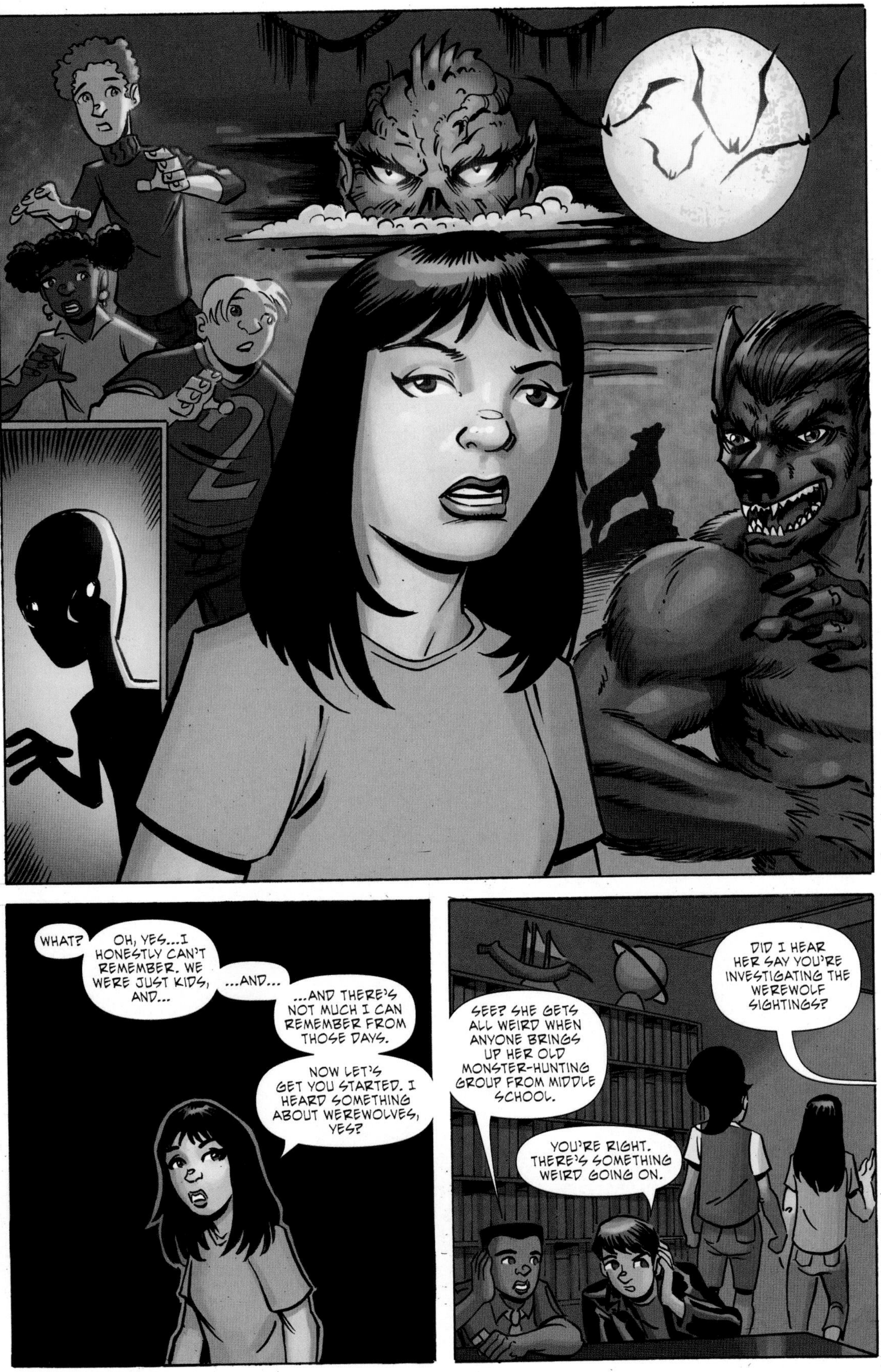
WHAT?
OH, YES...I HONESTLY CAN'T REMEMBER. WE WERE JUST KIDS, AND...
...AND...
...AND THERE'S NOT MUCH I CAN REMEMBER FROM THOSE DAYS.
NOW LET'S GET YOU STARTED. I HEARD SOMETHING ABOUT WEREWOLVES, YES?
SEE? SHE GETS ALL WEIRD WHEN ANYONE BRINGS UP HER OLD MONSTER-HUNTING GROUP FROM MIDDLE SCHOOL.
YOU'RE RIGHT. THERE'S SOMETHING WEIRD GOING ON.
DID I HEAR HER SAY YOU'RE INVESTIGATING THE WEREWOLF SIGHTINGS?

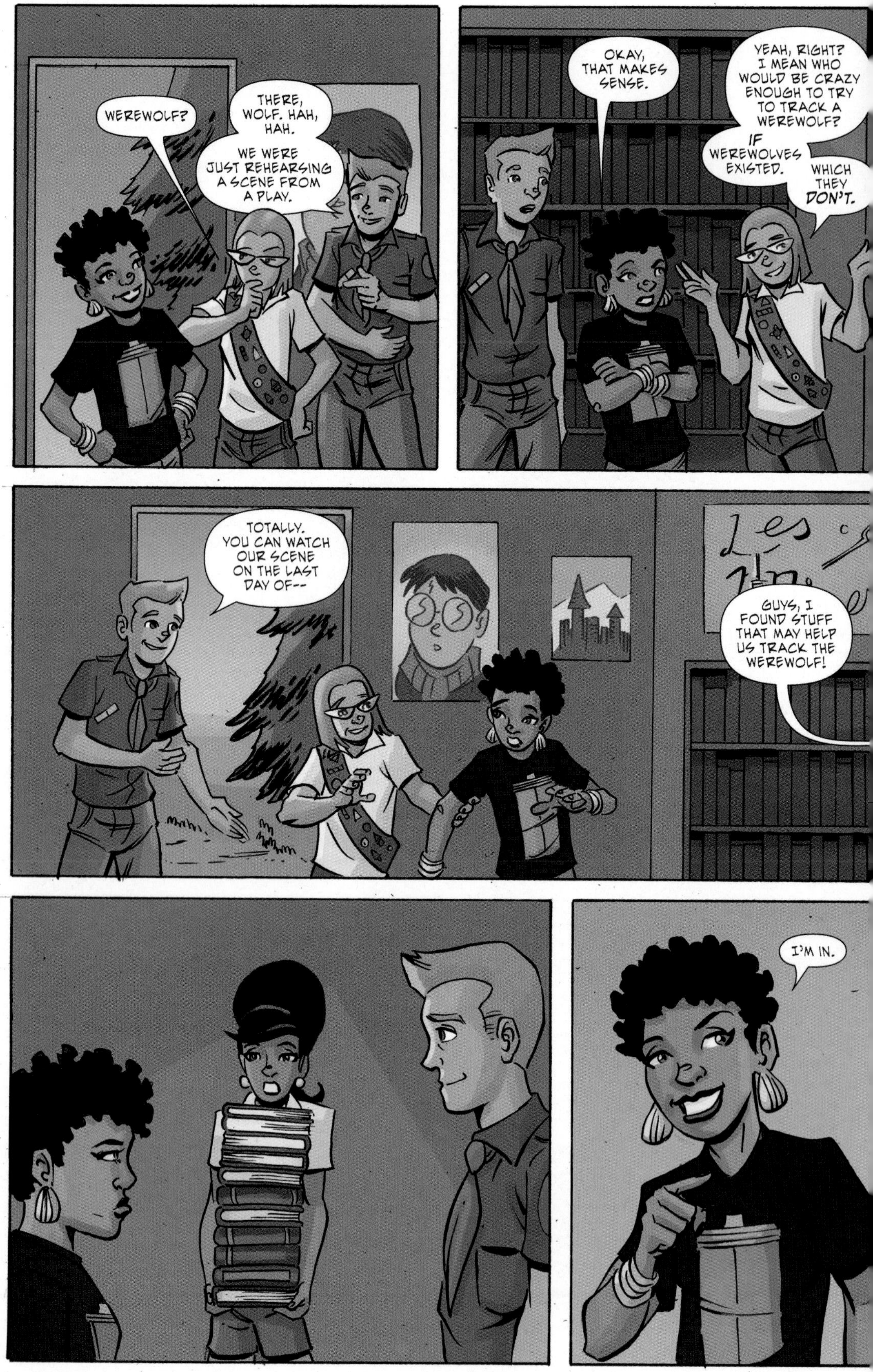
WEREWOLF?
THERE, WOLF. HAH, HAH.
WE WERE JUST REHEARSING A SCENE FROM A PLAY.
OKAY, THAT MAKES SENSE.
YEAH, RIGHT? I MEAN WHO WOULD BE CRAZY ENOUGH TO TRY TO TRACK A WEREWOLF?
IF WEREWOLVES EXISTED.
WHICH THEY DON'T.
TOTALLY. YOU CAN WATCH OUR SCENE ON THE LAST DAY OF--
GUYS, I FOUND STUFF THAT MAY HELP US TRACK THE WEREWOLF!
I'M IN.

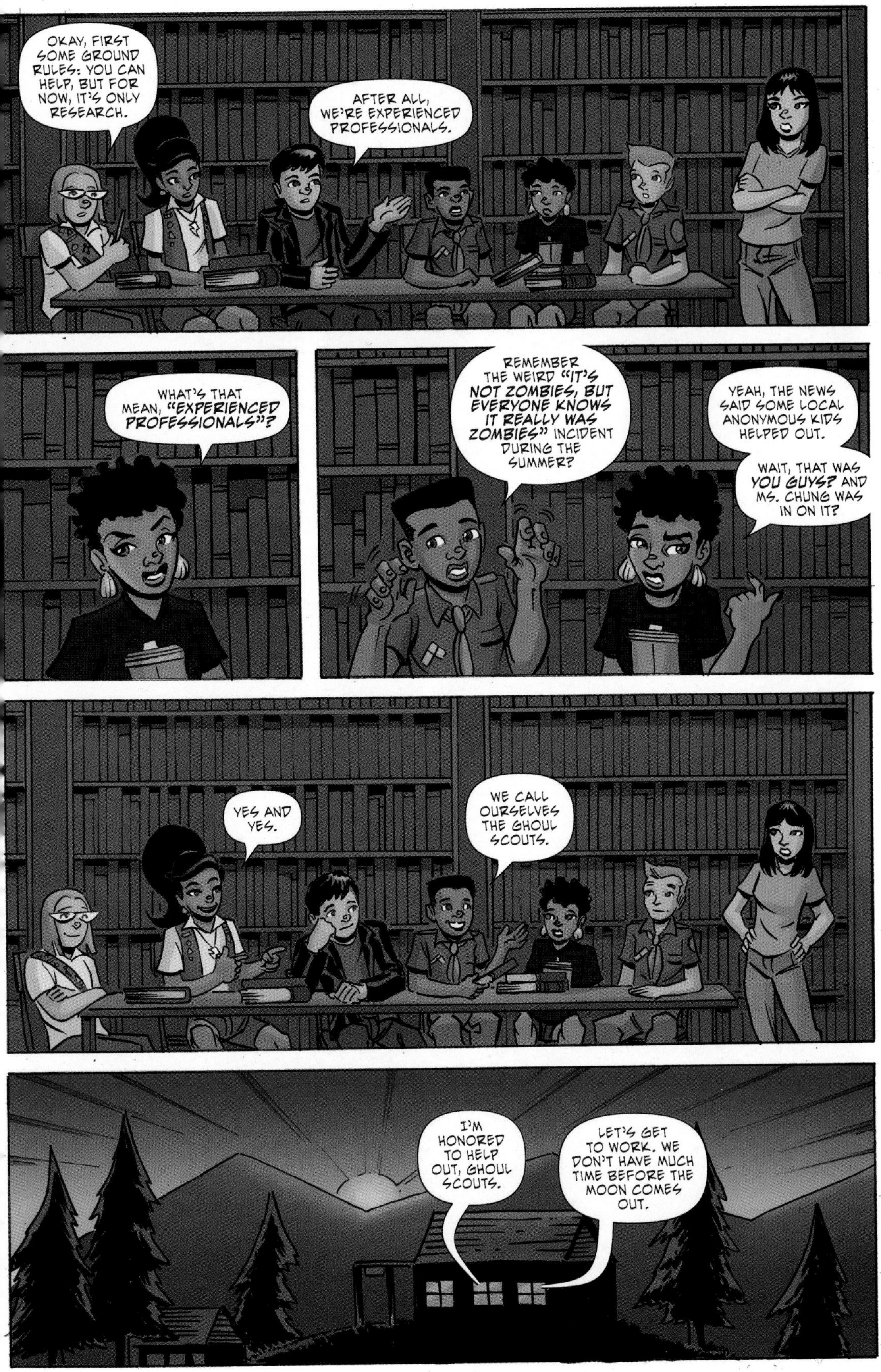
OKAY, FIRST SOME GROUND RULES: YOU CAN HELP, BUT FOR NOW, IT'S ONLY RESEARCH.
AFTER ALL, WE'RE EXPERIENCED PROFESSIONALS.
WHAT'S THAT MEAN, "EXPERIENCED PROFESSIONALS"?
REMEMBER THE WEIRD "IT'S NOT ZOMBIES, BUT EVERYONE KNOWS IT REALLY WAS ZOMBIES" INCIDENT DURING THE SUMMER?
YEAH, THE NEWS SAID SOME LOCAL ANONYMOUS KIDS HELPED OUT.
WAIT, THAT WAS YOU GUYS? AND MS. CHUNG WAS IN ON IT?
YES AND YES.
WE CALL OURSELVES THE GHOUL SCOUTS.
I'M HONORED TO HELP OUT, GHOUL SCOUTS.
LET'S GET TO WORK. WE DON'T HAVE MUCH TIME BEFORE THE MOON COMES OUT.

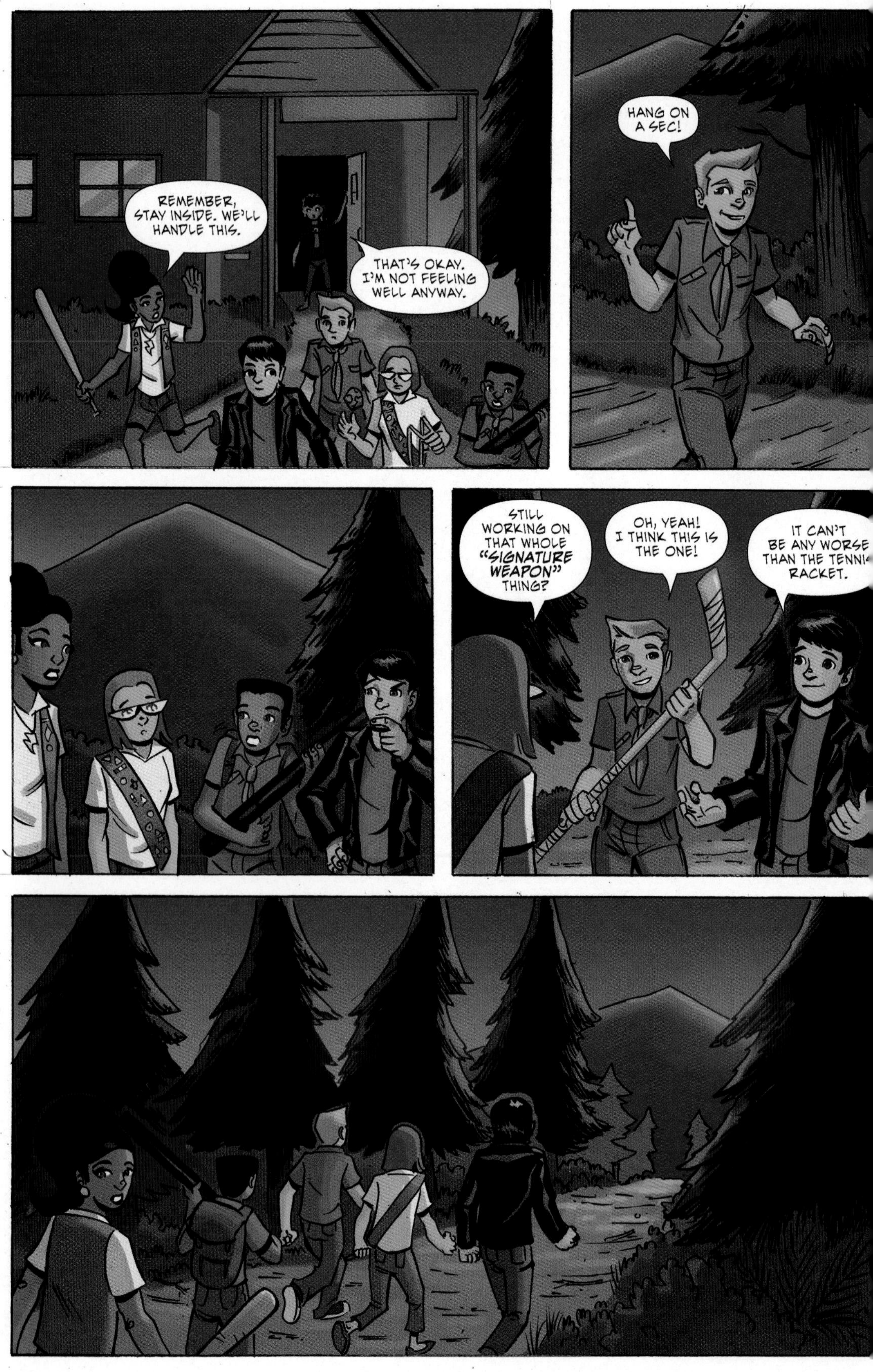
REMEMBER, STAY INSIDE. WE'LL HANDLE THIS.
THAT'S OKAY. I'M NOT FEELING WELL ANYWAY.
HANG ON A SEC!
STILL WORKING ON THAT WHOLE "SIGNATURE WEAPON" THING?
OH, YEAH! I THINK THIS IS THE ONE!
IT CAN'T BE ANY WORSE THAN THE TENNI
RACKET.

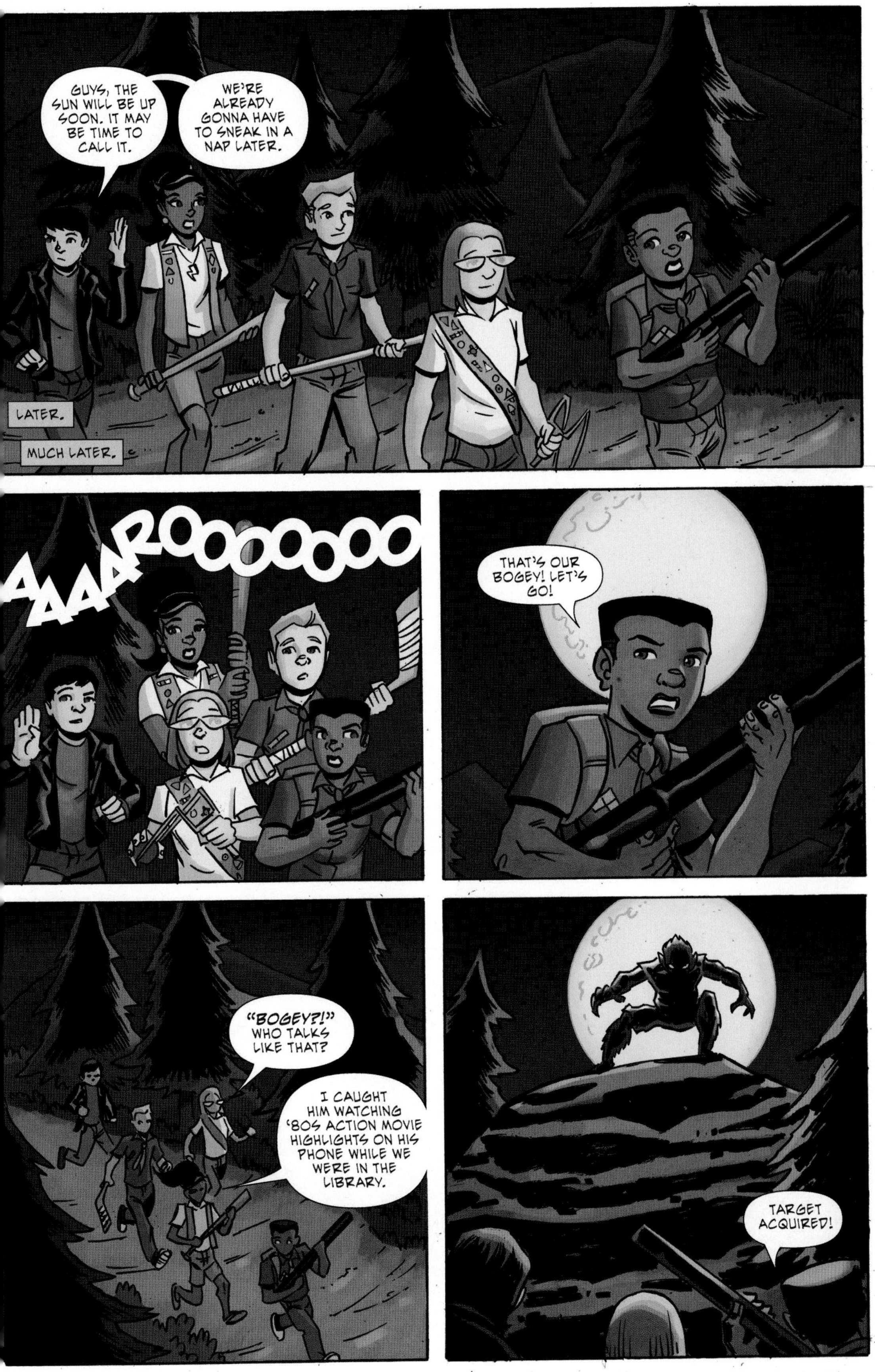
GUYS, THE SUN WILL BE UP SOON. IT MAY BE TIME TO CALL IT.
WE'RE ALREADY GONNA HAVE TO SNEAK IN A NAP LATER.
LATER.
MUCH LATER.
AAAAROOOOOOOO
THAT'S OUR BOGEY! LET'S GO!
"BOGEY?!" WHO TALKS LIKE THAT?
I CAUGHT HIM WATCHING '80S ACTION MOVIE HIGHLIGHTS ON HIS PHONE WHILE WE WERE IN THE LIBRARY.
TARGET ACQUIRED!

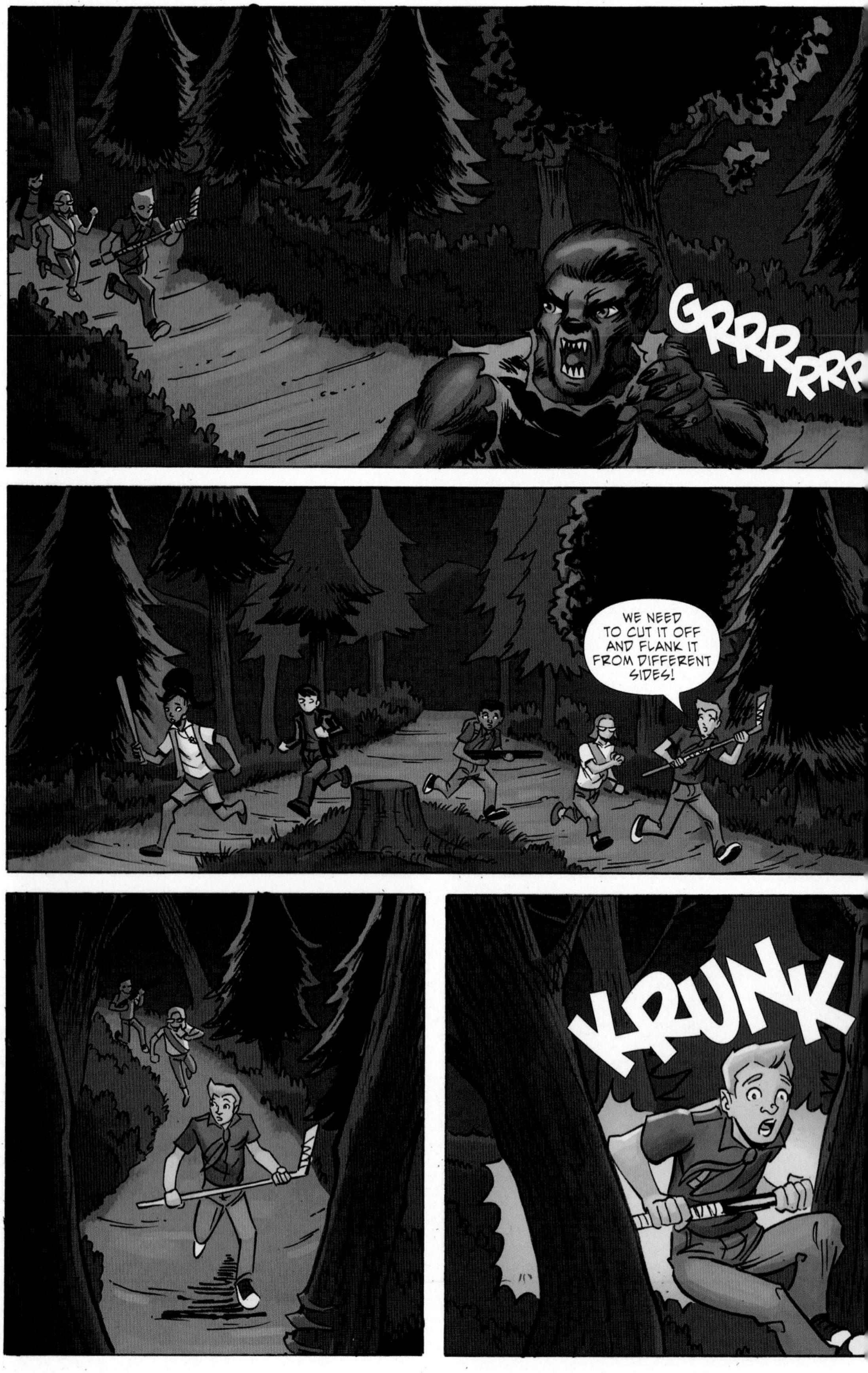
GRRRRRP
WE NEED TO CUT IT OFF AND FLANK IT FROM DIFFERENT SIDES!
KRUNK

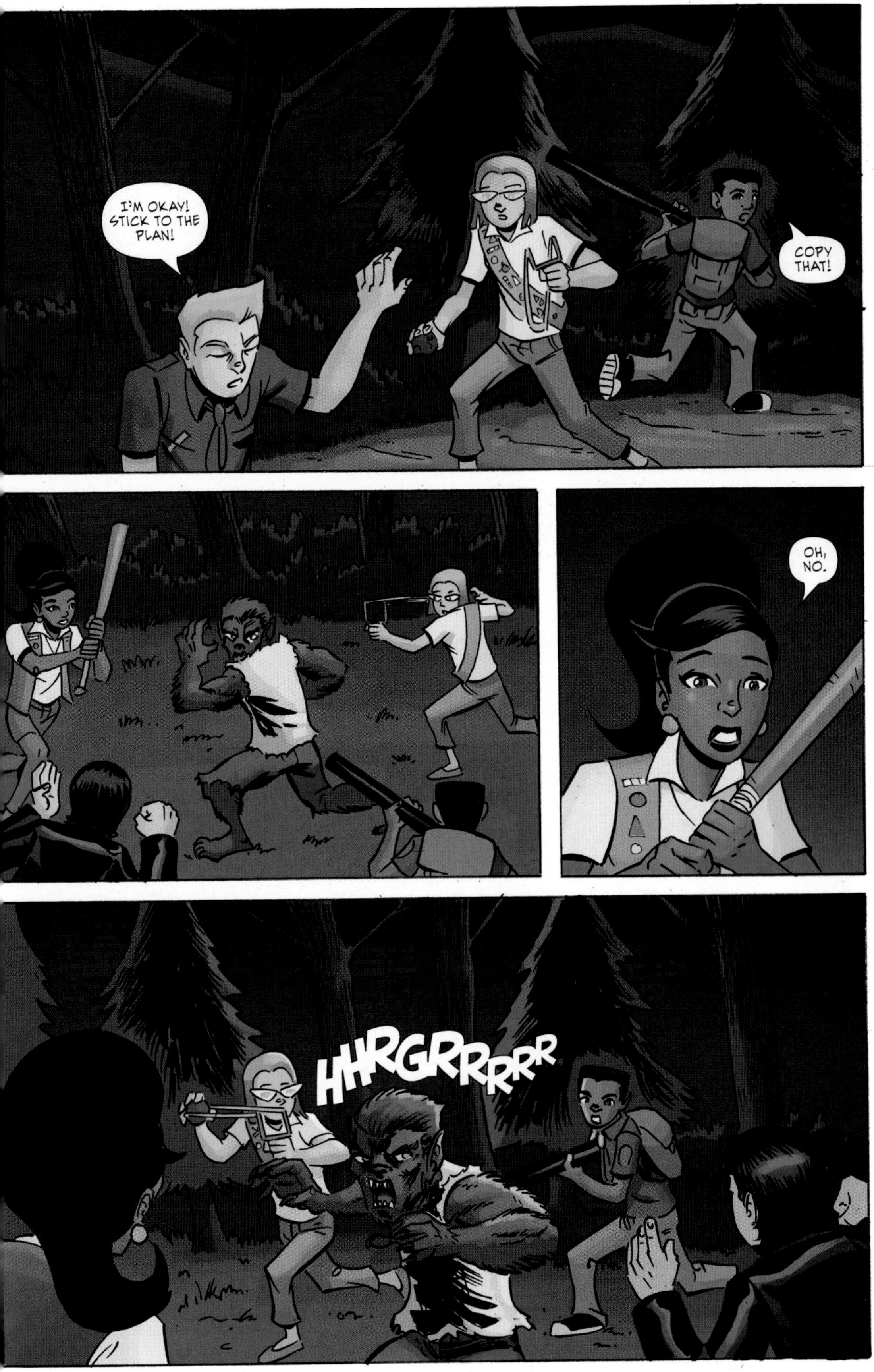
I'M OKAY! STICK TO THE PLAN!
COPY THAT!
OH, NO.
HHRGRRRRR

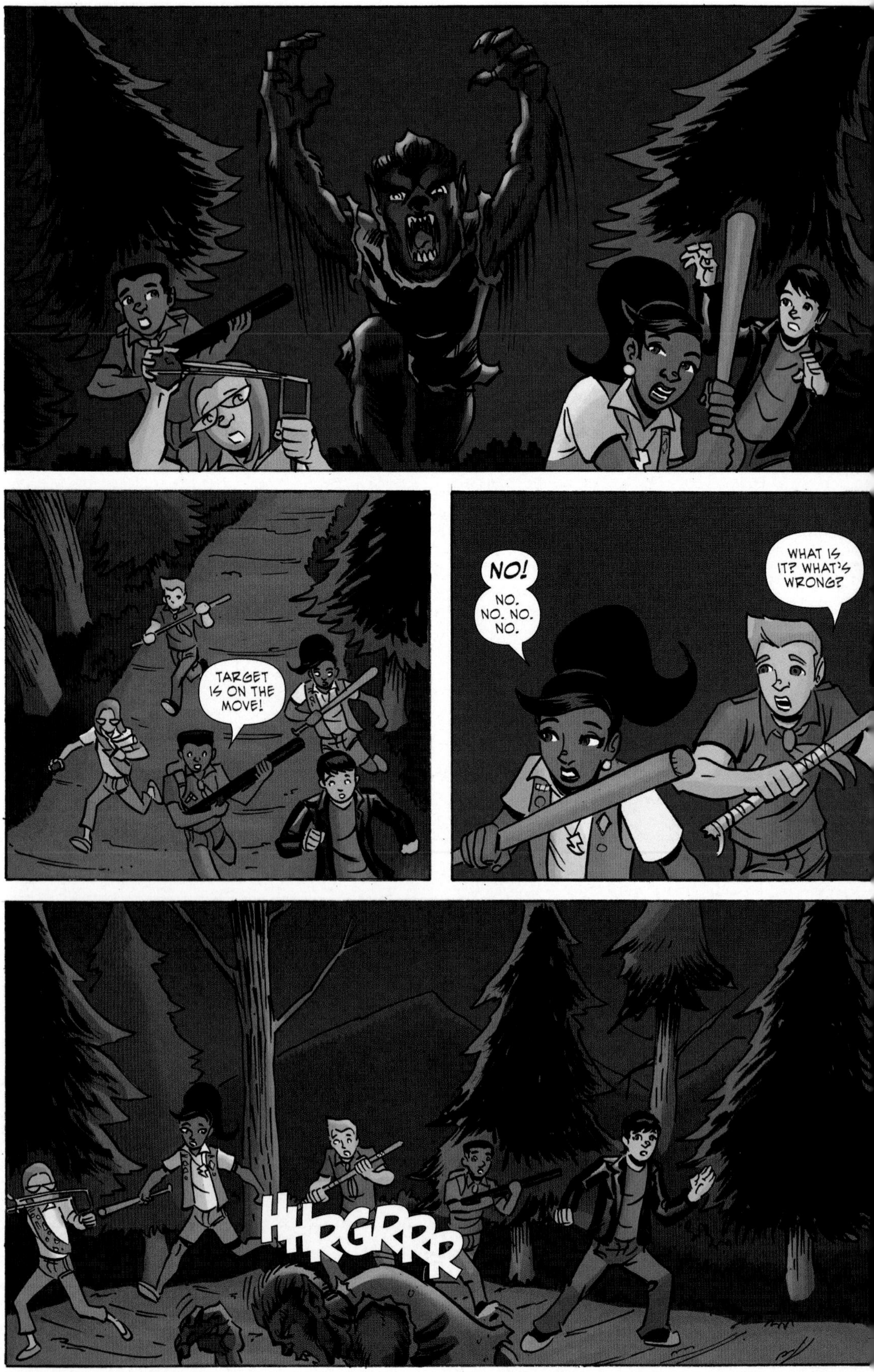
TARGET IS ON THE MOVE!
NO!
NO. NO. NO. NO.
WHAT IS IT? WHAT'S WRONG?
HHRGRRR

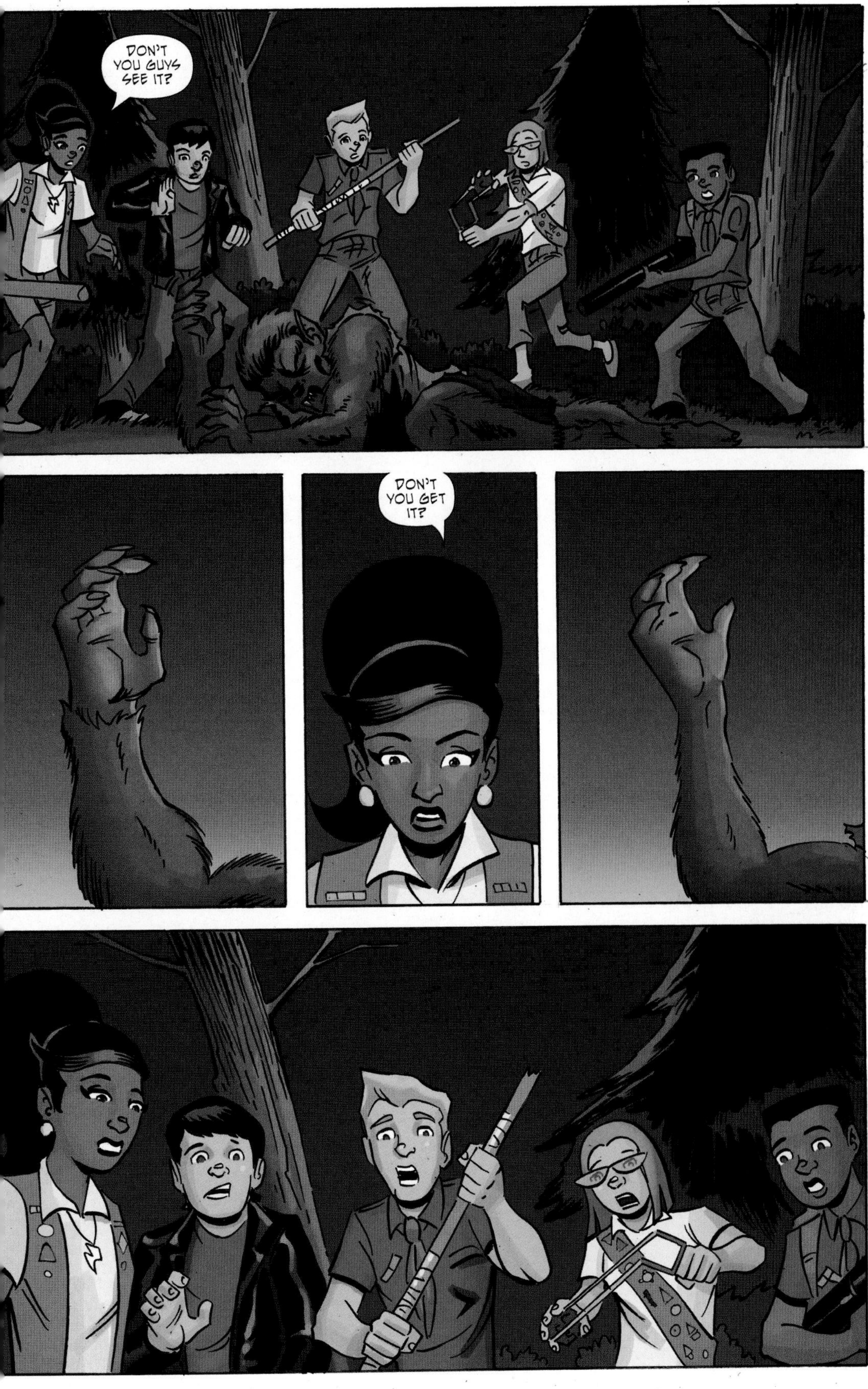
DON'T YOU GUYS SEE IT?
DON'T YOU GET IT?

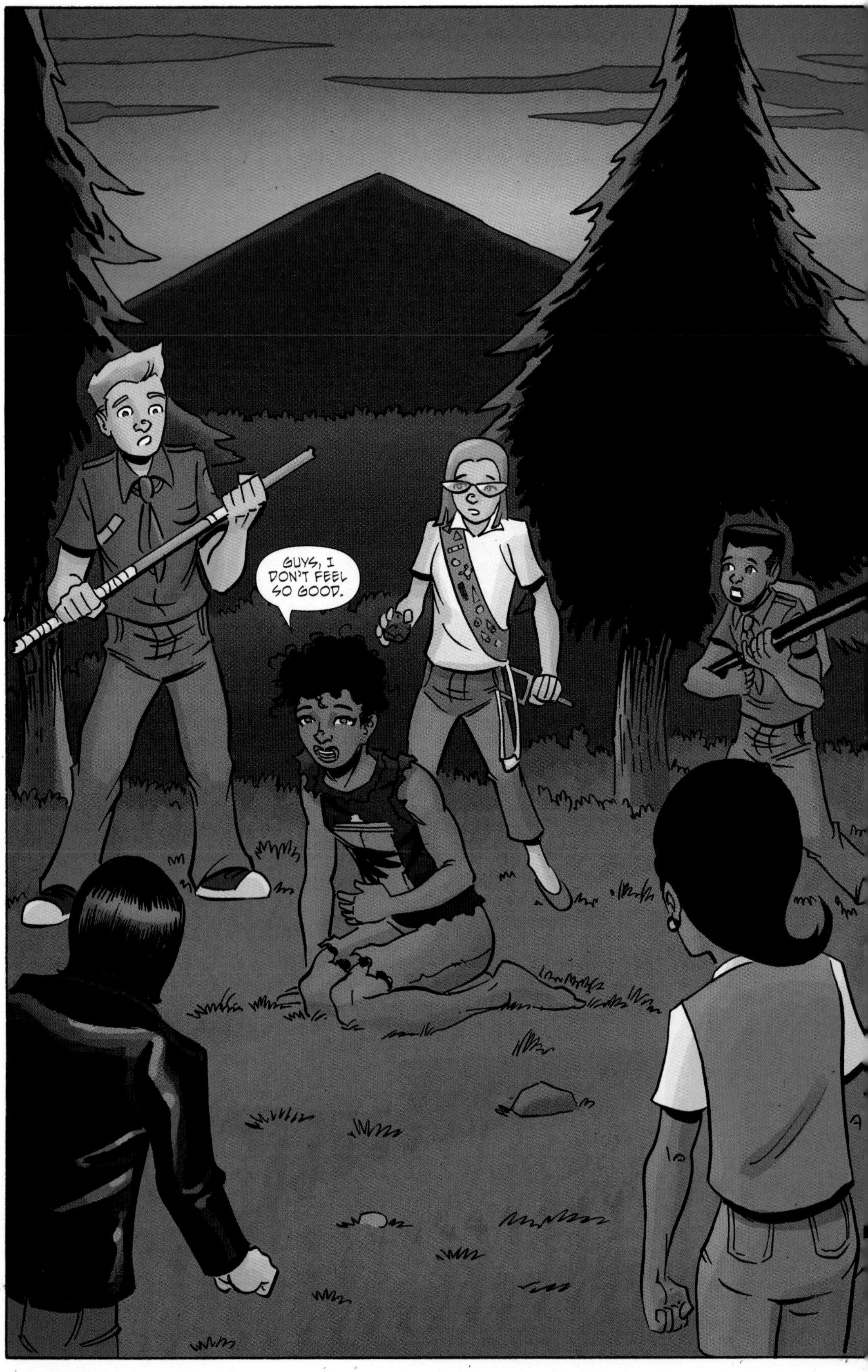
GUYS, I DON'T FEEL SO GOOD.

GHOUL SCOUTS BONUS FEATURE

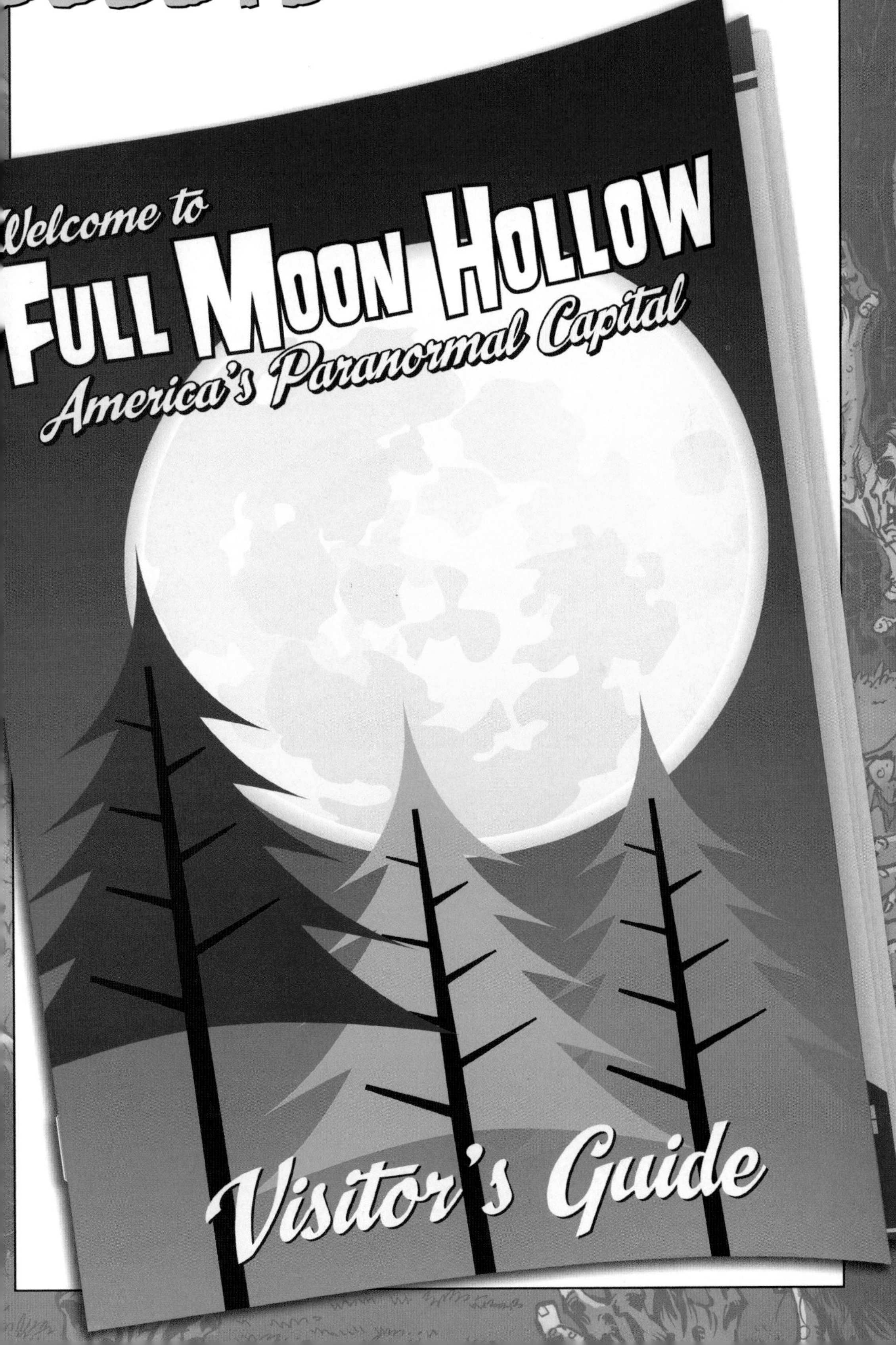
Welcome to
FULL MOON HOLLOW
America's Paranormal Capital
Visitor's Guide

GHOUL SCOUTS BONUS FEATURE

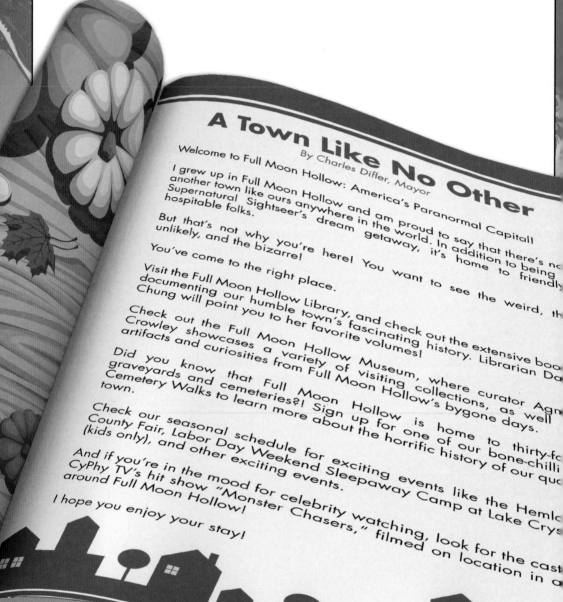

A Town Like No Other
By Charles Difler, Mayor

Welcome to Full Moon Hollow: America's Paranormal Capital!

I grew up in Full Moon Hollow and am proud to say that there's no another town like ours anywhere in the world. In addition to being a Supernatural Sightseer's dream getaway, it's home to friendly, hospitable folks.

But that's not why you're here! You want to see the weird, the unlikely, and the bizarre!

You've come to the right place.

Visit the Full Moon Hollow Library, and check out the extensive book documenting our humble town's fascinating history. Librarian Da Chung will point you to her favorite volumes!

Check out the Full Moon Hollow Museum, where curator Agn Crowley showcases a variety of visiting collections, as well artifacts and curiosities from Full Moon Hollow's bygone days.

Did you know that Full Moon Hollow is home to thirty-fo graveyards and cemeteries?! Sign up for one of our bone-chilli Cemetery Walks to learn more about the horrific history of our quo town.

Check our seasonal schedule for exciting events like the Hemlo County Fair, Labor Day Weekend Sleepaway Camp at Lake Crys (kids only), and other exciting events.

And if you're in the mood for celebrity watching, look for the cast CyPhy TV's hit show "Monster Chasers," filmed on location in a around Full Moon Hollow!

I hope you enjoy your stay!

GHOUL SCOUTS BONUS FEATURE

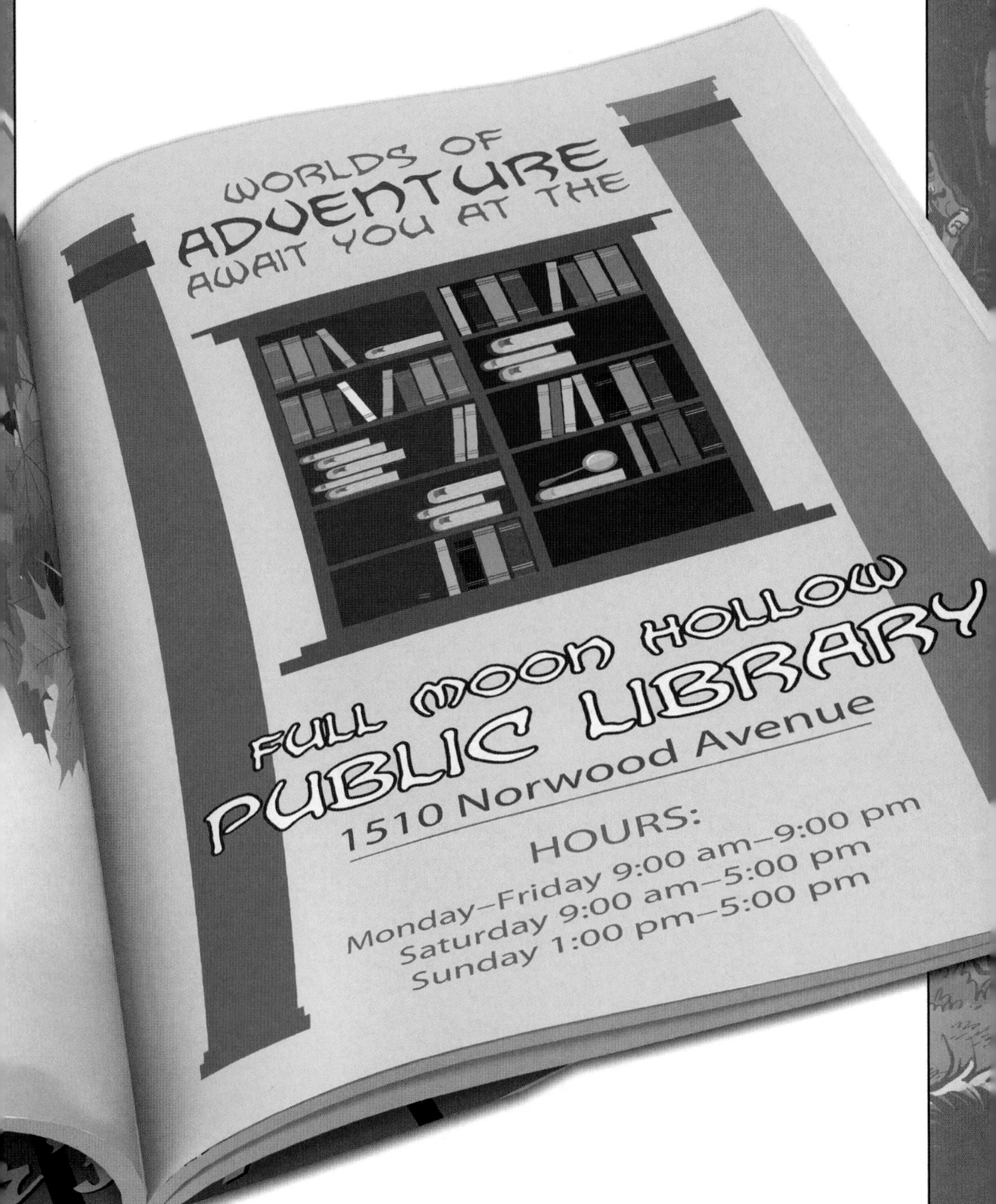
WORLDS OF
ADVENTURE
AWAIT YOU AT THE
FULL MOON HOLLOW
PUBLIC LIBRARY
1510 Norwood Avenue
HOURS:
Monday–Friday 9:00 am–9:00 pm
Saturday 9:00 am–5:00 pm
Sunday 1:00 pm–5:00 pm

GHOUL SCOUTS BONUS FEATURE

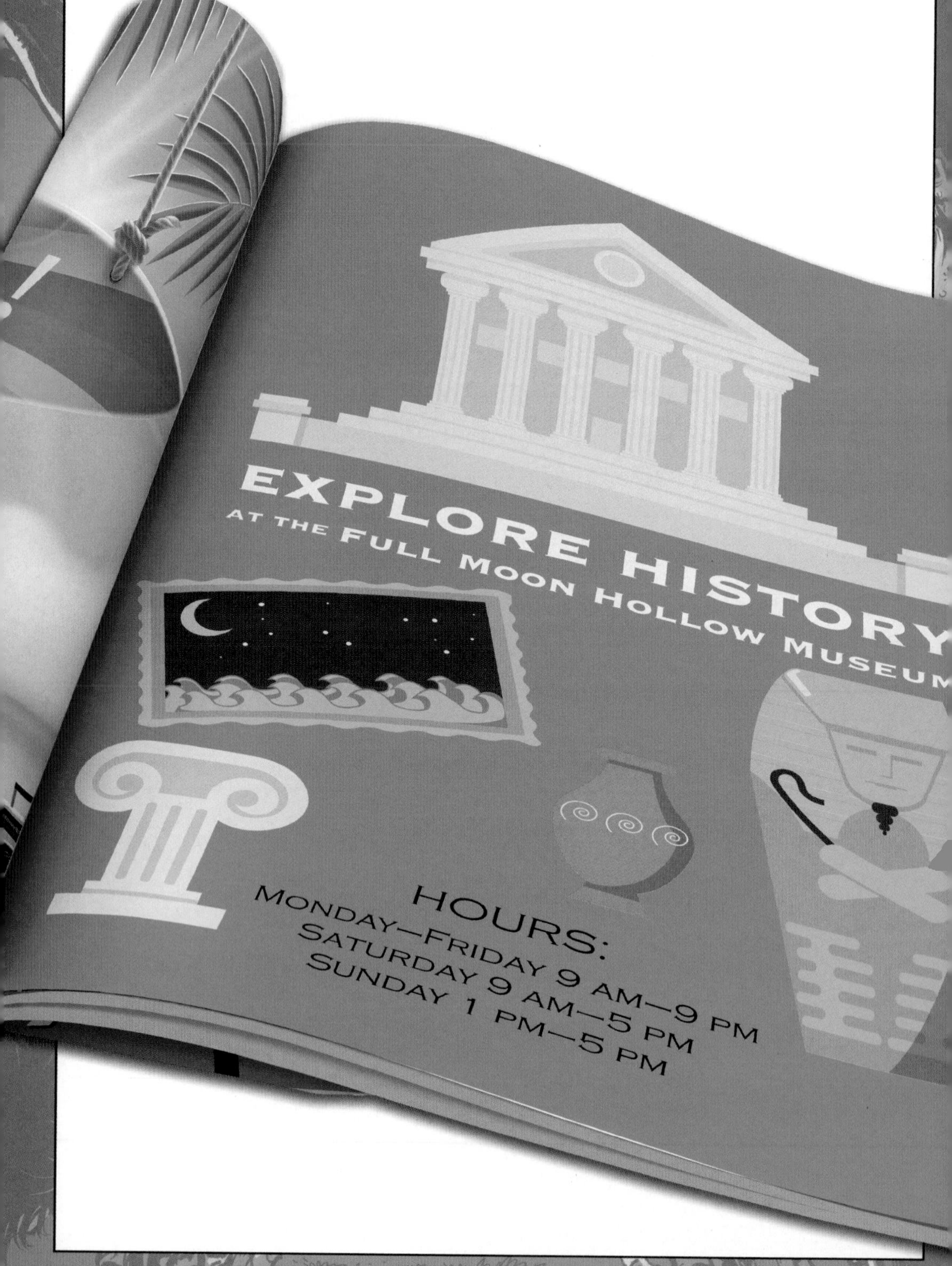

EXPLORE HISTORY
AT THE FULL MOON HOLLOW MUSEUM
HOURS:
MONDAY—FRIDAY 9 AM—9 PM
SATURDAY 9 AM—5 PM
SUNDAY 1 PM—5 PM

GHOUL SCOUTS BONUS FEATURE

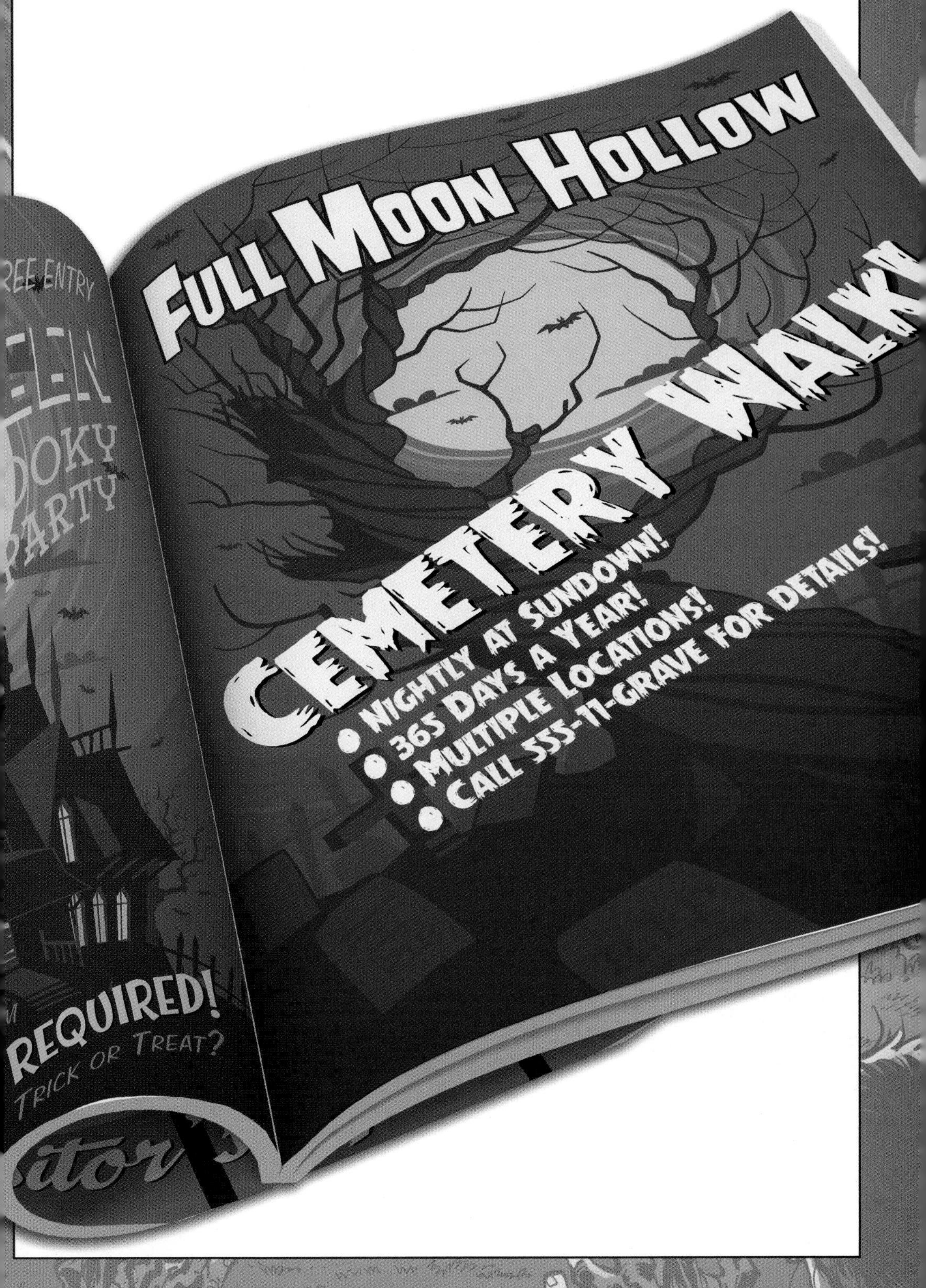
FULL MOON HOLLOW
CEMETERY WALK!
• NIGHTLY AT SUNDOWN!
• 365 DAYS A YEAR!
• MULTIPLE LOCATIONS!
• CALL 555-11-GRAVE FOR DETAILS!
REQUIRED!
TRICK OR TREAT?

GHOUL SCOUTS BONUS FEATURE

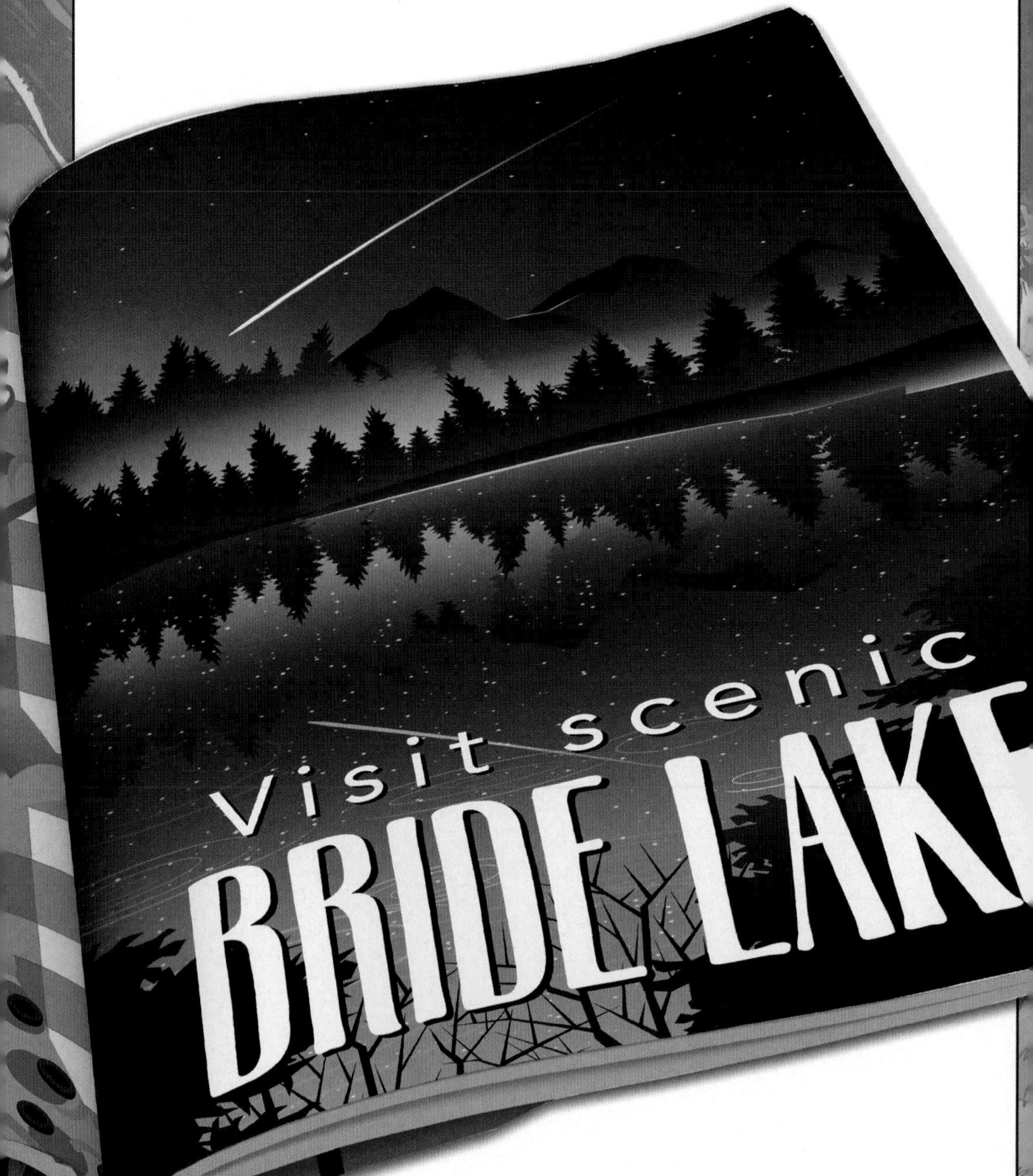
Visit scenic
BRIDE LAKE

GHOUL SCOUTS BONUS FEATURE

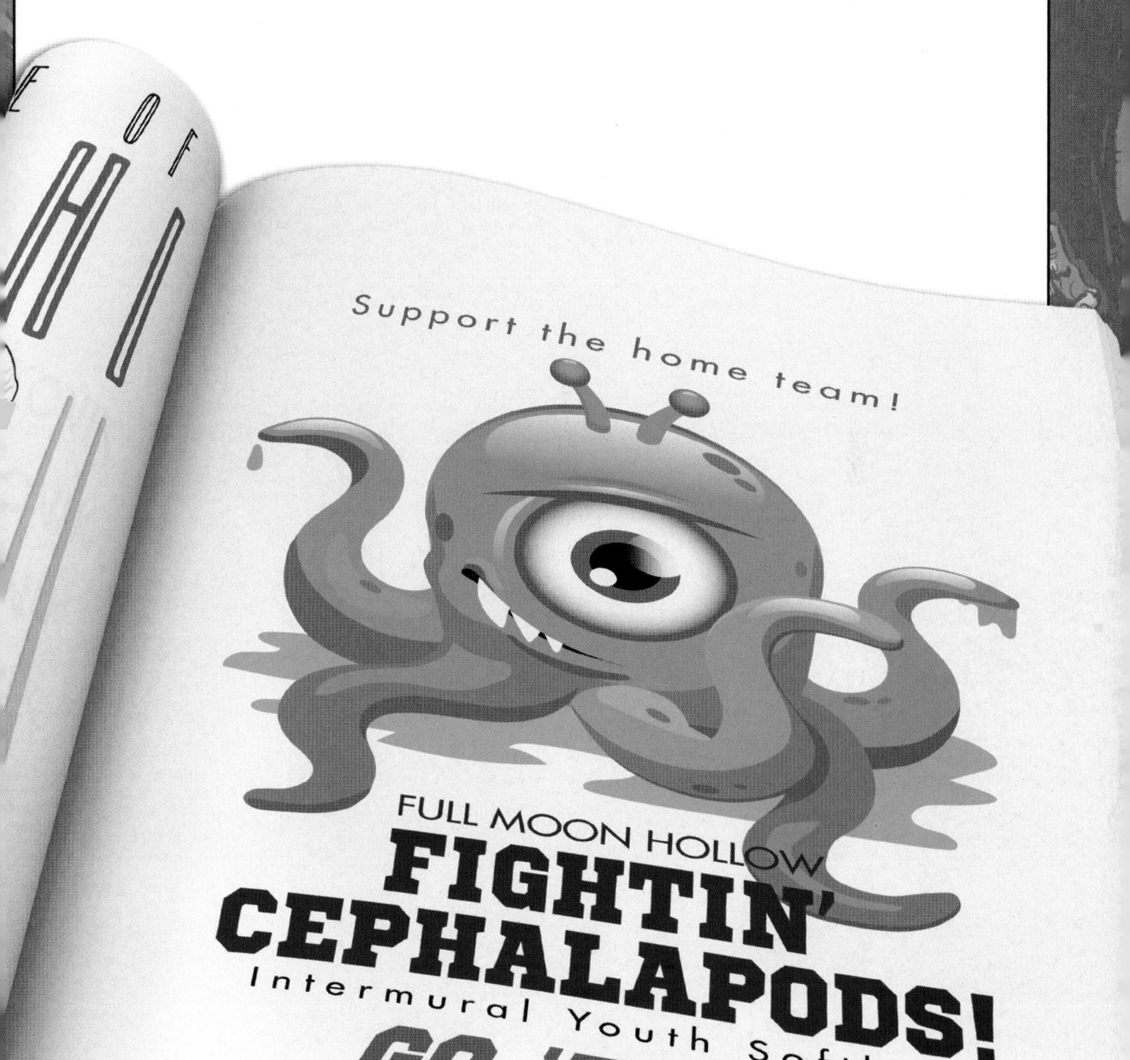

GHOUL SCOUTS BONUS FEATURE

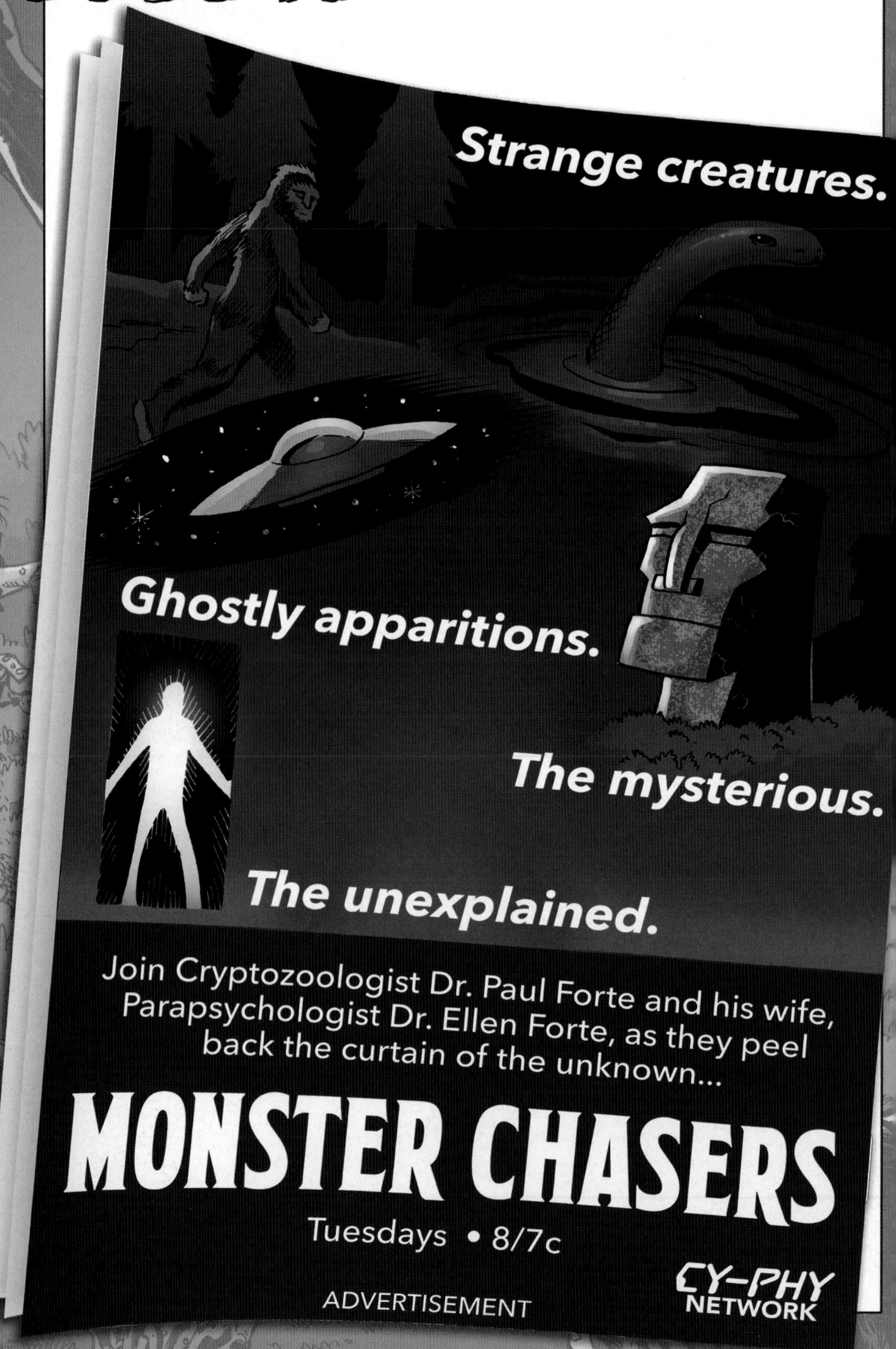

Strange creatures.
Ghostly apparitions.
The mysterious.
The unexplained.
Join Cryptozoologist Dr. Paul Forte and his wife, Parapsychologist Dr. Ellen Forte, as they peel back the curtain of the unknown...
MONSTER CHASERS
Tuesdays • 8/7c
ADVERTISEMENT
CY-PHY NETWORK

I WAS A TWEENAGE WEREWOLF!

CHAPTER

THREE

GHOUL SCOUTS

Story and Letters
STEVE BRYANT
@SteveBryantArt

Art
MARK STEGBAUER
@MarkStegbauer

Colors
JASON MILLET
@Jason_Millet

Edited by
CHRIS MURRIN
@ChrisMurrin

Color Assist
DREW BROWNE
@TheDrewBrowne

Cover
MARK STEGBAUER
& JASON MILLET

Bryan Seaton: Publisher/CEO **| Shawn Gabborin:** Editor In Chief **| Jason Martin:** Publisher-Danger Zone
Nicole D'Andria: Marketing Director/Editor **| Jim Dietz:** Social Media Manager **| Danielle Davison:** Executive Administrat
Chad Cicconi: Camp Cook **| Shawn Pryor:** President of Creator Relations

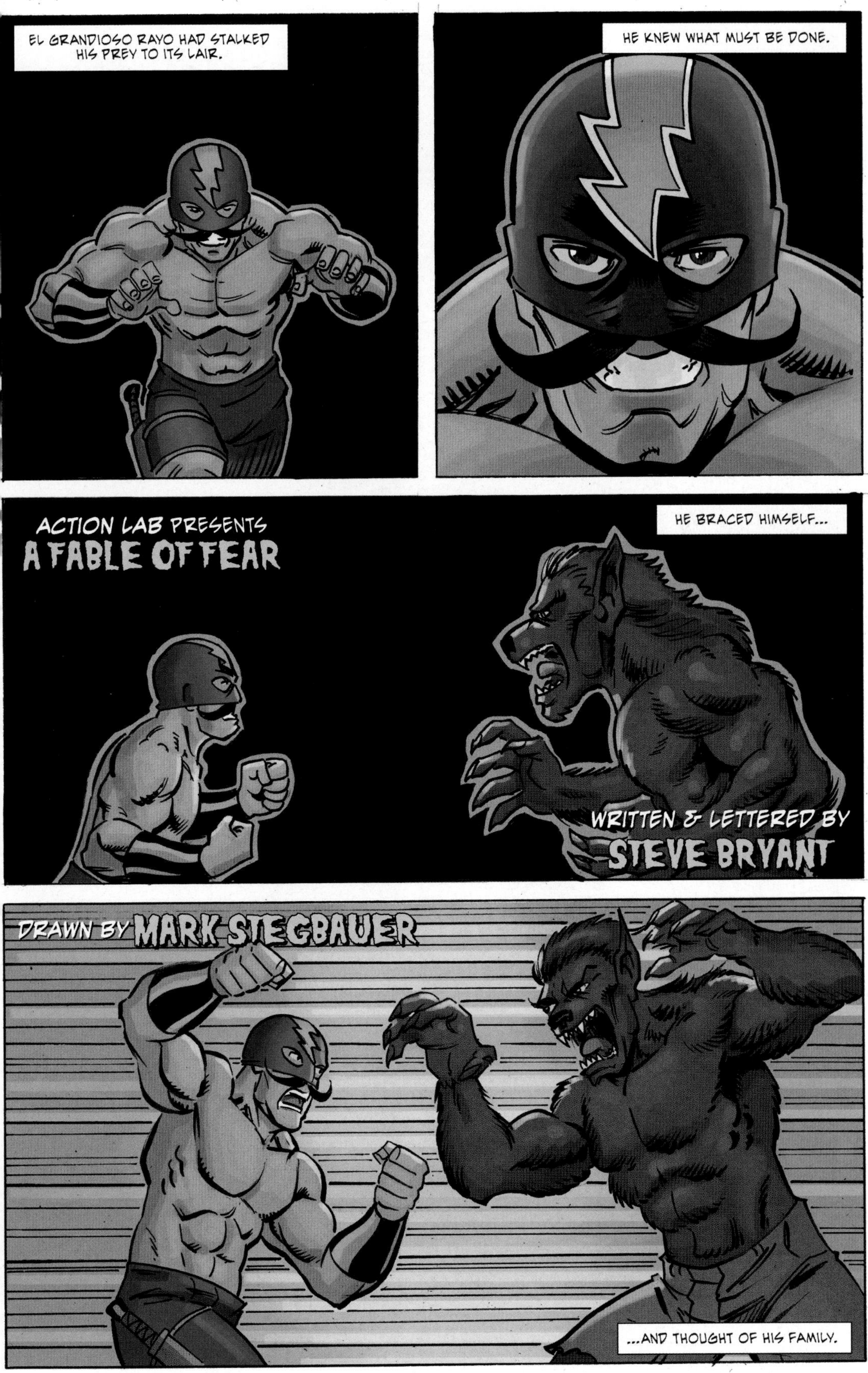
EL GRANDIOSO RAYO HAD STALKED HIS PREY TO ITS LAIR.
HE KNEW WHAT MUST BE DONE.
ACTION LAB PRESENTS
A FABLE OF FEAR
HE BRACED HIMSELF...
WRITTEN & LETTERED BY
STEVE BRYANT
DRAWN BY MARK STEGBAUER
...AND THOUGHT OF HIS FAMILY.

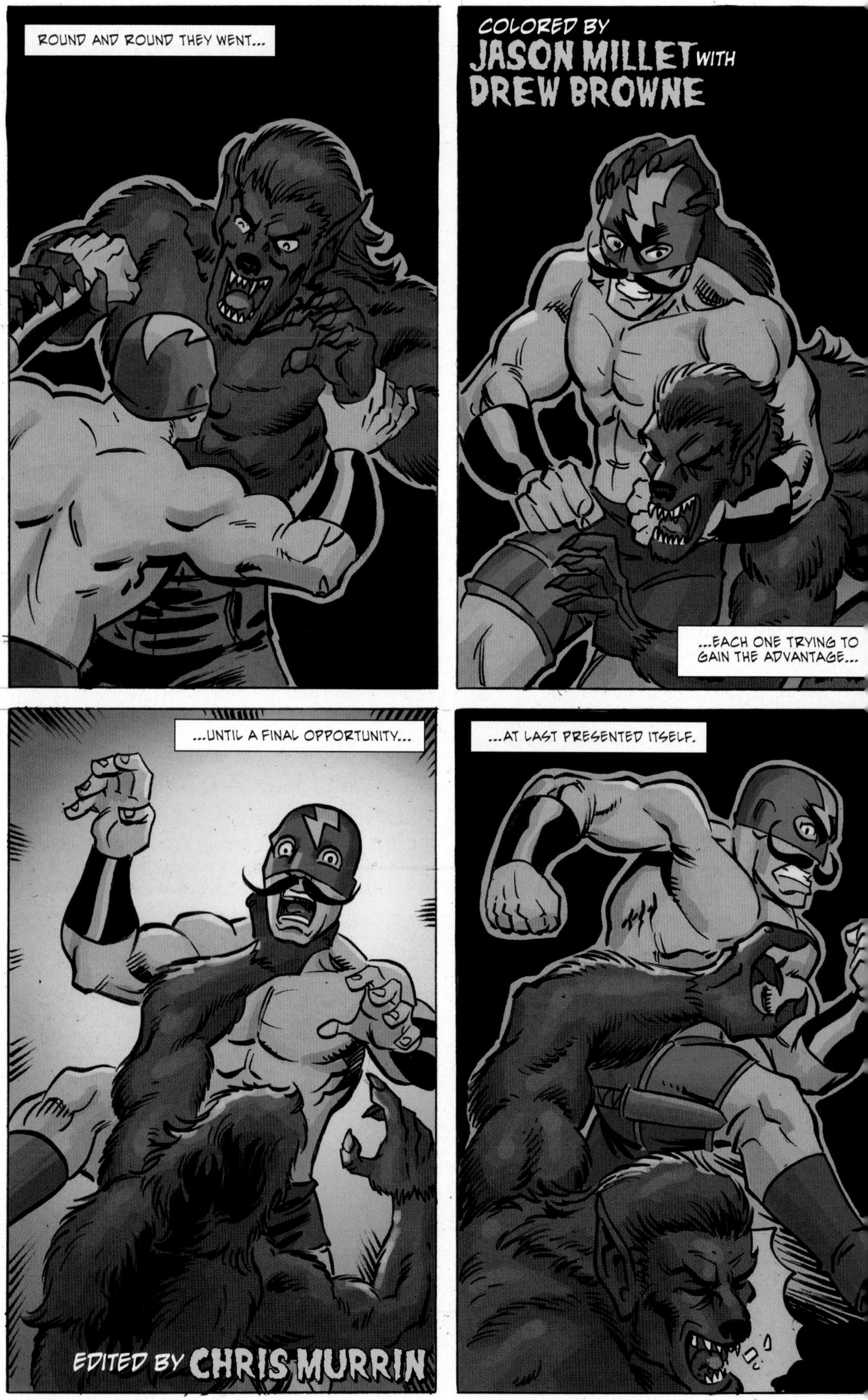
ROUND AND ROUND THEY WENT...
COLORED BY
JASON MILLET WITH
DREW BROWNE
...EACH ONE TRYING TO GAIN THE ADVANTAGE...
...UNTIL A FINAL OPPORTUNITY...
EDITED BY CHRIS MURRIN
...AT LAST PRESENTED ITSELF.

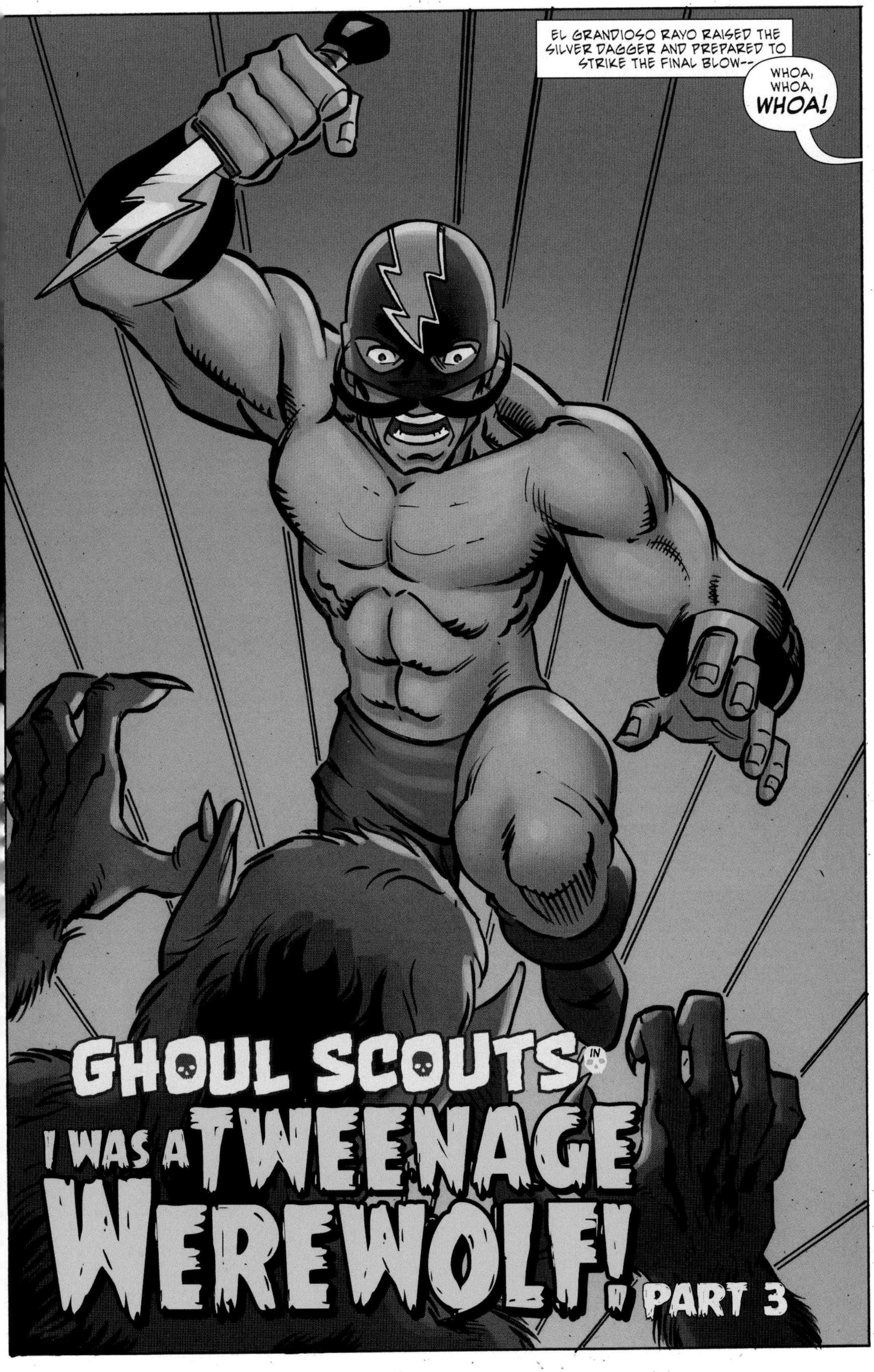

EL GRANDIOSO RAYO RAISED THE SILVER DAGGER AND PREPARED TO STRIKE THE FINAL BLOW--
WHOA, WHOA, WHOA!
GHOUL SCOUTS IN
I WAS A TWEENAGE WEREWOLF! PART 3

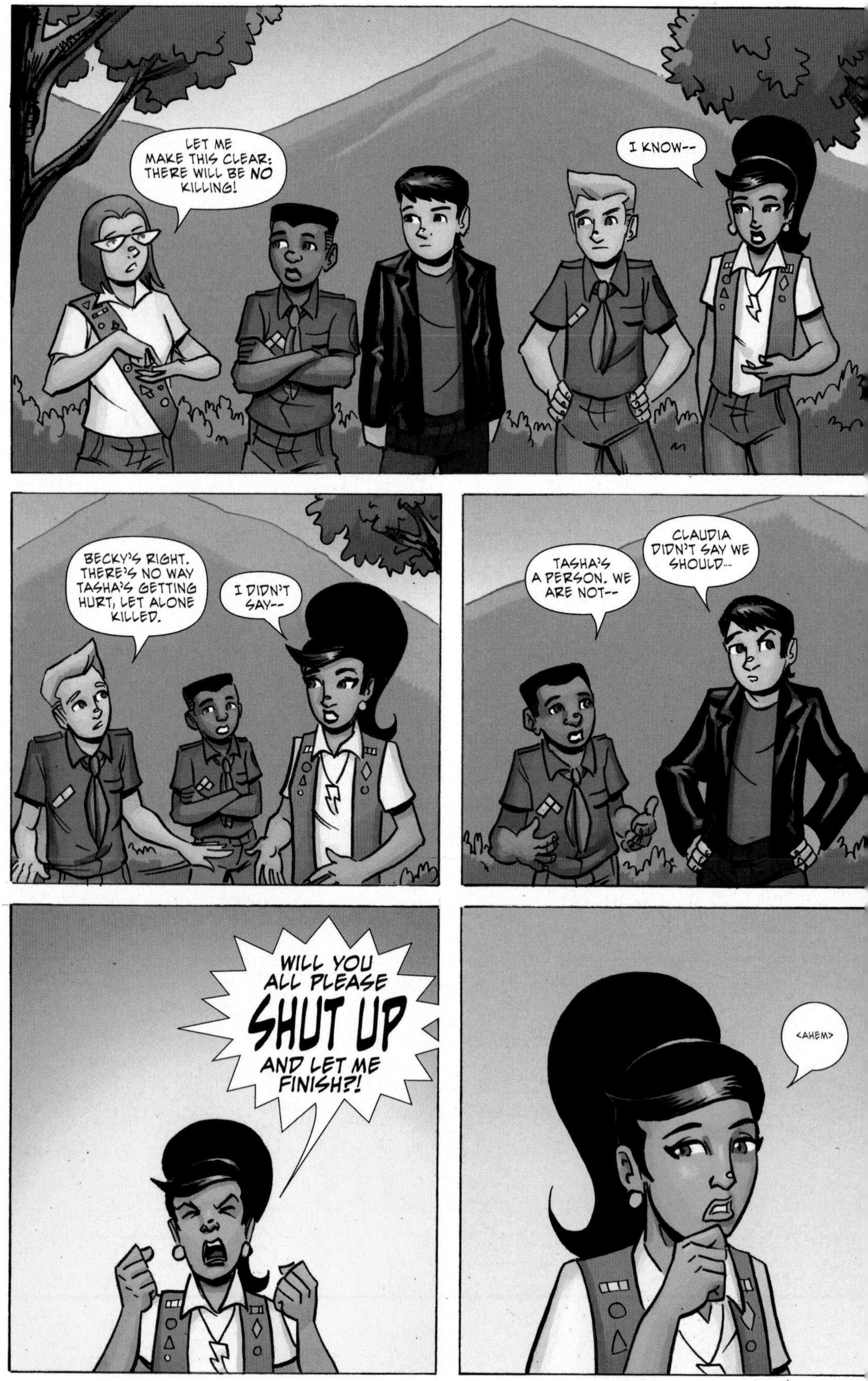
LET ME MAKE THIS CLEAR: THERE WILL BE NO KILLING!
I KNOW--
BECKY'S RIGHT. THERE'S NO WAY TASHA'S GETTING HURT, LET ALONE KILLED.
I DIDN'T SAY--
TASHA'S A PERSON. WE ARE NOT--
CLAUDIA DIDN'T SAY WE SHOULD--
WILL YOU ALL PLEASE SHUT UP AND LET ME FINISH?!
<AHEM>

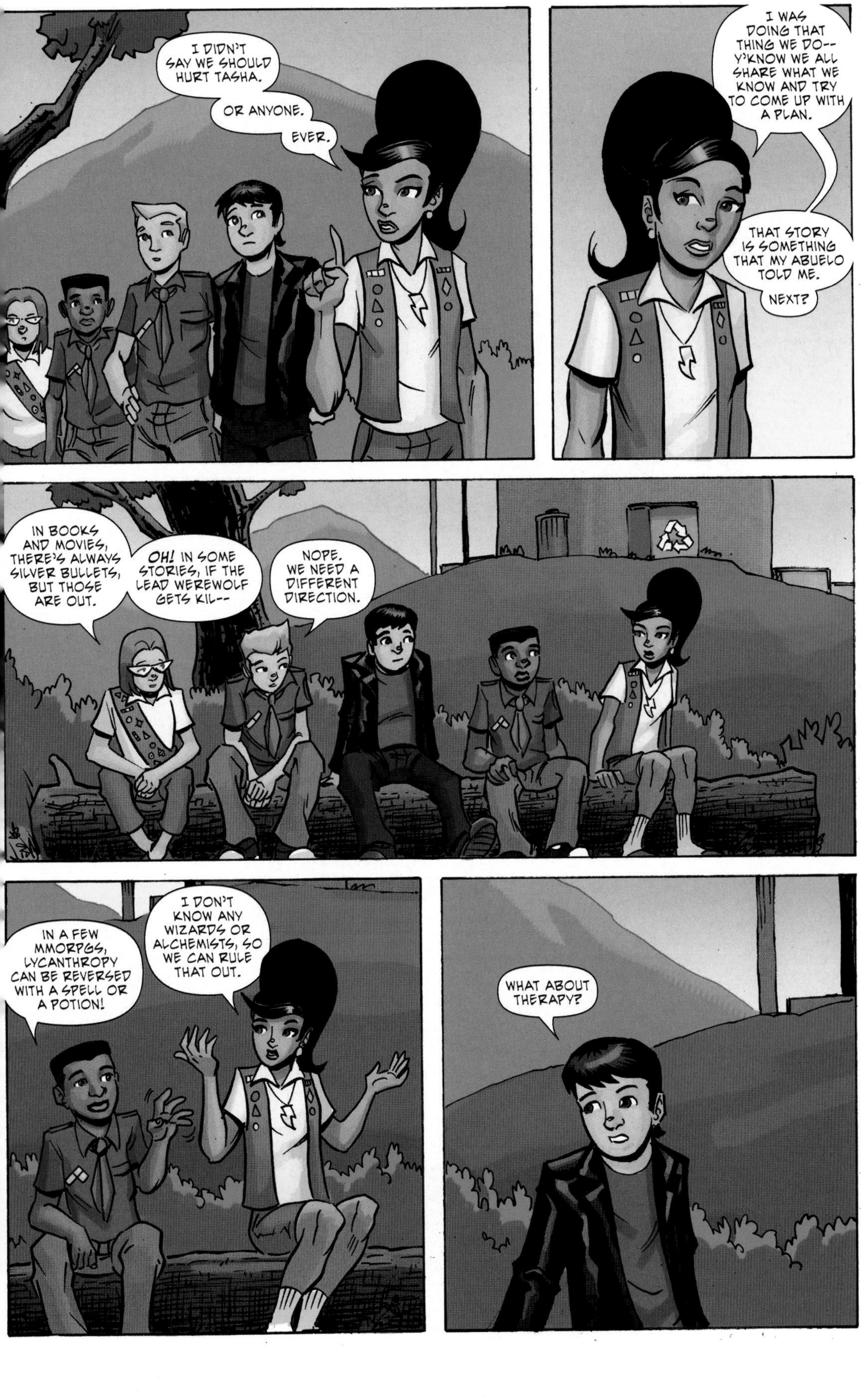
I DIDN'T SAY WE SHOULD HURT TASHA.
OR ANYONE.
EVER.
I WAS DOING THAT THING WE DO-- Y'KNOW WE ALL SHARE WHAT WE KNOW AND TRY TO COME UP WITH A PLAN.
THAT STORY IS SOMETHING THAT MY ABUELO TOLD ME.
NEXT?
IN BOOKS AND MOVIES, THERE'S ALWAYS SILVER BULLETS, BUT THOSE ARE OUT.
OH! IN SOME STORIES, IF THE LEAD WEREWOLF GETS KIL--
NOPE. WE NEED A DIFFERENT DIRECTION.
IN A FEW MMORPGS, LYCANTHROPY CAN BE REVERSED WITH A SPELL OR A POTION!
I DON'T KNOW ANY WIZARDS OR ALCHEMISTS, SO WE CAN RULE THAT OUT.
WHAT ABOUT THERAPY?

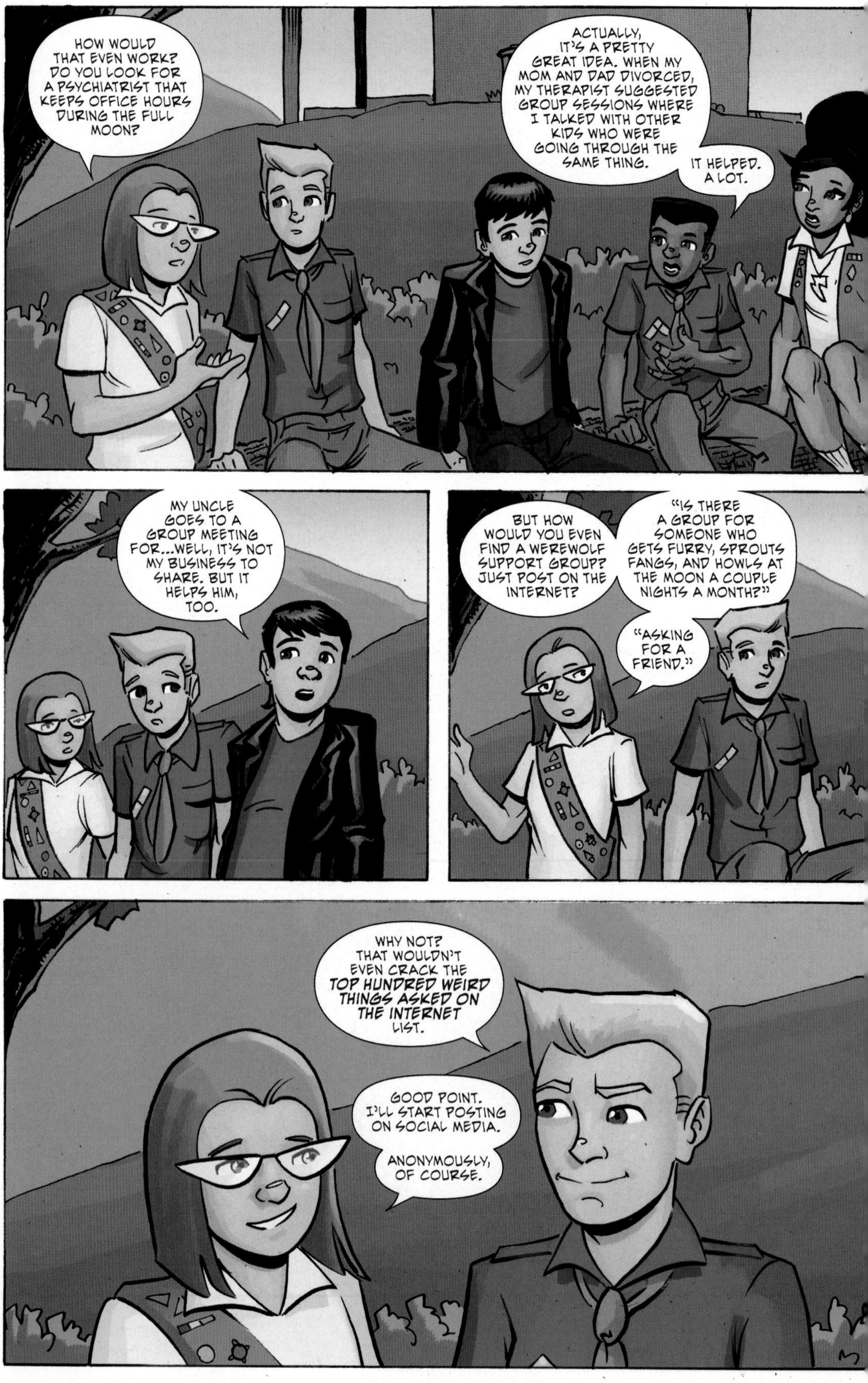
HOW WOULD THAT EVEN WORK? DO YOU LOOK FOR A PSYCHIATRIST THAT KEEPS OFFICE HOURS DURING THE FULL MOON?
ACTUALLY, IT'S A PRETTY GREAT IDEA. WHEN MY MOM AND DAD DIVORCED, MY THERAPIST SUGGESTED GROUP SESSIONS WHERE I TALKED WITH OTHER KIDS WHO WERE GOING THROUGH THE SAME THING.
IT HELPED. A LOT.
MY UNCLE GOES TO A GROUP MEETING FOR...WELL, IT'S NOT MY BUSINESS TO SHARE. BUT IT HELPS HIM, TOO.
BUT HOW WOULD YOU EVEN FIND A WEREWOLF SUPPORT GROUP? JUST POST ON THE INTERNET?
"IS THERE A GROUP FOR SOMEONE WHO GETS FURRY, SPROUTS FANGS, AND HOWLS AT THE MOON A COUPLE NIGHTS A MONTH?"
"ASKING FOR A FRIEND."
WHY NOT? THAT WOULDN'T EVEN CRACK THE ***TOP HUNDRED WEIRD THINGS ASKED ON THE INTERNET*** LIST.
GOOD POINT. I'LL START POSTING ON SOCIAL MEDIA.
ANONYMOUSLY, OF COURSE.

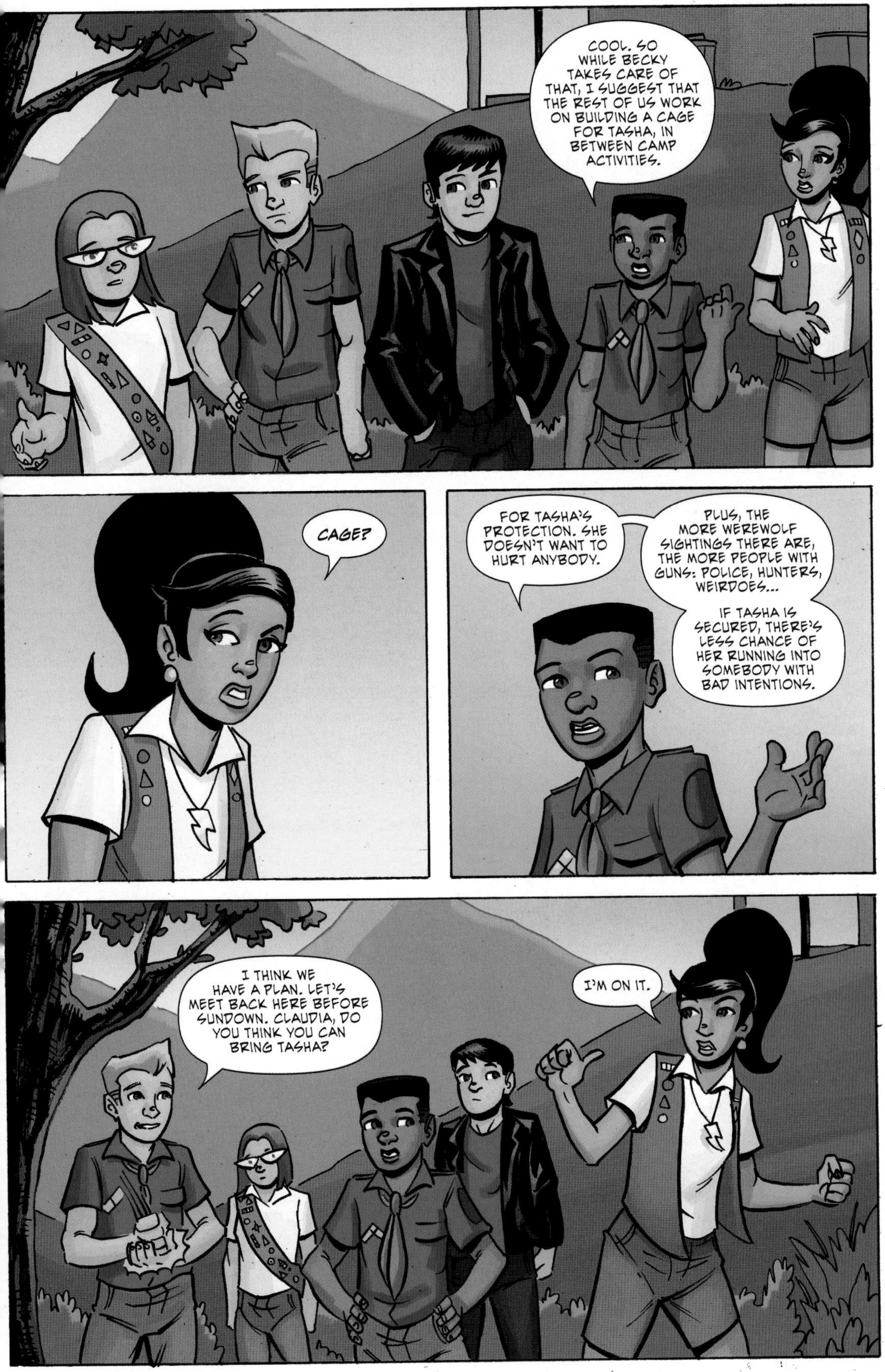
COOL. SO WHILE BECKY TAKES CARE OF THAT, I SUGGEST THAT THE REST OF US WORK ON BUILDING A CAGE FOR TASHA, IN BETWEEN CAMP ACTIVITIES.
CAGE?
FOR TASHA'S PROTECTION. SHE DOESN'T WANT TO HURT ANYBODY.
PLUS, THE MORE WEREWOLF SIGHTINGS THERE ARE, THE MORE PEOPLE WITH GUNS: POLICE, HUNTERS, WEIRDOES...
IF TASHA IS SECURED, THERE'S LESS CHANCE OF HER RUNNING INTO SOMEBODY WITH BAD INTENTIONS.
I THINK WE HAVE A PLAN. LET'S MEET BACK HERE BEFORE SUNDOWN. CLAUDIA, DO YOU THINK YOU CAN BRING TASHA?
I'M ON IT.

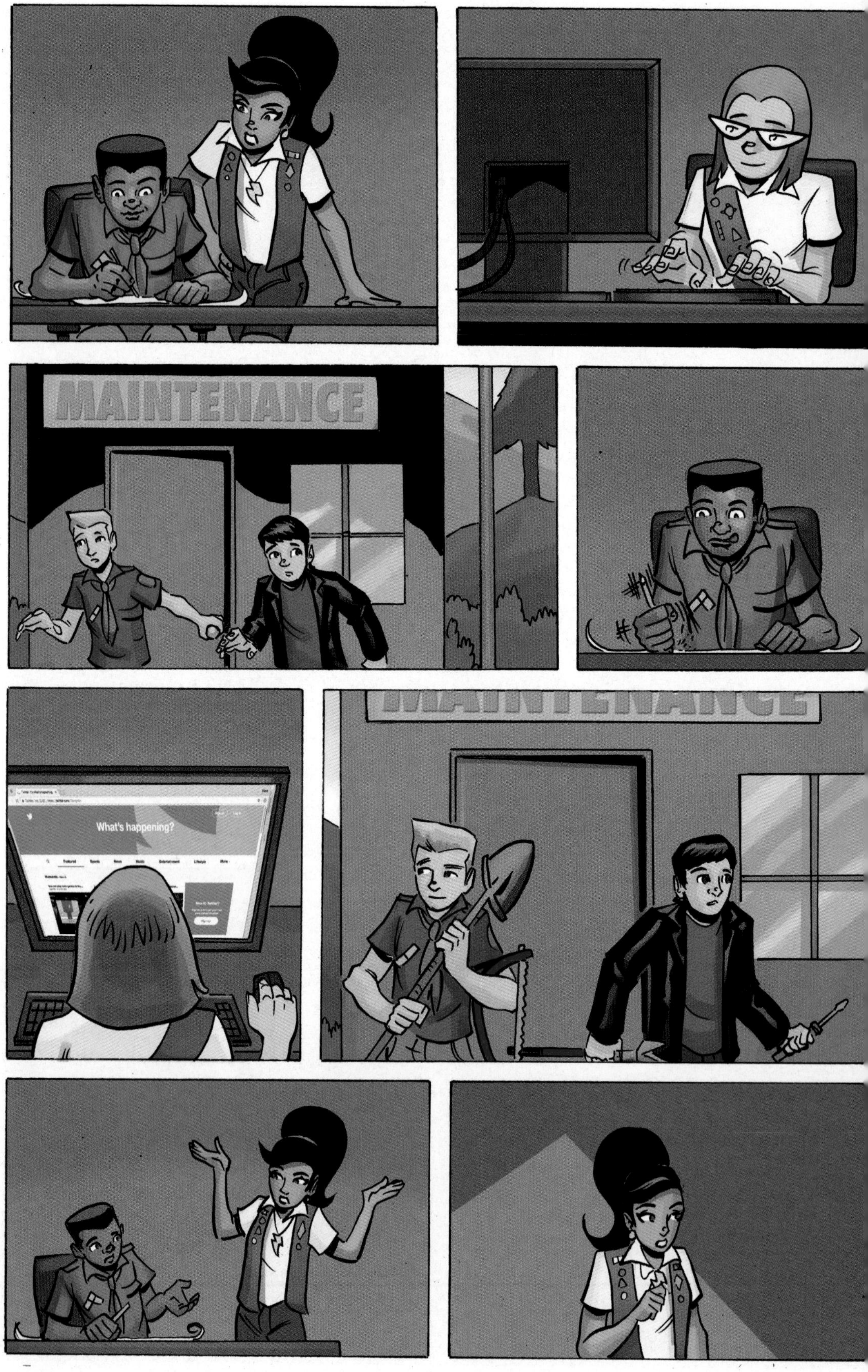
MAINTENANCE
What's happening?

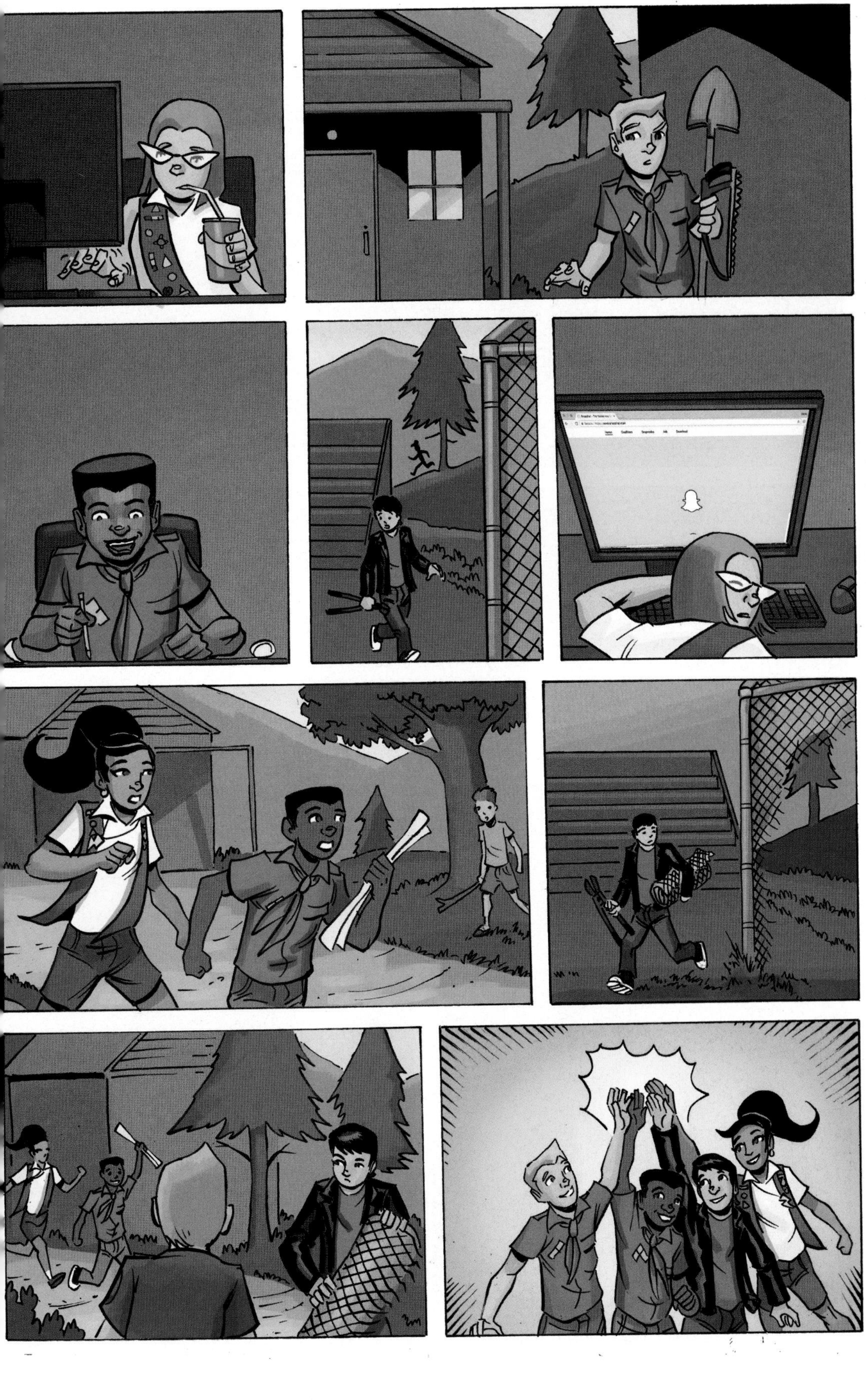

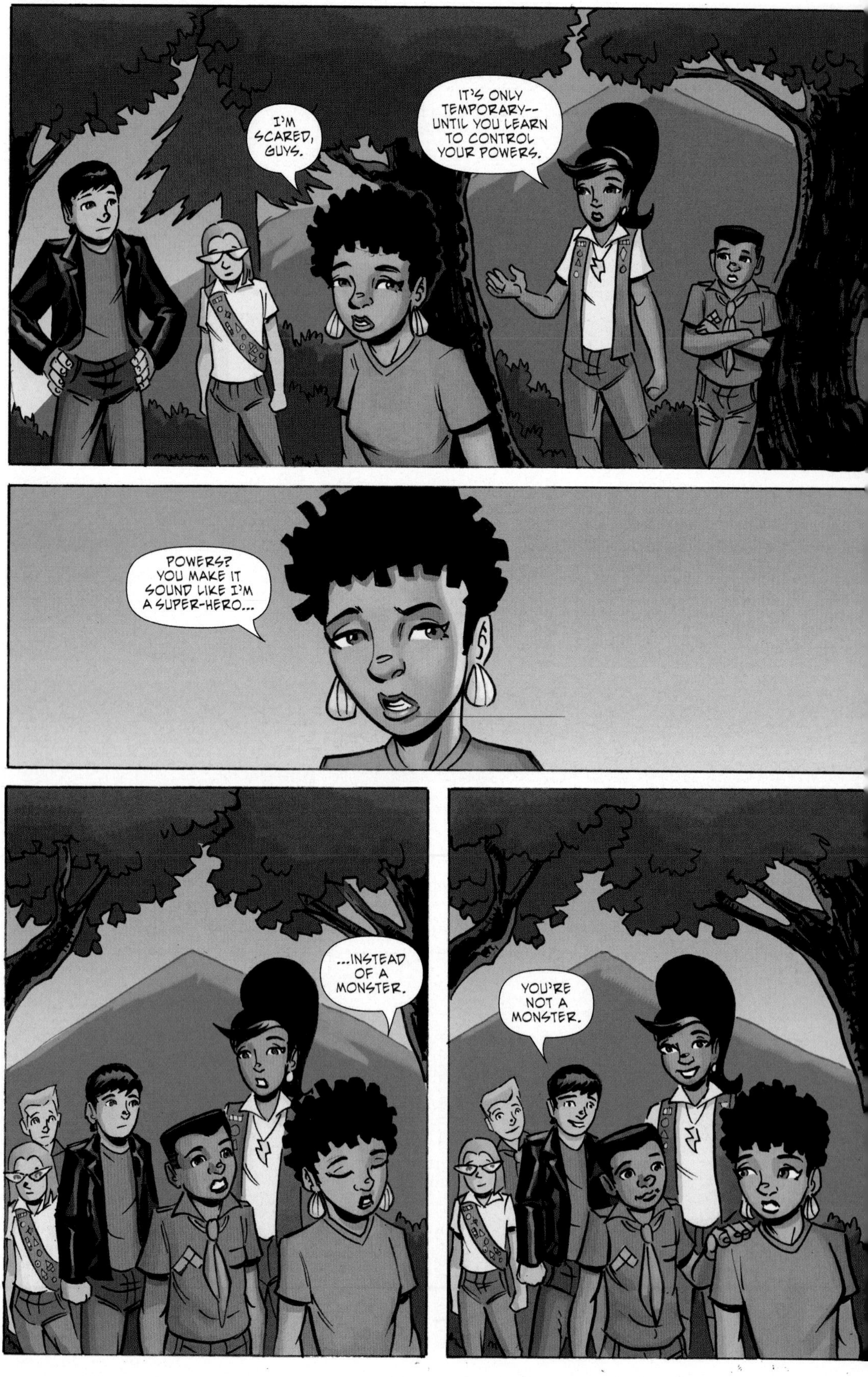
I'M SCARED, GUYS.
IT'S ONLY TEMPORARY-- UNTIL YOU LEARN TO CONTROL YOUR POWERS.
POWERS? YOU MAKE IT SOUND LIKE I'M A SUPER-HERO...
...INSTEAD OF A MONSTER.
YOU'RE NOT A MONSTER.

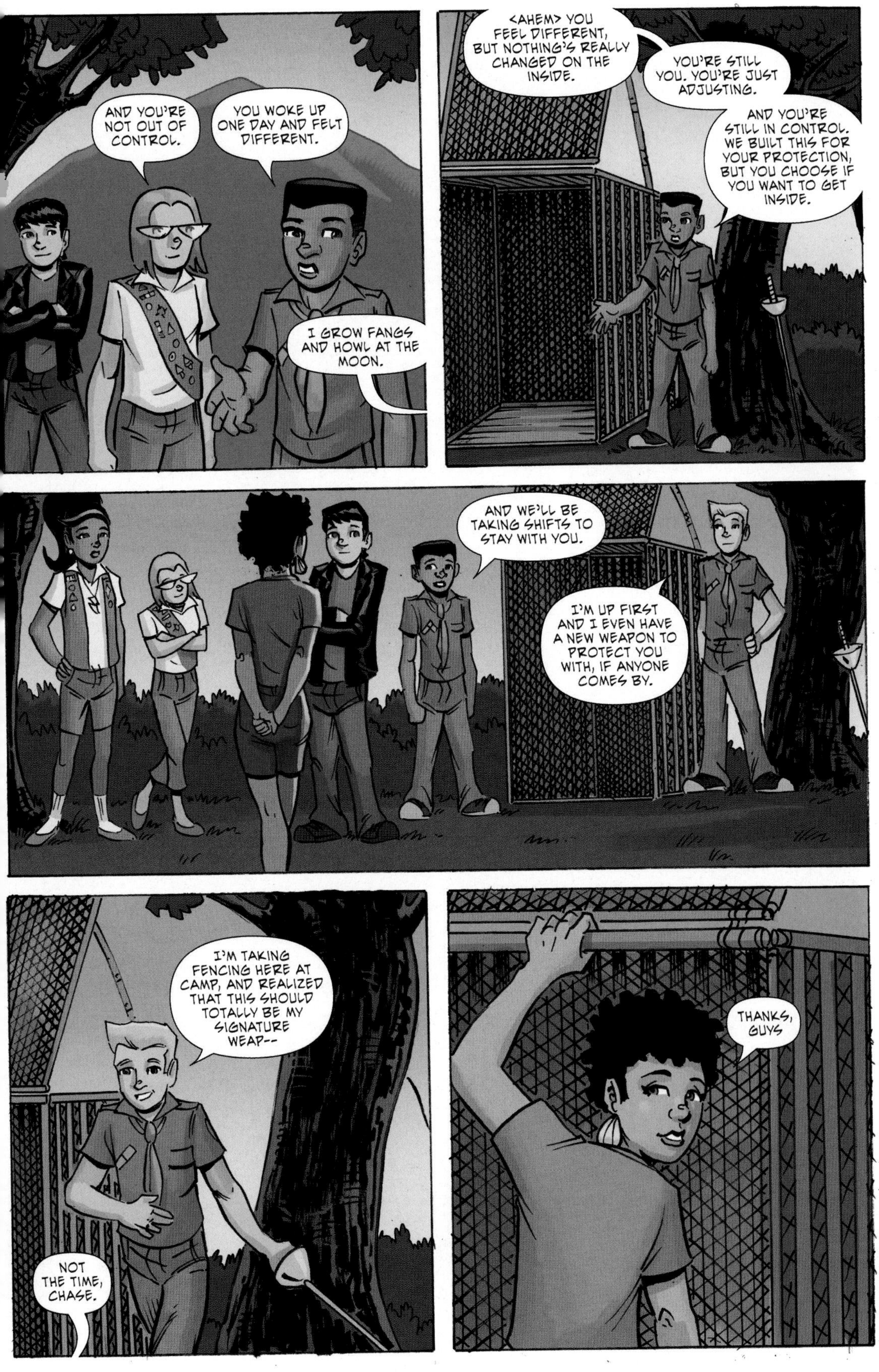
AND YOU'RE NOT OUT OF CONTROL.
YOU WOKE UP ONE DAY AND FELT DIFFERENT.
I GROW FANGS AND HOWL AT THE MOON.
<AHEM> YOU FEEL DIFFERENT, BUT NOTHING'S REALLY CHANGED ON THE INSIDE.
YOU'RE STILL YOU. YOU'RE JUST ADJUSTING.
AND YOU'RE STILL IN CONTROL. WE BUILT THIS FOR YOUR PROTECTION, BUT YOU CHOOSE IF YOU WANT TO GET INSIDE.
AND WE'LL BE TAKING SHIFTS TO STAY WITH YOU.
I'M UP FIRST AND I EVEN HAVE A NEW WEAPON TO PROTECT YOU WITH, IF ANYONE COMES BY.
I'M TAKING FENCING HERE AT CAMP, AND REALIZED THAT THIS SHOULD TOTALLY BE MY SIGNATURE WEAP--
NOT THE TIME, CHASE.
THANKS, GUYS

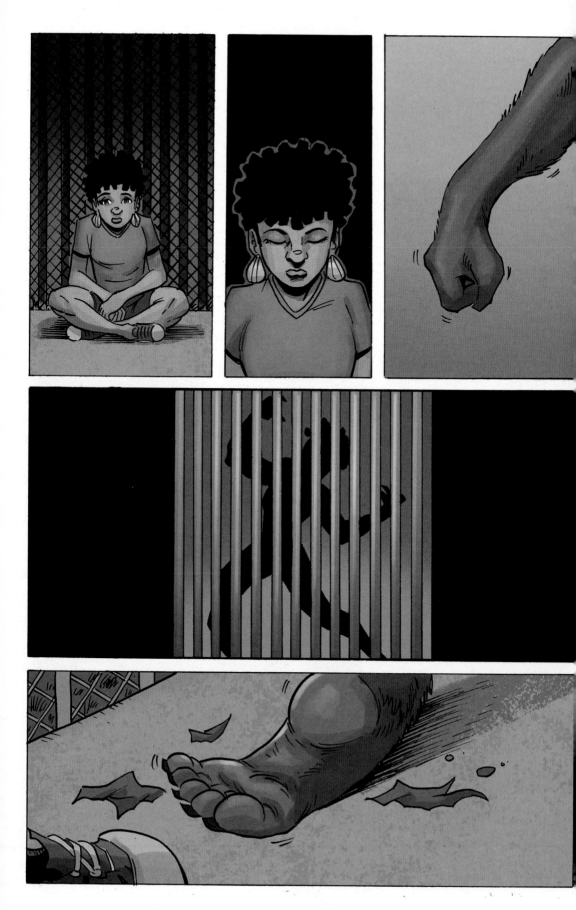

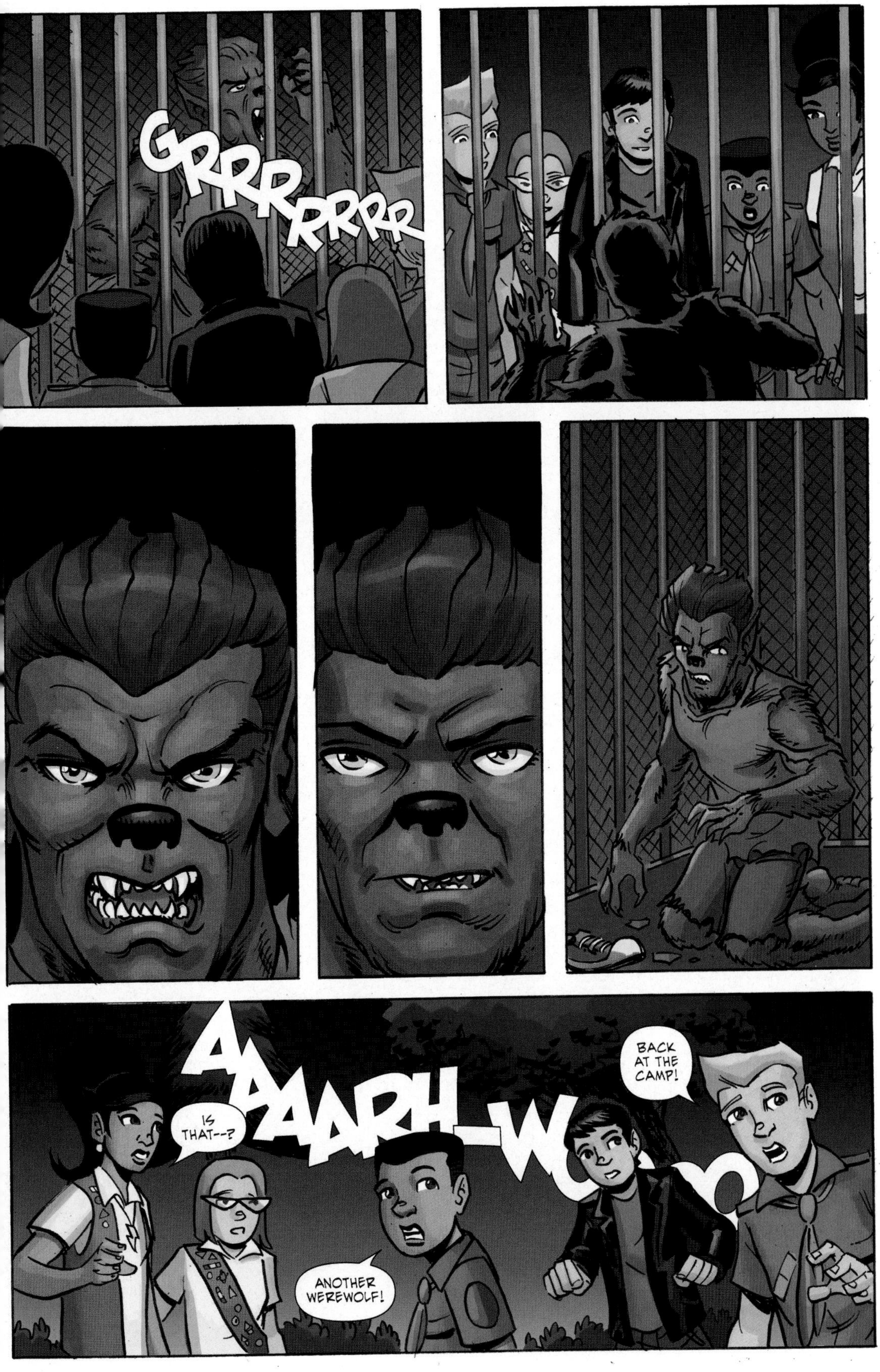
GRRRRRRR
AAAARH-WOOO
IS THAT--?
BACK AT THE CAMP!
ANOTHER WEREWOLF!

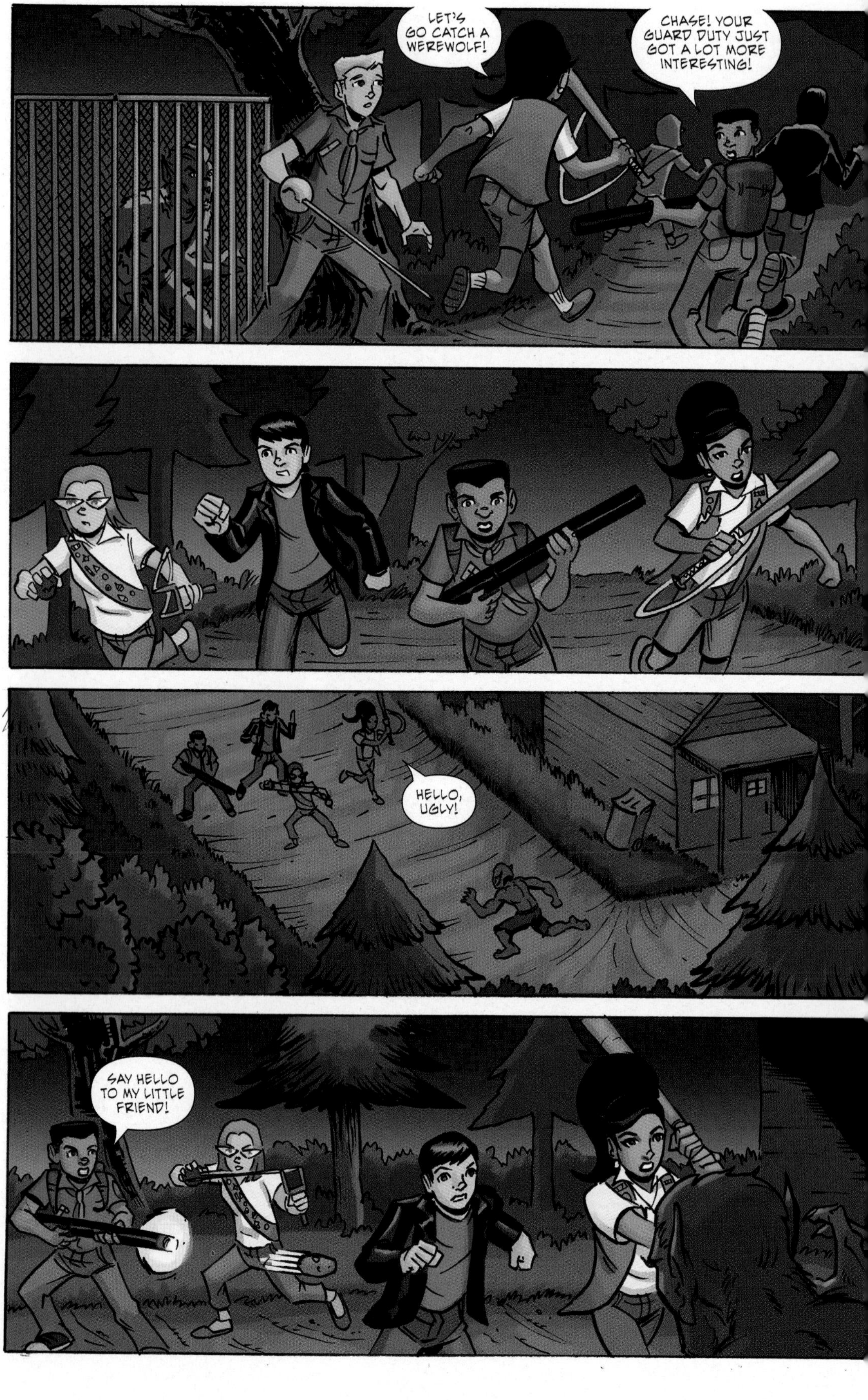
LET'S GO CATCH A WEREWOLF!
CHASE! YOUR GUARD DUTY JUST GOT A LOT MORE INTERESTING!
HELLO, UGLY!
SAY HELLO TO MY LITTLE FRIEND!

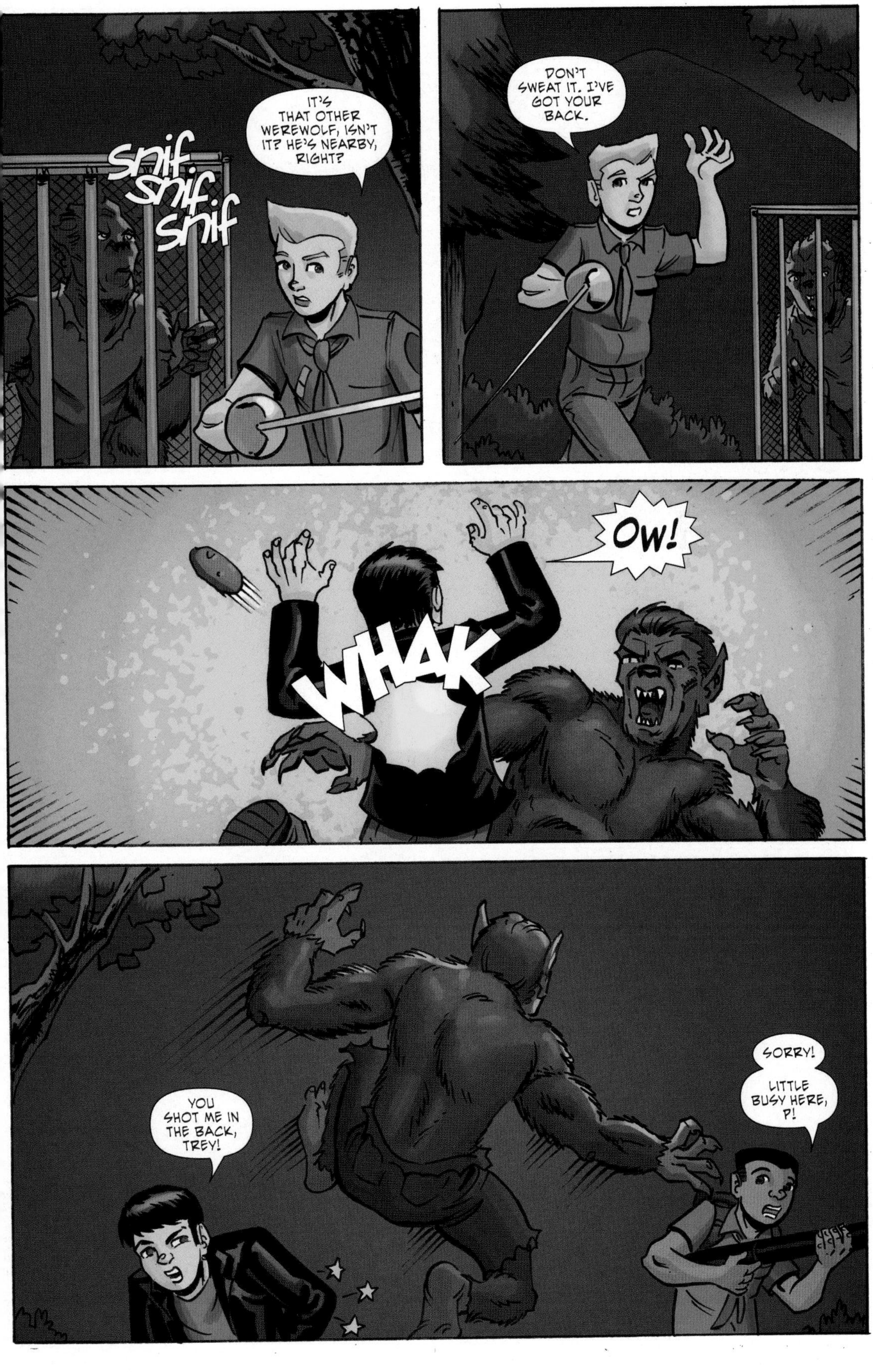
IT'S THAT OTHER WEREWOLF, ISN'T IT? HE'S NEARBY, RIGHT?
snif snif snif
DON'T SWEAT IT. I'VE GOT YOUR BACK.
OW!
WHAK
YOU SHOT ME IN THE BACK, TREY!
SORRY!
LITTLE BUSY HERE, P!

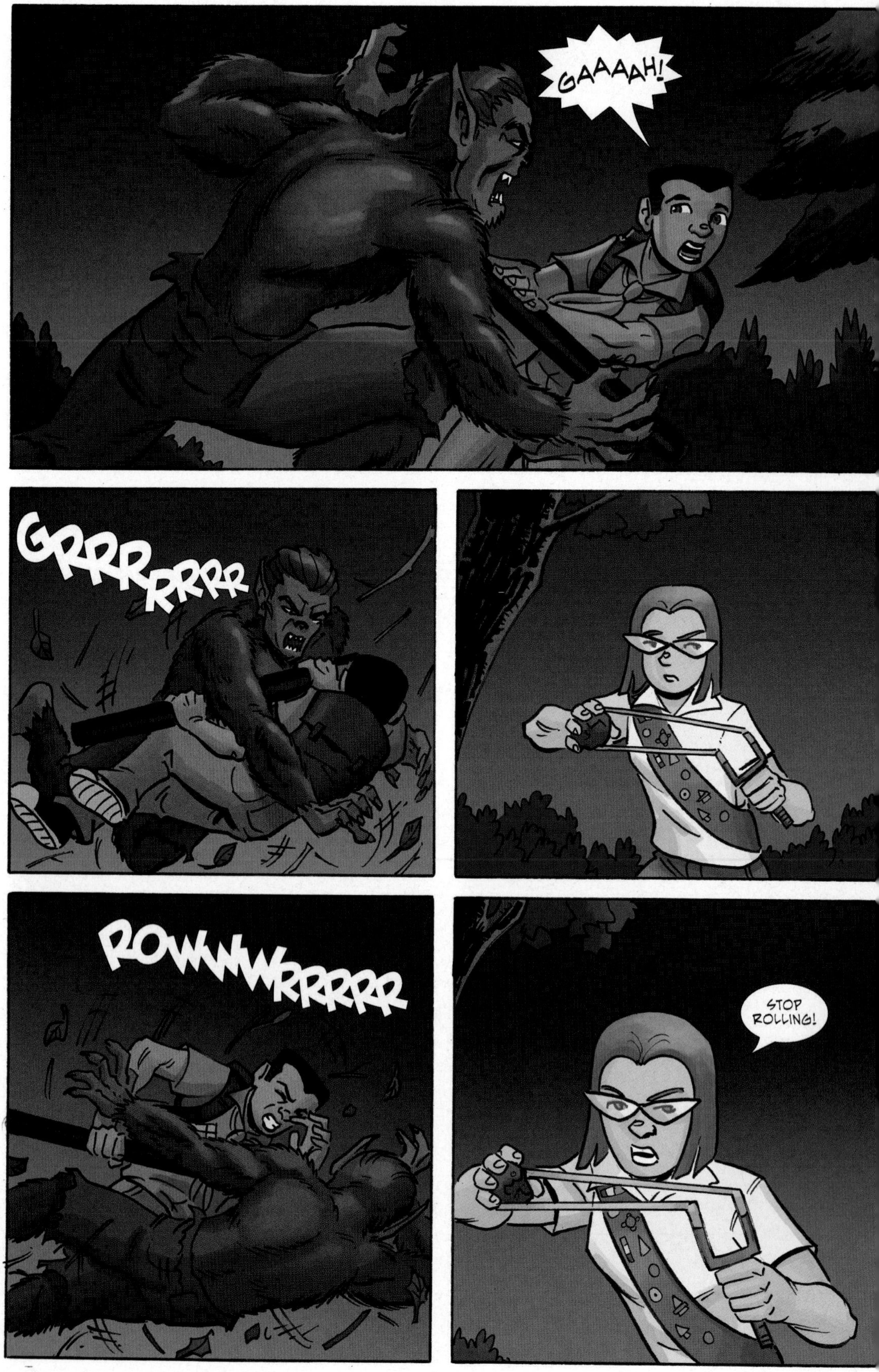
GAAAAH!
GRRRRRRR
ROWWWRRRRR
STOP ROLLING!

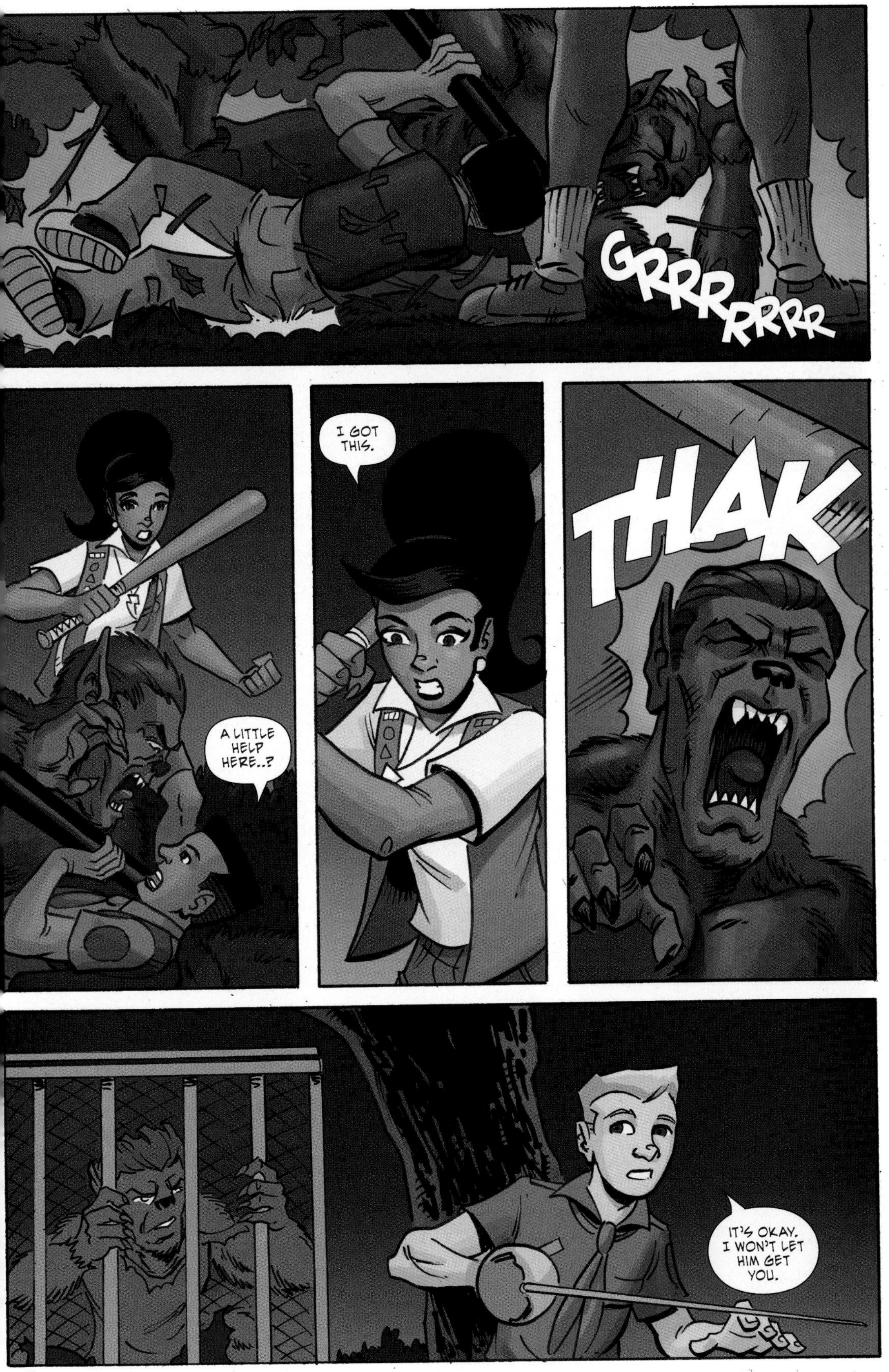
GRRRRRRR
A LITTLE HELP HERE..?
I GOT THIS.
THAK
IT'S OKAY. I WON'T LET HIM GET YOU.

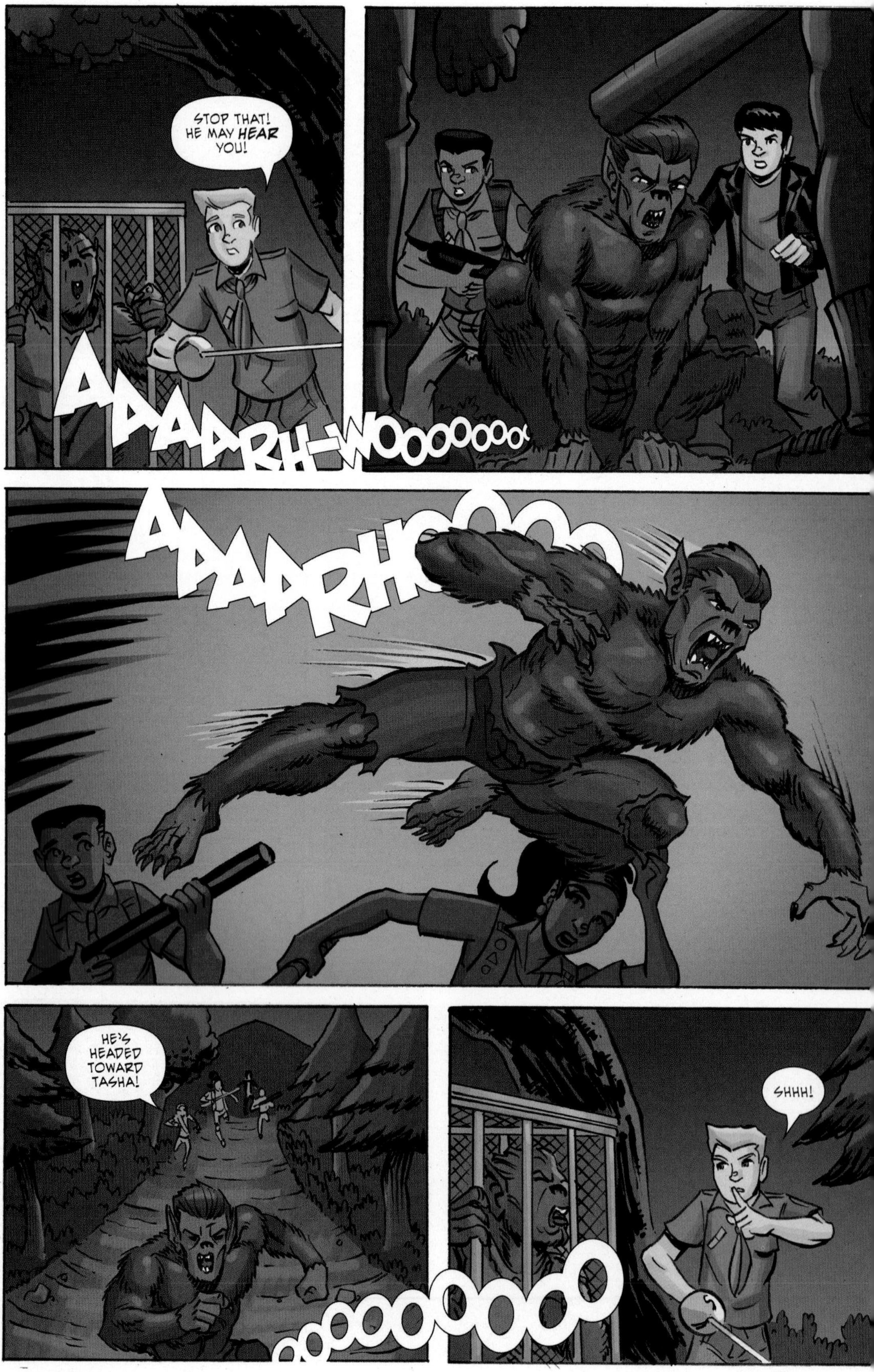
STOP THAT! HE MAY HEAR YOU!
AAARH-WOOOOOO
AAARHOOOO
HE'S HEADED TOWARD TASHA!
SHHH!
OOOOOOOOO

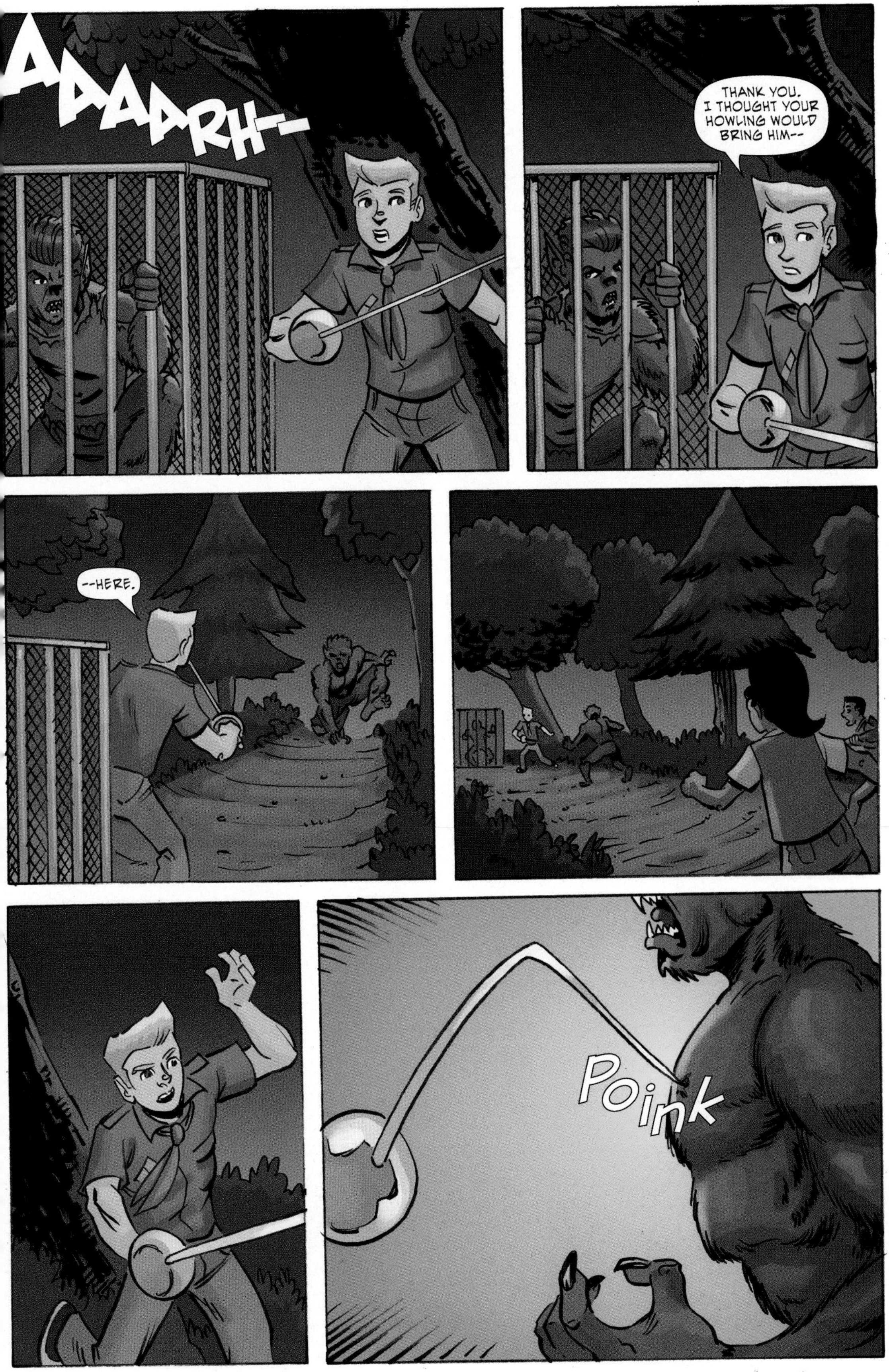
AAARH--
THANK YOU. I THOUGHT YOUR HOWLING WOULD BRING HIM--
--HERE.
Poink

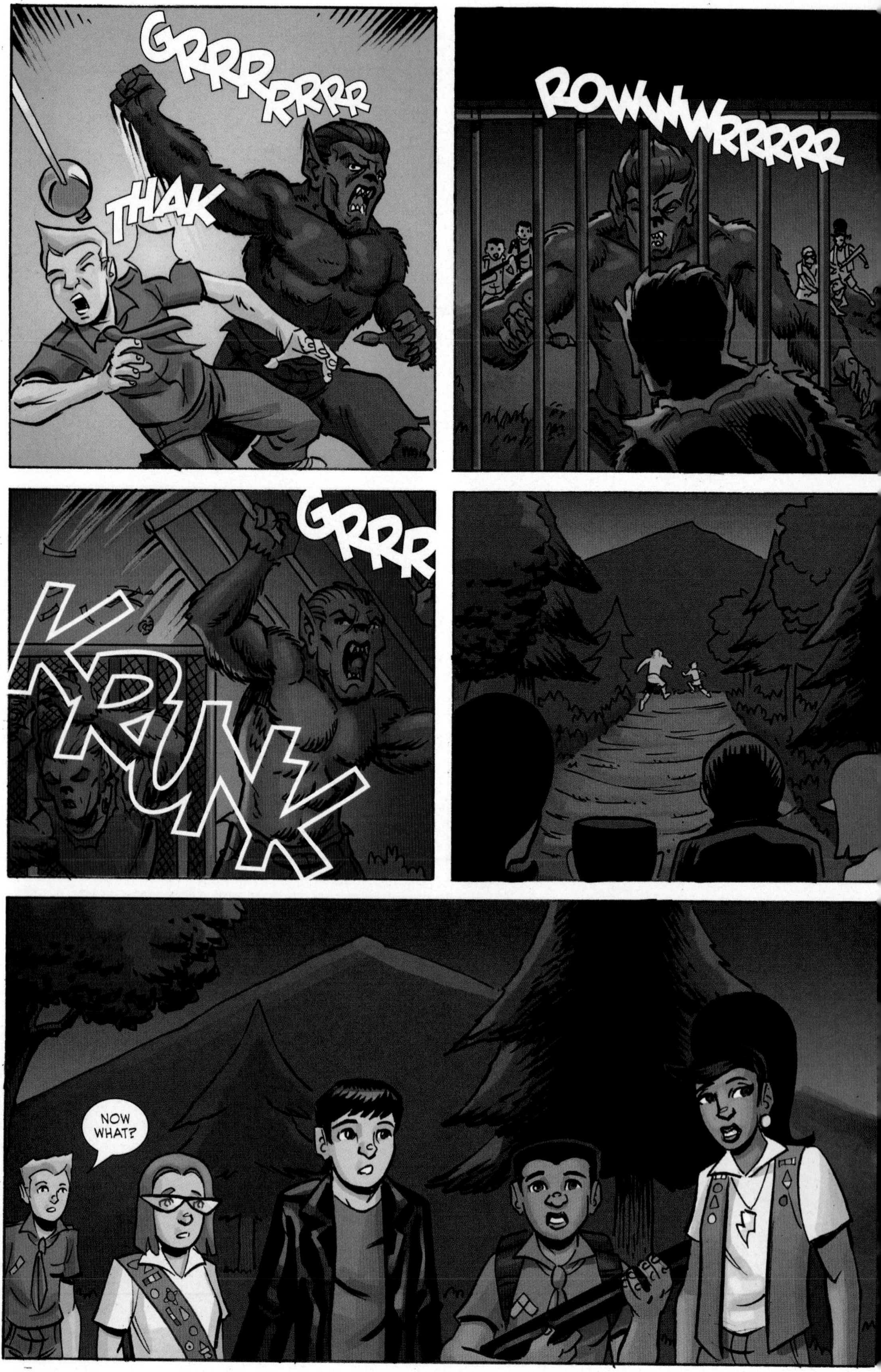
GRRRRRRR
THAK
ROWWWRRRRR
GRRR
KRUNK
NOW WHAT?

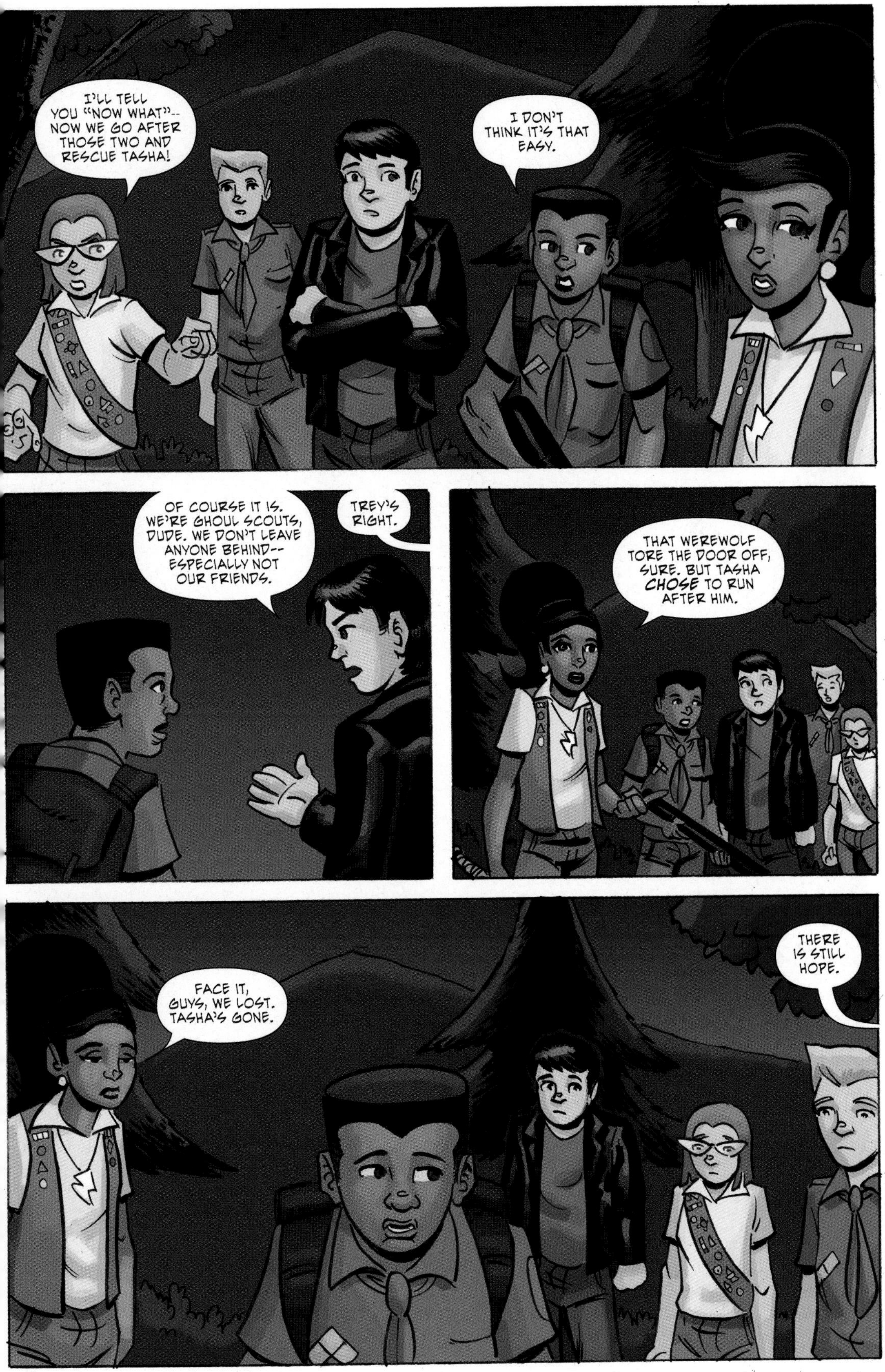
I'LL TELL YOU "NOW WHAT"-- NOW WE GO AFTER THOSE TWO AND RESCUE TASHA!
I DON'T THINK IT'S THAT EASY.
OF COURSE IT IS. WE'RE GHOUL SCOUTS, DUDE. WE DON'T LEAVE ANYONE BEHIND-- ESPECIALLY NOT OUR FRIENDS.
TREY'S RIGHT.
THAT WEREWOLF TORE THE DOOR OFF, SURE. BUT TASHA CHOSE TO RUN AFTER HIM.
FACE IT, GUYS, WE LOST. TASHA'S GONE.
THERE IS STILL HOPE.

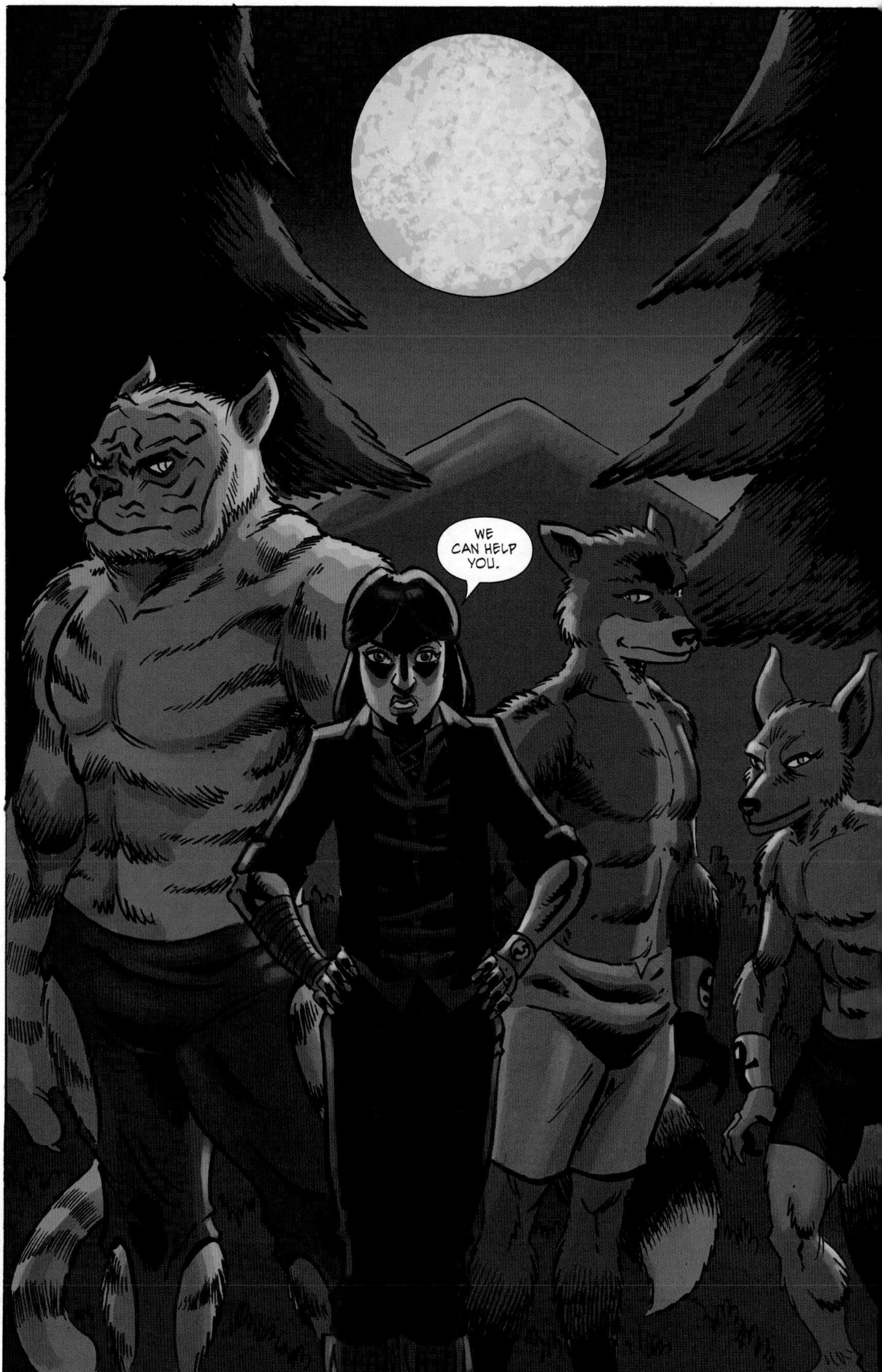
WE CAN HELP YOU.

GHOUL SCOUTS BONUS FEATURE

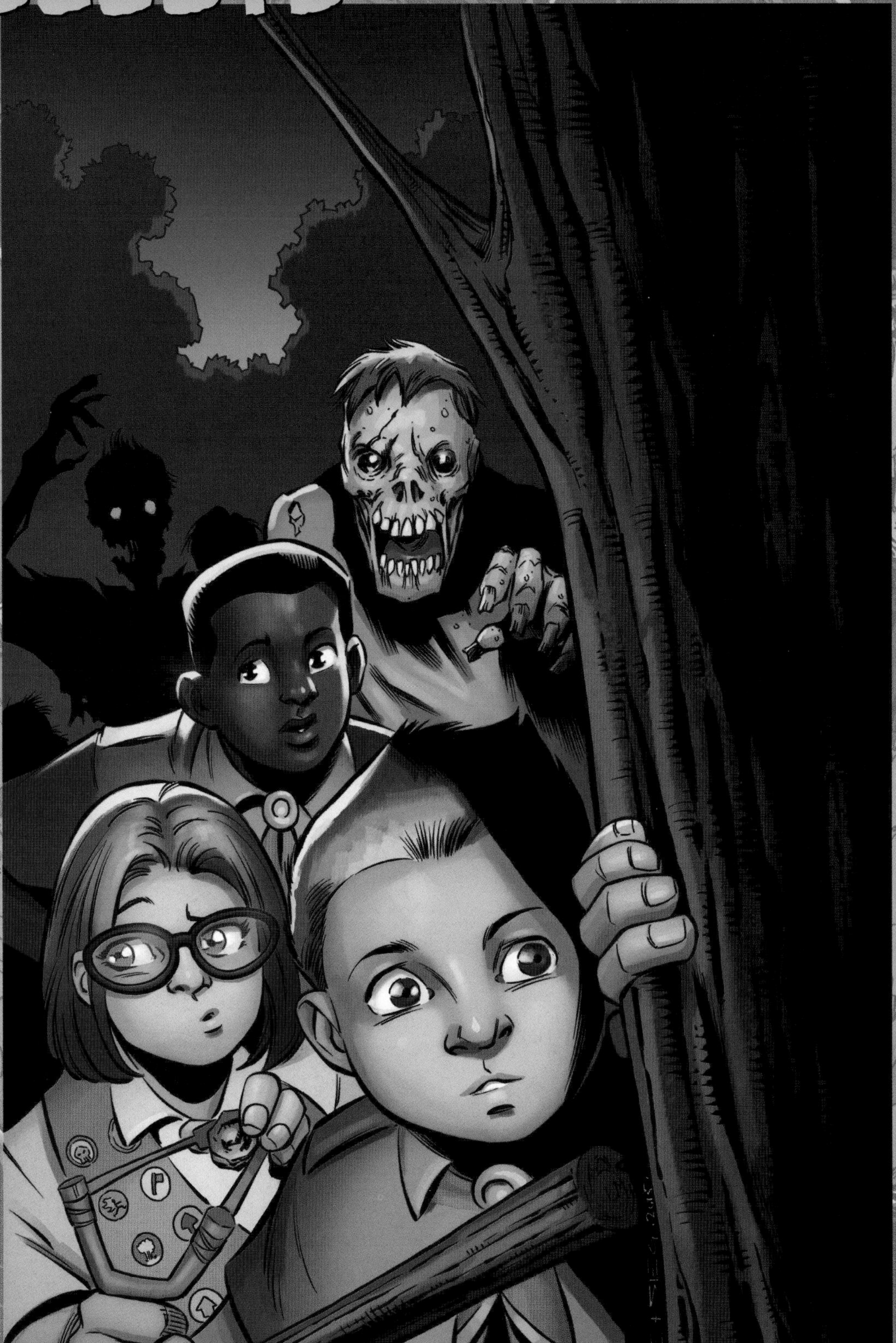

Variant cover by MIKE **NORTON**, MARK **STEGBAUER** & JASON **MILLET**

GHOUL SCOUTS BONUS FEATURE

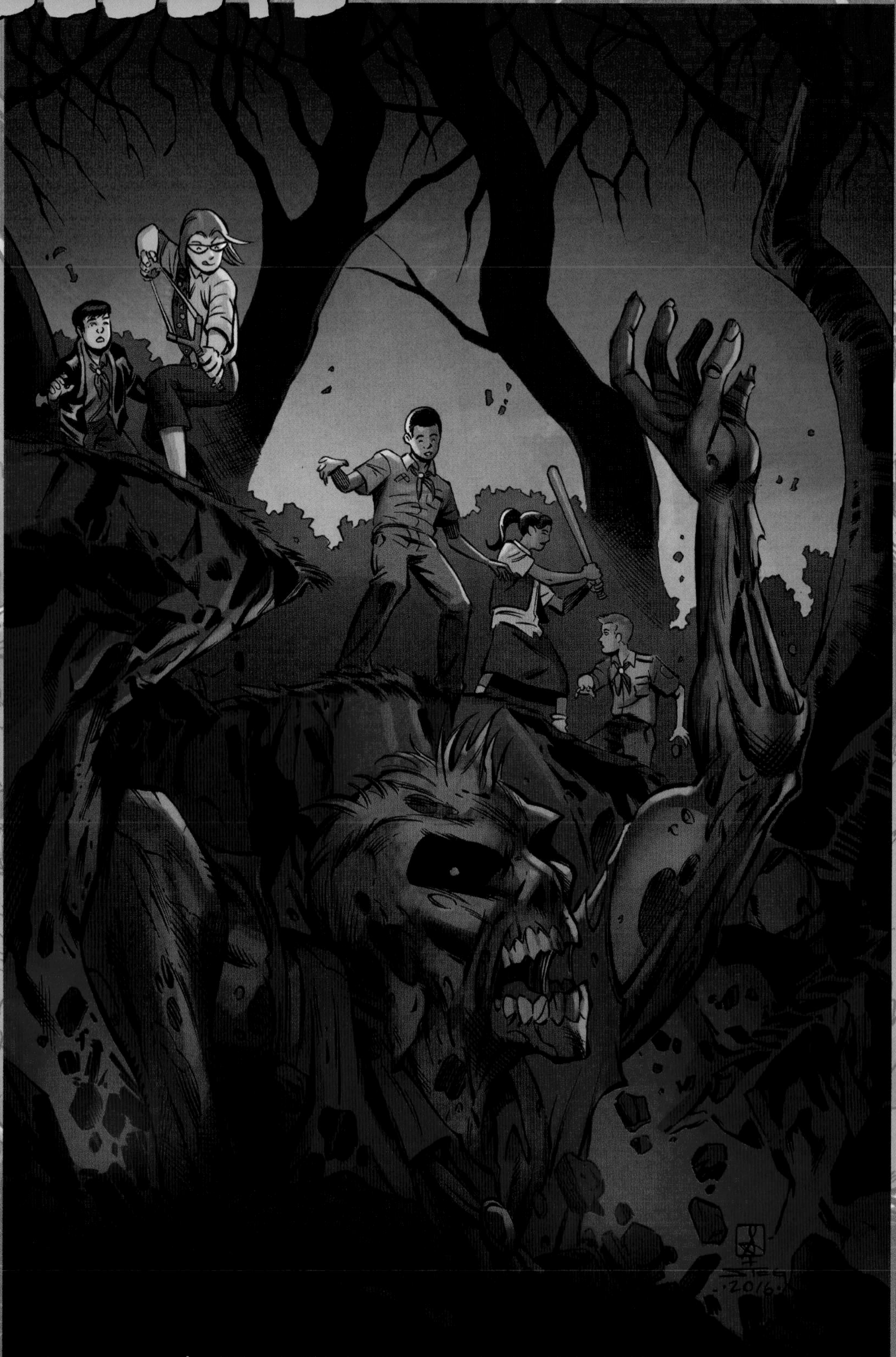

Variant cover by SEAN **IZAAKSE,** MARK **STEGBAUER** & JASON **MILLET**

GHOUL SCOUTS BONUS FEATURE

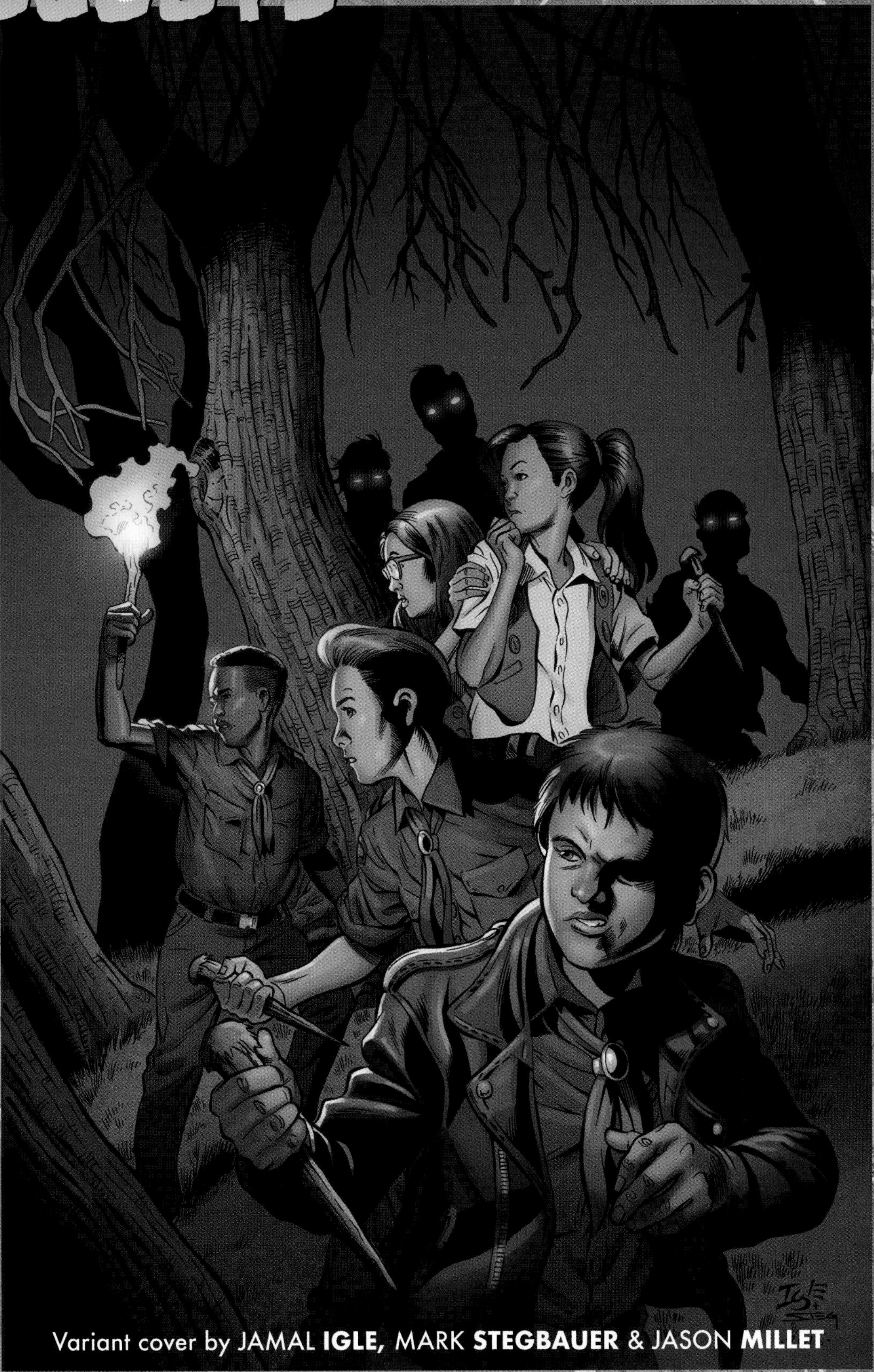

Variant cover by JAMAL **IGLE,** MARK **STEGBAUER** & JASON **MILLET**

GHOUL SCOUTS BONUS FEATURE

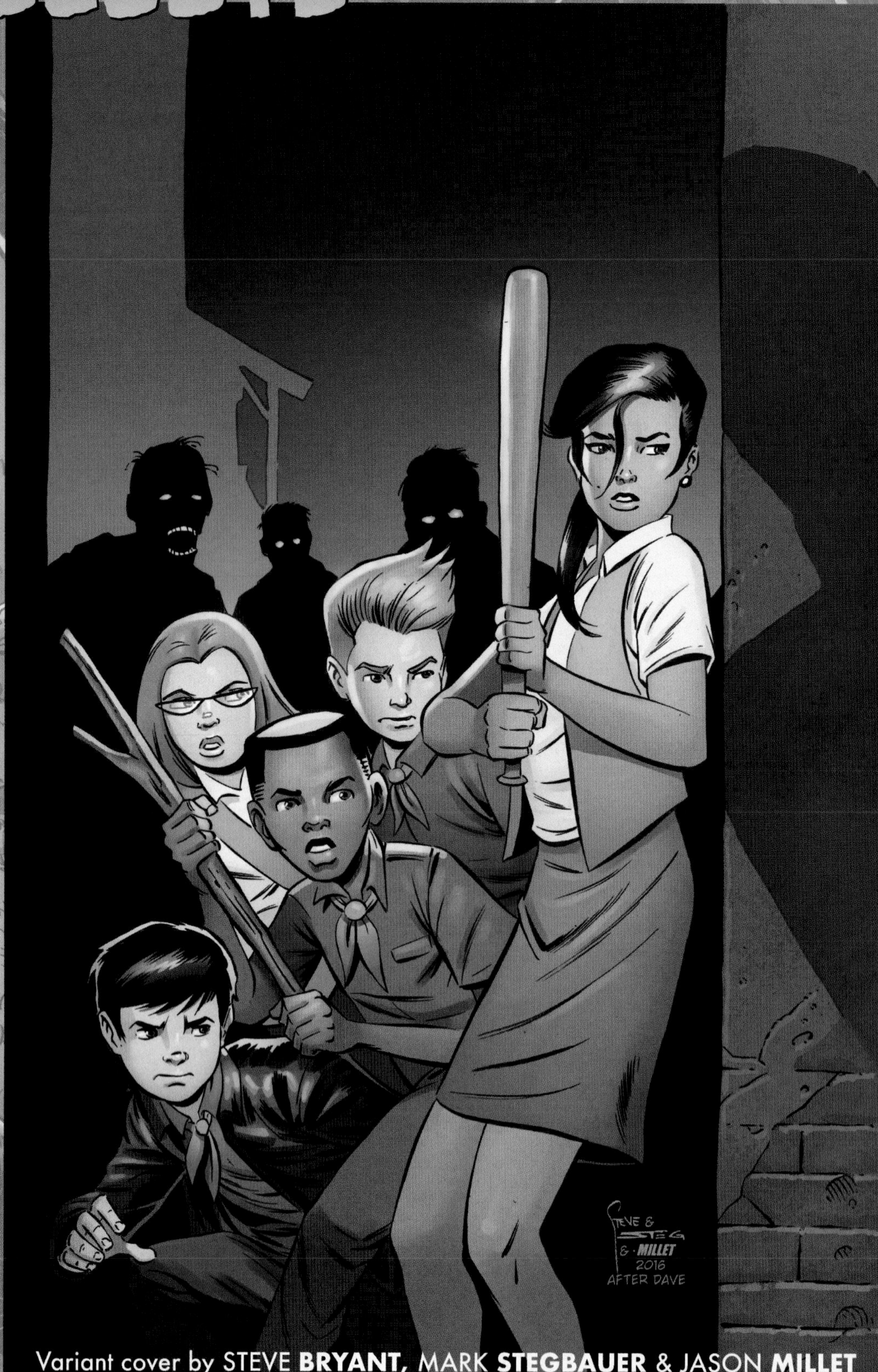
STEVE & STEG & MILLET 2016 AFTER DAVE

Variant cover by STEVE **BRYANT,** MARK **STEGBAUER** & JASON **MILLET**

GHOUL SCOUTS BONUS FEATURE

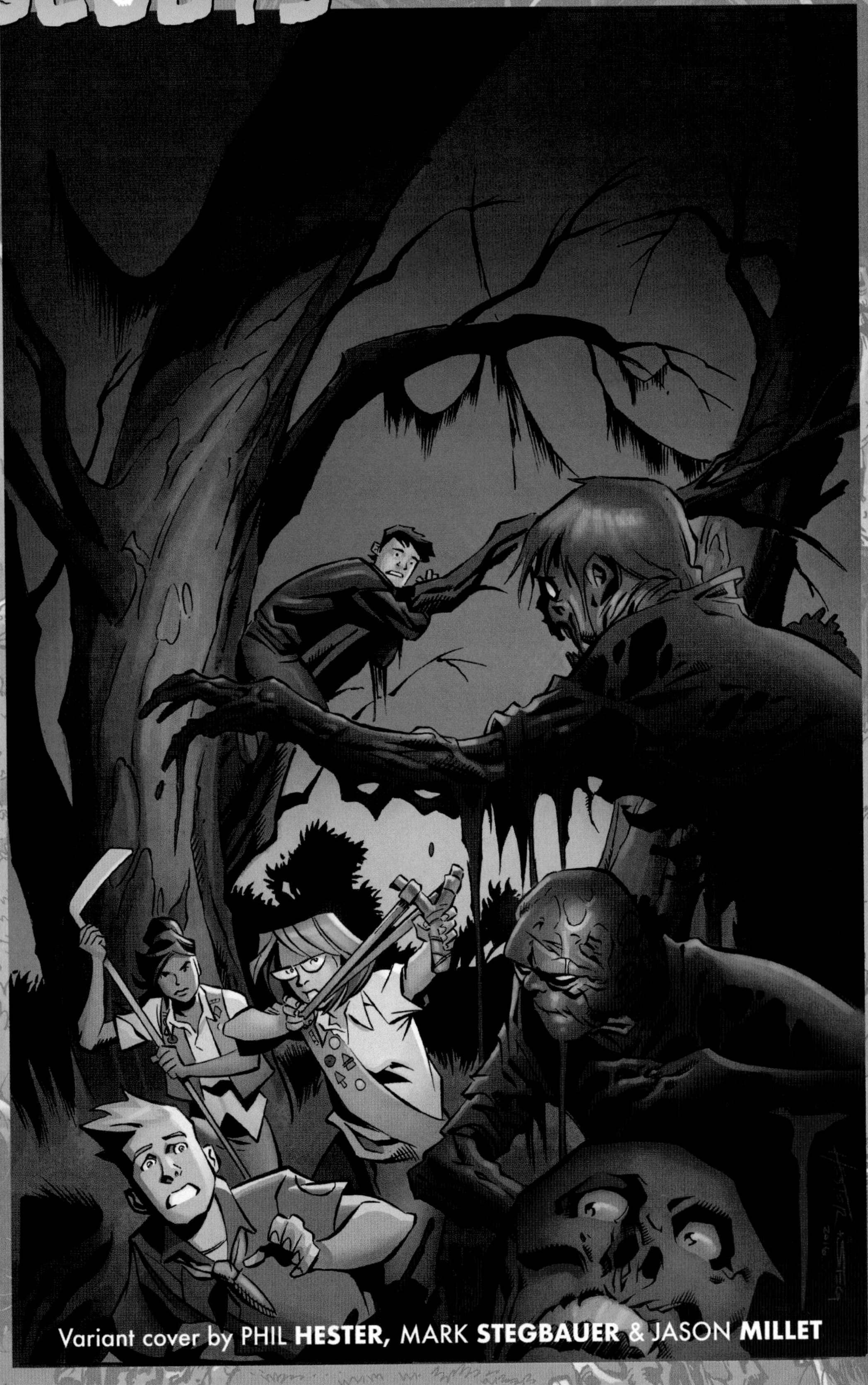

Variant cover by PHIL **HESTER,** MARK **STEGBAUER** & JASON **MILLET**

GHOUL SCOUTS BONUS FEATURE

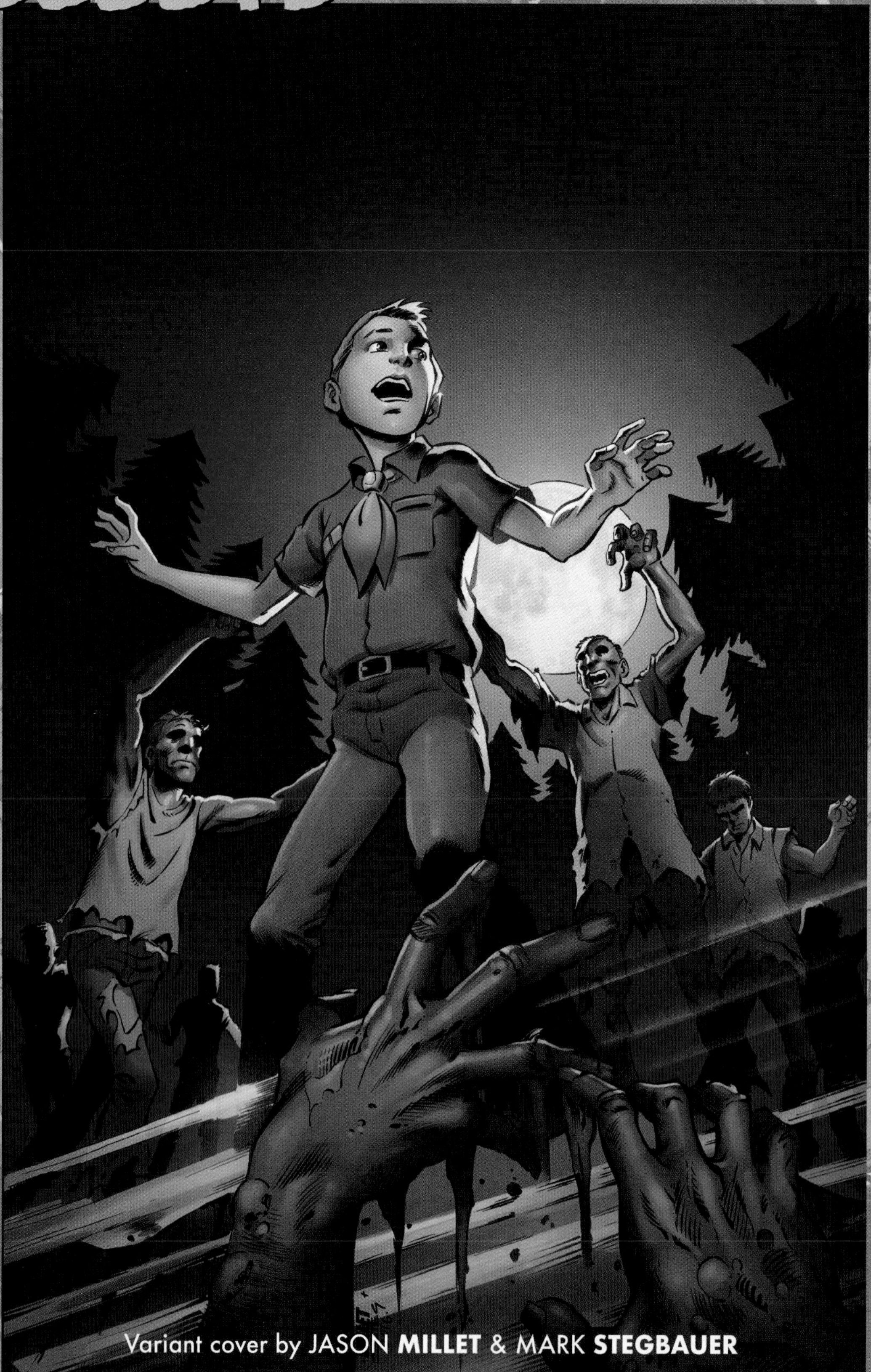

Variant cover by JASON **MILLET** & MARK **STEGBAUER**

GHOUL SCOUTS BONUS FEATURE

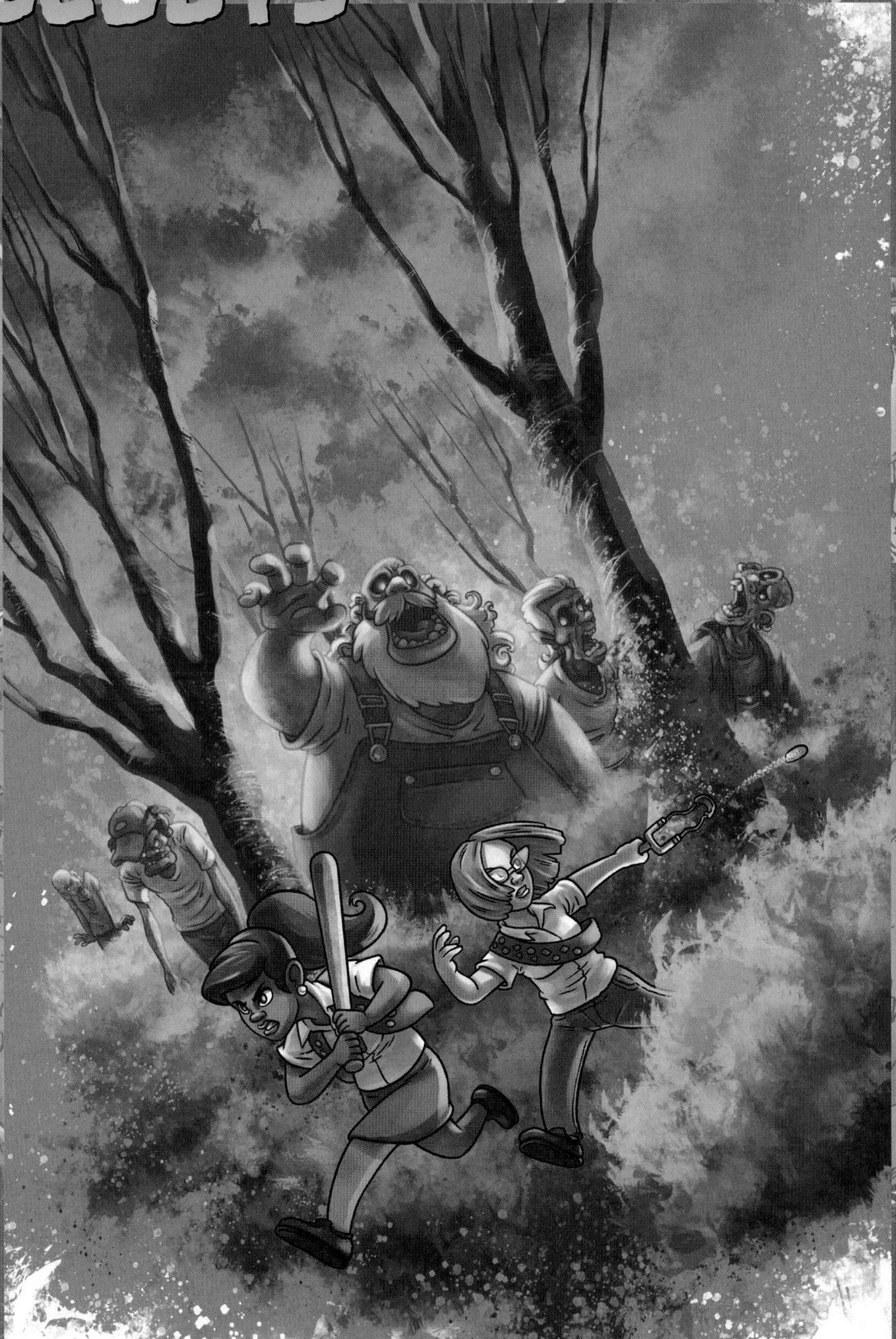

Variant cover by AXUR **ENEAS**

GHOUL SCOUTS

BONUS FEATURE

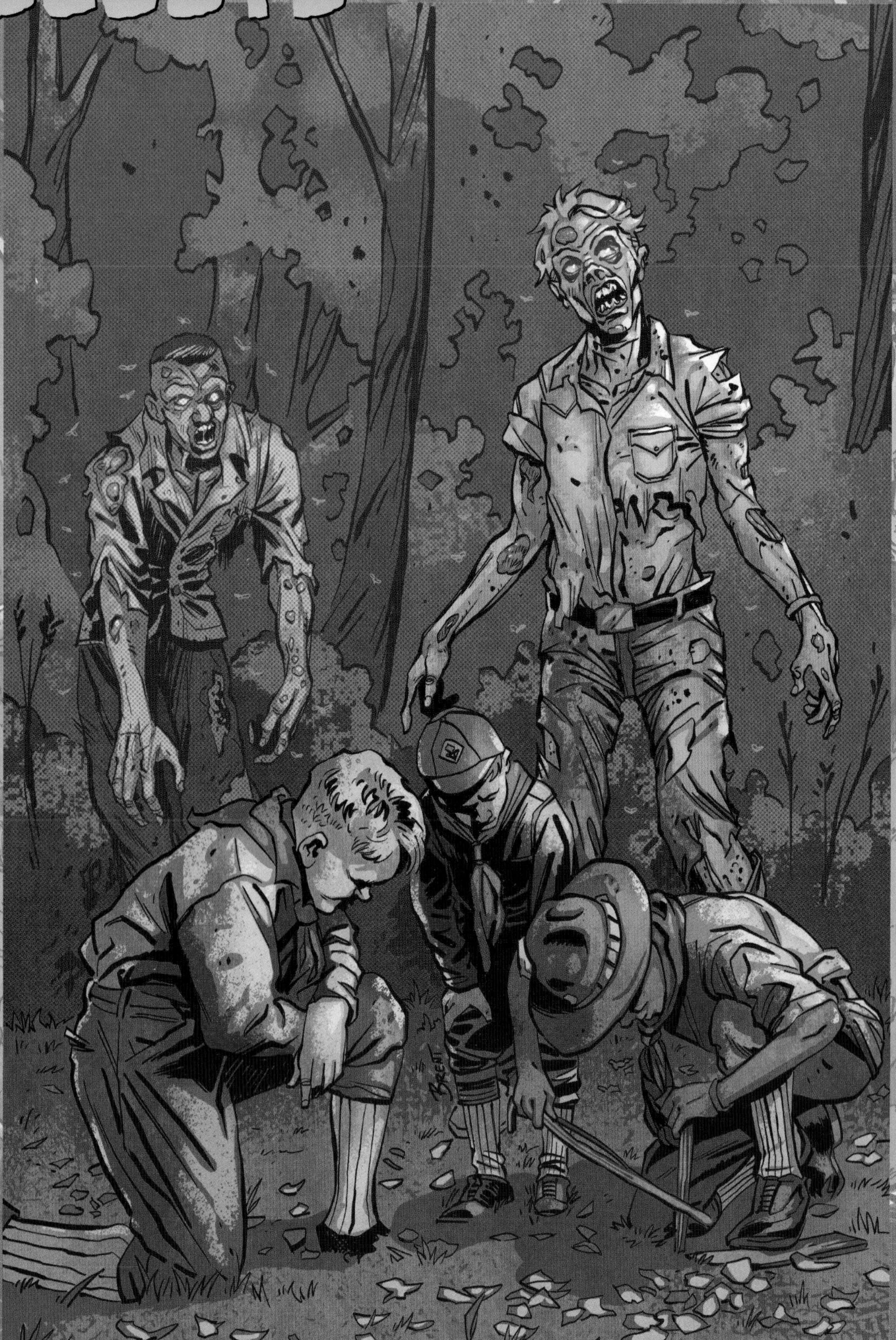

Variant cover by BRENT **SCHOONOVER** & ROBT **SNYDER**

I WAS A TWEENAGE WEREWOLF!

CHAPTER
FOUR

GHOUL SCOUTS ™

Story and Letters
STEVE BRYANT
@SteveBryantArt

Art
MARK STEGBAUER
@MarkStegbauer

Colors
JASON MILLET
@Jason_Millet

Edited by
CHRIS MURRIN
@ChrisMurrin

Color Assist
DREW BROWNE
@TheDrewBrowne

Cover
MARK STEGBAUER
& JASON MILLET

Bryan Seaton: Publisher/CEO **| Shawn Gabborin:** Editor In Chief **| Jason Martin:** Publisher-Danger Zone
Nicole D'Andria: Marketing Director/Editor **| Jim Dietz:** Social Media Manager **| Danielle Davison:** Executive Administrat
Chad Cicconi: Camp Maintenance **| Shawn Pryor:** President of Creator Relations

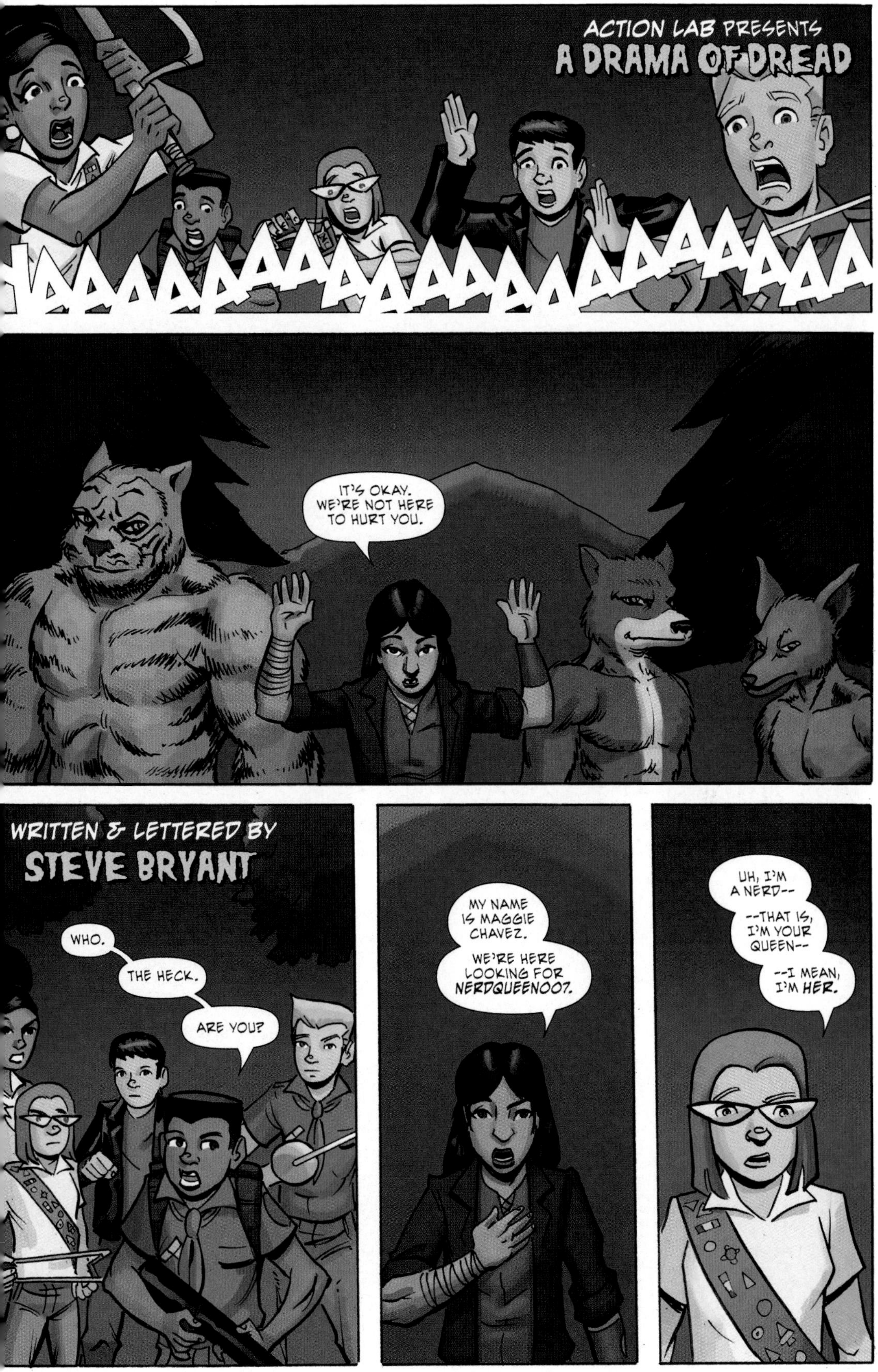
ACTION LAB PRESENTS
A DRAMA OF DREAD
HAAAAAAAAAAAAAAAAAAAAAAAAAAAA
IT'S OKAY. WE'RE NOT HERE TO HURT YOU.
WRITTEN & LETTERED BY
STEVE BRYANT
WHO.
THE HECK.
ARE YOU?
MY NAME IS MAGGIE CHAVEZ.
WE'RE HERE LOOKING FOR NERDQUEEN007.
UH, I'M A NERD--
--THAT IS, I'M YOUR QUEEN--
--I MEAN, I'M HER.

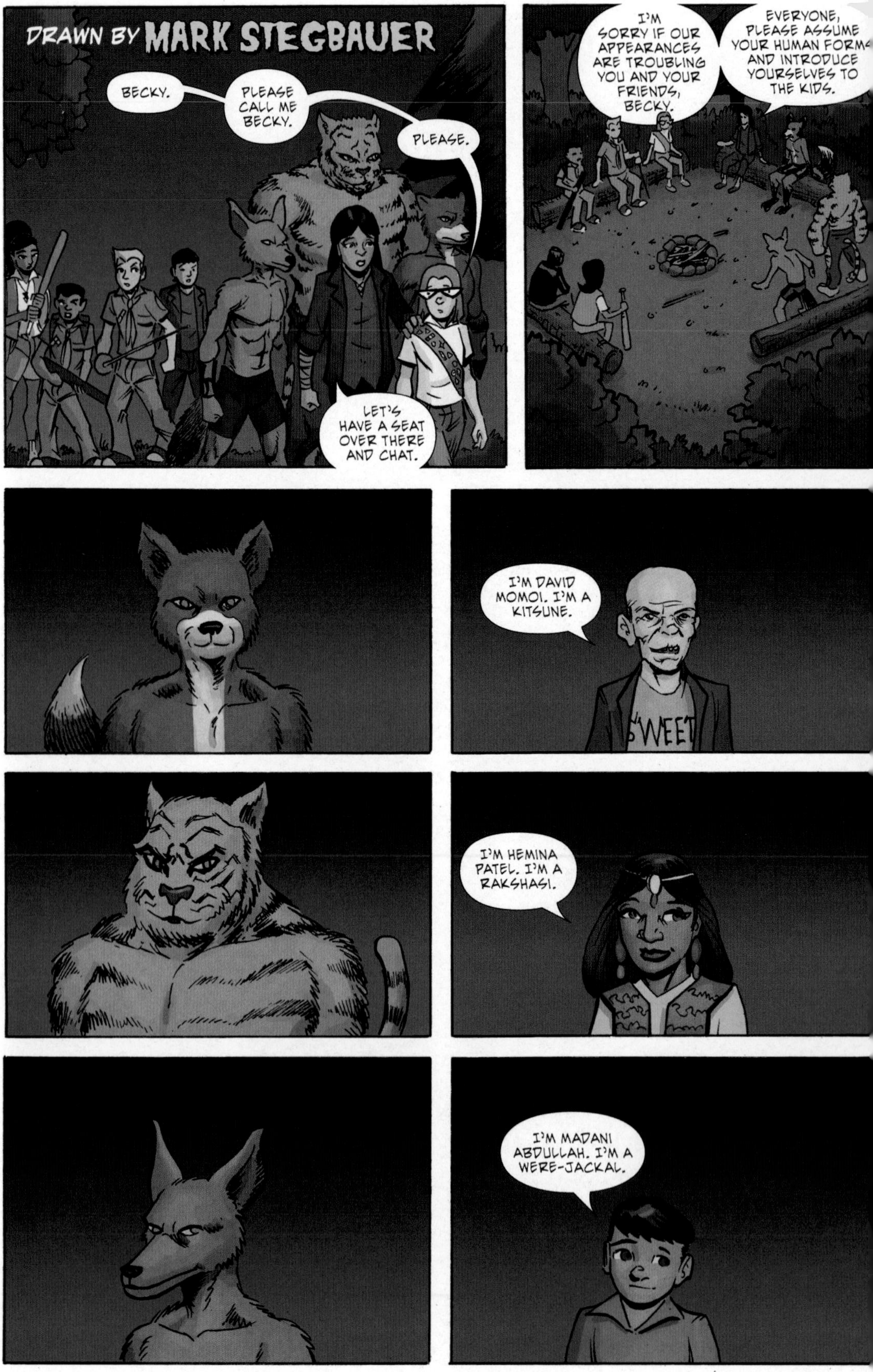
DRAWN BY MARK STEGBAUER
BECKY.
PLEASE CALL ME BECKY.
PLEASE.
LET'S HAVE A SEAT OVER THERE AND CHAT.
I'M SORRY IF OUR APPEARANCES ARE TROUBLING YOU AND YOUR FRIENDS, BECKY.
EVERYONE, PLEASE ASSUME YOUR HUMAN FORMS AND INTRODUCE YOURSELVES TO THE KIDS.
I'M DAVID MOMOI. I'M A KITSUNE.
SWEET
I'M HEMINA PATEL. I'M A RAKSHASI.
I'M MADANI ABDULLAH. I'M A WERE-JACKAL.

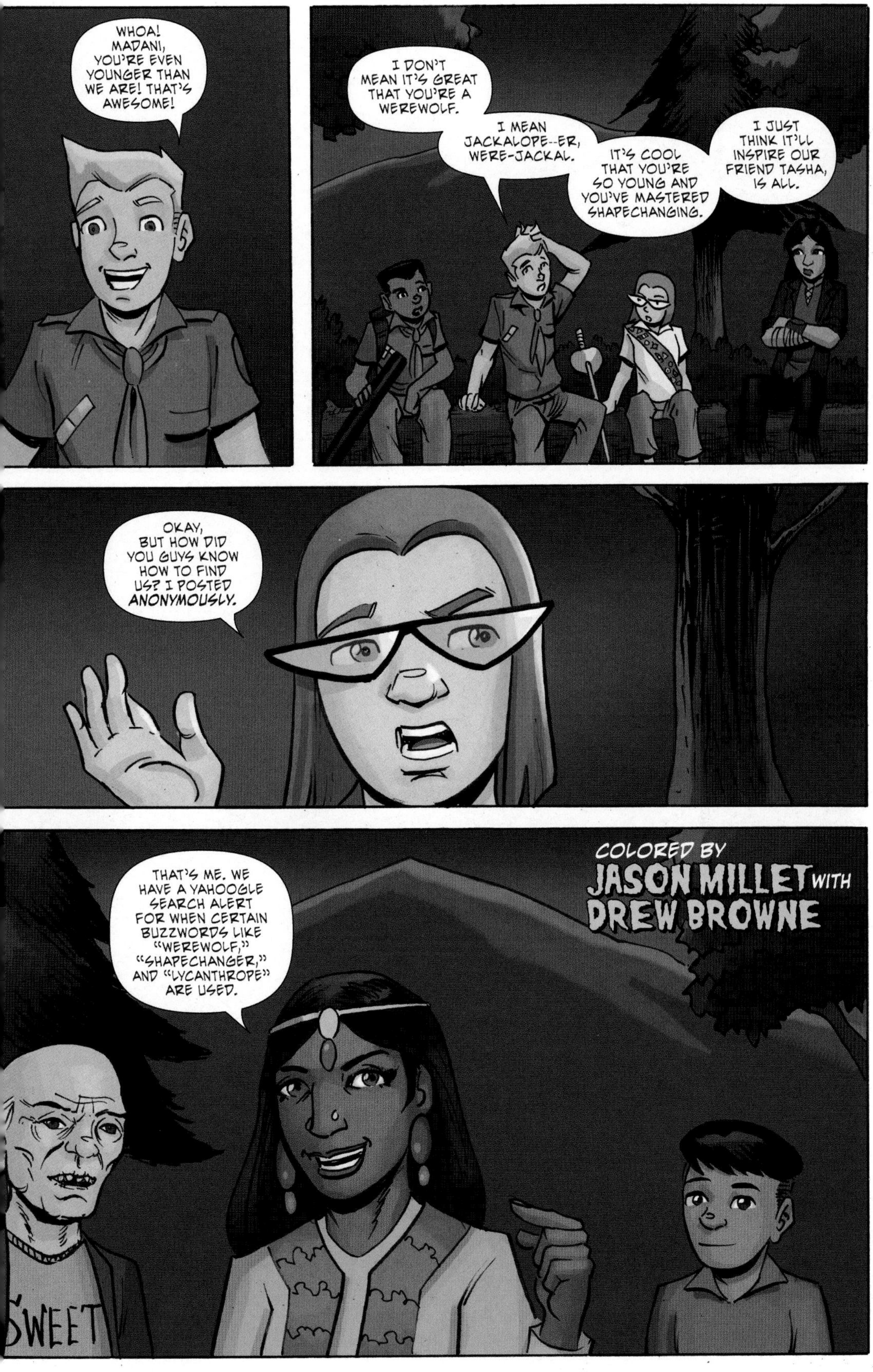
WHOA! MADANI, YOU'RE EVEN YOUNGER THAN WE ARE! THAT'S AWESOME!
I DON'T MEAN IT'S GREAT THAT YOU'RE A WEREWOLF.
I MEAN JACKALOPE--ER, WERE-JACKAL.
IT'S COOL THAT YOU'RE SO YOUNG AND YOU'VE MASTERED SHAPECHANGING.
I JUST THINK IT'LL INSPIRE OUR FRIEND TASHA, IS ALL.
OKAY, BUT HOW DID YOU GUYS KNOW HOW TO FIND US? I POSTED ANONYMOUSLY.
THAT'S ME. WE HAVE A YAHOOGLE SEARCH ALERT FOR WHEN CERTAIN BUZZWORDS LIKE "WEREWOLF," "SHAPECHANGER," AND "LYCANTHROPE" ARE USED.
COLORED BY JASON MILLET WITH DREW BROWNE
SWEET

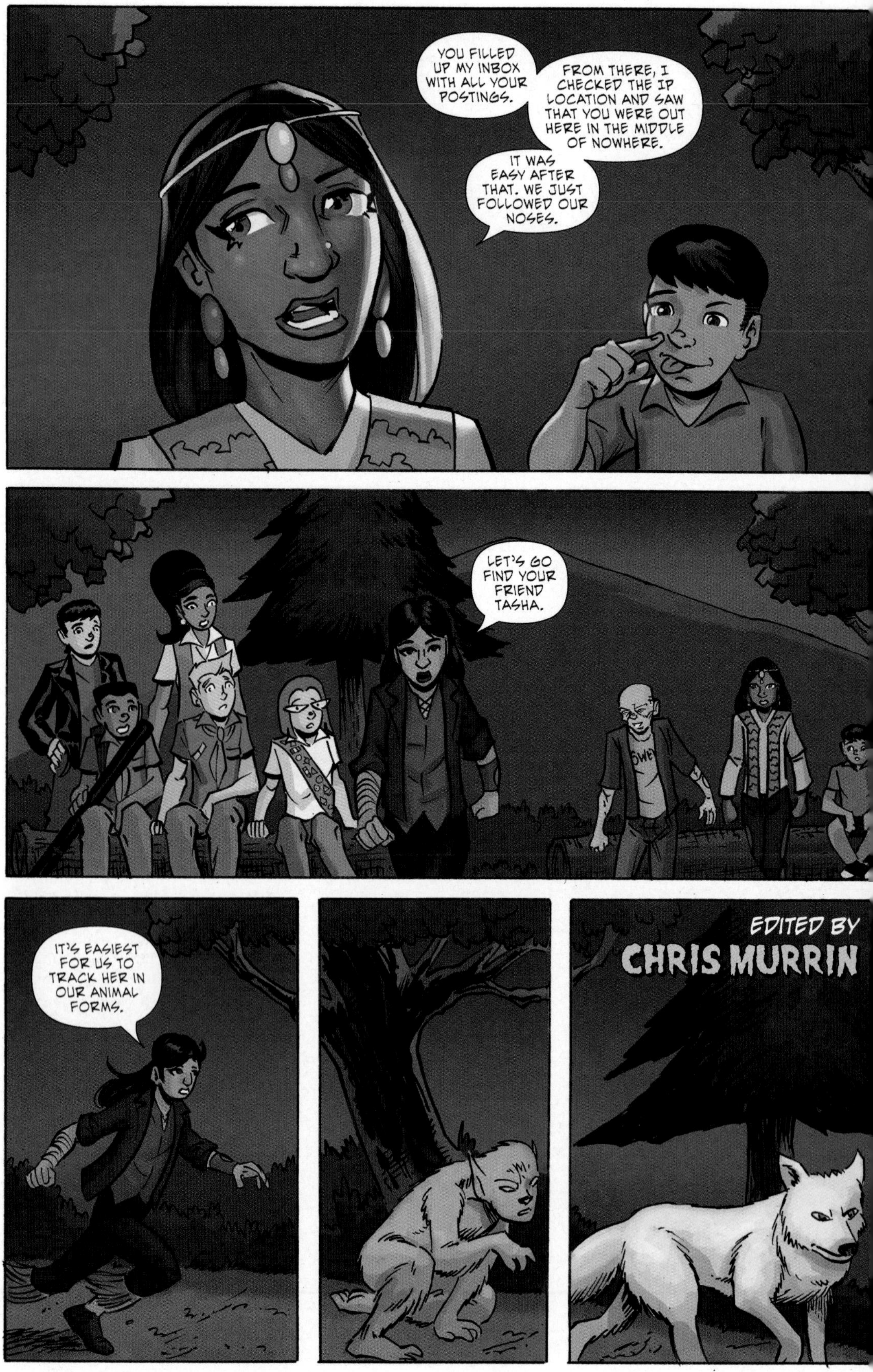
YOU FILLED UP MY INBOX WITH ALL YOUR POSTINGS.
FROM THERE, I CHECKED THE IP LOCATION AND SAW THAT YOU WERE OUT HERE IN THE MIDDLE OF NOWHERE.
IT WAS EASY AFTER THAT. WE JUST FOLLOWED OUR NOSES.
LET'S GO FIND YOUR FRIEND TASHA.
IT'S EASIEST FOR US TO TRACK HER IN OUR ANIMAL FORMS.
EDITED BY
CHRIS MURRIN

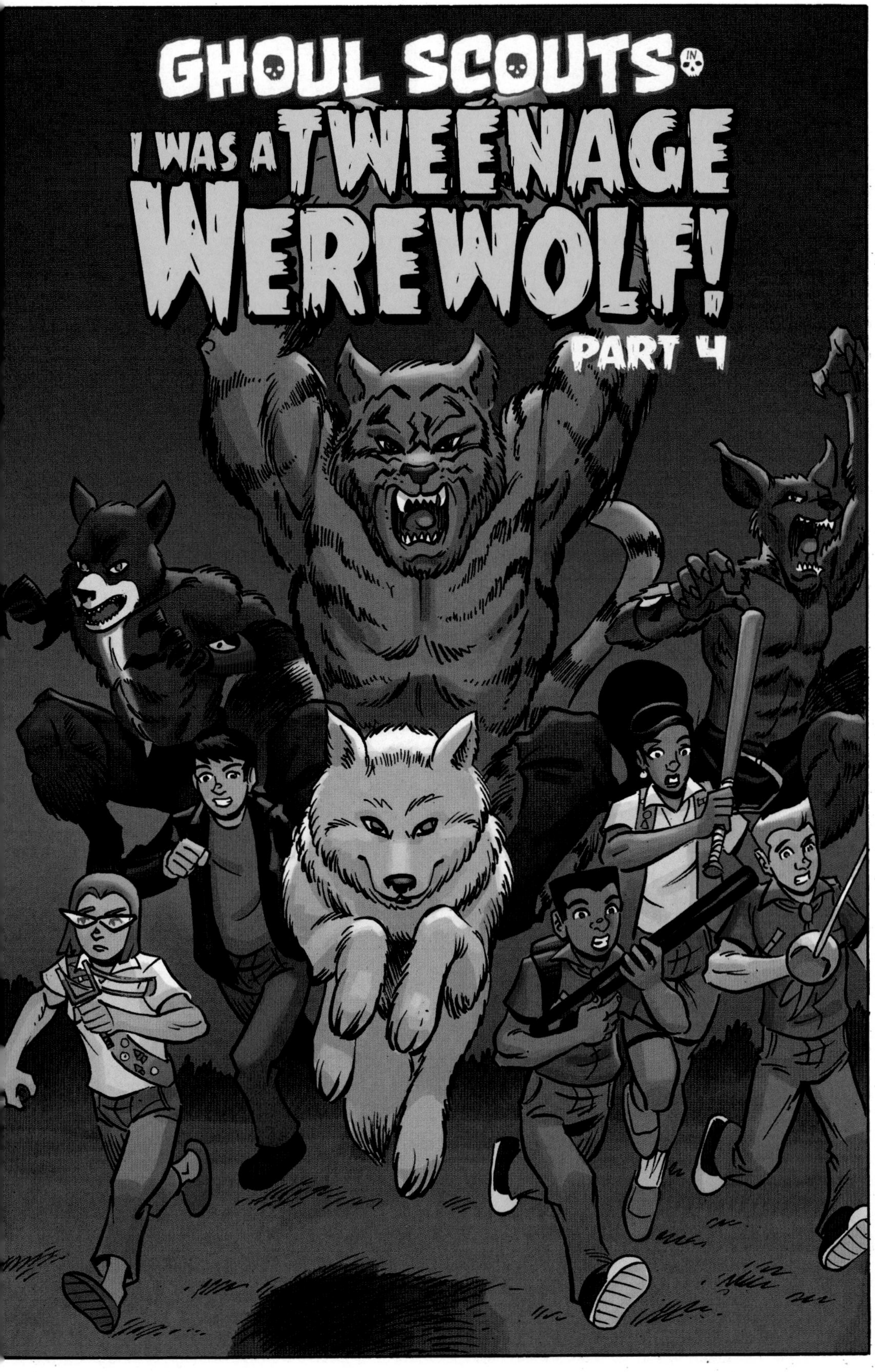
GHOUL SCOUTS
IN
I WAS A TWEENAGE WEREWOLF!
PART 4

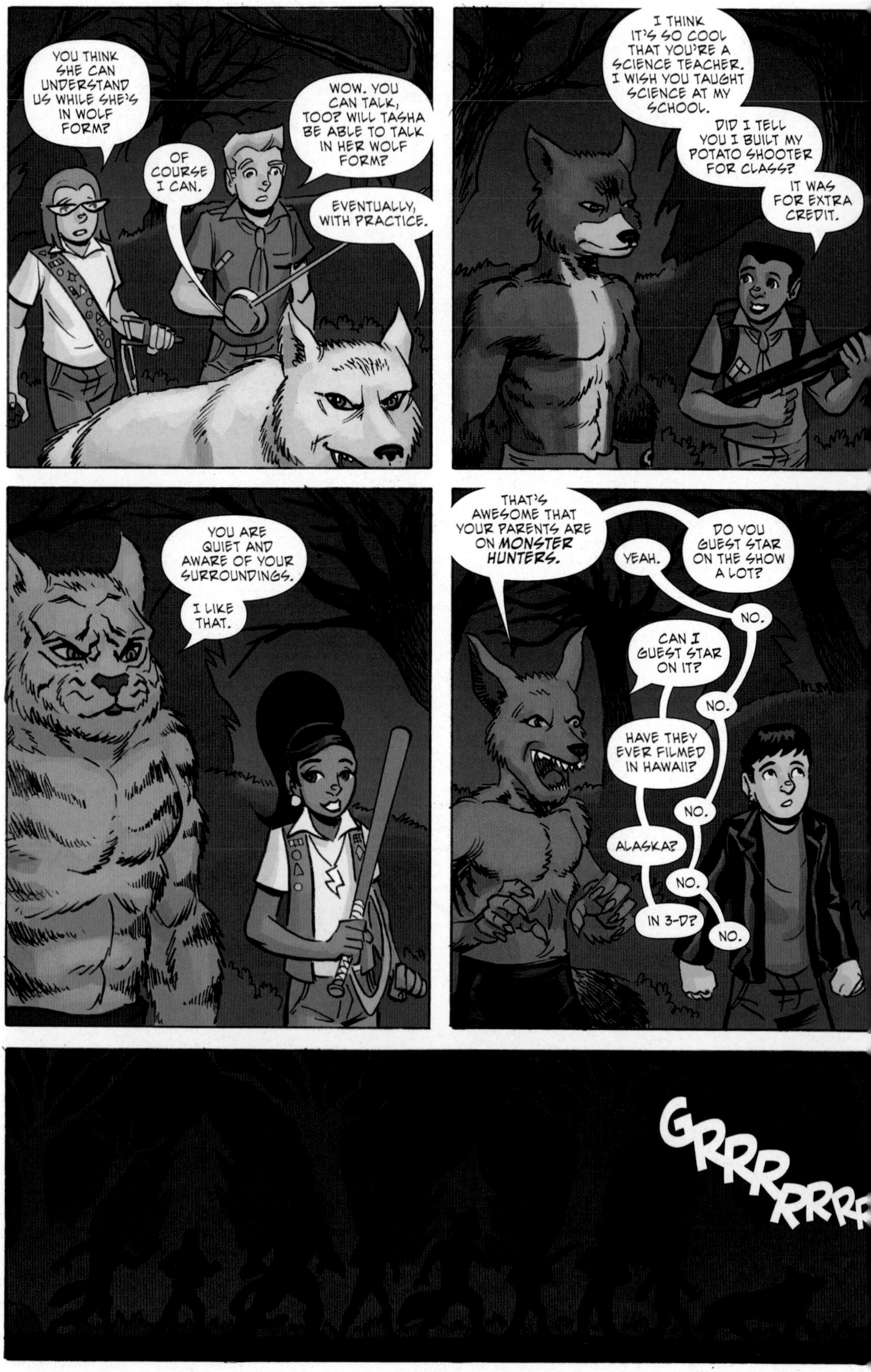
YOU THINK SHE CAN UNDERSTAND US WHILE SHE'S IN WOLF FORM?
OF COURSE I CAN.
WOW. YOU CAN TALK, TOO? WILL TASHA BE ABLE TO TALK IN HER WOLF FORM?
EVENTUALLY, WITH PRACTICE.
I THINK IT'S SO COOL THAT YOU'RE A SCIENCE TEACHER. I WISH YOU TAUGHT SCIENCE AT MY SCHOOL.
DID I TELL YOU I BUILT MY POTATO SHOOTER FOR CLASS?
IT WAS FOR EXTRA CREDIT.
YOU ARE QUIET AND AWARE OF YOUR SURROUNDINGS.
I LIKE THAT.
THAT'S AWESOME THAT YOUR PARENTS ARE ON MONSTER HUNTERS.
YEAH.
DO YOU GUEST STAR ON THE SHOW A LOT?
NO.
CAN I GUEST STAR ON IT?
NO.
HAVE THEY EVER FILMED IN HAWAII?
NO.
ALASKA?
NO.
IN 3-D?
NO.
GRRRRRR

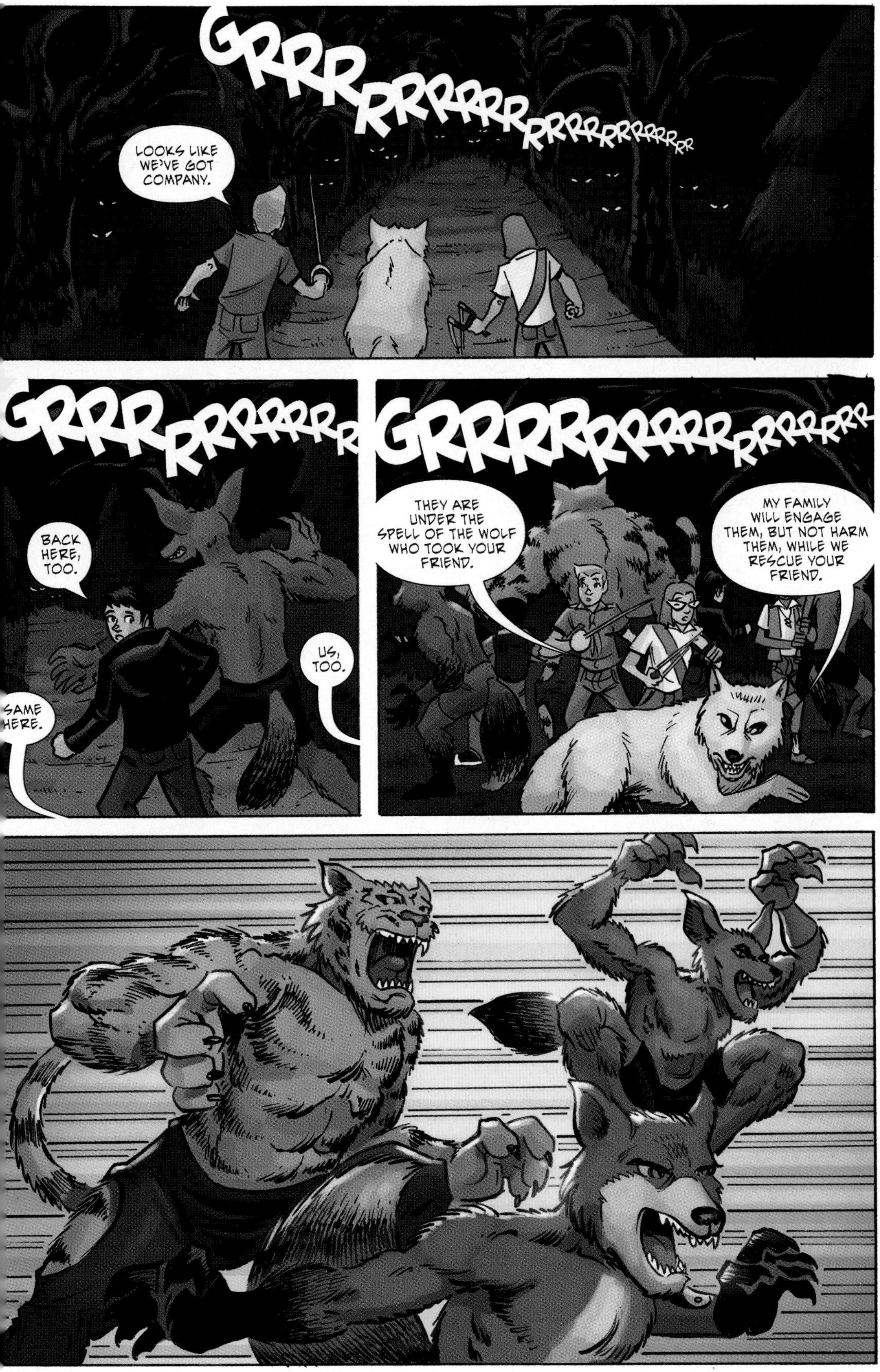
GRRRRRRRRRRRRRRRRRRRRR
LOOKS LIKE WE'VE GOT COMPANY.
GRRRRRRRRRR
BACK HERE, TOO.
US, TOO.
SAME HERE.
GRRRRRRRRRRRRRRRRR
THEY ARE UNDER THE SPELL OF THE WOLF WHO TOOK YOUR FRIEND.
MY FAMILY WILL ENGAGE THEM, BUT NOT HARM THEM, WHILE WE RESCUE YOUR FRIEND.

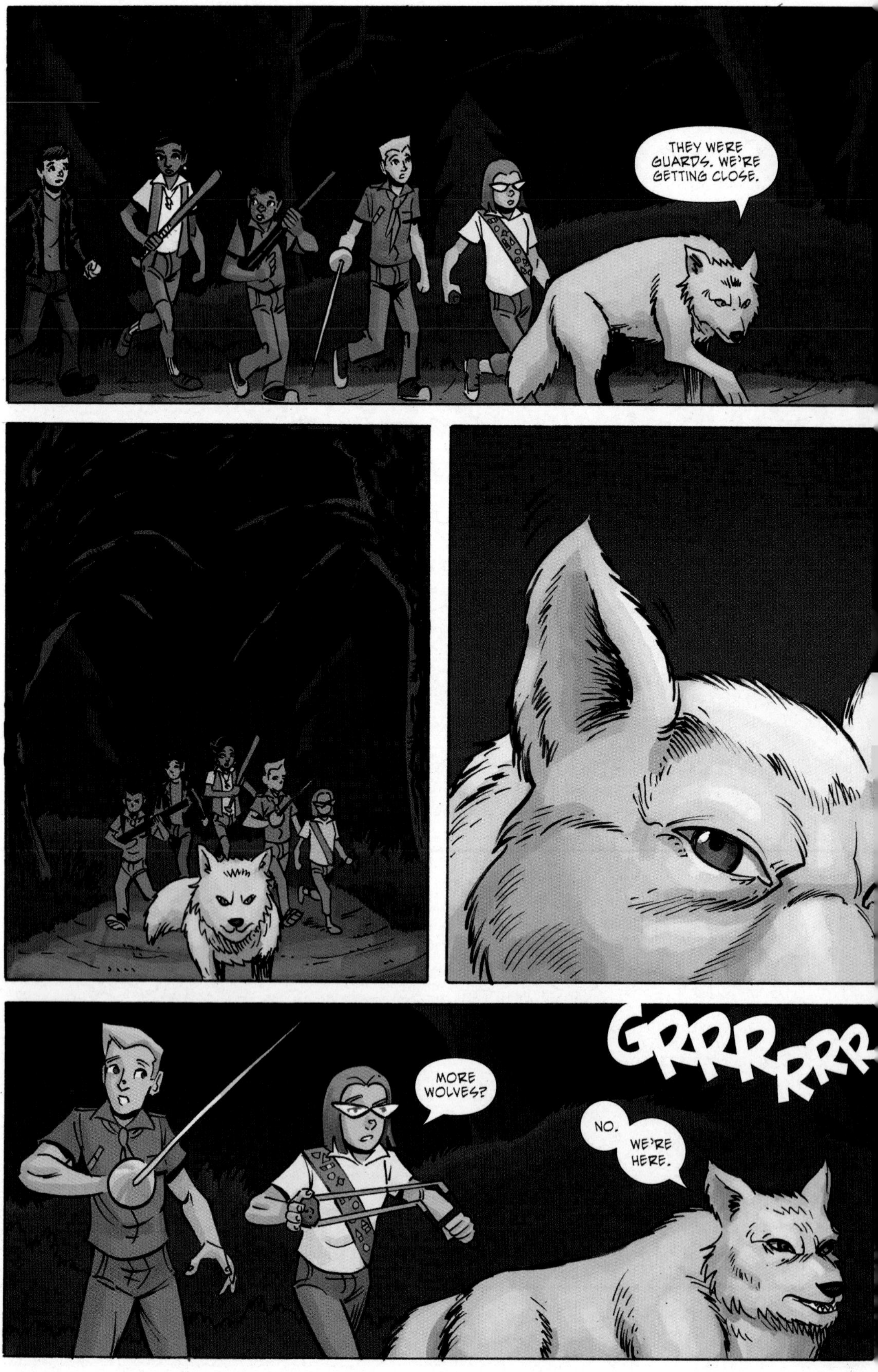
THEY WERE GUARDS. WE'RE GETTING CLOSE.
GRRRRRR
MORE WOLVES?
NO.
WE'RE HERE.

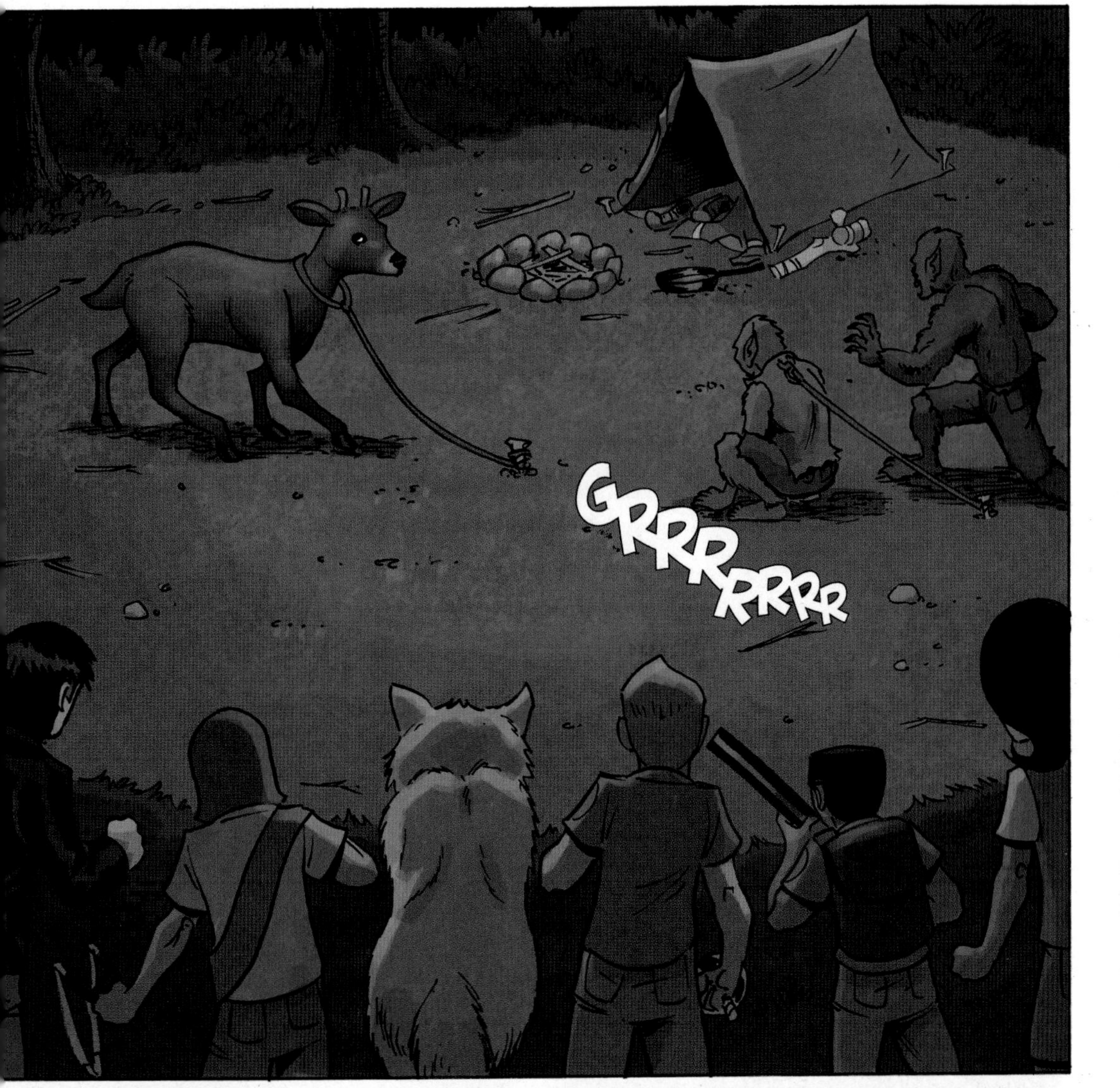
GRRRRRRR

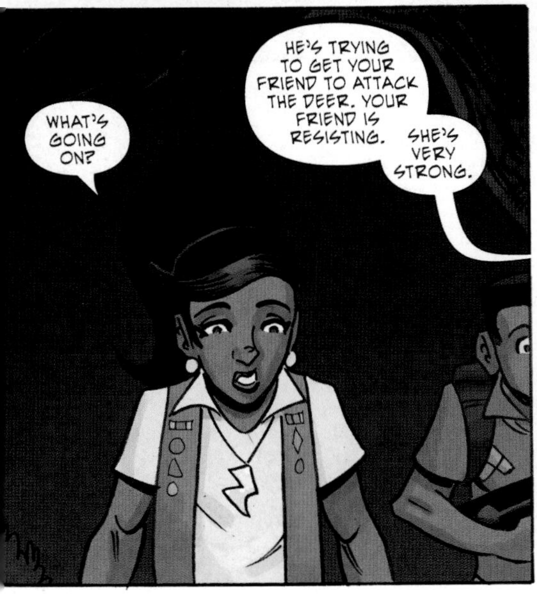
WHAT'S GOING ON?
HE'S TRYING TO GET YOUR FRIEND TO ATTACK THE DEER. YOUR FRIEND IS RESISTING.
SHE'S VERY STRONG.

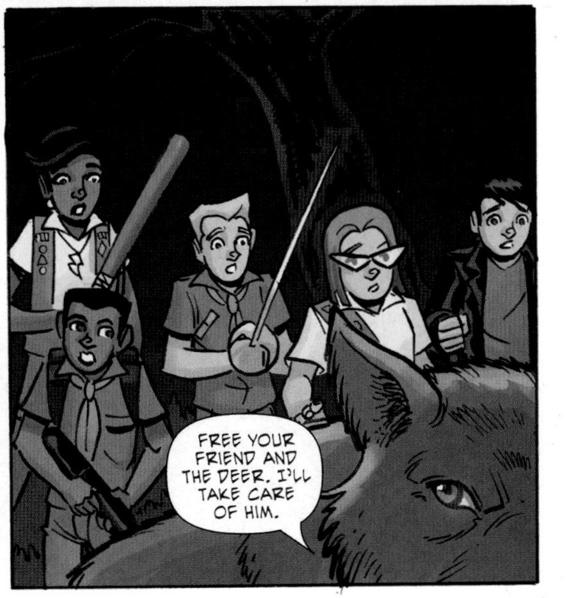
FREE YOUR FRIEND AND THE DEER. I'LL TAKE CARE OF HIM.

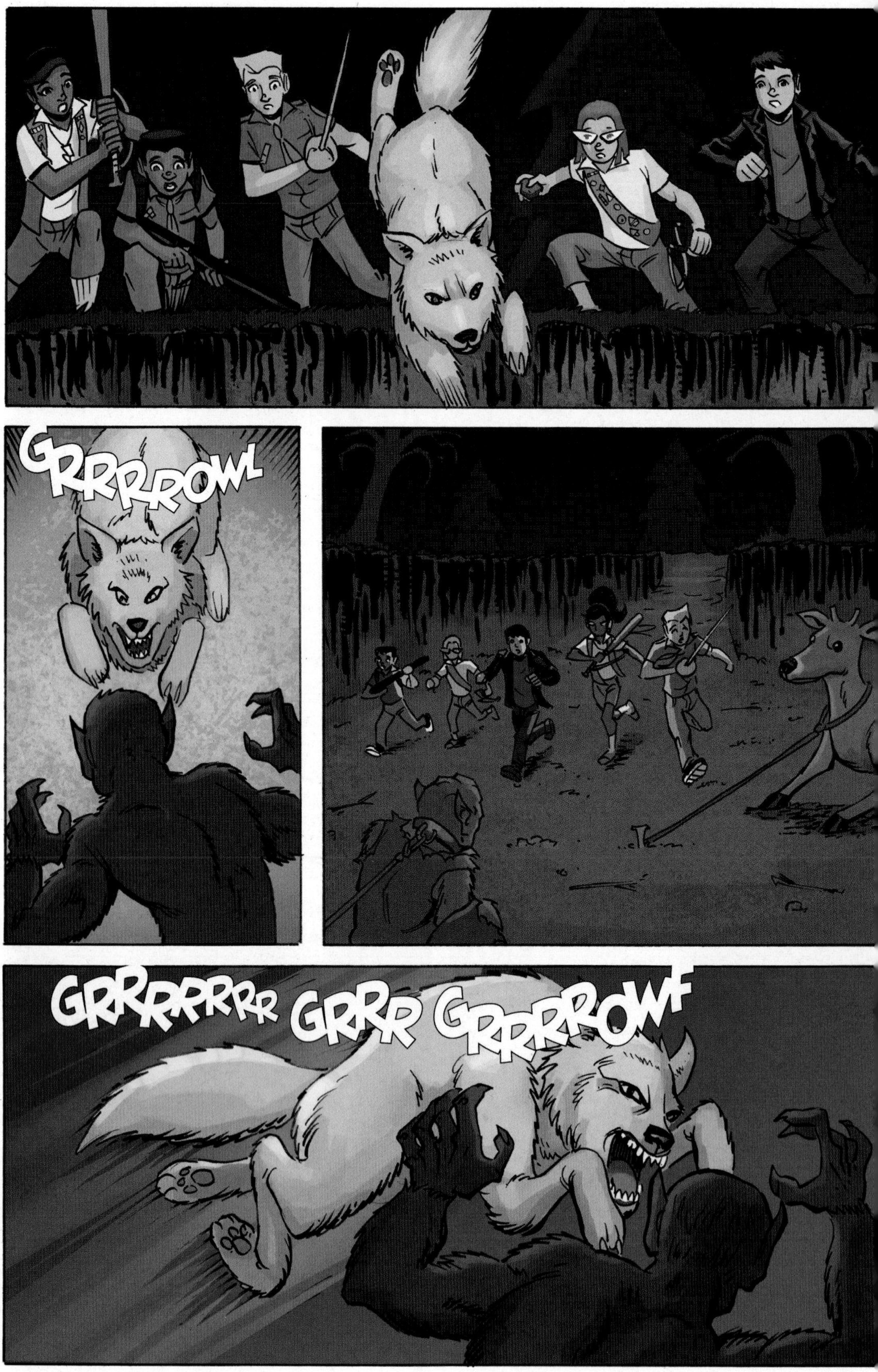
GRRRROWL
GRRRRRRR GRRR GRRRROWF

GEEZ, WAS THIS GUY A SAILOR OR SOMETHING? THIS IS A TOUGH KNOT!
GRRR GRRRRROWURK
PEYTON, YOU IDIOT! SHE'LL BITE YOU!
NO, WE'RE COOL.
JUST HOLD HER ATTENTION...

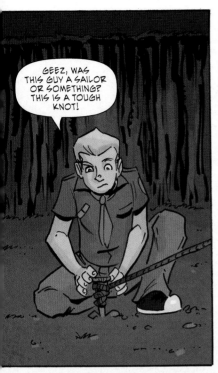

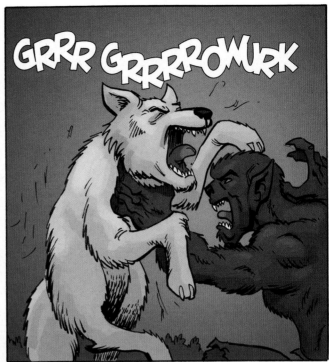

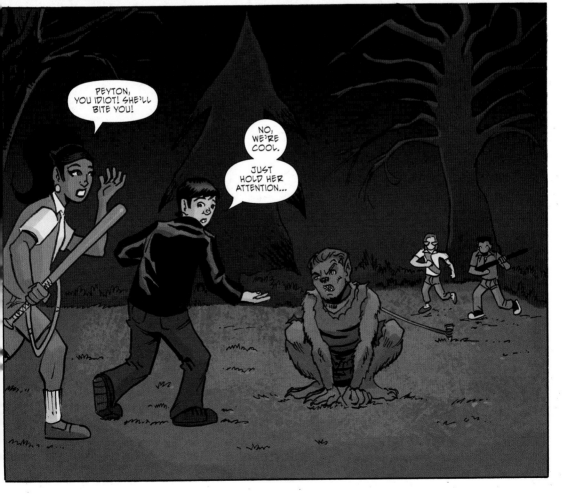

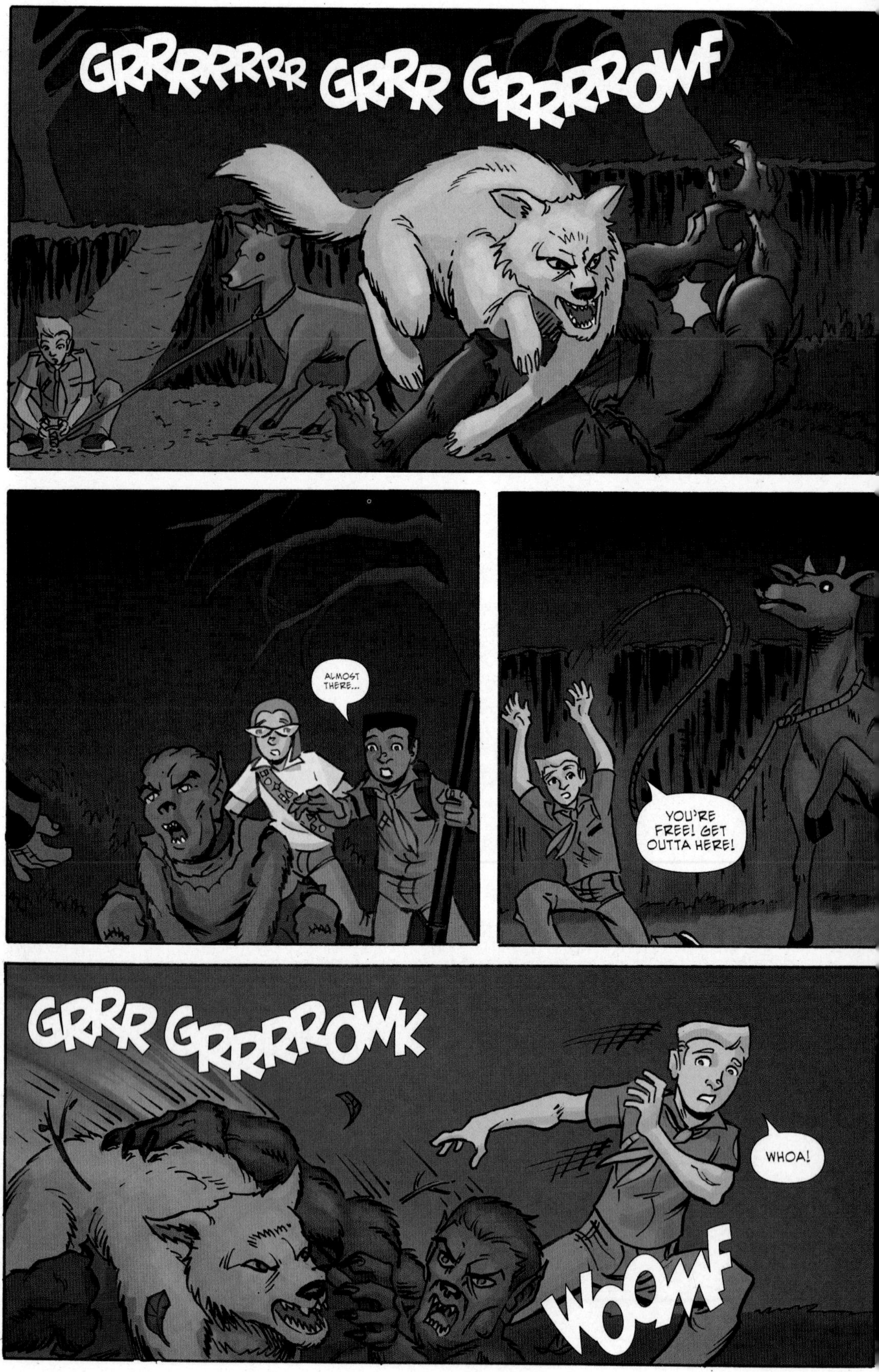
GRRRRRRR GRRR GRRRROWF
ALMOST THERE...
YOU'RE FREE! GET OUTTA HERE!
GRRR GRRRROWK
WHOA!
WOOMF

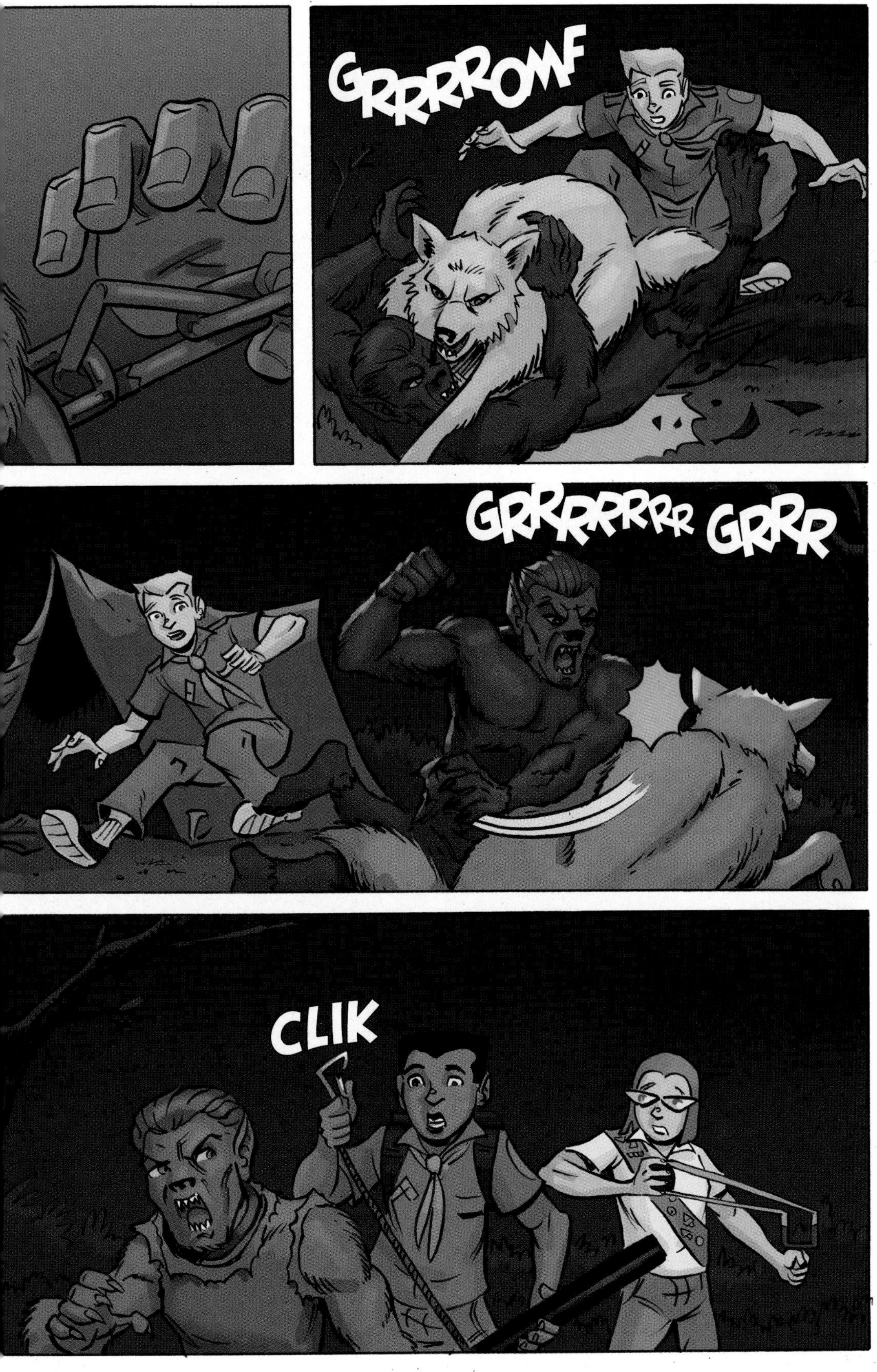
GRRRROMF
GRRRRRR GRRR
CLIK

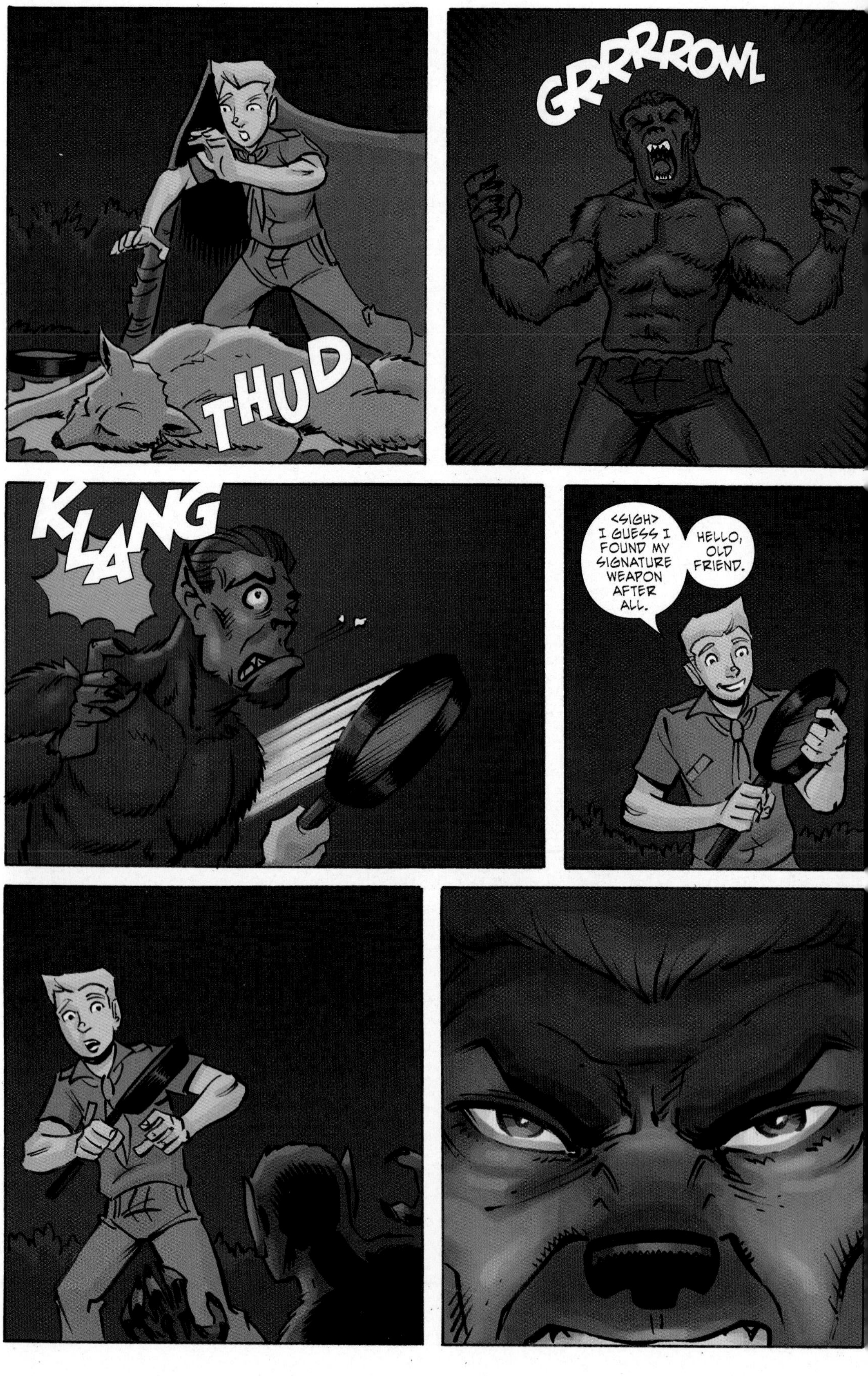
THUD
GRRRROWL
KLANG
<SIGH> I GUESS I FOUND MY SIGNATURE WEAPON AFTER ALL.
HELLO, OLD FRIEND.

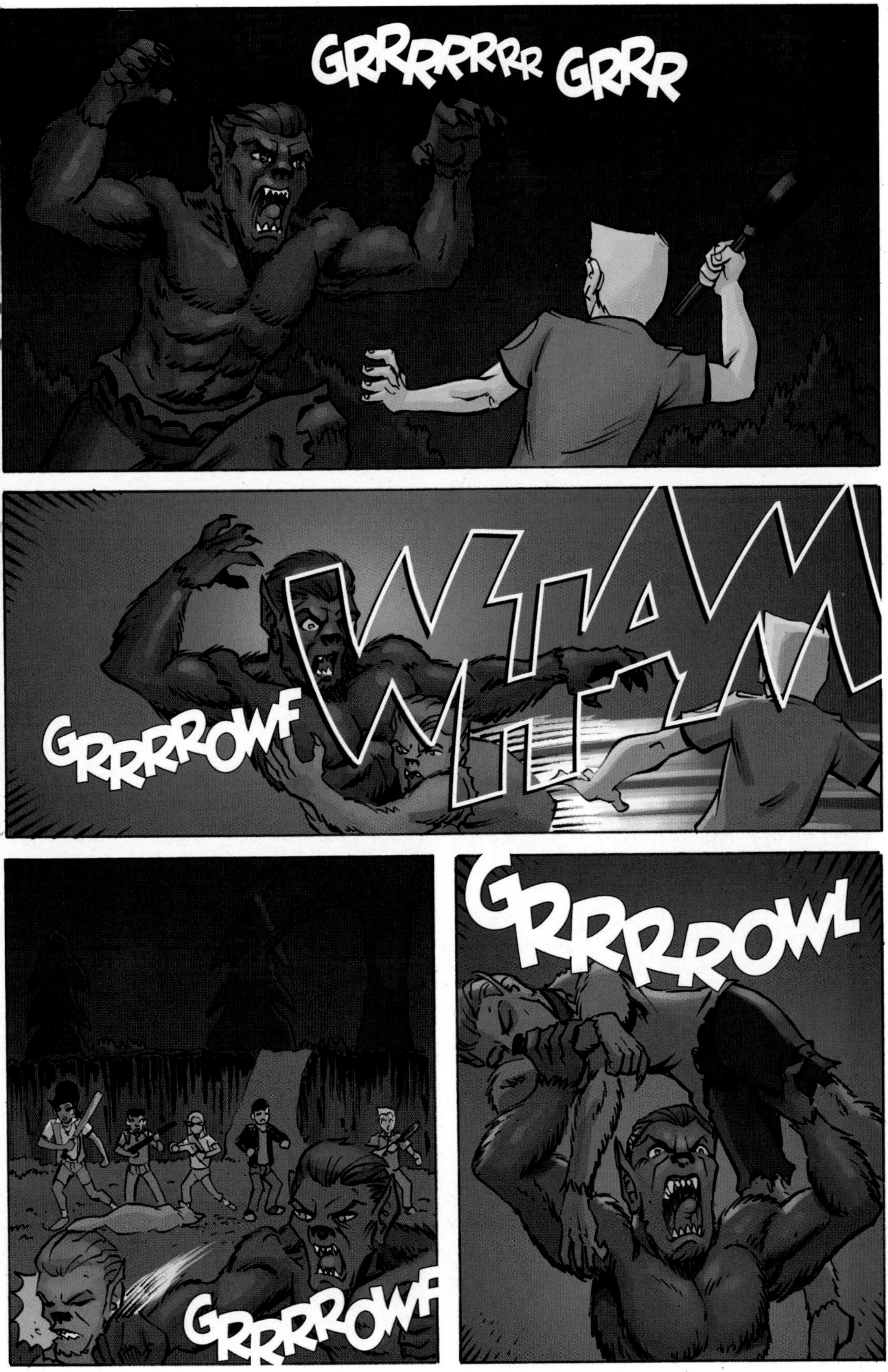
GRRRRRRR GRRR
GRRRROWF
WHAM
GRRRROWF
GRRRROWL

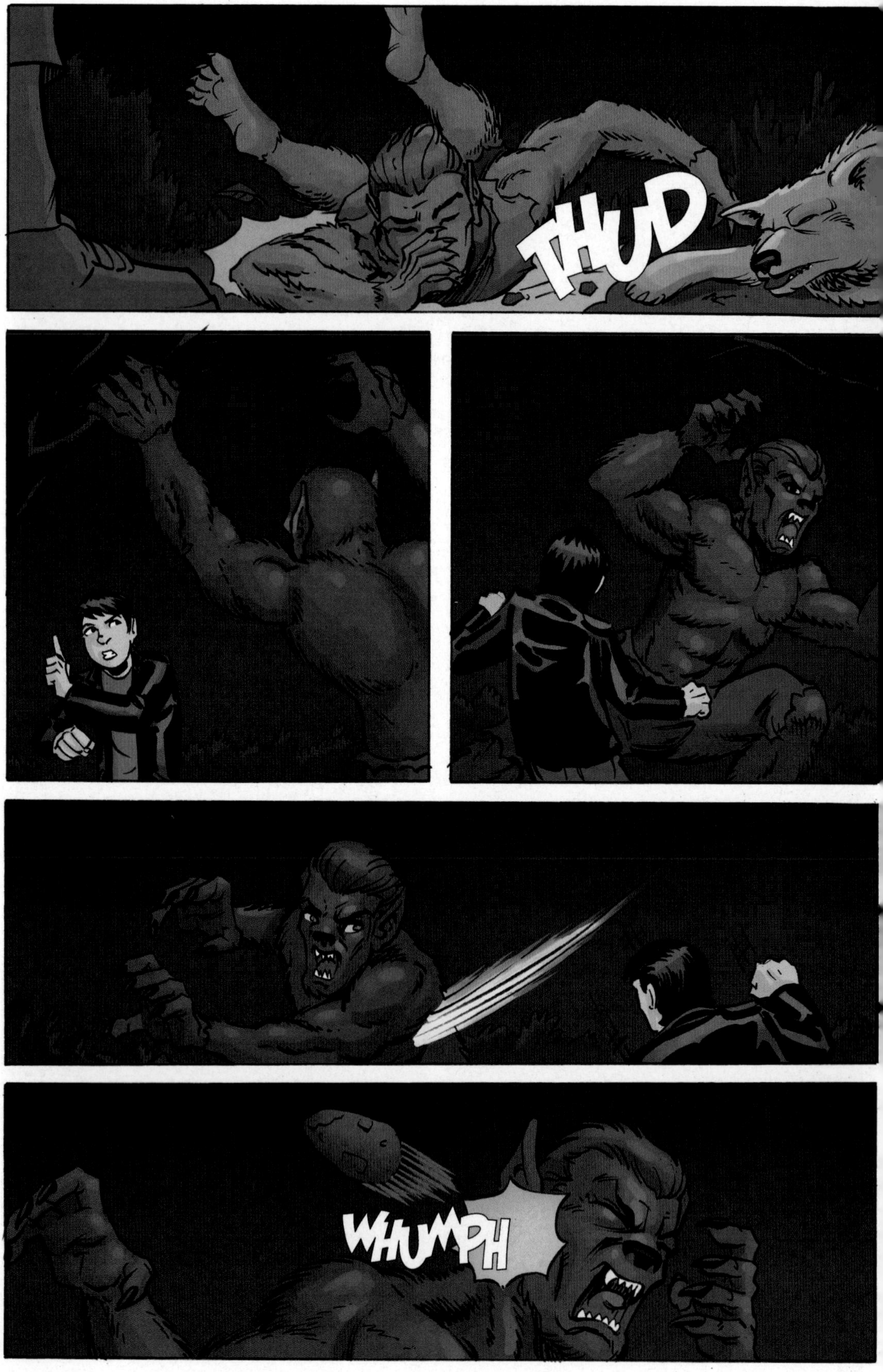
THUD
WHUMPH

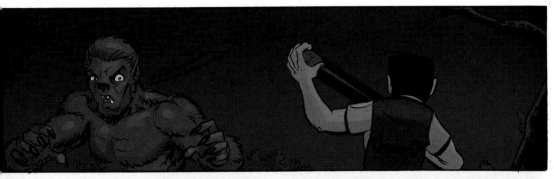

GRRRRRRr

KER-KRRRAK

POK

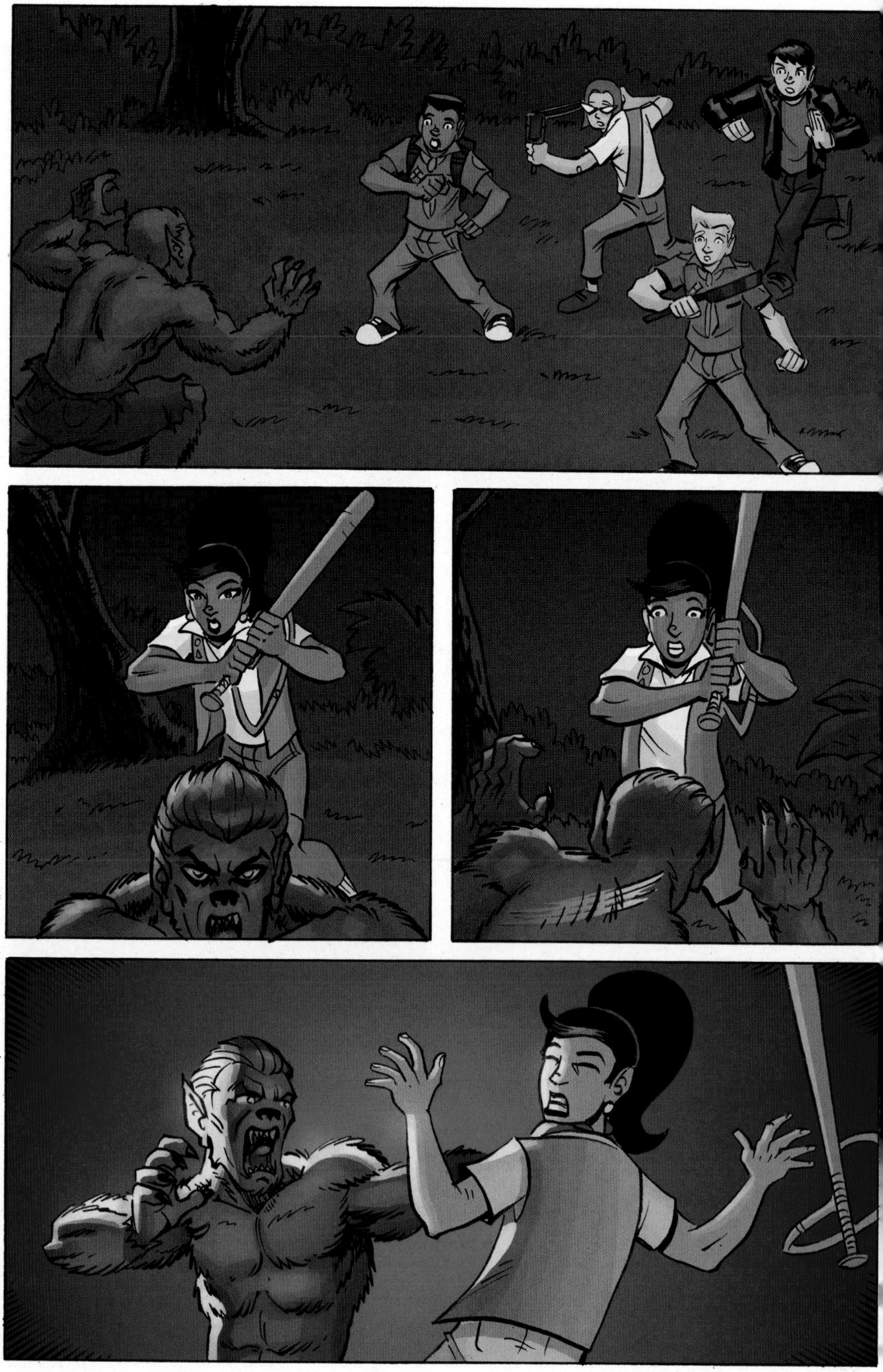

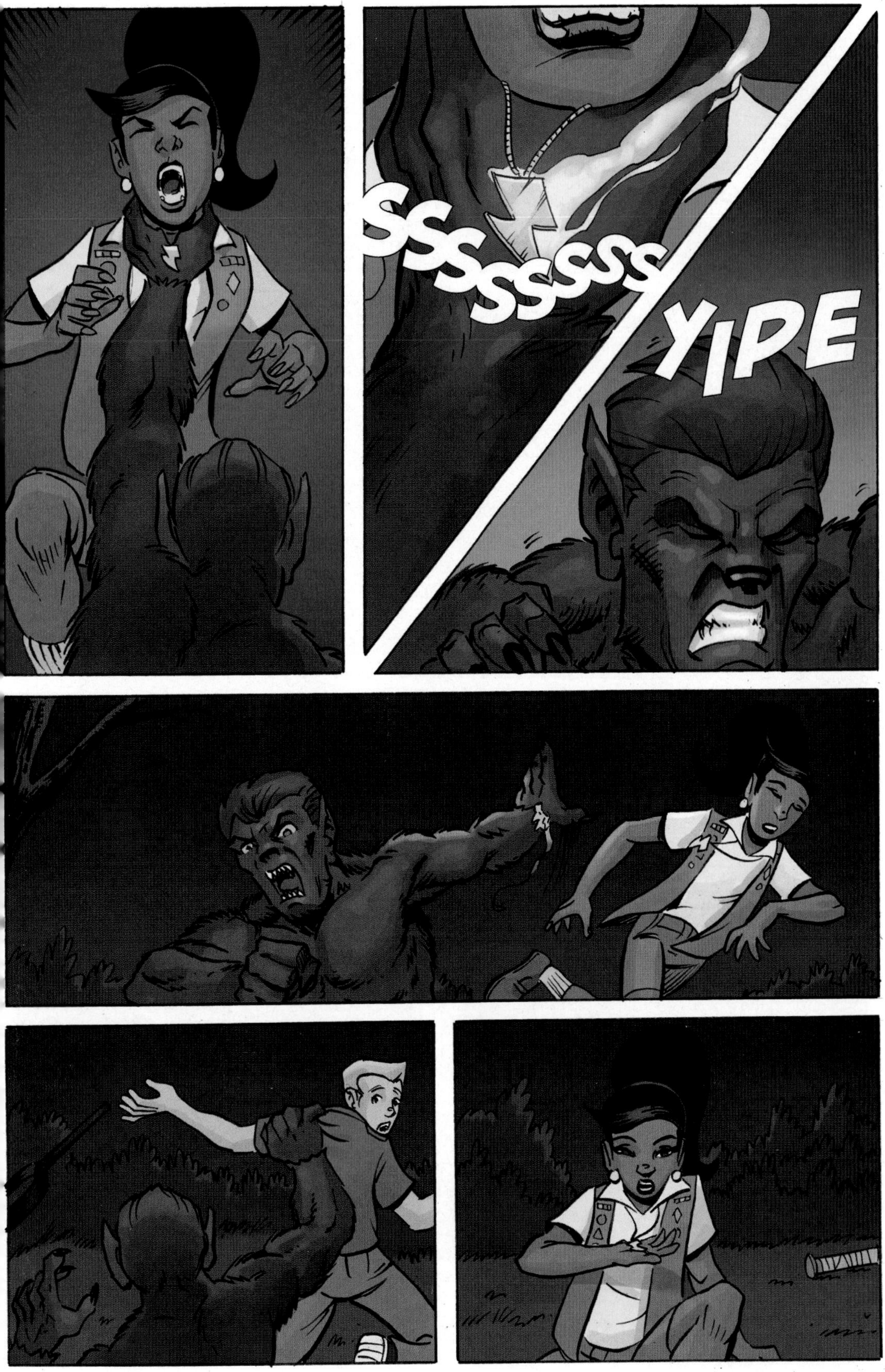
SSSSSSSSS
YIPE

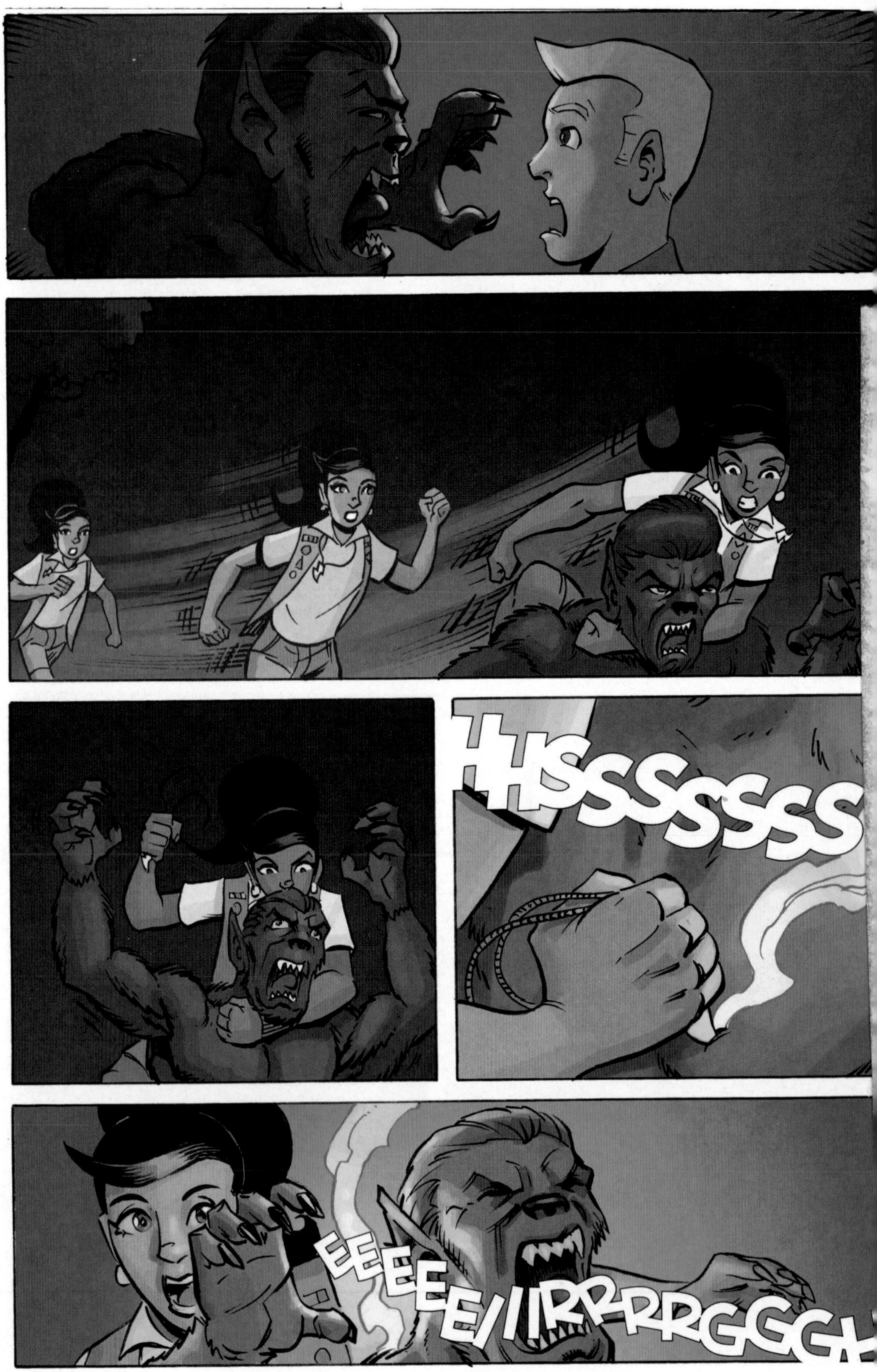
HHSSSSSSS
EEEEE!!RRRRGGGH

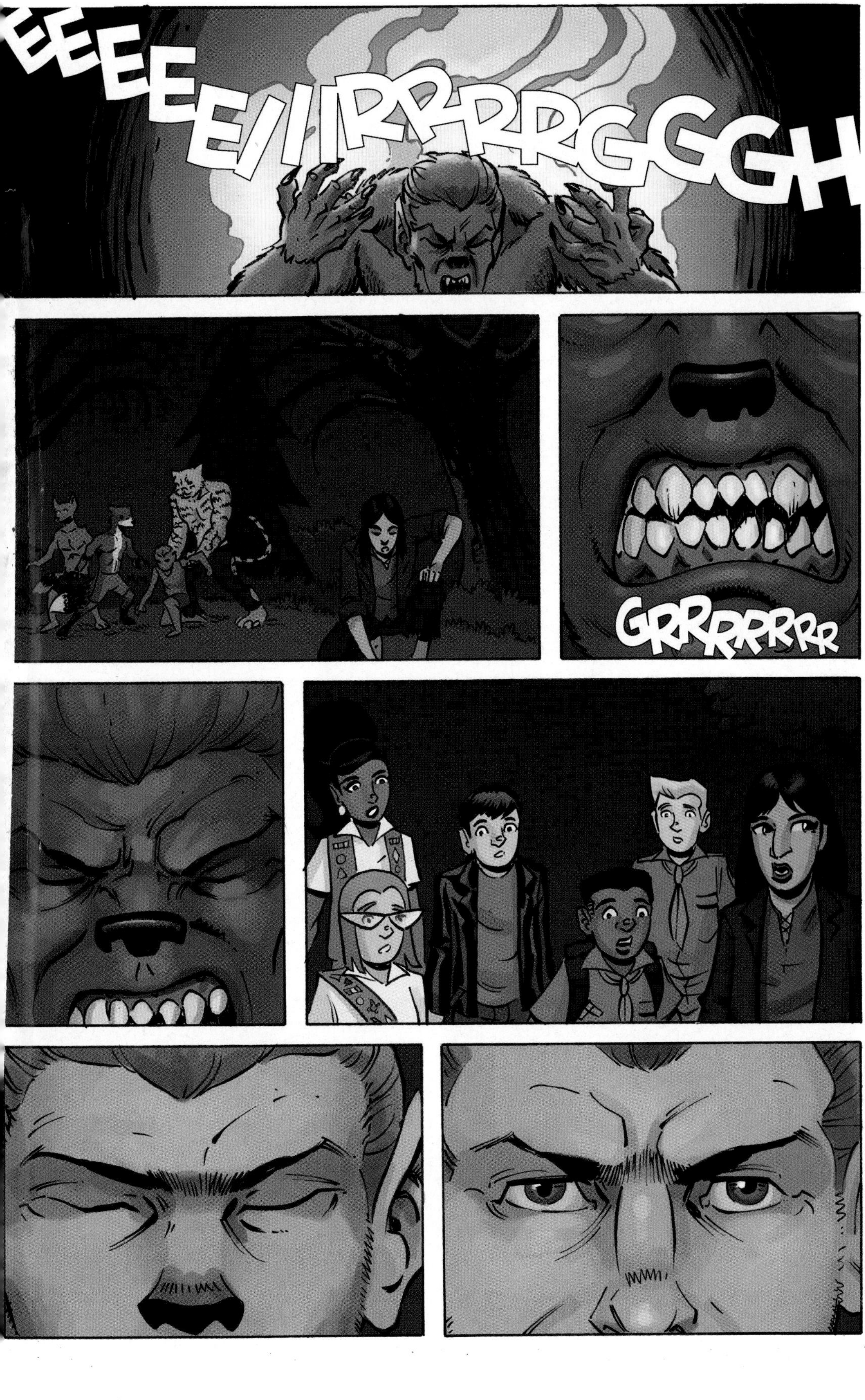
EEEEE//IRRRRGGGH
GRRRRRRR

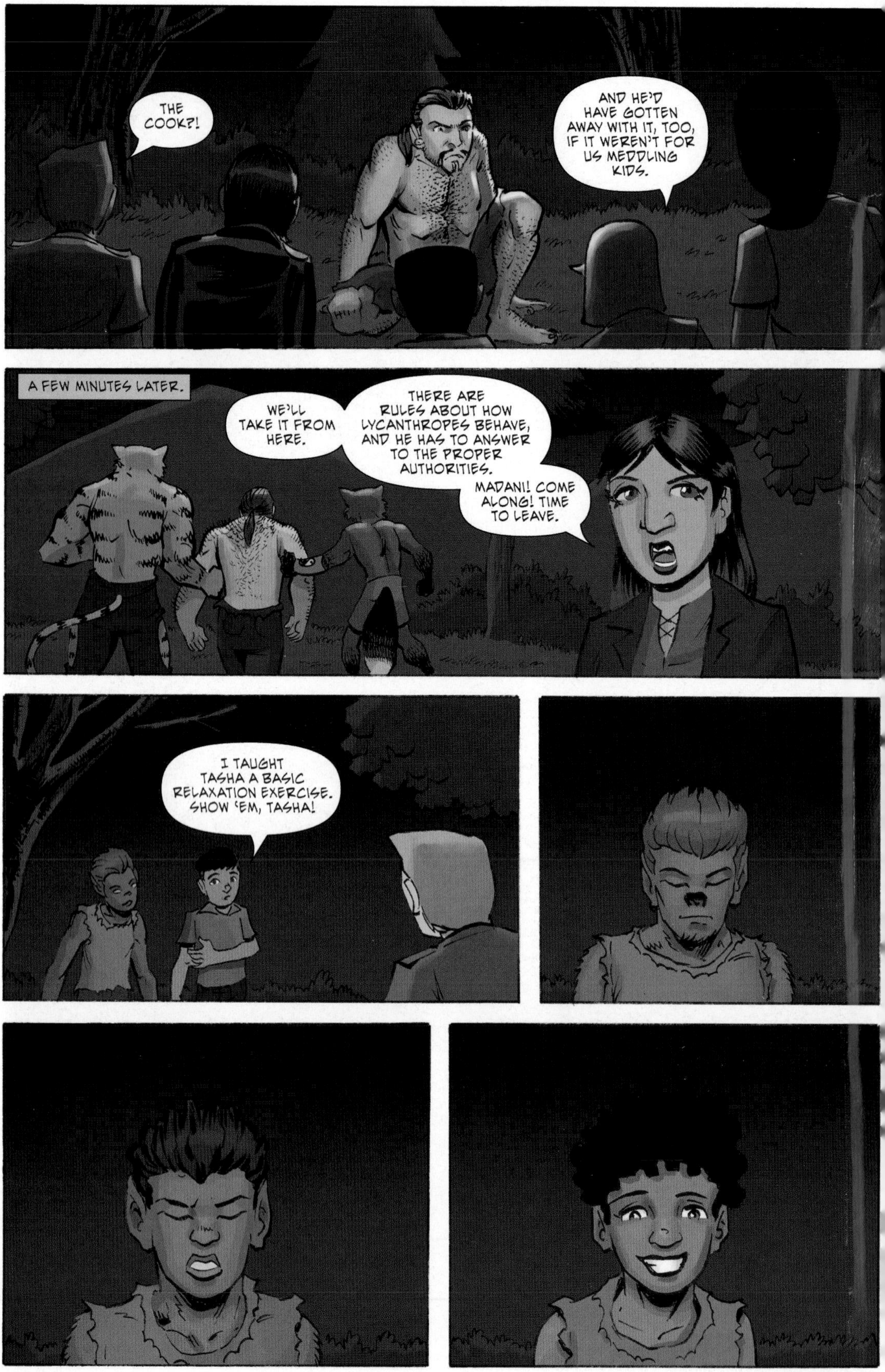

THE COOK?!
AND HE'D HAVE GOTTEN AWAY WITH IT, TOO, IF IT WEREN'T FOR US MEDDLING KIDS.
A FEW MINUTES LATER.
WE'LL TAKE IT FROM HERE.
THERE ARE RULES ABOUT HOW LYCANTHROPES BEHAVE, AND HE HAS TO ANSWER TO THE PROPER AUTHORITIES.
MADANI! COME ALONG! TIME TO LEAVE.
I TAUGHT TASHA A BASIC RELAXATION EXERCISE. SHOW 'EM, TASHA!

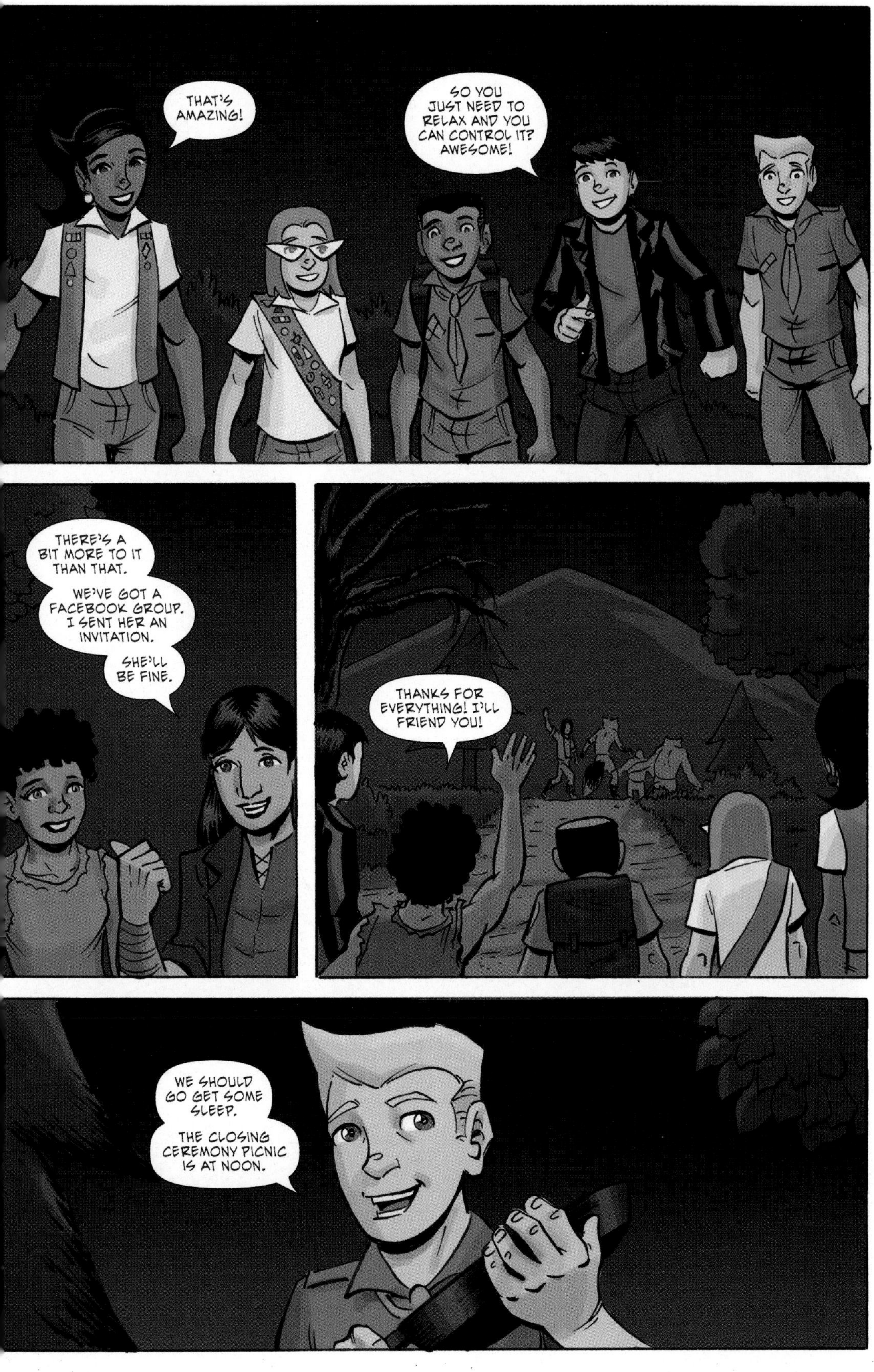
THAT'S AMAZING!
SO YOU JUST NEED TO RELAX AND YOU CAN CONTROL IT? AWESOME!
THERE'S A BIT MORE TO IT THAN THAT.
WE'VE GOT A FACEBOOK GROUP. I SENT HER AN INVITATION.
SHE'LL BE FINE.
THANKS FOR EVERYTHING! I'LL FRIEND YOU!
WE SHOULD GO GET SOME SLEEP.
THE CLOSING CEREMONY PICNIC IS AT NOON.

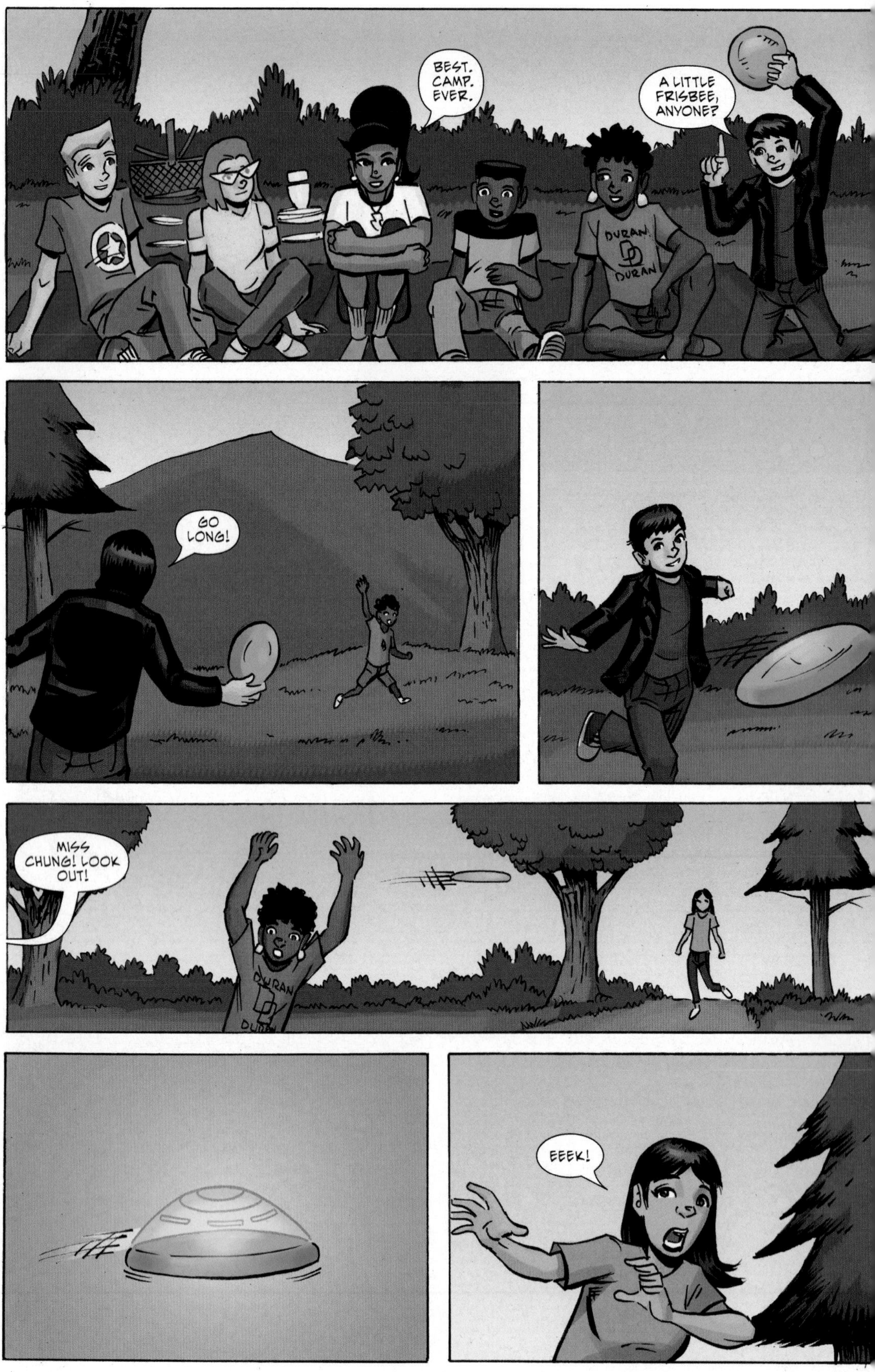
BEST. CAMP. EVER.
A LITTLE FRISBEE, ANYONE?
GO LONG!
MISS CHUNG! LOOK OUT!
EEEK!

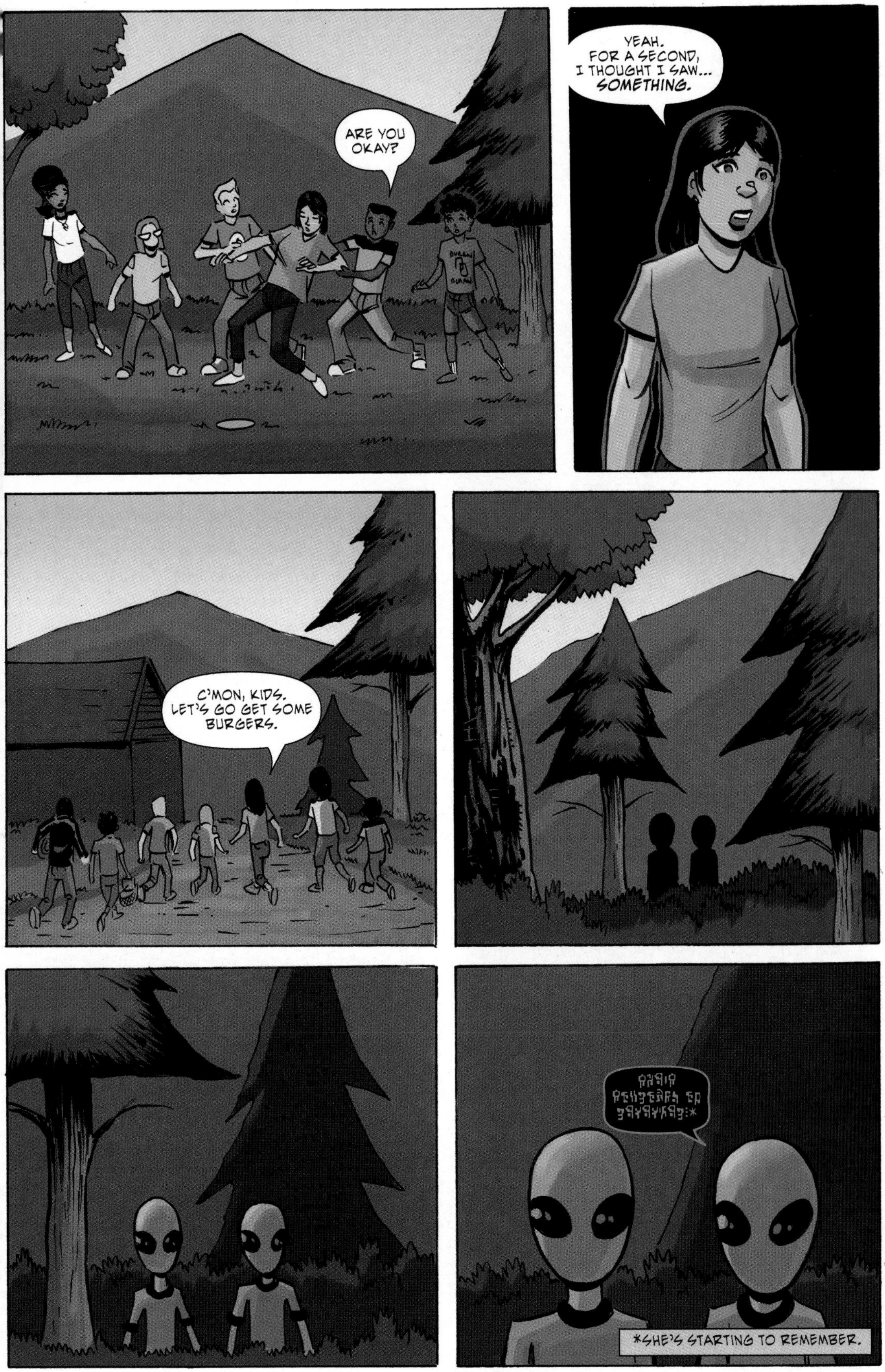
ARE YOU OKAY?
YEAH. FOR A SECOND, I THOUGHT I SAW... SOMETHING.
C'MON, KIDS. LET'S GO GET SOME BURGERS.
*SHE'S STARTING TO REMEMBER.

GHOUL SCOUTS BONUS FEATURE

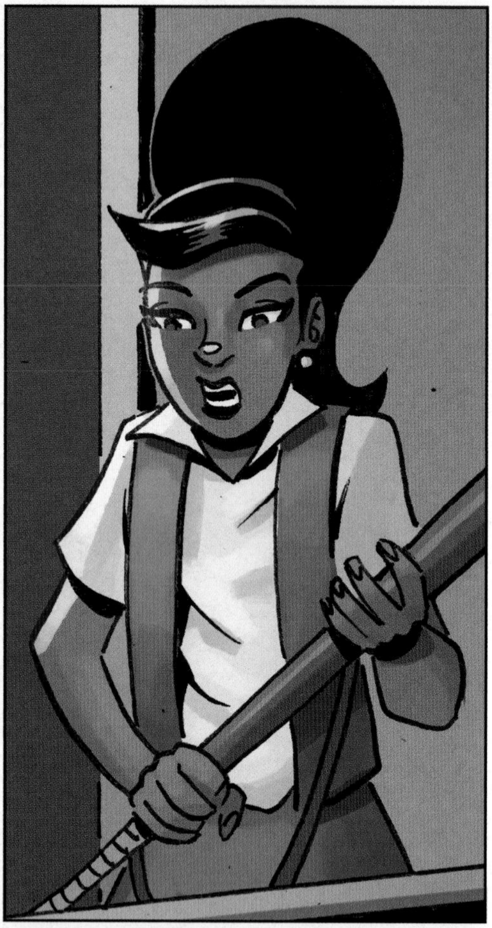

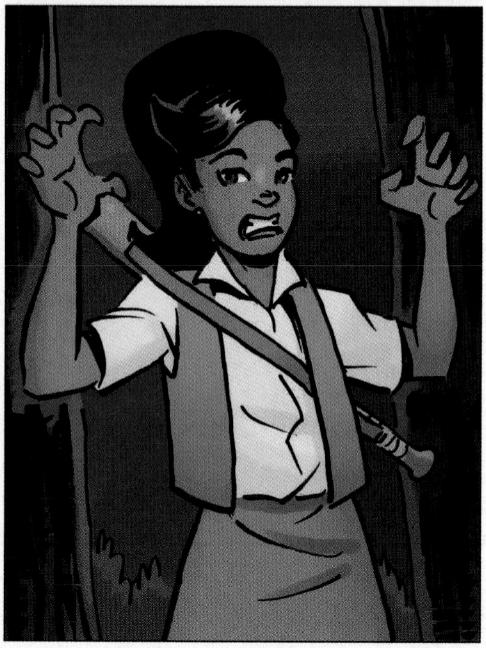

CLAUDIA

Full Name: Claudia Adriana Rivera

Age: 13

Height: 5' 11 ¾"

Weight: 118 lb.

Hair: Black

Eyes: Brown

Grade: Eight

Favorite Subject: Social Studies, I guess.

Jam: *reputation* by Taylor Swift

Throws: Right

Bats: Both

Badges Earned: 5

Claudia was born in Castle Hills, Texas, but her family moved to Full Moon Hollow ten years ago, so the Hollow is really the only home she remembers. Her father, Axel, manages a grocery store, and her mother, Laura, works part time at a department store so she can be home when Claudia and her two younger brothers, Marcus and Peter, get out of school.

A natural athlete, Claudia excels at many sports, but she WILL NOT play basketball. In the fall she prefers to play indoor volleyball, but in the spring Claudia gets to play her favorite sport, softball. Claudia hits for both power and average, and her defensive skills at first base have made her a two-time all-star in her age group.

When she's not at school, on the softball diamond, or exploring the forest with the Gaia Scouts, Claudia volunteers at the Full Moon Hollow Library. There, she shelves returned books, helps borrowers find materials, and reads all she can about world history. She loves having so much clearly organized information at her fingertips without having to wade through a million inaccurate internet search results!

Someday she hopes to be an historian, museum curator, archivist, or maybe a librarian like her mentor, Ms. Chung.

GHOUL SCOUTS BONUS FEATURE

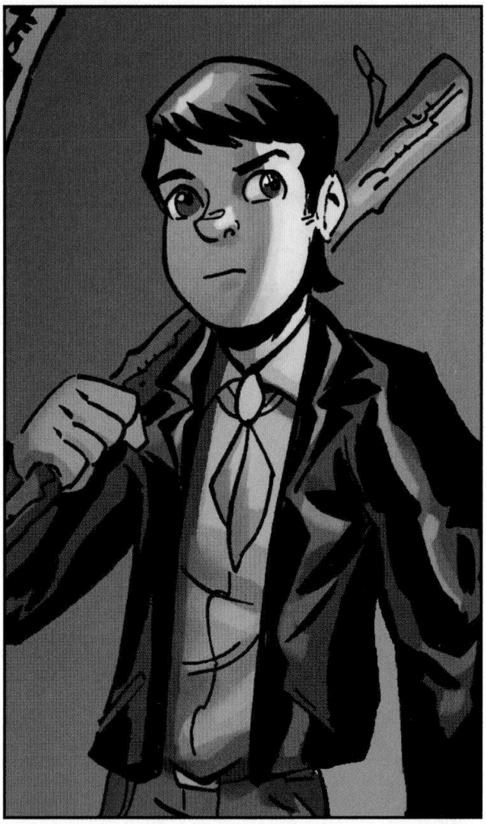

PEYTON

Full Name: Peyton Thomas Forte

Age: 11

Height: 5' 3"

Weight: 104 lb.

Hair: Black

Eyes: Brown

Grade: Six

Favorite Subject: Science

Jam: *Moving Pictures* by Rush

IMDB STARmeter: Up 65 this week

Badges Earned: 3

Though he has always lived in Full Moon Hollow, Peyton used to travel all over the world with his parents as they filmed their long-running hit "reality" TV show "The Monster Chasers." When he was a toddler, Peyton even appeared on the show, playing the ghost of Ottie Cline Powell in an episode on the Appalachian Trail.

Once Peyton reached kindergarten age, though, his parents wanted him to have a stable home and school life, so they asked his grandmother to move in and watch over him whenever they need to travel for the show, which is more often than Peyton would like. Not that he doesn't love his grandma—he absolutely does—he just misses his mom and dad sometimes.

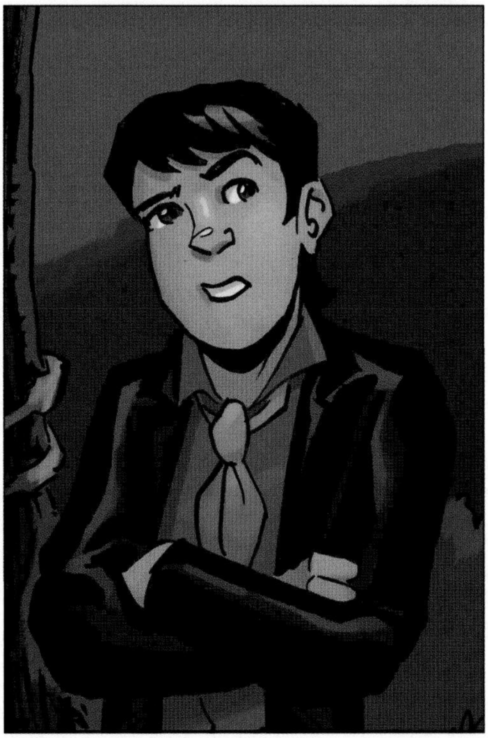

While on the "Monster Chasers" set, the men and women on the crew taught Peyton some of their skills, helping him succeed in the Wilderness Scouts. But that's not all he learned. From his parents' stories and his glimpses behind the scenes of their show, Peyton saw first-hand how special-effects teams can manufacture phony ghosts, ghouls, and other creatures of the night for the cameras. If nothing else, Peyton learned for sure that there are no such things as monsters.

At least that's what he thought...

...Until now!

GHOUL SCOUTS BONUS FEATURE

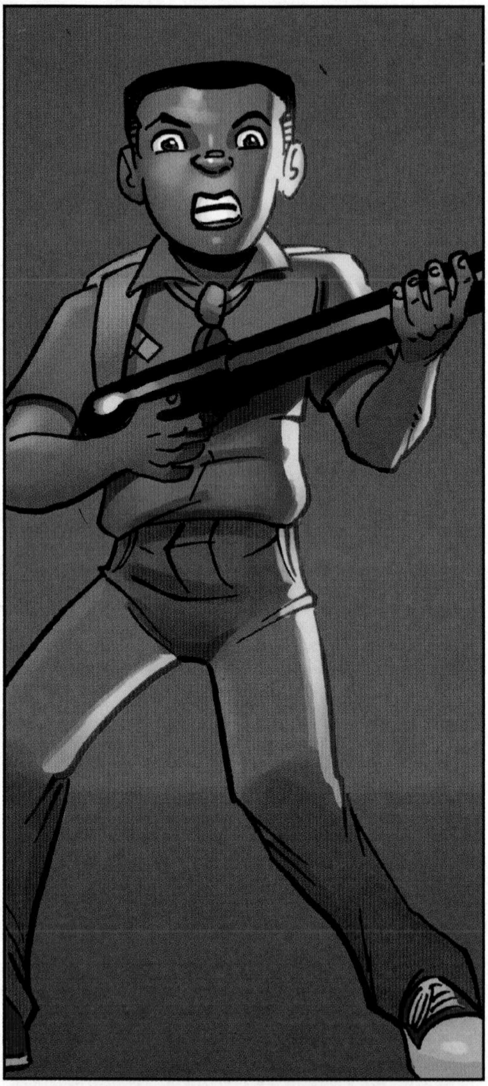

TREY

Full Name: Alexander Richard Dent III

Age: 13

Height: 4' 11 ½"

Weight: 93 lb.

Hair: Black

Eyes: Brown

Grade: Eight

Favorite Subject: Do I have to pick just one?

Jam: *Random Access Memories* by Daft Punk

Potato Gun PSI* *(Pounds per square inch):* 80

Badges Earned: 3

Five years ago, Trey's father, Alex Dent, Jr., bought the Radley Avenue Bank and moved their family to Full Moon Hollow. To keep the small bank profitable, Mr. Dent had to work long hours, and his absence put a lot of stress on his marriage to Trey's mom, Angela. They divorced recently, and his mom has since started dating Tom O'Quinn.

Since Trey and his younger brother, Lewis, were toddlers, their parents stressed the importance of learning and education. Trey took that lesson to heart, immersing himself in his studies to distract him from the tension building up in his home. All that hard work has earned Trey straight As for the last few years and a membership in the National Junior Honor Society.

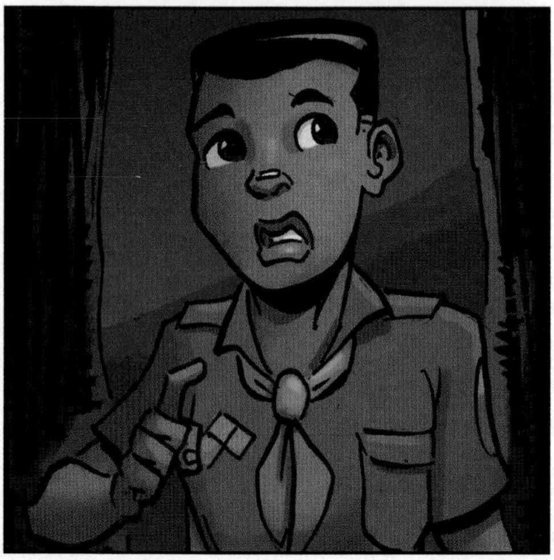

In his spare time at home, Trey spends hours in the garage working on "experiments" and "projects" like his potato gun*, sometimes using Lewis as his guinea pig. On the weekends that he and Lewis visit their dad, they like to go to the movies before hitting Dishman Lanes for pizza, bowling, and pinball.

The thing Trey most wants to be when he grows up is grown UP. Shorter than most kids his age and barely taller than his younger brother, Trey has grown tired of looking up at the world.

**Kids, do not build or play with any type of potato gun without adult supervision.*

GHOUL SCOUTS BONUS FEATURE

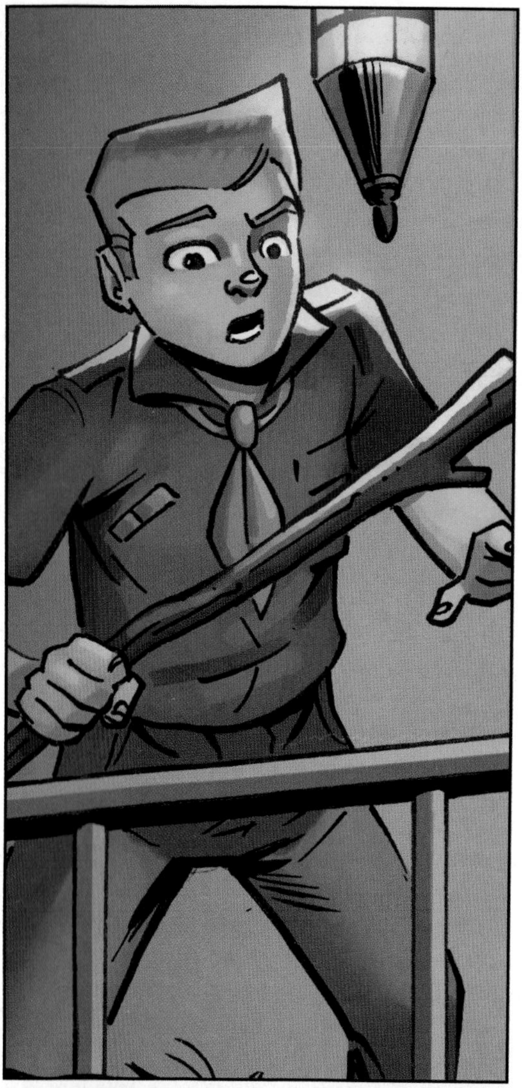

CHASE

Full Name: Chase Douglas Bannon
Age: 12
Height: 5' 5"
Weight: 112 lb.
Hair: Blonde
Eyes: Brown
Grade: Eight
Favorite Subject: Lunch?
Jam: *Church Clothes 3* by Lecrae
Badges Earned: 2

Chase Bannon's family had only lived in Full Moon Hollow for a year when Chase's father lost his job as an Ad Sales Manager. With his older sister only a year and a half from graduating high school, Chase worried that the family might have to move somewhere more affordable and with better job opportunities in order to afford both college tuition and a decent home. This couldn't have come at a worse time for Chase.

Fortunately, his dad managed to get a job teaching at Full Moon Hollow Junior High. While it's good to stay in town, having one of your parents at school with you isn't always fun.

Chase earns mostly Bs in school and plays both soccer and tennis well, but isn't an all-star at either. In all things, he does well enough to succeed, but not so well that he gets noticed. Sometimes Chase feels invisible. On top of that, being naturally shy, Chase has found making friends in Full Moon Hollow difficult.

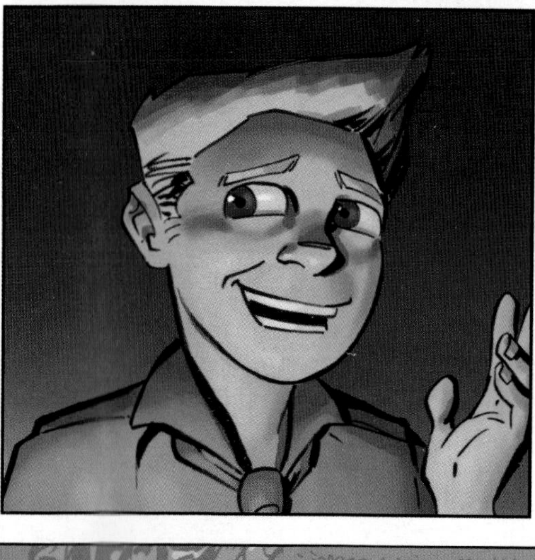

Through the Wilderness Scouts, however, Chase has found both friendship and confidence. His levelheadedness has made him a bit of a leader among his group of buddies. That leadership will be put to the test as the Ghoul Scouts try to uncover the mysterious, dark forces wreaking havoc in Full Moon Hollow.

When he's not hunting down the supernatural, Chase spends his time—too much time, his mom would say—playing *Minecraft* and watching English Premier League football, rooting for Arsenal.

GHOUL SCOUTS BONUS FEATURE

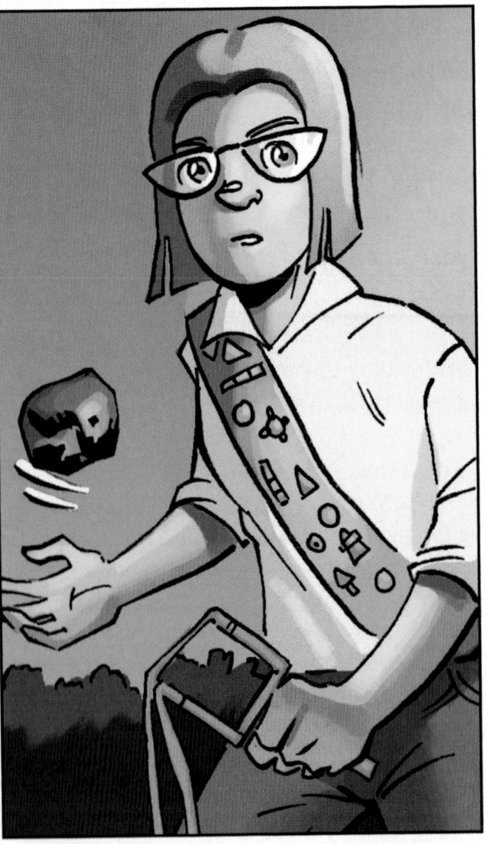

BECKY

Full Name: Rebecca Shannon Palmer

Age: 12

Height: 4' 10"

Weight: 89 lb.

Hair: Pink at the moment

Eyes: Blue

Grade: Seven

Favorite Subject: Biology

Jam: *Start Here* by Maddie & Tae

Slingshot* Range: 40-50 yards

Badges Earned: All of them

After working with horses for years, Becky's parents, John and Daisy Palmer, bought a tract of land outside Full Moon Hollow and opened up a small ranch of their own. Whenever her parents and her schoolwork allow it, Becky works right alongside them. All that time on the ranch has helped Becky develop a love for animals of all kinds and has taught her many of the skills that have made earning Gaia Scout badges a breeze. Also, learning to train horses—some from the moment they were born—has made Becky sure of herself, a strong leader.

Anytime Becky gets a free minute, whether at school or on the ranch, she enjoys reading. For a while, Becky was really into the *Hunger Games* books, so much so that she made herself a slingshot, just like the one carried by her favorite character, Rue. Her favorite books right now are the eerie steampunk mysteries of the *Stoker and Holmes* novels by Colleen Gleason.

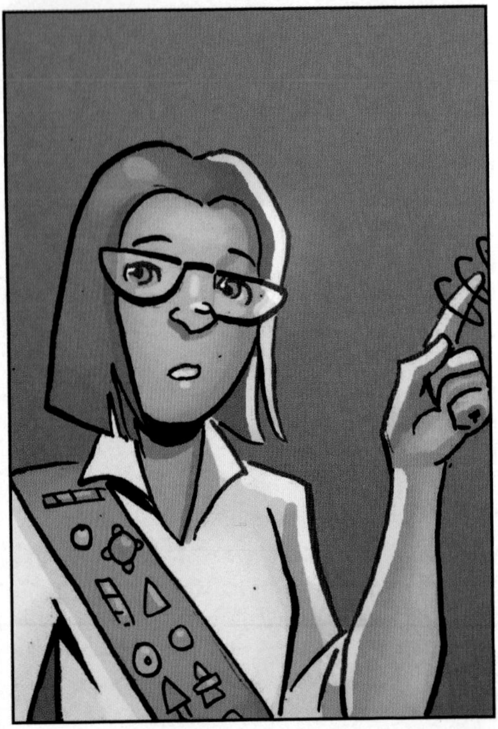

Becky's fascination with the supernatural goes beyond her love of books, though. She is also an avid fan of "The Monster Chasers," the show hosted by Peyton's mom and dad. She and her parents never miss an episode.

One day Becky hopes to go to veterinary school and either open her own practice or continue working with her parents on their ranch.

**Kids, do not build or play with any type of slingshot without adult supervision.*